ROUGH JUSTICE

ROUGH JUSTICE

STEPHEN LEATHER

ISIS
LARGE PRINT
Oxford

Copyright © Stephen Leather, 2010

First published in Great Britain 2010
by
Hodder & Stoughton

Published in Large Print 2011 by ISIS Publishing Ltd.,
7 Centremead, Osney Mead, Oxford OX2 0ES
by arrangement with
Hodder & Stoughton,
An Hachette UK Company

British Library Cataloguing in Publication Data
Leather, Stephen.
    Rough justice.
    1. Shepherd, Dan (Fictitious character) - - Fiction.
    2. Police corruption - - Fiction.
    3. Undercover operations - - England - - London
    - - Fiction.
    4. Suspense fiction.
    5. Large type books.
    I. Title
    823.9'14–dc22

ISBN 978–0–7531–8720–3 (hb)
ISBN 978–0–7531–8721–0 (pb)

Printed and bound in Great Britain by
T. J. International Ltd., Padstow, Cornwall

For Tracey

There were three men in the black Humvee, tall, lanky Jamaicans with diamond earrings, chunky gold chains around their necks and diamond-studded Rolex watches on their wrists. They were all wearing expensive leather jackets, Armani jeans and limited-edition Nike trainers, and had dreadlocks hanging halfway down their backs. The driver was Carlton Richie: he had just turned thirty and was taking his friends to an illegal drinking den in Willesden, north-west London. Sitting next to him was Glenford Barrow, the youngest member of the crew. Barrow's nickname was Shotty because of his predilection for resolving disputes with a sawn-off shotgun. In the back seat was Kemar Davis, the biggest of the three men. He tipped the scales at a little over a hundred and twenty kilos and it was all solid muscle.

Davis looked at his watch. "Are we there yet, man? I need a piss."

"How old are you — six?" asked Richie. "Why didn't you go before you got into the car?"

"I didn't want to go when I got into the car," said Davis. "Now I do. And if you don't get me there soon I'll be pissing all over the back of your seat."

"Like fuck you will," said Richie.

They stopped arguing when they heard the blip of a siren being switched on and off and saw flashing lights. "Fuck," said Richie, looking in his rear-view mirror. "Five-O."

Davis twisted around in his seat and looked through the back windscreen. Behind them was a grey police van with fluorescent stripes along the sides. "Pork in a can," he said. "What the fuck do they want? We didn't do nuffink."

"Is anyone carrying?" asked Richie, pulling over to the kerb. They were in a side-street about half a mile from their destination. His two companions shook their heads. "What about the boot — anything in there?"

"Nuffink," said Davis.

"And no one's got any gear?"

More shaking heads.

Richie parked the car and sat with his hands on the steering-wheel. He shrugged his shoulders. "Just chill," he said. "We're carrying nothing, we've done nothing, they've got nothing."

"Fucking Babylon pigs," spat Davis.

"Chill," repeated Richie. "They just wanna give the black man a hard time, that's all. Ten minutes, we'll be on our way. Keep your hands where they can see them — don't give them no excuse."

They sat where they were as two uniformed police officers carrying flashlights walked from the van, one either side of the Humvee. The policeman on Richie's side of the car tapped on the window with the base of his flashlight and motioned for him to wind it down.

2

Richie did as he was told and smiled up at him, showing a single gold canine among his pristine white teeth. "Good evening, Officer," he said. "Is there a problem?"

"Driving licence," said the policeman. He was about Richie's age, with a sallow complexion and a small white scar across his chin. He was wearing a fluorescent jacket over his uniform and a peaked cap.

Richie moved his hand slowly down to his jeans and took out his wallet. "I wasn't speeding, was I?" he asked.

The policeman said nothing and continued to stare impassively at him. Richie slid out his licence and handed it over. The officer studied it, then shone his flashlight into Richie's face. "Name?"

"It's on the licence, innit?"

"Name," repeated the policeman.

The second bent down and shone his flashlight through the passenger window, playing the beam over Barrow's chest and arms.

"Carlton Richie," said Richie.

"Date of birth?"

Richie took a deep breath, sighed, then recited his birth date in a bored voice.

"Get out of the vehicle, please," said the policeman.

"What's the problem?" asked Richie.

"Just get out of the car or I'll drag you out." He shone his torch into Richie's eyes.

"I haven't done anything," protested Richie, putting his hand up to shade them.

"Get out of the car," repeated the policeman.

Richie sighed again and opened the door. The officer stepped back as he climbed out, glaring. "This is wrong," he said.

The policeman sneered at him, then grabbed him by the collar of his jacket, spun him around and slammed him against the car. He kicked Richie's legs apart. "Keep your hands on the car," he said. He went through Richie's pockets, pulling out his wallet and mobile phone and placing them on the roof. "I ain't carrying nuffink," said Richie.

The second policeman opened the passenger door. "You, out!" he snapped at Barrow. Barrow did as he was told and placed his hands on the roof of the car.

"This is bullshit, man," said Richie.

The policeman slammed the flashlight against the back of Richie's neck. "When I want you to talk I'll tell you," he hissed.

"You are in so much fucking shit," said Richie. "I know my rights and you're trampling all over them."

"Fuck your rights."

"You can't say that." Richie turned to face the officer. "You can't say that to me. I've got me rights. Me human rights."

"I can say what I want," said the policeman. "It's a free country. And it's my free country. You see, we know who you are, and we know what you've done."

"What?" said Richie.

"Your name's Orane Williams, and you're wanted for three murders in St Catherine, back in Jamaica."

"Like fuck."

"Yeah, just like fuck. You're a big wheel in the Clansman Massive. Drugs, extortion, prostitution." The policeman pointed his flashlight at the man in the back seat. "And the big man there, he's Leonardo Sachell but the Clansman crew call him Da Vinci."

"So?" said Richie.

"So you're a murdering scumbag, and we're fed up with you running amok in our country." He prodded Richie in the chest with the flashlight. "Our country, scumbag. You hear that? This is our country. And we've had enough."

"That's assault," said Richie. "You've just assaulted me."

The policeman prodded him again, harder this time.

Richie picked up his mobile phone. "I'm calling me lawyer," he said. "I'm allowed me phone call."

The policeman smiled as Richie tapped out a number on his mobile. When he put the phone against his ear, the officer grabbed it, threw it to the ground and stamped on it.

Richie stared at the shattered pieces of metal and plastic, shaking his head in disbelief. "I'm gonna report you to the Commission for Racial Equality, the Human Rights Commission, the Police Complaints Authority! I'm gonna —"

The policeman hit him across the face, splitting his lips and breaking two of his front teeth. Richie clasped a hand across his bleeding mouth, his eyes wide and fearful.

The side door of the police van opened and three officers climbed out. They were wearing riot gear —

black overalls, boots and blue helmets with visors. "You're not going to do anything, scumbag," said the first policeman.

"You can't do that!" shouted Barrow. The second officer kicked him in the knee and he went down, howling.

Now Davis roared and kicked open the rear passenger door. He stormed out, his hands bunching into fists, his dreadlocks flailing behind him.

Two of the men in riot gear pulled blue and yellow Taser guns from nylon holsters on their thighs. They pointed them at Davis and fired. Twin barbed darts shot out from each gun, trailing fine wires behind them. All four hit Davis in the chest. He immediately went rigid, then fell to the ground, every muscle in his body in spasm.

"Who are you going to report that to, arsehole?" the officer asked. "The RSPCA?"

"What do you want?" asked Richie, lowering his voice to a conspiratorial whisper. "Do you want a piece? Is that it? Is this a shakedown? Because all you gotta do is ask. How much do you want?" He prodded his broken teeth and winced.

The policeman grinned. "What have you got?"

Richie shrugged. "I could go a grand," he said. "A grand a week."

"Sounds like a plan."

"You didn't have to break me fucking teeth, man," said Richie. He rubbed his hand across his bleeding lips.

6

The officer's grin widened. "That? That's just the start," he said. He raised his flashlight and brought it crashing down on the side of Richie's head.

Richie opened his eyes. His head was throbbing and he could taste blood in his mouth. He cleared his throat and spat. Bloody phlegm trickled down his nose and across his forehead. He realised he was hanging upside-down, his head a few inches above the floor and his dreadlocks dragging across the concrete. His hands were tied behind his back and when he strained to look up he saw that his ankles were chained to a girder in the roof. His chest hurt every time he breathed. He looked to his left and saw Barrow, also suspended upside-down. His eyes were closed, the left puffed up; the cheek was cut and bruised.

"You awake there, Orane, or Carlton, or whatever you want to call yourself?" It was the policeman who'd hit him with the flashlight.

"What the fuck do you want?" gasped Richie.

Something hard slammed into his chest and he felt a rib crack. He roared in pain and struggled but his wrists were tightly bound. He thrashed around and then gradually went still. The policeman walked in front of him, swinging a cricket bat. "Do you play cricket, Orane?" he said.

Richie shook his head. His chest felt as if it was on fire.

A second policeman appeared behind the first. He was holding a crowbar. "What about you, Shotty?" he said. "I'd put you down as a spin bowler." He smacked the crowbar against Barrow's left knee, which cracked like a dry twig. Barrow screamed in pain and tears ran down his face as he thrashed from side to side.

"What do you want?" yelled Richie. "What the fuck do you want?"

He heard a footfall behind him and twisted around, trying to see who it was. The movement made him start to spin and his stomach lurched. He threw up. Vomit spewed over his dreadlocks and stung his eyes.

"That's fucking disgusting," snarled the policeman with the cricket bat. The three in riot gear fanned out behind him. Two were carrying large spanners and one was holding a broom handle — he was black, Richie realised.

"Yeah, look at the mess he's made," said the black officer. "Don't they teach them Yardies any manners?" He bent down and grinned at Richie. "What da problem, my man? You eat somefink you shouldn't oughta have, huh?" he said, in a mock Jamaican accent. He pushed the end of his broom handle between Richie's teeth. "Why doncha chew on this, man?"

Richie gagged and tried to turn his head but the man pushed the broom handle harder. "What da problem, man? Doncha like to swallow?"

The two men with spanners circled Davis. "He's a big lad, isn't he?" said one. He swung the spanner and slammed it into the man's hip. Davis grunted and glared at him. "Hard as nails, aren't you, Da Vinci?" He hit him again, harder this time. Davis kept his teeth clamped together and made no sound.

"Yeah, he's a right hard bastard all right," said the policeman with the cricket bat. "Especially where little girls are concerned. Raped a thirteen-year-old in Kingston, he did." He walked over to where Davis was hanging. His head was almost touching the floor, his dreadlocks piled around him like a nest of snakes. "Raped her and then slashed her so that she'd never forget." He swung his cricket bat through the air. "You know what I'm gonna do, Da Vinci? I'm going to smash your balls to a pulp." He patted the bat against Da Vinci's groin. "Think about that for the next minute or two. I'm going to smack your balls and your dick so hard that you'll never be able to have sex again. Ever." He grinned. "I reckon your dick's going to look like a dinner plate by the time I've finished."

He walked around to stand in front of Richie again. Blood was trickling down Richie's face, dripping through his dreadlocks and pooling on the concrete floor. "So, let me tell you how it's going to be, Orane. Are you listening?"

Richie tried to speak but his mouth was filling with blood and he gagged. He spat out bloody phlegm. "Yeah, I hear you."

"My friends and I are going to beat the crap out of you. We're going to break a few bones and smash a few kneecaps and Da Vinci there is gonna lose the use of his gonads. When we're finished we're going to cut you down and then you can crawl to the local hospital and they can patch you up, courtesy of the good old National Health. That's one of the great things about this country. We'll treat any foreign scumbags because, deep down, we're basically too nice for our own good. And once they've patched you up, Orane, you and your two dickhead mates are going to get on the next Air Jamaica flight to Kingston. Do you understand what I'm saying?"

Richie looked up at the black officer. "You gonna let them treat a brother like this, man?" he asked.

Even through the visor, Richie could see the contempt in the man's eyes. "You're no brother of mine, scumbag," he said.

The officer with the cricket bat walloped Richie's shins again. "Talk to me, not him," he said. "Now, do you understand what I've said to you or do you want me to run through it again?"

Richie closed his eyes. "I hear you," he said.

"Because, my scumbag friend, if you're still in this country next week, me and my mates are gonna pick you up again, and we won't be as gentle with you. In fact, my little scumbag friend, we'll kill you. We'll kill you stone dead." He smacked the cricket bat against Richie's left ankle. Richie screamed in agony. "And if you ever tell anyone what happened, we'll kill you. Do you understand that?"

Richie nodded. The officer hit his ankle again, harder this time, and the pain was so agonising that Richie almost passed out. "I can't hear you, Orane."

"I understand!" howled Richie.

"Believe me, we'll do it," he said. "Because what you've got to remember, my little scumbag friend, is that we are the police and we can do what we fucking want." He rested the cricket bat on his shoulder and grinned at the two men with spanners. "Let's get started," he said. "I'm taking the girlfriend out for dinner tonight."

Langford Manor had been built on the blood of slaves. Every stone and slate, every window frame, every feature in the five reception rooms and two dozen bedrooms had been chosen personally by the Honourable Jeremy Langford, one of the most successful slave-traders ever to operate out of the port of Bristol. He was born in 1759, the same year as the slavery abolitionist William Wilberforce. But while Wilberforce had devoted his life to ending the vile trade, Langford had made a fortune from it. By the time the Society for the Abolition of the Slave Trade was founded in 1787, Langford's ships were transporting hundreds of thousands of slaves from West Africa to the sugar plantations of the West Indies. He had begun designing Langford Manor when he was in his teens and building work had started when he was just short of his twenty-fifth birthday. It had taken three years to complete.

In 1806, a year before the British Parliament abolished the transatlantic slave trade, Langford sold his shipping line and used some of the money to purchase several thousand acres around the house he had built. The rest he invested wisely and spent the remainder of his life following country pursuits and sitting as a local magistrate. He died in 1833, just days after the Abolition of Slavery Act was passed, lying in his four-poster in the master bedroom of Langford

Manor, surrounded by his wife, five children and twenty-three grandchildren.

Not that the four men in the dark blue Transit van cared about the history of Langford Manor or the man who had commissioned it. All they cared about were the works of art hanging on its walls, which were conservatively valued at close to fifteen million pounds, and the contents of a small safe in the master bedroom.

The man driving the van was a stocky Scotsman with a greying moustache and slicked-back hair. Like his three companions, he was wearing dark clothing and black leather gloves. "Are we going or what?" he growled. His name was Carrick Thompson and he tapped his fingers on the steering-wheel as he stared at the house in the distance.

"We'll go when I say we go," said the man in the front seat. He took the binoculars away from his face and stared at Thompson with cold blue eyes. "Have you got somewhere you'd rather be?" His name was Alex Grimshaw, but everyone called him Lex.

Thompson stared impassively back at him. "I'm just saying time's a-passing, that's all."

"Time's a-passing because there's still a light on in the library, which means that someone's still up, and if there's someone still up then they're probably going to pick up the Batphone if we go charging in, so let's just wait until whoever it is pops up to bed, okay?" Grimshaw sneered at Thompson. "I've spent three months casing this place. We're not going to blow it just because you've got a short attention span."

"Forget I spoke," mumbled Thompson.

Grimshaw put the binoculars back to his eyes and scrutinised the house. They were parked about half a mile away, on a hill that overlooked Langford Manor. From where they were sitting they had a clear view of the front of the house and, at the main entrance, the lodge, which was occupied by an elderly gamekeeper and his wife. As usual they had gone to bed before nine o'clock. There were three cars parked in front of the manor: a Bentley, a Land Rover and a Ford Focus. Grimshaw knew that the present owner of the house owned all three. The Bentley was for show, the Land Rover for driving over the estate, and the Ford Focus was the vehicle of choice for the wife when she visited the local supermarket. Tobias Rawstorne had bought Langford Manor five years earlier and spent more than two million pounds on improvements, including a state-of-the-art security system. One of the men who had helped fit the burglar alarm and CCTV system was married to a good friend of Grimshaw's and for ten thousand pounds in cash had been more than happy to provide the information necessary to gain trouble-free access to the premises.

Grimshaw scanned the road leading towards the main gate. A white Transit van was parked in a lay-by about a hundred yards away from the lodge. Its lights were off. Grimshaw cursed and pulled out his mobile phone. He tapped out a number, then barked, "Turn your bloody lights on, Matt," he said. "Anyone who drives by is gonna wonder why three grown men are sitting by the side of the road in the dark." The lights of the white Transit van flicked on. Grimshaw swore and ended the call.

"What's happening?" asked the man sitting directly behind Grimshaw. He was holding a sawn-off shotgun in his lap. They weren't expecting any trouble but Rawstorne had half a dozen shotguns in a cabinet in his study. The man with the shotgun was Eddie Simpson: he was a newcomer to Grimshaw's crew and was tapping his fingers nervously on the stock of the shotgun. In his mid-thirties, with brown hair that needed cutting, he was chewing gum noisily.

"Nothing's happening until whoever it is in the library heads upstairs," said Grimshaw.

The man sitting next to Simpson had the build of a wrestler, a shaved head, and a tattoo on his left forearm of a British bulldog wearing a Union flag waistcoat. His name was Geoff Maloney and he was a good ten years older than Simpson, but most of those years had been spent behind bars. He patted Simpson on the knee with a shovel-sized hand and winked. "Relax," he said.

"I'm relaxed," said Simpson.

Grimshaw twisted around in his seat. "Don't go all soft on me now," he said.

"I'm fine," said Simpson, defensively. "I just don't like waiting, that's all." He scowled at Maloney. "And get your bloody hand off my knee."

Grimshaw turned back and took a drink from a pewter hip flask. "The waiting's the key," he said. "Waiting means we know what we're doing. Amateurs rush in because they're all hyped up on adrenalin, and

14

that's when mistakes are made. I don't make mistakes, which is why I've never been caught."

"That, and the fact that you've got one of the best drivers in the business," growled Thompson.

"Yeah, but he was busy tonight, so I had to use you," said Grimshaw. He chuckled and checked out the house again through the binoculars. The light went out. "Right, here we go," he said. He nodded at Thompson. "Wagons roll," he said, and pointed down the road.

Thompson started the engine and drove slowly down the hill, then turned left and followed the high wall that ran around the entire estate. They had used satellite photographs on Google Earth to find the best place to go over the wall, well away from any other houses and with large trees that would make it easy to hide from any passing vehicles. Thompson stopped the van as the three passengers put on night-vision goggles and switched them on. "All working?" Simpson and Maloney nodded.

Grimshaw climbed out. "Let's do it," he said. He took out his phone and hit redial. "We're going over the wall, Matt," he said. "I'll call you when we've secured the house."

"Roger," said Matt Burrowes, at the other end of the line.

"I'll give him bloody roger," said Grimshaw, ending the call. Burrowes was a professional thief and Grimshaw had worked with him more than a dozen times over the years, but he could be careless and had a big mouth. Maloney opened the side of the van and got out, then pulled a pair of aluminium stepladders after him. He jogged over to the wall as Simpson jumped out and slammed the door.

Maloney opened the ladders as Grimshaw and Simpson ran over. Simpson went first, passing the sawn-off shotgun to Grimshaw before straddling the top of the wall and leaping down. He grunted as he hit the ground and rolled to absorb the impact. He stood up and held out his hands to catch the shotgun. He moved away from the wall while Grimshaw clambered over and, a few seconds later, Maloney.

As they moved together through the trees towards the stables at the rear of the house, Thompson ran to the wall, retrieved the stepladders, put them back in the van and drove to a nearby lay-by.

The three men moved quickly, bending low, Simpson cradling the shotgun. They skirted around the stables, following the edge of a paddock and then moving through a small orchard of fruit trees. There was no moon and the sky was cloudy, but the night-vision goggles gave them a perfect view of the house and grounds.

To the right was a clay tennis court, and beyond it concentric circles of flowerbeds around a fountain in the shape of an angel with outstretched wings.

They went around the tennis court and headed to the kitchen. There was a door but their inside man had told them it was always locked and bolted from the inside. They crept around the building and reached a conservatory. They kept low, even though it was in darkness, and made for the staff entrance.

Grimshaw took a key from his pocket. It had been supplied by the technician who had fitted the burglar alarm and worked perfectly. The console began to beep quietly so Grimshaw walked quickly over to it and tapped in the four-digit master code to deactivate it. The beeping stopped.

Maloney padded across the kitchen as Simpson closed the door. The three men strode quietly along a corridor, past the study and the library, into a large hallway. Two stairways led up to the first floor. Grimshaw reached into his jacket, pulled out a semi-automatic and waved for Maloney and Simpson to go up the staircase on the right while he ascended the one on the left. Maloney slid a revolver from a holster under his arm as he went up. Simpson followed, holding his shotgun across his chest.

Grimshaw knew that none of the staff lived in and there were only three people in the house — Rawstorne, a fifty-year-old businessman, his trophy second wife, a former model and actress who had once done a two-year run in *Emmerdale*, and their daughter Amy. Rawstorne had a son by his first wife but he was away at university.

Rawstorne had made his money from an employment agency that specialised in bringing gangs of workers from EU countries where the British minimum wage was a big improvement on the pittance they earned at home. It wasn't quite slavery, but there was a certain irony in the fact that he had ending up owning Langford Manor. Rawstorne's wife liked to think that she was a gifted interior designer so she had done up the house from top to bottom, then invited *Country Life* magazine to do a photo-shoot. The photographs, and the hours he had spent keeping the house under surveillance, meant that Grimshaw knew where the master bedroom was, and where the teenager slept.

They reached the upstairs landing. Simpson joined Grimshaw and they tiptoed towards the master bedroom. The man of the house was the only one likely to put up any resistance so it was important that he saw the heavy artillery. Maloney headed down the landing towards the bedroom where the girl slept.

Simpson reached for the doorknob. Grimshaw looked over his shoulder at Maloney, held up his hand and made a fist. "Go," he whispered to Simpson.

Simpson twisted the doorknob and pushed the door open. They padded across the plush bedroom carpet, Simpson heading for Rawstorne's side of the bed, Grimshaw covering the sleeping woman with his automatic.

Simpson placed his gloved hand across Rawstorne's mouth. He woke almost immediately and tried to sit up, but Simpson pressed the barrel of the shotgun against his forehead. "Don't move, don't speak, don't do a damn thing," he whispered. "Do exactly as we say and no one needs to get hurt."

Rawstorne glared at Simpson but he stopped struggling. Grimshaw tapped the barrel of his gun against the wife's cheek. "Wake up, Sleeping Beauty," he said.

She opened her eyes. There was just enough light for her to make out Grimshaw standing over her and she opened her mouth to scream. Grimshaw clamped his hand over it. "Sssh!" he hissed. "We've got your daughter. Just lie still and everything will be all right. Nod if you understand."

She nodded slowly, her eyes wide and fearful.

"Good girl," he said. "Now, I'm going to take my hand away from your mouth. If you make a sound, I'll smash your pretty little teeth with this gun. Okay?" She nodded again. Grimshaw slowly removed his hand. She was panting, close to hyperventilating. She looked across at her husband but Grimshaw grabbed her face and squeezed. "Don't look at him," he said. "He can't help you." He released his grip and told her to lie still. He pulled a handkerchief from his pocket and pushed it into her mouth, then placed the gun on the bedside table and took a roll of duct tape. "Put your wrists together," he said. She did as she was told and he used plastic ties to fasten her wrists, then wound tape around her mouth. He went over to the door, flicked on the lights and took off his night-vision goggles. Simpson did the same, keeping the gun trained on Rawstorne with his right hand.

"You can take whatever you want — just don't hurt us," said Rawstorne.

"That's very kind of you, Squire," said Grimshaw. "But forgive me if I don't tug my forelock, us having the guns and all." He took out his mobile phone, hit redial, and held it to his ear while he waited for Burrowes to answer. "Yeah," he said eventually. "The eagle has bloody landed. Get your arses in here." As he put the phone away, the bedroom door opened wide

19

and Maloney pushed the girl in. She had been bound and gagged like her mother.

Rawstorne tried to sit up but Simpson prodded him in the chest with the barrel of the shotgun. "Stay put," he snarled.

The girl struggled to get away from Maloney. He laughed and pushed her towards the bed. She stumbled and fell against it, but managed to scramble up to lie next to her mother.

"What do you want?" asked Rawstorne.

"Sit up," said Simpson. "That'll do for a start."

Rawstorne sat up. Grimshaw walked around the bed and bound his wrists with two plastic ties. Then he put a hand around the man's throat. "You do exactly as we say and give us what we want, and nobody will get hurt," he said.

Rawstorne nodded.

"But you screw us around and . . ." He left the sentence unfinished, but slowly released his grip on Rawstorne's throat.

Rawstorne coughed and cleared his throat. "Okay, okay," he said. "Whatever you want."

Grimshaw nodded at Maloney. "Go down and let the boys in," he said. "Get them started on the downstairs rooms." The *Country Life* spread had featured several works of art on the walls of the library and sitting rooms, paintings that Rawstorne had spent hundreds of thousands of pounds on. And in several of the photographs there were valuable antiques that Grimshaw had already priced with a fence in London.

20

Maloney headed downstairs. Grimshaw pointed his gun at Rawstorne. "Right. Now here's the thing, Squire," he said. "We're taking the paintings and we're taking the antiques, and I need you to tell me where the safe is."

Rawstorne frowned. "We don't have a safe."

Grimshaw looked at Rawstorne's wife. "Is that right, Angela? He doesn't keep all your jewellery in a safe? What about all the watches you've got? You collect old watches, don't you? That's what you told *Country Life*. Where do you keep them?"

The woman stared at Grimshaw, the tape over her mouth pulsing in and out as she fought to breathe.

Grimshaw used his left hand to take a Stanley knife out of his pocket and flicked open the blade with his thumb. "Are you going to tell me, Squire, or shall I cut your lovely wife's face? And your daughter's? How would you like that? Every day for the rest of your life you'll look at the scars and remember that they're there because you put money before your family's safety. Is that what you want, Squire? Because I've cut women before and I'm happy to do it again."

"I don't have a safe," said Rawstorne, flatly. "If I did have a safe I'd tell you. We keep our valuables in the bank."

"Of course you do," sighed Grimshaw. He walked around the bed, shaking his head as he put his gun back into his shoulder holster. "I'm sorry, Angela, sorry, Amy, but he obviously doesn't give a shit about either of you." Amy and her mother huddled together, their cries muffled by the duct-tape gags. Grimshaw glared at Rawstorne. "I know for a fact that there's a safe in this bedroom," he said. "The one thing I don't know is where it is. Now, I could tear the place down looking for it but it'd save me a lot of time and effort if you'd just bloody well tell me where it is." Grimshaw grabbed Angela's hair and yanked it hard, exposing her throat. Tears were streaming down her face. He placed the blade against her cheek.

"Tell him, you bastard!" hissed Simpson. "He'll do it — he'll cut her."

Angela Rawstorne was crying hysterically. She kicked out with her legs but Grimshaw put his knee on her chest to hold her down.

"You're insured, you bastard — why are you putting your family through this?" said Simpson. "Just tell us."

Rawstorne stared in horror as the blade pierced his wife's flesh and a trickle of blood ran down her cheek. "Okay, okay!" he shouted. "Behind the painting over there, by the dressing-table."

"Thank you," said Grimshaw. "That wasn't so hard, was it?" He stood up, retracted the blade of the Stanley knife, and put it back in his pocket.

The painting was a family portrait with Rawstorne standing next to his wife, his hand on his son's shoulder while his wife rested her head against her daughter's. Rawstorne hadn't changed much since the portrait had been painted, but the girl was clearly five or six years older. In the picture she was just a child, but now, tied up on the bed, she was almost a woman.

Grimshaw grabbed the frame and pulled. It was hinged and swung to the side to reveal a grey metal wall safe. "Combination, Squire," said Grimshaw.

22

Downstairs they heard the front door open, footsteps and muffled talking. The door closed.

"Combination, Squire," Grimshaw repeated. "Don't make me get my knife out again."

Rawstorne gave him the combination. Grimshaw tapped out the four digits, and scowled. "Don't screw me around," he growled. "Give me the right number now or I'll cut your bitch of a wife."

"I'm sorry, I'm sorry," said Rawstorne. He shook his head. He repeated the combination, this time reversing the last two digits.

Grimshaw tapped it in and smiled as he pulled open the door. There were bundles of cash, new notes still in their wrappers. Grimshaw pulled out one of the bundles and flicked through it. A thousand pounds in fifties. There were twenty bundles in all. He piled them on the dressing-table. "Bet this won't be covered by insurance," said Grimshaw. "Keeping a little something from the taxman, are we?"

"Just take it and go," said Rawstorne.

"I'll be setting the schedule, thank you very much," said Grimshaw. "Just keep your trap shut or my mate there will shut it for you." Simpson gestured with the shotgun to reinforce the message.

There were a dozen watch boxes in the safe. Grimshaw took them out and put them next to the money. He opened one. It was an antique gold Rolex, studded with diamonds. "Nice," he said. "Your missus has got taste, all right."

He reached back into the safe and brought out several jewellery boxes. He opened a heart-shaped red velvet box and whistled when he saw the diamond necklace it contained.

They heard footsteps on the stairs and a few seconds later Maloney appeared at the bedroom door. "All present and accounted for," he said, throwing Grimshaw a fake salute. He tossed him a nylon holdall.

Grimshaw caught it and filled it with the money, watches and jewellery boxes. Maloney went over to the bed. "Come here, darling," he said, and grabbed the girl by the back of her nightdress. He pulled her to her feet. "You and me can have some fun."

"Leave it out," said Simpson.

"You can have her after me," said Maloney. "Sloppy seconds." He pushed the girl towards the door.

Simpson looked across at Grimshaw. "Are you going to let him do this?"

Grimshaw shrugged. "The boy's got urges, what can I say?" He zipped up the holdall.

"Nobody said nothing to me about rape."

"He's just gonna have some fun," said Grimshaw.

"You're supposed to be pros," said Simpson. "Art thieves, the Scarlet bloody Pimpernels, you said."

"If it upsets you that much, you can have the wife," said Maloney. The struggling girl tried to get back to the bed but Maloney dragged her away. "Feisty little thing, isn't she? Bet she's a virgin — they always fight harder, virgins."

"This is a bloody liability," Simpson said to Grimshaw. "I'm not working with a rapist. Thieving's one thing, raping young girls is something else."

24

"You're just here to rob. Don't begrudge him his fun. It's one of the perks."

"He's done this before? No one told me that."

"Look, it's cool," said Grimshaw. "He always gives them a little speech afterwards, along the lines of 'We know where you live and if you tell anyone what I did I'll come back and kill your whole family,' and that seems to do the trick." Grimshaw pointed the Stanley knife at Rawstorne. "You'll do as you're told, won't you, Toby boy? You won't tell the cops what happened to your little girl, will you? No, of course you won't. Besides, what will the neighbours think? They might think that little Amy here enjoyed it."

"Don't hurt her — please, don't hurt her," begged Rawstorne. "I'll get you more money. Anything you want."

"Have you got more money in the house, Toby boy? Something you're keeping for a rainy day? Because, believe me, it's about to pour down on your life."

"I've money in the bank. Just please don't hurt my family."

"The banks are shut, in case you hadn't noticed," said Grimshaw. "It's Friday night and I'm buggered if I'm going to wait here all weekend." He waved the knife at Maloney. "Do what you have to do and then give the guys a hand loading the vans," he said.

"Please, don't do this," begged Rawstorne. "She's only fifteen."

Grimshaw walked over to Rawstorne, pulling the gun from his holster. He slammed the butt against the side of his head and Rawstorne screamed in pain. Grimshaw dragged him off the bed and kicked him in the stomach, hard. Rawstorne curled into a ball, his knees against his chest as he moaned in pain. "I told you, shut the hell up!" shouted Grimshaw.

"Hey, leave it out!" roared Simpson.

Grimshaw ignored him. He kicked Rawstorne in the back, then stamped on him, grunting with the exertion. He was about to kick the man again when Simpson's shotgun went off, blowing chunks of plaster from the ceiling. Simpson pointed it at Grimshaw's groin. "This stops right now!" he yelled.

"Are you bloody crazy?" Grimshaw pointed his gun at Simpson's face. "What the hell are you playing at?"

"I'm not playing at anything! This isn't a bloody game, Lex!" shouted Simpson. "I didn't sign up to start raping kids."

They heard running footsteps on the stairs, then muttering in the hallway. "What's going on in there?" called a man. It was a Scottish accent. Carrick Thompson.

"First one through that door gets shot in the balls!" bellowed Simpson.

"Boss, are you okay?" asked Thompson.

"It's all under control," replied Grimshaw. "Go back to loading the vans — we've got to be out of here in five minutes."

Maloney threw the girl to the floor and pointed his gun at Simpson "Just remember you've only got one cartridge left in that thing," said Maloney.

Simpson pumped another shell into the breech. "It's a Remington 870 Marine Magnum pump action with a magazine that holds seven shells, you stupid prick," he said, not taking his eyes off Grimshaw. "And seven minus one is six. And even if you were a good enough shot to put a bullet in my head from there, which I doubt, the reflex would still be enough to blow Lex's private parts to kingdom come. Might not kill him outright, but he won't be having sex ever again."

"Will you stop using my sodding name?" said Grimshaw.

"Why? Are you ashamed of being Lex Grimshaw of forty-seven Cleveland Gardens, Exeter? Explain that to me. Not ashamed of aiding and abetting rape, are you?"

"I'll bloody well do you!" yelled Maloney, taking a step closer to Simpson. The girl rolled over to a corner and lay there, sobbing.

"You do and I'll blow Lex's balls off," said Simpson. "And if there's any life left in me I'll let you have the next one in your groin, too. Look at the ceiling, Maloney, and imagine what your prick's going to look like."

"No one's going to shoot anyone," said Grimshaw.

"Yeah, well, that's down to me, not you," said Simpson. "I'm the one with the shotgun."

"Let's just calm down," said Grimshaw. "We're in the middle of something here and we don't want it all to go tits up."

"As far as I'm concerned, the tits are already up," said Simpson. "I didn't sign up for rape. And I sure as hell didn't know that Maloney here had form for it."

"Can we at least stop using names?" said Grimshaw. "We're not bloody amateurs."

"It's too late for that," said Maloney. "The damage is done. We're gonna have to top them all. Are you happy now, Simpson? We're going to have to kill all three of them, however this pans out."

"Nobody has to kill nobody," said Grimshaw. "Look, guys, let's just put the guns down, get the stuff in the vans and drive off into the bloody sunset. Then we can all go our separate ways."

"They know our bloody names!" shouted Maloney.

"How many bloody Maloneys do you think there are in the phone book, you tosser?" sneered Grimshaw. "And a name's no good without forensics or a face to put to it. We're cool. Are we cool, Eddie?"

"No, Lex, we're as far from cool as you can get without falling out of the fridge."

"What? What the hell does that mean?"

Simpson waved his shotgun. "I don't know what it means. I just mean we're not cool because Maloney's a vengeful bastard and as soon as I lower my gun he's going to shoot me. Aren't you, Geoff?"

"See?" shouted Maloney. "Now he's told them my first name."

"Forget the bloody names — the names don't mean shit," said Grimshaw. He put his hands up as if he was trying to calm a startled horse. "Look, Eddie, tell me what you want to make this right. I don't want you to pull that trigger and I'm pretty sure you don't want to either. We can still make a good score here — we can all walk away with our heads held high."

"Tell Maloney to go downstairs."

"Sod that," said Maloney.

"Go downstairs, Geoff," said Grimshaw.

"Will you stop using my bloody name!"

"It's too late now. They already know your name."

"So we top them."

"We're not topping anybody, Geoff."

Maloney waved his gun at Grimshaw. "I'm not going down for this. I'm not going to prison again. Not for you, not for anyone."

"No one's going to prison," said Grimshaw. "We leaving no forensics. No one's seen our faces, we'll all have alibis. Names mean nothing. Now, get the hell downstairs and help the guys load the vans."

Maloney hesitated.

"Now!" roared Grimshaw. "Or I'll bloody well shoot you myself."

Maloney muttered under his breath and left the bedroom, pointing a warning finger at Simpson as he went.

"Thank you," Rawstorne said to Simpson. He had rolled onto his back and managed to get into a sitting position next to the bed.

"Don't thank me," snapped Simpson. "Just keep your mouth shut and let us do what we're here to do."

Grimshaw picked up the holdall. "What do you want to do, Eddie? You wanna stay here with your new-found friends?"

"This isn't about choosing sides, it's about not wanting to get involved in rape," said Simpson. "My sister was attacked a few years back. Got into a pirate mini-cab, bastard beat her up and screwed her without a condom. She got pregnant, had to have an abortion.

Ruined her life. So don't get in my face about this, okay?"

Grimshaw nodded. "Okay, I get the picture. Fair enough." He put his gun back and pointed at the door. "Time to go."

"Haven't you forgotten something?"

Grimshaw frowned. "What?"

Simpson gestured with his shotgun at Rawstorne's mobile phone on the bedside table. "You're going to leave that there, are you?"

Grimshaw growled and went to pick it up.

Simpson pointed his gun at Rawstorne. "Don't even think of trying anything," he said. "Maloney's still downstairs and he's just looking for an excuse. Stay here and keep quiet. We'll be gone in five minutes. You wait at least half an hour before you try to get free."

Rawstorne forced a smile. "Thank you," he said.

"I already said don't thank me," said Simpson. He nodded at Grimshaw. "Okay, let's go."

Simpson followed Grimshaw out of the bedroom, and closed the door. The two men walked down the landing. The front door was open. Thompson, now wearing a ski-mask, looked up when he saw them coming down the stairs. "What's going on?" he asked. "Maloney's as mad as hell."

"Screw Maloney," said Grimshaw. "How are we doing?"

"Half a dozen paintings already. The guys are in the library now, fetching the Monet."

As he spoke, Matt Burrowes, dressed in black and wearing a ski-mask, jogged out of the library, holding a large painting sheathed in bubble-wrap.

"Come on, Matt, get a bloody move on," said Grimshaw.

"Be nice if you'd give us a hand," panted Burrowes, heading out of the door.

Grimshaw tossed the holdall down to Thompson. "Shove that in the van," he said. Thompson headed outside.

"Come on, Eddie, help load the vans," said Grimshaw.

Just then they heard staccato shouts outside. "Armed police! Hands in the air — now!"

"What the hell . . . ?" said Grimshaw.

Maloney came running out of the library, holding his gun in the air. "There's cops outside — hundreds of cops!"

Three men in black overalls wearing bulletproof vests and black helmets and pointing Heckler & Koch carbines appeared at the front doorway. Maloney dropped his gun and threw his hands up. "Don't shoot!"

The three men fanned out across the hall and another five armed officers rushed in through the door. "Armed police, drop your weapons!" shouted one of the new arrivals.

Grimshaw raised his hands. Simpson flicked the safety on the shotgun but before he could throw it to the floor one of the armed police fired. Simpson's head jerked back and he slumped to the ground as the gun fell from his nerveless fingers.

Two armed policemen dragged Grimshaw roughly across the driveway to a waiting van. "Okay, okay, I'm not resisting," he said, but his captors ignored him.

The three men who had arrived in the second van were all lying face down while six armed officers covered them with their MP5s. Thompson was standing spreadeagled against a wall while an officer in a bulletproof vest patted him down.

A paramedic was attending to Simpson, dabbing at a graze on his forehead where the police marksman's bullet had narrowly missed splattering his brains across the hallway. Two armed police stood guard over him, cradling their MP5s. "You were lucky," said the paramedic.

"Yeah, well, I'd have been even luckier if the idiot had held his fire for another second or two," sneered Simpson. "I was bloody well surrendering." He scowled up at the two armed policemen. "Was it one of you pricks that shot me?"

The two men stared at him impassively.

"Yeah, well, you'll be hearing from my lawyers, you trigger-happy morons." He winced as the paramedic used a Q-tip to apply antiseptic.

There were half a dozen patrol cars in a semicircle facing the house, their doors open and lights off, with two ambulances. Two paramedics in green overalls and yellow fluorescent jackets wheeled Rawstorne out of the house on a stretcher towards one of the ambulances. His wife, a blanket around her shoulders, hurried after them, dabbing at her face with a tissue. Two female police officers, one wearing a bulletproof vest and a black helmet with the visor up, came out with Amy. She was trembling and hugging herself as she stared blankly at the activity around her.

A female detective with a chestnut bob, wearing a beige raincoat with the collar turned up, hurried over to Angela Rawstorne. "Are you all right?" she asked.

"Of course I'm not all right," she said acidly. "I want to go with my husband."

"That's not a problem, Mrs Rawstorne," said the detective. She nodded at the paramedics and they helped the woman into the back of the ambulance. Mrs Rawstorne looked over at her daughter and held out a hand. "Amy, come on! Come with us!"

"He's going to be all right," said one of the paramedics, as Amy climbed in after them.

Mrs Rawstorne put a protective arm around her daughter. "Just bloody drive," she snapped. "Get him to a real doctor — now!"

Two cops pulled Maloney out of the house. He was struggling and two more rushed over to grab a leg each. They lifted Maloney up and carried him to the van. He bucked and kicked but the four officers were big men and used to dealing with uncooperative prisoners. Maloney cursed and spat at them, but his struggling intensified when he saw Simpson in the back of one of the ambulances. "This is all your bloody fault, Simpson!" he roared. "I'll bloody well have you for this."

The detective looked up when she heard Maloney verbally abusing Simpson and went over to the four officers who were restraining him. "Put him in with the other one," she said, gesturing at the van that contained Grimshaw. "Cuff him first and, judging by the way he's kicking, I'd restrain his legs too." The four armed officers had never met the detective before and didn't know her rank but her tone was enough to convince them to do as she said.

"You're bloody dead, Simpson," screamed Maloney. "When I get my hands on you, you're dead meat."

"A gag wouldn't go amiss either," said the woman, as she walked over to the ambulance where the paramedic was attending to Simpson. She pointed at the injured man. "Keep them apart," she said, to the two armed officers guarding him. "Put him in the van over there." A third vehicle was parked next to one of the armed-response vehicles.

The paramedic finished applying a plaster to the graze. "He's good to go," he said. "It's just a scratch."

The two armed officers frogmarched Simpson to the back of the police van. The rear doors were already open and they shoved him inside. The uniforms were just about to slam the mesh door on him when the detective told them to wait. "I'll ride with him," she said, and climbed in.

"Are you sure, ma'am?" said one of the uniforms.

"Don't worry, boys, I can take care of myself," she said.

The officers closed and locked the mesh door, then closed the two outer doors.

The detective looked at Simpson and smiled. "Well, Spider, that didn't go as well as we hoped, did it?"

Dan "Spider" Shepherd, undercover operative with the Serious Organised Crime Agency, scowled at her. He wanted to shout and swear but Charlotte Button was a lady and his boss so he just smiled thinly. "I've had better days, Charlie," he said. He put his hand up to touch the plaster and winced. "I've got one hell of a headache."

"Would you like some paracetamol?"

"I nearly bloody well died, Charlie. I'm supposed to be one of the good guys and the cops came this close to putting a bullet in my head."

"Moan, moan, moan," said the van's driver, as he twisted around in his seat. Shepherd grinned: it was his dour Scottish colleague, Jimmy Sharpe. "Where to, m'lady?" he asked.

"Take us back to the safe-house in Bristol," said Button.

"Can I use the siren?"

"No, you can't," said Button. "Any more backchat and I'll drive and you can walk."

The safe-house was an office above an estate agent's in north Bristol. There were two designated parking spaces in the yard behind it and Sharpe parked the police van next to his Lexus. He got out, walked around to the rear and opened the doors, then the cage.

Button stepped out, unlocked a green door that was covered by a CCTV camera and led Shepherd and Sharpe up a flight of stairs where she unlocked a second door. They went into a large, open-plan office with two sash windows overlooking the street below and a small kitchenette off to the right. One wall was lined with surveillance photographs of Alex Grimshaw and his gang. Shepherd dropped down onto a faded tartan sofa. "Why didn't we know that Maloney was a rapist?" he asked.

"I honestly don't know," said Button, taking off her raincoat and hanging it on the back of the door.

"The victims were interviewed, presumably. Didn't anyone pick up the signs?"

"Spider, if someone doesn't want to tell the police they were raped, there's not much the police can do about it." She picked up the kettle. "Do you want coffee?"

Shepherd nodded. "Please, yeah."

"I don't get it. What happened?" asked Sharpe.

"You don't get it because, as usual, you weren't anywhere near the sharp end," said Shepherd. "No pun intended."

"Hey, it's not my fault," said Sharpe. "It was hard enough getting you in the gang. Two of us would have been overkill."

"Let's not argue the point, boys," said Button, as she switched on the kettle.

"I'm sorry, I'm just a bit stressed," said Shepherd. "Maloney was planning on shooting me, I'm sure he was. I could feel him staring at the back of my head and almost feel his finger tightening on the trigger." He grinned ruefully. "I spun him that old tale about death spasms being enough to pull the trigger. Has anyone ever done any research on that?"

Button smiled. "I don't think they have." She poured milk into three mugs.

"Well, I'm pretty sure that Maloney didn't believe it."

36

"Any booze around?" asked Sharpe, sitting behind the one desk in the office.

Button ignored him and carried on talking to Shepherd. "He didn't pull the trigger, so all's well that ends well."

"Let's not forget that the boys in blue went for a head shot because I didn't drop my gun fast enough," said Shepherd. He put a hand up to the plaster on his forehead. "An inch to the left and I'd be dead, Charlie."

"I know, but you're not, so let's be grateful for that."

"Didn't they know there was an undercover agent in the gang?"

"They didn't, no. But it wouldn't have made any difference because you were all wearing ski-masks."

"Well, I hope whoever fired the shot gets his balls ripped off," said Shepherd. "Even if I had been one of the bad guys, what he did was bang out of order. I was dropping my weapon — my finger was nowhere near the trigger."

"Looking on the bright side, no one's ever going to think you're working for SOCA," said Sharpe. "Your legend's well intact."

"I'm not sure that's true," said Shepherd. "After what happened in the bedroom, they must have realised I'm not kosher."

"They might just assume that you're a villain with a soft heart," said Button. "Anyway, we'll put it out that you escaped from custody while you were in hospital and the rest of the gang will go down for at least ten years." The kettle finished boiling and she stood up.

"I'll make us all a coffee and then I'll run you along to the hotel. I've got rooms booked for us all."

"I'd rather get back to Hereford," said Shepherd. "It's been a while since I saw Liam."

"No problem," said Button, spooning coffee into a cafetière. "I'll arrange a car. What about you, Razor?"

"Minibar included?"

"Within reason," said Button.

Sharpe rubbed his hands together. "I'll phone the wife and tell her to expect me tomorrow."

"And I'm going to need to see you both in London on Monday."

"A new job?" asked Shepherd.

"All lined up and ready to go," she said.

"Care to give us clue?"

She smiled brightly. "Now, Spider, that would spoil the surprise."

The occupants of the six cells looked up as Shepherd walked into the block. Six pairs of brown eyes gazed at him hopefully. He was the key to their salvation: one word from him and they would be released. The floors were bare concrete, the rear walls whitewashed brick, and there was a single metal-barred gate fronting each three-feet-by-eight cell.

"How long have they been here?" he asked the middle-aged woman who had escorted him into the block.

She indicated the occupant of the first cell. "He's been here two years," she said. The Alsatian-Labrador cross growled softly and wagged its tail. "He's six years old and most people want a puppy."

"What do you think, Liam?" asked Shepherd. "Do you see anything you like?"

"I like them all, Dad," said Liam. He bent down and pushed his fingers between the bars. The dog licked them, its tail swishing from side to side like a metronome. "We can really have one? Really?"

"I promised you, didn't I? I said we'd get a dog after I'd finished the job I was on." The investigation into Alex Grimshaw and his gang of armed robbers had taken the best part of two months and for most of that time Shepherd had been in the West Country. He'd managed a few weekend trips back to Hereford but he knew he hadn't been spending enough time with his son.

He'd arrived back in Hereford just as Liam was waking up and had realised he hadn't brought him a present. He'd been promising to let his son have a dog for months, so he'd offered to take him to the local RSPCA kennels. The dog was a bribe, Shepherd knew, to make up for him being such an absentee father, but it was clear from the look on Liam's face that it was more than acceptable.

"What happens to the ones you don't find homes for?" Shepherd asked the woman. She was dressed in a tweed suit and sensible shoes, and had her RSPCA identification hanging on a long chain around her neck. "Do you . . ." He left the sentence unfinished.

"Oh, these days it's quite rare to put down a healthy dog," said the woman. "If a dog is very old or sick or

39

has an impossible temperament then we might be forced to, but generally they just stay here until a home becomes available. The local paper is very good. Whenever we get close to capacity they run a story with photographs of our more appealing animals and that always gets results."

Liam had moved on to the next cage, where a small beagle wagged its tail and made a fuss of him. "Look, Dad, it's Snoopy."

"She's a pure beagle," said the woman. "That's quite unusual for us — generally we get the Heinz 57 varieties. She's probably from a good home and just got lost. But we've had her for two weeks and no one has claimed her so we've put her up for adoption. She'll go quickly — pedigrees are always popular. You'd pay several hundred pounds to buy a dog like that from a breeder."

Liam scratched the animal behind an ear. "It's so cute, Dad," he said.

"Beagles need a lot of exercise," said Shepherd.

"You have a house and garden?" asked the woman.

"Quite a large garden," said Shepherd. "And we live close to a lot of open space. Liam here has promised to walk the dog at least once a day."

"And you're married, are you?"

Shepherd frowned. "Why's that important?" he asked.

"We don't want the dogs left on their own for long periods," she said. "We need to know that there's someone around for them."

"We have an au pair, and she's home all the time," said Shepherd.

"That'll be fine," said the woman. "We'll need to do a home visit, of course."

"A home visit?"

"To check that it's the sort of environment that's suitable for a dog. A lot of our dogs have been mistreated and we need to know that their new home will give them the stability they need."

"It's probably easier to adopt a child than a dog," said Shepherd.

"Sadly, Mr Shepherd, that could well be true. But we do our bit by making sure that our dogs only go to good homes."

"Can we have this one, Dad?" asked Liam. The beagle was scrabbling at the cage door, trying to get to him.

"You remember the rules?" asked Shepherd.

Liam sighed theatrically. "Walk her at least twice a day, feed her, clean up after her, and take responsibility for any damage she does."

"The kennel maids have been calling her Lady," said the woman, "but she's only been here two weeks so there wouldn't be a problem calling her something else."

"Lady's a good name," said Liam. He looked up at his father. "Can we take her now, Dad?"

Shepherd looked at the woman. "There's some paperwork to do," she said. "And we still have the home visit to arrange. Where do you live?"

Shepherd told her his address and she agreed to do the home visit early the following day, even though it was Sunday.

"That'll give us a chance to get some supplies in," said Shepherd.

"Supplies?" queried Liam.

"Bedding, food, brushes, a lead, a collar — dogs need almost as much stuff as children," said Shepherd.

"But we can have her, right?"

"Sure," said Shepherd. He crouched next to Liam and put his hand through the bars of the cage. The dog licked his fingers enthusiastically.

"You're great, Dad. Thanks."

"Just remember the rules," said Shepherd. "Six months down the line, I don't want to be the one feeding her and taking her out whenever she needs a pee."

"That's what we've got Katra for," said Liam.

Shepherd glared at his son and pointed a warning finger at him.

"Dad, I'm joking," said Liam. "She's my responsibility, I'll take good care of her, I swear."

"Just make sure that you do."

The waitress was a pretty Chinese girl with waist-length hair, flawless olive skin and long fingernails painted bright red to match the figure-hugging cheongsam dress that she was wearing. All the men at the table turned to watch her walk away.

"She's a cracker," said the youngest of the group of five. Ben Portner had just turned nineteen and had only

42

been in the army for six months. He had a shock of ginger hair and a mass of freckles across his nose and cheeks, so he wasn't at all surprised to be nicknamed "Ginge" before he'd even got off the bus that had taken him to basic training.

"Yeah, a prawn cracker," said the man sitting next to him. Greg Massey was two years older than Ginge but had gone through basic training at the same time and, like Ginge, was preparing for his first overseas posting. Afghanistan.

The men around the table laughed, including the one officer, Captain Tommy Gannon. Gannon was in his mid-twenties, a career soldier, good-looking with a strong chin and piercing blue eyes. Like all the men, he was casually dressed, wearing a dark blue polo shirt and brown cargo pants, with a leather bomber jacket hanging on the back of his chair.

"What are the girls like in Afghanistan, sir?" Massey asked Gannon.

"No idea," said Gannon. "They always have their faces covered, once they're past puberty. And they keep well away from us."

"What about female suicide bombers?"

"It happens," said Gannon. "They've been using kids, too. But in Afghanistan the main hazards for us are going to be Taliban fighters, snipers and IEDs. Most of the Taliban suicide bombers are for their own people."

The pretty waitress returned with bottles of Chinese Tsingtao beer on a tray. "Hey, darling, do you go out with round-eyes?" asked the soldier sitting on Gannon's left. He was in his late twenties, the most experienced squaddie at the table. Craig Broadbent had already done one tour of Iraq and had the scars from a car bomb down his back to prove it.

The waitress scowled at him. "I don't go out with squaddies," she said, her accent pure Northern Irish.

"You should try Mr Gannon, then," said Massey, pointing his chopsticks at Gannon. "He's an officer."

The waitress looked at Gannon and raised her eyebrows. "A sergeant?" she said.

"Sergeants aren't officers," he said. "I'm a captain. *Ney ho mah?*"

She looked surprised. "You speak Cantonese?"

"*Siu siu,*" he said. "Just a bit. I was in Hong Kong last year, picked some up while I was there." He gestured at the men sitting around the table. "Don't worry about these guys. They're off to Afghanistan next week."

"Are you going with them?" asked the waitress.

"We wouldn't go without the captain," Massey put in. "We've got it written into our contracts."

"Is that true?" asked the waitress.

"No," laughed Gannon. "But they can't even put on their boots without me, so I've got to go with them. What's your name?"

"May," said the waitress.

"Well, I tell you what, May, as soon as I get back I'll pop in and you can teach me more Cantonese, okay?"

She grinned. "Okay."

He held out his hand. "Tommy Gannon," he said. The waitress shook it timidly.

"Captain Tommy Gannon," said Massey. "Killer of the Taliban and breaker of hearts."

Gannon's men cheered and the waitress hurried back to the kitchen, blushing.

The door to the street opened and two men in ski-masks and long dark coats walked in. Gannon's jaw dropped and a prawn slipped from between his chopsticks. His first thought was that the restaurant was about to be robbed, but then both men swung Kalashnikov assault rifles from under their coats. He looked around for a weapon but there was nothing, just the chopsticks, plates and bottles. He started to get to his feet. "Get down!" he screamed to his men, as he grabbed the beer bottle nearest to him.

The gunmen stood with their feet shoulder-width apart, the stocks of the Kalashnikovs tucked into their hips, braced for the recoil to come.

Gannon drew back his hand but before he could throw the bottle the guns burst into life. He felt two thumps in the chest and saw Massey's head explode, blood splattering across the tablecloth. Bullets thudded over the table, shattering bottles and kicking food into the air. Gannon saw Broadbent fall backwards with a gaping wound in his neck.

The gunfire was deafening in the confined space and the cordite stung his eyes. The bottle fell from his hand as he felt another thud, this time in his guts, and bent forward. His shirt and trousers were drenched with blood.

Still the guns kept firing, a non-stop rat-tat-tat of burning lead that ripped through the men at the table.

Portner was on his hands and knees, crawling towards the kitchen, until half a dozen bullets thudded into his back and he went down, his hands clawing at the carpet.

Gannon put his hands to his chest, trying to stem the flow of blood, but he knew it was a waste of time. He couldn't feel anything — the body's natural painkillers had flooded into his system, dulling the pain and making him almost sleepy. His last thought before his eyes closed and he slumped to the floor was that sometimes life was so bloody unfair.

The two men jumped into the back of the Toyota and the driver stamped on the accelerator as they slammed the door. Both were breathing heavily. The bigger of the two grabbed his companion's knee. "Perfect," he said. "Fecking perfect."

"How many do you think we got?"

"Four. Five. Six, maybe," said the Big Man. "Did you see the look of surprise on their faces, the stupid Brit bastards? Didn't have a clue what was happening." The man pulled off his ski-mask. "We bloody well showed them, Sean. We bloody well showed them that the fight's not over."

Sean pulled off his ski-mask and twisted around in his seat. The road was clear behind them. He turned back and cradled the Kalashnikov.

The driver took a hard left and the tyres squealed in protest. "Easy there, Joe," said the Big Man. "Nice and easy now."

"The shit's going to hit the fan, right enough," said the driver.

"And that's how it should be," said the Big Man. Now he removed his own mask. He was in his late forties with pale blue eyes and skin the texture of old leather, reddened and roughened from years out in the sun. "The shit should be flying left, right and centre till they get the hell out of our country. *Tiocfaidh ár lá.*"

"*Tiocfaidh ár lá*," echoed Sean and the driver. Our day will come.

Shepherd's alarm woke him early on Sunday morning. He pulled on a sweatshirt and tracksuit bottoms, went downstairs and made himself a cup of black coffee. Then he put on a pair of old army boots and took his rucksack out from the cupboard under the stairs. Inside the rucksack, a dozen bricks were wrapped in newspaper. He took his running seriously. He didn't believe in state-of-the-art trainers with gel insoles and Lycra shorts: he believed in doing it the hard way, in heavy boots with weight on his back.

He left the house and ran on the roads for two miles at a medium pace until he'd worked up a good sweat, then cut off into the countryside along a route through fields and woods that he knew was exactly six miles. At the halfway point two men in black tracksuits passed him. They were both in their early twenties with full bergens on their backs. Shepherd smiled to himself. They were obviously in the Regiment, SAS troopers at the peak of physical condition and probably carrying twice the weight he had on his back. Shepherd's bergen

47

was a GS issue, general service. The troopers were running with SAS-issue, bigger, with a zipped compartment on the lid, a zip on the outer central pouch, buckles on the lid straps and spaces for skis or a shovel behind the side pouches. When fully packed, an SAS bergen weighed between thirty-six and forty kilos. Shepherd was still in good condition but he doubted that he'd be able to run more than five miles with that amount of weight on his back. The two troopers pulled away from him and Shepherd let them ago. His racing days were over.

By the time he'd done his countryside route he was bathed in sweat, his shoulders ached from the weight of the rucksack and his feet were sore. He vaulted over a five-bar gate and started running on the pavement again. He upped the pace, his chest heaving, and ran the last two miles at full pelt.

When he got home, Katra was in the kitchen preparing breakfast. Shepherd went upstairs, showered and changed into a clean polo shirt and black jeans. By the time he was back in the kitchen, Liam was already tucking into scrambled eggs and bacon, the eggs done with cheese the way he liked them.

Katra gave Shepherd a mug of coffee. "What would you like, Dan?" she asked.

"Tomato omelette would hit the spot," said Shepherd, ruffling his son's hair and sitting down next to him. "Homework done?"

"Almost."

"Need any help?"

Liam shook his head as he shovelled a forkful of egg into his mouth.

"How's school?"

"School's school."

"Don't speak with your mouth full," said Shepherd.

"You asked me a question!" protested Liam.

"And don't answer back." Shepherd grinned and sipped his coffee.

The doorbell rang and Liam sprang up from the table. "That'll be Lady," he shouted.

"Calm down," said Shepherd, amused by his son's enthusiasm. "Remember what they said — everything has to be calm until she's settled. No loud noises, no rough games."

"Got it, Dad," said Liam, hurrying to the front door.

"Can you put my breakfast in the oven, please," Shepherd asked Katra, as he followed his son out of the kitchen.

Liam had already opened the front door and was on his knees petting the beagle. A girl in her twenties with short, spiky black hair, wearing blue jeans and a grey duffel coat, was holding the dog's leash and grinning at the fuss Lady was making of her new owner. She grinned at Shepherd and waved. "Hi," she said. "I'm Zoe, from the dogs' home."

"I guessed that," said Shepherd. "Come on in. Do you want a coffee or tea or something?"

"I'm fine," she said, stepping into the hallway. She handed the leash to Liam. "Here you are," she said. "Take her out into the garden and show her around. Keep her on the leash until she gets used to you."

Liam grabbed it and ran down the hall. The dog scrabbled after him, her tail lashing wildly. "She seems happy enough," said Shepherd.

"She's a lovely dog, great temperament and already house-trained," said Zoe. She took a small notebook from the pocket of her jacket and a ballpoint pen. "Have you had a dog before, Mr Shepherd?"

Shepherd shook his head. "Lady's our first, but we've bought a couple of books and we've already been along to see a local vet in case we have any problems."

"Who did you see?"

"Susan Heaton — she has a surgery on Lanhill Road. We were asking about inoculations — she said if we'd got the dog from you she would have had all her shots. But she said we should take her in for a check-up once she'd settled in."

"You're well prepared," she said, making a note in her book.

"It was one of my conditions for getting a dog that Liam read up on it," said Shepherd. "What exactly is it you need to see?"

"Just the state of the house generally," said Zoe. "And that's fine — I could tell from the outside." She grinned. "Actually, it's a lot better than a lot of the homes I visit. I just need to see where you'll be feeding her, where she sleeps and where she'll exercise."

"Kitchen's this way," said Shepherd, and took her along the hallway. Katra was loading the dishwasher. Shepherd introduced her to Zoe.

"I put the food and water bowls by the back door," said Katra. "I wasn't sure if inside or outside was best."

"Either works," said Zoe, making another note in her book. "What food will you be giving her?" Shepherd showed her the dried and tinned food that he and Liam had bought and Zoe nodded her approval. "And give her the occasional bone to gnaw on. Beagles can turn into chewers if they get bored," she said. "Everything looks fine. Just give me a quick look at the garden and I'll be out of your hair."

Shepherd opened the kitchen door and Zoe did a quick walk around outside, pronounced herself satisfied and handed Shepherd a printed form, which she'd already signed. She bent down and patted the dog. "You'll have a good life here, Lady," she said.

The dog woofed, as if she'd understood what Zoe had said, then sat down by Liam's feet, her tail still swishing from side to side.

Katra took Zoe back into the house while Shepherd watched Liam try to teach the dog to walk to heel. The beagle kept getting herself tangled in Liam's feet and Shepherd laughed out loud as the boy stumbled. "Dad!" Liam protested.

"We'll fix you up with training classes, don't worry," said Shepherd.

"I'll teach her," said Liam.

"I meant for you," said Shepherd. "The dog's fine — it's you that can't walk in a straight line." Liam grinned and took his Nokia mobile phone from his pocket. "Video me, Dad," he said.

"What's the magic word?"

"Please," said Liam. He held out the phone. "Come on, Dad, I want a video of the first time I walked her."

Shepherd took the phone from his son. He scrolled through the menu to the video camera and filmed Liam as he walked the dog around the garden. Every few steps Lady would jump up at him and by the time he'd gone around the lawn his jeans were splattered with mud.

"Make sure you clean her paws before you take her inside," warned Shepherd, as he gave Liam back the phone.

He went back into the kitchen. Katra took his breakfast out of the oven and put the plate on the table. "She's a lovely dog," she said.

"Just make sure that Liam looks after her," said Shepherd, sitting down. "I don't want to find you feeding and exercising her. She's Liam's responsibility, that's the deal."

Katra brushed a lock of hair behind her ear. "I understand, Dan," she said. "Do you want more coffee?"

"Please."

She refilled his mug. Liam rushed in, grabbed a kitchen roll and rushed out. A few minutes later he came in with Lady. "I've cleaned her paws, Dad."

"I'm glad to hear it."

"Can she go in the sitting room and watch TV?"

"Dogs don't watch TV, Liam," said Shepherd.

"You know what I mean," said Liam.

"She stays off the furniture, remember," said Shepherd.

Liam hurried into the sitting room and the dog scurried after him. Shepherd polished off his omelette, then picked up his coffee mug and went to join his son.

Liam was sprawled on one of the sofas, using the remote to flick through the channels. The dog was lying on the floor, her head resting on her paws.

"Just choose something and watch it," said Shepherd, as Liam continued to channel-hop. "You're making me dizzy."

"It's all rubbish," said Liam.

"Put on a DVD, then."

Liam carried on switching channels as Shepherd sipped his coffee. Five head-and-shoulders photographs of soldiers in uniform flashed onto the screen. It was Sky News and Shepherd was only half listening, but he heard, "Real IRA," just before Liam changed channels again. "Back, back, back, quick," he said.

Liam fumbled with the remote but after a few seconds he managed to get back to Sky News. The five photographs had been replaced by a video outside a Chinese restaurant. There were ambulances with lights flashing and officers of the Police Service of Northern Ireland hurrying back and forth while helmeted soldiers cradled their carbines.

"Hit the volume," said Shepherd, and Liam did as he was told.

"The five soldiers were eating a meal in a Chinese restaurant last night when the gunmen burst in," said a female voice. "Witnesses said they fired Kalashnikovs and fled to a waiting car outside. A waiter was also shot but is recovering in hospital. The five men were all with the 2nd Battalion, The Rifles, based at Ballykinler Barracks in County Down, and were due to fly out to Afghanistan on Wednesday. Last night the Prime

Minister paid tribute to the murdered servicemen and called the attack a cowardly assault on brave men who were serving their country. He said the attack was not a political act but was premeditated mass murder and he had no doubt that the perpetrators would be brought to justice."

The Prime Minister appeared on the screen, standing in front of 10 Downing Street, looking sombre. "This was not a political act, but was premeditated mass murder. Those who are trying to disrupt and destroy the political process that is working for the people of Northern Ireland are doomed to fail and will be brought to justice. The people of Northern Ireland do not want a return to guns on the street, and the murderers of our brave soldiers will not be allowed to destroy or undermine the political process."

"What is it, Dad?" asked Liam.

"Hush, Liam, let me listen," said Shepherd, leaning forward.

The newsreader reported that the Northern Ireland Secretary had said that he was sure the attack would not spell the end to the Peace Process and that everything possible would be done to track down the killers. The pictures of the five soldiers flashed up again. Under each picture was the soldier's name and rank. Shepherd's stomach churned as he stared at the screen.

"Dad, what's wrong?"

Shepherd stood up. "I've just got to make a call, Liam. I'll explain when I've finished."

He went back into the hall, picked up his mobile phone and pulled out the charger. He scrolled through his contacts list and called Major Gannon's number as he walked through the kitchen and into the back garden. The Major answered almost immediately. "Hi, Spider, you've seen the news, then?"

"I'm so sorry about your loss, boss," said Shepherd. "If there's anything you need, you know you just have to ask."

"I'm on the way to the airport as we speak. I'll call you from Ireland."

"Tell your brother my thoughts are with him," said Shepherd. "And, Major, anything you need — anything, okay?"

"I understand, Spider, and thanks for that. I've got to go. I'll call you later."

The Major ended the call. Lady ran up and began to sniff at Shepherd's shoes. Shepherd bent down to pat her and saw that Liam was standing at the kitchen door. "Sorry about that, Liam. I had to call the Major."

"Major Gannon?"

Shepherd nodded. The dog began biting his hand, playful nips but painful nevertheless. He straightened up and the dog tried to nibble his ankles. "Hey, put her on the lead for a while and stop her biting," said Shepherd.

"How do I do that?" asked Liam.

"Just give the lead a jerk and say, 'No,' whenever she does it."

"She's got a name, Dad."

"She's a dog," said Shepherd. "And dogs, like children, have to be trained."

"That's a joke, right?"

"It's sort of a joke."

Shepherd went back into the kitchen with his son. Liam picked up the lead and clipped it to the beagle's collar.

"You saw the story on TV about the soldiers getting shot?" asked Shepherd.

Liam nodded.

"One of the soldiers was Major Gannon's nephew."

"Who killed them?"

"The Real IRA. Terrorists."

"I thought the IRA had given up?"

"They had, supposedly. Their political wing is now a political party, part of the government, but the terrorists were supposed to have given up their guns. But that was the IRA. The men who killed the soldiers say they are with the Real IRA."

"And what's the difference between the IRA and the Real IRA?"

"That's a very good question," said Shepherd. "There are some people who say there's no difference, that the IRA terrorists just started using a different name."

"And why are they killing soldiers now?"

"That's another very good question, Liam. I would guess that the politicians are trying to answer that themselves, as we speak."

Shepherd got to Paddington station ten minutes before he was due to meet Jimmy Sharpe and waited for him at Caffè Ritazza. He sipped a coffee and read the *Daily Mail*. The killings in Downpatrick were the main story on the front page. There were five head-and-shoulders photographs of the soldiers, identical to the ones that had been shown on the television news, and inside the paper was a large photograph of the inside of the Chinese restaurant. There were two bodies covered with sheets under one of the tables. Shepherd scanned the article. According to the newspaper's security correspondent, the South Antrim unit of the Real IRA had claimed responsibility in a phone call to the *Sunday Tribune* paper in Dublin, using an established codeword to confirm their identity.

The Real IRA said they intended to continue killing members of the British armed forces until they withdrew in full from the island of Ireland, and that they made no apologies for the death of the soldiers or for the injuries of the Chinese waiter who was hurt in the attack. According to the Real IRA, the restaurant staff "were collaborating with the British by servicing them and were therefore legitimate targets".

Shepherd read through the story. "Dinosaurs," he muttered. The public had assumed that when the Provisional IRA announced it had given up its armed struggle it would be the end of violence in Northern Ireland, but sectarian killings had continued under the guise of criminal activity. Now troops were being targeted again, even though the British government was clearly moving towards granting everything the IRA had ever wanted or demanded. The men behind the restaurant killings weren't motivated by politics, or by a desire for a united Ireland. They were hate-filled, vicious sociopaths who killed because it was in their nature to do so. The soldiers they had murdered had been about to go to Afghanistan, to fight for democracy, and the cowardly thugs had ambushed them while they were out for a Chinese. Shepherd had respect for soldiers, for men who put on a uniform and picked up a weapon to fight for their country or for their beliefs, but he had no respect for terrorists who killed unarmed men while they ate, or used bombs to kill and maim civilians. He put down the paper, shaking his head.

He spotted Sharpe, reflected in the front window of Marks & Spencer, skulking around the ATMs. He was wearing a bulky sheepskin jacket with the collar turned up. Shepherd smiled to himself. Sharpe was trying to creep up behind him. Shepherd's choice of table hadn't been random: he'd sat where he was precisely because it gave him a view of the station concourse and the shopping area, and the stairs that led to the upper level. He sat back in his chair and tapped his fingers on the table as he waited for Sharpe to finish his little game.

Sharpe edged around the ATMs, then circled the Caffè Ritazza tables. Shepherd looked to his right and caught Sharpe's reflection in a glass door that led to the concourse. He waited until Sharpe was about six feet behind him before raising his hand and giving him the finger. "When are you going to grow up, Razor?" he said, without turning.

"What?" said Sharpe. "I was just testing your powers of observation."

"By skulking around Paddington station like Sylvester stalking Tweety Pie?"

Sharpe sat down at Shepherd's table. "I thought of it more as a lion stalking a wildebeest," he said.

58

"Did you ever play that game Fairy Footsteps when you were a kid? One kid turns his back on the rest and they have to creep up on him? Whenever he turns around, everyone has to freeze."

"I'm from Glasgow, remember," growled Sharpe. "You don't turn your back on anyone. Anyway, how did you know I was there?"

Shepherd waved his coffee mug at the Marks & Spencer window. "Your reflection."

"My problem for not being a vampire," he said. "Anyway, you passed. You now officially have eyes in the back of your head." He looked at his watch. "I make it almost ten thirty."

Shepherd checked his own and nodded. "Come on, let's get Charlie her tea and we'll head on over," he said, as he stood up.

"Why not get her a nice rosy apple while you're at it?" said Sharpe.

"I'm just being polite," said Shepherd. "I was going to get you a coffee, but if you're making a big thing out of it you can get it yourself."

"*Latte*," said Sharpe. "Tall or big or *grande* or whatever passes for large here."

Shepherd bought two *lattes* and a cup of breakfast tea for Button, then the two men walked out of the station and along Praed Street. The office was above a travel agent's. There were eight buttons on a panel by the entrance and he pressed number five. They both waved up at the CCTV camera covering the door and the lock clicked open.

Sharpe went in first and Shepherd followed him along a scruffy hallway, with a threadbare carpet that had once been scarlet but was now a muddy brown, and up a flight of wooden stairs.

Button already had the door open for them. She smiled as she took the tea from Shepherd. "You're always such a sweetie," she said.

"Teacher's pet," whispered Sharpe. He dropped down onto a black vinyl sofa under the window overlooking the street. To the right of the door was a small kitchen area with a sink, a microwave and a fridge, and to the left a door led to a small bedroom.

Shepherd sat down at the table. Button closed the door and joined him. Her briefcase was on the floor. Behind her, a large whiteboard was fixed to the wall. "So, the good news is that it looks as if Grimshaw and his crew are all going to plead guilty," said Button. "I can't see them getting away with less than ten years. And Maloney's going to get a darn sight longer than that."

"Deserves it, too," said Shepherd. "Any joy getting him charged with rapes from the other jobs?"

"The cops are working on it," said Button. "It's the age-old problem, though, that rape victims don't want to appear in court."

"Yeah, well, who can blame them?" said Shepherd. "Would you want to stand up in front of a man like Maloney and describe to a court what he did to you? I can see the bastard standing there grinning and lapping it up."

"The line they're trying to sell is that if they can get enough evidence then he'll plead guilty."

"And his lawyer will get the sentences running concurrently, which means he won't serve any extra time for the rapes," said Shepherd. "Maloney's an animal. He should be locked away for life."

"He'll get close to that, Spider, don't worry. Even without a rape charge he'll go down for armed robbery and for GBH on Toby Rawstorne and sexual assault on the girl. The really bad news is that Rawstorne has lost his spleen and he's threatening to sue us all."

"For what?" said Shepherd.

"His lawyer's claiming that the police were using him as bait. And that because of police recklessness, his family was put at risk."

"I didn't know where we were going until we were there," said Shepherd. "I took a hell of a risk sending you the text when I did — if they'd caught me it would have ended then and there in the van."

"And we got the armed-response unit there as quickly as we could," said Button. "But Rawstorne's house is in the middle of nowhere and we were in the depths of Somerset when all is said and done. The armed cops out there are okay, but they're not up to the standards of CO19."

"We're lucky they didn't turn up on tractors," said Sharpe.

Button ignored the interruption. "Anyway, that's all been explained to him, but his lawyer's arguing that we were negligent and is threatening to sue us."

"If it hadn't been for the police turning up when they did, Maloney would have killed him and his family," said Shepherd. "We saved them. How stupid is he? If I hadn't infiltrated Grimshaw's gang the robbery would still have gone ahead and his daughter would have been raped. And the beating he got was nothing to do with me."

"No arguments there," said Button. "But he does have a point. We could have pulled them in the planning stage. Got them for conspiracy." She caught the look of disgust that flashed across Shepherd's face. "I'm just saying, Spider, that you can see it from their point of view. It was my call to let the operation run."

"And it was the right call," said Shepherd. "No one knew that Maloney was going to turn nasty. We needed to catch them with the gear."

"Their lawyer is demanding full details of the operation, including any undercover operatives."

"Which, of course, he isn't going to get," said Shepherd.

"Of course. I just wanted you to know where we stand, that's all."

"I sometimes wonder if it's worth us doing what we do," said Shepherd. "The courts go easy on the guys we do put away, and the people we're trying to help want to sue us."

"Everyone's a victim," said Sharpe, sourly. "Everyone except the cops. And us."

Button laughed. "Looks like I'd better give you your next assignment before you start talking about quitting," she said. She picked up her briefcase, opened it and took out a thick file. Sharpe finished his coffee and joined them at the table as Button stuck a large photograph onto the whiteboard. It had been taken using a long lens but the detail was sharp. Three men in wheelchairs were being wheeled away from an Air Jamaica jet. Two had leg casts, one had his arm in a sling and all had facial injuries. "Orane Williams, Leonardo Sachell and Dwayne Brand, a.k.a. Glenford Barrow, big wheels in the Clansman Massive gang and frequent visitors to our shores," said Button. "Shown here returning to Kingston." She used a black marker pen to write the names on the whiteboard.

"Good riddance, I'd say," said Sharpe.

"I can't argue with that," said Button. "But someone gave them a hell of a going over before they left the UK. Broken legs, fractured arms, smashed kneecaps, broken teeth, a ruptured spleen and other assorted injuries. The guy in the middle there lost both his testicles."

"I've heard of the Clansman Massive," said Shepherd. "Didn't I read somewhere that raping an underage girl formed part of their initiation ceremony?"

"You don't want to believe everything you read," said Button. "But they're hard bastards, that's for sure. They were dealing drugs and running hookers in north London and are thought to be responsible for a number of shootings being investigated by Operation Trident. It's not the first time — they got very busy in 2006 but when things got too hot they went back to Jamaica and returned with new identities." She stuck another surveillance photograph onto the whiteboard. This one showed Jamaican police officers surrounding the three injured men. "Someone tipped off the Jamaican cops. There were outstanding warrants against all of them and they're now in custody. They'll be sent down for a long, long time."

"Rum and Cokes all round," said Sharpe. "What's SOCA's interest?"

"In the past year a dozen Yardies have returned to Jamaica in a similar state. Beaten to a pulp but not prepared to say a word to the police here."

"Good riddance to bad rubbish," said Shepherd. "Someone's giving them a taste of their own medicine. I doubt anyone's shedding any tears for them."

Button stuck a police photograph onto the whiteboard, a front view and two side views. It was a man in his fifties, rat-faced with a small moustache and thinning hair. "Oliver Barrett," she said. "Convicted paedophile, served eight years back in the nineties for assaulting two toddlers. He was murdered two months ago. His body was found under a railway arch in Kilburn." She stuck several scenes-of-crime photographs onto the board. "Strangled with a length of rope," she said.

"A dead paedophile. Again, I don't see why SOCA would be interested," said Shepherd.

"Stick with me, Spider," said Button. "But I will tell you that a police van was seen driving away from the railway arch a couple of hours before the body was discovered." She put up another photograph. A black man with short hair and a jagged scar across his cheek stared sullenly at the camera. "Jake Fellows, known to his friends as Screwball." Button wrote the name and nickname on the whiteboard. "He was recently sent down for life for murdering a rival drug-dealer, and this is where it all gets very interesting."

"Another Yardie?"

Button shook her head. "British born," she said. "Jamaican mother, Geordie father. Brought up in Newcastle but moved down to London in the nineties. Nasty piece of work. Operation Trident had been looking at him for years until one day he was handed to them on a plate. Anonymous phone call that he had crack cocaine in his car. Drugs Squad picked him up and it was a good tip — he had half a kilo hidden in his spare tyre. But what was much more interesting was the Glock they found with the drugs. It had been used to kill another drug-dealer, guy by the name of Winston Cameron — Churchill to his friends. Cameron was shot twice in the head and the bullets were a match to the gun in Screwball's car."

"Which he denied all knowledge of, presumably," said Sharpe.

"Why, Razor, have you become psychic in your old age?" said Button. "Screwball denied all knowledge of the drugs and the gun, but the forensic evidence and the gun did for him. Police had found an oil leak in the road opposite Cameron's house, and it was a match to the oil in the sump of Screwball's car. There were half a dozen cigarette butts on the pavement and the DNA on them was a match to Screwball's."

"Bang to rights," said Sharpe.

"The jury certainly thought so," said Button. "Took them less than an hour to reach a verdict and the judge sent him down for twenty-five years. That was three months ago, but last week someone else confessed to killing Cameron. And we've no reason to think that he was lying. The killer is another Yardie drug-dealer, who was arrested after a road-rage incident in Harlesden." She put another police photograph on the board. "Name of Sexton Packer. Sixpack is his gang name. A man in a van pulled in front of him and gave him the finger, so Packer got out and broke it. Snapped it in half. At the time an Operation Trident unit had him under surveillance so they pulled him in and found a gun in his glove compartment and a kilo of Colombia's finest. He was processed at Harlesden police station and the cops put an undercover guy in with Packer."

"Risky."

"The cop's been under cover for over a decade. Very hush-hush, one of the few black undercover cops the Met has. They won't even tell me who he is." She smiled. "Probably because they know I'd try to poach him. Anyway, this undercover guy spent twelve hours in a police cell and another three days on the remand wing of Wandsworth prison with Packer. Packer's still on remand, but he's got a top brief and is claiming that the car wasn't his and he didn't know about the drugs or the gun, and if his track record is anything to go by he'll probably walk. But what got Operation Trident all hot and bothered was that Packer told their man he'd killed Cameron and that he reckoned the police had fitted up Screwball."

"The forensics were faked?"

"Packer doesn't know how they did it, or why, but he's adamant that he killed Cameron. Knew the make of gun, and when and where it happened."

"So now what?" said Shepherd. "Screwball gets out?"

"It's not as simple as that," said Button. "There's no hard evidence and Packer isn't likely to stand up in court and repeat what he said. And there's no way that the undercover cop can give evidence. No, the way things stand at the moment, Screwball continues to serve his sentence. But we need to find out who set him up. Because it was almost certainly cops that did it."

"That's a jump, Charlie," said Shepherd.

"Not necessarily," said Button. "If it was one of Packer's competitors, they wouldn't bother with a set-up, they'd just arrange a drive-by. No, whoever did it had to have access to the gun in the first place — and who better to relieve a bad guy of his weapon than the police? Packer was regularly turned over by the cops, and during one search they could have found the gun and kept it."

"And you think it's the same cops that have been riding roughshod over the Yardies?"

"That seems logical enough," said Button. "What's the alternative? That we've got two groups of vigilantes on the go?" She shook her head. "The commissioner thinks it's one group and so do I." She reached into her file and took out three photographs, all of young white men who were bruised and bloodied, and put them up on the whiteboard. "Three of north London's most prolific housebreakers have ended up in Casualty over the past year," continued Button. "All three had horrific hand injuries and all claimed to have been involved in unlikely accidents."

Sharpe grinned, and Button glared at him. "It's not funny, Razor. One of them was a sixteen-year-old kid."

"Yeah, well, when I walked a beat in Strathclyde, we had ten-year-olds breaking into houses," he said. "They'd get in through the bathroom window and let their mates in. Steal everything that wasn't nailed down and trash the place for good measure. Scum of the earth, burglars, and the courts these days let them off with a slap on the wrist. Same with car thieves and joy-riders. Maybe if a few more got their hands smashed, they'd be less likely to do it."

"Maybe you'd be better off applying for a job with the Saudi police," said Button. "These men were assaulted and nearly crippled, and no matter how you cut it, that's not the role of the police in a civilised society."

"Charlie, nothing that you've said directly points to the cops," said Shepherd.

"Yeah, it could be the militant wing of Neighbourhood Watch," said Sharpe.

Button opened her mouth to snap at Sharpe, but Shepherd put up a hand to interrupt her. "Razor actually has a point," he said. "It could be civilians. There are plenty of anti-drug groups that have got fairly violent in the past. Could be civilian workers within the Met. I don't see why you're assuming it's cops that have gone bad."

"The van that was seen near to where the dead paedophile was found. We have a partial number plate."

"And how did we get that, pray tell?"

"A dosser with a pretty good memory, considering he's an alcoholic who's been on the streets for going on twenty years," said Button. "He remembered the first two numbers and there were three letters in the plate that were his daughter's initials, so that was enough to tie it to one of three vans used by the Territorial Support Group in north-west London." She wrote the numbers and letters on the whiteboard and underlined them.

"The TSG?" said Sharpe. "I remember the good old days when they were the SPG, the Special Patrol Group. A rose by any other name."

"The SPG was disbanded in 1987," said Button, archly. "But, yes, the TSG, or CO20, carries out the same function as the SPG used to, pretty much."

"They're the heavy mob," said Sharpe. "They go in with shields and truncheons where other bobbies fear to tread."

"They have an anti-terrorism role, these days," said Button. "But you're right. They are there to provide a level-one response to disorder throughout the capital, and reducing crime that has been determined to be a priority."

"Like I said, the heavy mob," said Sharpe.

Shepherd nodded thoughtfully. "And the plan is to send me and Razor in as cops?"

"Just you," said Button. "I doubt we'd get away with two new faces appearing at the same time. I'll arrange

69

for you to report for duty next Monday so you'll have the rest of the week off. I'll talk to Jenny Lock and get a place fixed up for you in north London." Jenny Lock was one of SOCA's dressers, providing the props necessary to back up an undercover legend. Shepherd had met her two years previously when she'd helped provide his background for a job in Belfast. Button slid a sheet of blank paper across the desk. "We'll need a signature for the warrant card and ancillary ID. Name of Terry Halligan."

"Terry or Terrence?"

"Terry," said Button.

Shepherd signed the sheet of paper and gave it back to Button. She took a thick file from her briefcase and gave it to him. "Some light reading for you," she said. "There's a lot to absorb there so take it home with you. I'll need you back in London on Sunday — bring it with you then. It's got all the details of the Serials you'll come across."

"Serials?"

"The operational units of the TSG. Basically three vans each with a sergeant and six constables, all reporting to an inspector. We know that the van seen in Kilburn came from the TSG base at Paddington Green, just down the road from here. We think, because of the operational duties they were on that day, that we can narrow it down to two of the Serials. But in the file I've included photos and details on all the TSG staff at the station, plus any other senior officers you might come across. I've already checked that there's no one at Paddington Green that you've run into before."

"I'm not happy about going under cover against cops," said Shepherd.

"Your legend will be watertight," said Button.

"That's not what I'm worried about," said Shepherd. "They're cops, Charlie. We're on the same side."

"They've committed assault, GBH, perjury, they've faked evidence, and there's a very good chance that they've committed murder," said Button.

"They've beaten up Yardies, put a drug-dealer behind bars and maybe killed a paedophile," said Shepherd.

"They've broken the law, Spider. We can't be selective about justice. People either obey the law or they don't."

Shepherd tapped the photographs of the three injured Yardies on the airport Tarmac. "Don't tell me you feel sorry for them. We're better off without them in our country, and if the government was doing its job they wouldn't be here in the first place. And don't get me started on paedophiles. You know as well as I do that there's no curing a paedophile. They'll keep on offending until they die. The only way of dealing with them is to lock them up so they can't get near kids."

"There's a few psychologists that would argue with you there" said Button.

"Once a nonce, always a nonce," said Sharpe. "And that's a fact."

"Thank you for your input, Razor," said Button. "But it's also a fact that murder is a crime, no matter who the victim is."

"You're a mother, Charlie. How would you feel if someone molested her? Or worse?" said Shepherd.

"I'd rather not think about it but, frankly, it's irrelevant."

"I know that if anyone ever deliberately hurt Liam, they'd have me to deal with."

"I do hope you're not condoning vigilantism, Spider."

"I'd do what I had to do," said Shepherd.

"Is that what you think these cops have become?" asked Sharpe. "Vigilantes?"

"That's exactly what we think," said Button.

"There's no profit involved? They're not ripping off their cash or drugs?"

"There's no evidence of that, no."

Sharpe sat back and folded his arms. "Then I for one think we should just leave them to it. Or give them a medal."

"Well, thankfully, the fate of the British criminal justice system doesn't rest in your hands," said Button.

"Again, Razor does have a point," said Shepherd. "We're SOCA, the Serious Organised Crime Agency. My understanding is that we'd be going after drug-dealers, people-traffickers, armed robbers."

"What these guys are doing is serious and organised," said Button.

"But they're cops. We go after villains."

"In this case, the cops are villains," said Button.

"Professional Standards investigate bad cops," said Sharpe. "That's what they do."

"In this case, the commissioner for the Met has asked for our assistance."

"Then you should just say we're too busy," said Shepherd. "I didn't sign up to investigate cops."

"Perhaps 'asked' is the wrong word," said Button. "The commissioner spoke to the Home Secretary and the Home Secretary spoke to my boss and my boss spoke to me and now I'm telling you two that your next assignment is to investigate these cops. And you can huff and puff as much as you want but at the end of the day that's what you're going to be doing."

Shepherd sighed. "Has anyone looked at the crime stats for the area that these guys work in?"

"Crime's down, if that's what you're getting at," said Button.

"That's exactly what I'm getting at," said Shepherd. "If they're running drug-dealers out of town and crippling housebreakers and putting bad guys behind bars by whatever means, then I figure all the crime stats will be on the way down."

"Please don't even think about saying that the end justifies the means."

Shepherd opened his mouth to reply but then thought better of it. There was no point in arguing with Button because basically she was right. It didn't matter what the profession, a criminal was a criminal and SOCA was in the business of putting away criminals.

"And what am I doing while Spider's getting up close and personal with the TSG?" said Sharpe.

Button flashed him a sarcastic smile. "I'm so glad you asked, Razor," she said. "I've got the perfect job for you. Infiltrating a right-wing racist group."

Sharpe frowned. "What?"

"Do you remember a while back when a membership list of the British National Party was posted on-line and it turned out that there were police officers on it?"

Sharpe nodded.

"The powers-that-be already had the list, as it happens, but because it was in the public domain we had to act. We've been a bit more circumspect with another list that we got our hands on some time ago. It's an organisation called England First, made up of a lot of the heavies in the National Front who weren't palatable enough for the BNP. And it looks as if one of the TSG sergeants is a member. Gary Dawson." She put a photograph of a grey-haired man in his mid-forties on the whiteboard.

"How stupid is he to let his name appear on a membership list?" asked Shepherd.

"Give him some credit," said Button. "He used a false name, but there was a pay-as-you-go mobile on the list that we've traced to him. Razor, I need you to make contact with England First and worm your way in. With your tendency to make off-the-cuff racist statements, I'm sure you'll have no problem blending in."

"I resemble that remark," joked Sharpe. He grinned. "You know I'm a changed man after the racial-awareness course you sent me on?"

"Yes, Razor, we're all very impressed with how you've managed to drag yourself into the third millennium."

"But now you want me to undo all that good work by having me pretend to be a dyed-in-the-wool racist?"

74

Button flashed him another sarcastic smile. "I'm sure you'll do your best," she said. "I'll get someone to brief you on England First."

"A spook?" Sharpe grinned again. "And by that I mean a member of the Secret Service, of course."

"It'll be an intelligence briefing," said Button. "And I'm sure it'll make clear just how dangerous these people are. You're going to have to watch yourself, Razor. They're the guys who throw petrol bombs through the windows of Asian families and beat up black kids on the streets."

"What are you saying, Charlie?" asked Shepherd. "Are you saying these vigilante cops are racist?"

"It's a possibility," said Button. "A high proportion of the cases we're looking at involve Afro-Caribbean males."

"You're saying that they're targeting black criminals? Or is it that the criminals they're targeting happen to be black?"

"That's a question I hope you'll be able to answer, Spider."

"It's going to be messy, you know that. There'll be ramifications, either way."

"I'm aware of what a can of worms this is," said Button. "And so's the commissioner."

"Every case they've been involved in, any criminal they dealt with, they're all going to be given get-out-of-jail-free cards."

"Probably."

"And if it's racism, it'll rip the Met apart."

Button frowned. "Are you suggesting that we don't do anything? Let sleeping dogs lie?"

Shepherd shook his head. "Of course not," he said. "But if you know that Dawson's rotten, then split him and his team up. Disperse them. That'll put an end to it."

"Or spread the virus throughout the force," she said.

"Service," said Sharpe.

"What?" said Button.

"It's not a police force any more," said Sharpe. "It's a service. Which is part of the problem. If the public respected the police the way they used to, and if cops were allowed to deal with villains the way they used to, then there wouldn't be any need for vigilantes."

"Yes, well, we've moved on since the glory days of the eighties," said Button. "We're now dealing with policing in the third millennium and, be it a force or a service, we can't afford to let the bad apples infect the whole barrel. We have to find out which ones are rotten and weed them out."

"Publicly?" said Shepherd.

"That'll be up to the commissioner and the Crown Prosecution Service," said Button.

"Because the great British public is probably going to think they're heroes," said Shepherd.

"That's not our problem," said Button. "We go in, get the facts, and leave. What happens then is for someone else to decide. And as much as I understand your reservations, we don't get to pick and choose what we do." She waved at the photographs on the whiteboard. "These are our targets, and for the foreseeable future, you'll have them in your sights."

"I was hoping for a week or two's leave," said Shepherd. "It's been a month since I spent more than one night at home."

Button sat down and picked up her tea. "There's something else I have to tell you both," she said. Shepherd frowned. He could tell from her tone that it was bad news, and even before she spoke he knew what she would say. "I'm going to be leaving SOCA before the end of the year," she said.

"Back to Five?" asked Sharpe, putting into words exactly what Shepherd had been thinking.

Button nodded. "I'm to head up the International Counter-terrorism Branch," she said.

"It's a big job," said Shepherd. "You've earned it."

"I'll miss you guys," she said. "I mean that."

"We were always a stepping-stone," said Shepherd. "We knew that from the start."

Button raised her eyebrows. "Spider, the job meant more to me than that," she said.

Shepherd shrugged. He didn't want to get into an argument with his boss but he wasn't happy at her leaving. "I'm not saying you weren't committed or that you weren't good at the job, I'm just saying that you always saw SOCA as a temporary assignment."

"I'm not sure that's true," said Button. "But there aren't the opportunities within SOCA that I'll get within Five."

"Yeah, at least they let women run MI5, which is more than SOCA does," said Sharpe.

"Is that the plan, Charlie?" asked Shepherd. "Director General one day?"

Button smiled. "That's a long way off, Spider," she said.

Shepherd leaned back in his chair and stretched out his legs. "Do you know who your successor is going to be?"

"They haven't told me yet," she said. "As soon as I know, you'll know." She sipped her tea. "I'd be grateful if you wouldn't say anything for a day or two. I want to tell everyone in the unit personally, rather than having them hear second-hand."

Shepherd and Sharpe nodded.

"Hopefully we'll have tied this operation up before I go," said Button.

"And if we don't?" said Shepherd.

"Let's cross that bridge when we come to it," said Button.

The barman put the Jameson's and soda in front of Shepherd and gave Sharpe his pint of lager. "A rat deserting the sinking ship," said Sharpe. "I knew we couldn't trust her."

"SOCA isn't exactly a sinking ship," said Shepherd. The two men went to a corner table. They were in the pub around the corner from the office where Button had briefed them.

Sharpe tossed his sheepskin jacket over the back of a chair and sat down on a bench seat. "Let's face it, Spider, SOCA's successes are few and far between," he said. "It was set up to bust organised crime and what are we doing? Investigating plod. Why aren't we going after the real criminals? We know who they are, and we know what they're doing."

"Knowing and proving are different things," said Shepherd, sinking into a chair opposite Sharpe's bench.

"It's because SOCA's run by bean-counters," said Sharpe. "They work out what an investigation is going to cost, and it just costs too much to go after the big boys because they're so well protected. You and I know half a dozen guys in Amsterdam who are responsible for a quarter of the drugs coming into this country, but do we go after them? Do we hell. They send us after bank robbers and small-time drug-dealers and now they want us to investigate cops. Why? Because they're easy options, that's why. I think Button's doing the right thing, jumping ship now. She can see which way the wind's blowing. I tell you, I'm thinking about going back to the Met."

"Are you serious?"

"At least I'd be going up against real villains. This going up against cops really pisses me off. Professional Standards is supposed to investigate cops, not us. You heard me tell her. But did she listen?"

"She's between a rock and a hard place," said Shepherd. "If the Met commissioner asks the Home Secretary for SOCA's help, she can hardly say no."

"No, she can't, because it might put the brakes on her meteoric rise to the top."

"You're a cynical bastard," said Shepherd.

"And you cut her too much slack because you want to get into her pants."

Shepherd's eyes narrowed. "Screw you, Razor."

"I'm just saying — you've always had a thing for her, have done from day one. Which means you let her get away with a lot." Shepherd opened his mouth to reply, but Sharpe held up a hand to silence him. "Don't deny it because I saw the look on your face when she said she was leaving."

Shepherd shook his head. "There's no talking to you sometimes." He sipped his whiskey.

"Because you know I'm right," said Sharpe.

"She's not leaving because she's unhappy with SOCA — we were always just a stepping-stone. She needed to do a few years at the sharp end before going any further up the MI5 ladder."

"She told you that?"

"It was obvious," said Shepherd. "Once a spy, always a spy. We were just a temporary attachment."

"She used us," said Sharpe. He raised his glass to Shepherd. "She used us all."

"No one stays in the same job for ever," said Shepherd. "You were walking a beat in Strathclyde, then you moved to the Met, now you're with SOCA. I was in the army, then the cops, now I'm . . ." He grinned. "Now I'm a civil servant with powers of arrest," he said. "Sod it, Razor, let's both go back to the Met."

Sharpe frowned. "Now it's my turn to ask, are you serious?"

Shepherd sighed. "Maybe it's time for a move. I'm not sure that I want to break in a new boss."

Sharpe leaned over and clinked his glass against Shepherd's. "I'm going to hold you to this," he said.

"Let's see who we get," said Shepherd.

"I bet it'll be another woman," said Sharpe. "Probably black and disabled to boot so that they can tick all the boxes."

Despite himself, Shepherd smiled. "You're impossible," he said.

"No, I'm a cynical bastard," said Sharpe. "It's the job that's impossible."

The train journey from Paddington to Hereford was almost three hours, which gave Shepherd plenty of time to study the file that Charlotte Button had given him. The TSG had five bases around London. 1TSG, or Area One, was at Paddington Green police station in Harrow Road, the most secure police station in the UK where terrorism suspects were usually held and interrogated before being taken south of the river to Belmarsh prison. The van that had been seen near to the dead paedophile was one of the Mercedes Sprinters based at Paddington Green. The other four TSG bases were at Finchley, Chadwell Heath, Catford and Clapham.

The organisational structure was the same at all of the bases, though the Paddington Green group included trained firearms officers. As Button had said, the units were based around the vans. Each van had a sergeant and seven constables. Three vans formed an operational Serial, headed by an inspector, so a Serial was made up of an inspector, three sergeants and eighteen constables. There were five Serials at each base with senior officers taking the total establishment of the TSG up to 720 across the capital.

Assuming that the problem was at a relatively low level, that meant everyone from inspector down at Paddington Green was a suspect, a total of 132 men. Shepherd smiled to himself. And women, of course. The TSG was an equal-opportunity employer.

The TSG as a whole was headed by a commander, with a superintendent below him. Each of the five bases was run by a chief inspector, and under each chief inspector was an inspector in charge of operations and another five inspectors each running a Serial of three teams. The teams' Mercedes Sprinters were specially modified, their windscreens covered with mesh shields.

Button had included the TSG's handbook in the file and Shepherd speed-read it as the train powered towards Hereford. The TSG had three main functions: to secure the capital against terrorism, to react to violent situations that arose anywhere in London, and to help reduce crime by supporting the local police when needed.

Since the al-Qaeda attacks on the Twin Towers in New York, the TSG had been trained to deal with the aftermath of terrorist incidents in London, and the unit was equipped to deal with chemical, biological, radiological and nuclear attacks. So far as day-to-day policing was concerned, TSG officers could be used on patrols and surveillance, and were also available for undercover operations. Each Serial also took it in turns to stand as the Commissioner's Reserve, available to be sent anywhere within the capital to deal with riots, brawls or football hooligans.

In the file there was a printout of the TSG staff at Paddington Green with head-and-shoulders photographs and a brief description of their career to date. Shepherd effortlessly committed the information to memory. His memory had been virtually photographic for as long as he could remember.

The inspector in charge of the Serial that Shepherd was joining was Phillip Smith, a university graduate who was being fast-tracked through the ranks. He had joined straight from Oxford with a degree in Economics and had been promoted to sergeant before he was twenty-five. He had become an inspector at twenty-seven and had already done two years with the TSG. Under Smith there were three sergeants. Michael Keane was one. He had been with the TSG for six years and prior to that had been a traffic cop. Tony Drury had just turned thirty and had moved from CO19 shortly after being promoted. Roy Fogg was in his mid-thirties and in the TSG for five years. He was in charge of the team that Shepherd would be joining. Before the TSG he'd walked a beat in Battersea and had two Commissioner's Commendations for bravery. Fogg's team included Carolyn Castle, a twenty-eight-year-old constable who had recently been transferred to the TSG from a Sapphire team in Croydon, investigating rapes and looking after rape victims. Richard Parry was a West Indian who had worked for a Safer Neighbourhoods Team in Haringey and had a Commissioner's Commendation for bravery: he had disarmed, single-handed, two muggers who had just robbed a pensioner. Nick Coker was twenty-six, had joined the police straight from school and had been with the TSG for two years. He had receding hair, cut short, and a nose that looked as if it had been punched a few more times than was good for it.

According to the file, officers were generally assigned to the TSG for five years, but could stay on for longer if they wanted. Angus Turnbull, the driver of Fogg's van, was one of the long-timers and had been with the TSG for nine years. He was in his late thirties and had the look of a male model with jet-black hair, piercing blue eyes and a boyish smile. Darren Simmons was a relative newcomer and had only been with the unit for nine months. Like Smith, he had been placed on the Met's graduate-entry scheme, which meant he would be fast-tracked to sergeant three years after joining and inspector two years after that. The final member of the team was Barry Kelly, who had spent four years with the British Transport Police, based at King's Cross station, before switching to the Met. Kelly was a redhead with a sprinkling of freckles across his nose.

A page was devoted to the equipment that Shepherd would be expected to use as a member of the TSG. The officers weren't routinely armed, though specially trained firearms officers were based at Paddington Green and authorised to carry Glocks and MP5 carbines. The rank-and-file officers were equipped with the force's standard Monadnock batons and CS sprays but were also allowed to carry and use Tasers. In riot situations they wore fireproof overalls, visored helmets, elbow and shin pads, and held acrylic riot shields. Jimmy Sharpe hadn't been far wrong when he'd referred to them as the heavy mob.

About half an hour before the train was due to arrive at Hereford, Shepherd's mobile rang. It was Major Gannon. "The funeral's on Friday, in Sussex," said the Major. "They'll bury him in the churchyard near where my brother lives in Rotherfield. Two o'clock."

"I'll be there, boss. Do you want me to spread the word?"

"Just the guys who knew Tommy," said the Major. "My brother doesn't want to make a big thing of it. And he's made it clear that there are to be no uniforms. Tommy's regiment aren't happy but they'll respect his wishes, obviously."

"Your brother and his wife, how are they holding up?" asked Shepherd.

"My brother's a tough nut, always has been, but Grace has taken it really badly."

"I'm sorry, boss. If there's anything you need . . ."

"Everything's being taken care of, but thanks." The Major ended the call and Shepherd phoned Katra to tell her that he was on his way home. "Is Liam asleep?" he asked.

"He was in bed by nine. He wanted Lady to sleep in his bedroom — I hope that's okay."

"Katra, I said not to."

"I know, but Liam said he was lonely with you away and they both gave me puppy-dog eyes."

"Liam's pulling your strings," said Shepherd. "I guess it won't do any harm, but make sure that she's sleeping on the floor, I don't want her on the bed."

"I'll make sure," promised Katra. "I've got an *obara* in the oven for you."

Shepherd smiled. *Obara* was a traditional Slovenian stew, one of Katra's specialities. "Not dormouse, I hope," he said.

"That was a joke," said Katra. "I only told Liam that because he was asking about my grandparents."

"And your grandmother cooked dormouse *obara*. That's what you said."

"They were poor," said Katra, "and my grandfather always said it tasted delicious. Like chicken."

"Clearly a man who loved his wife," said Shepherd. "Whatever sort of *obara* it is, I'm sure it'll be delicious, too."

"It's beef," she said.

"Great."

"Really, beef. Good beef, from Waitrose."

Shepherd laughed and switched off the phone. He picked up Button's file again. He was finishing the last page just as the train pulled into Hereford station. He climbed into a waiting minicab and ten minutes later he was home. Katra already had a whiskey and soda waiting for him, the ice barely melted. He sipped it gratefully and sat down at the kitchen table. Katra put on oven gloves and carefully took out a green Le Creuset pot. She carried it to the table and spooned a generous helping of stew onto his plate. "It's beef," she said, before he could say anything.

"So you said." He sniffed it. "Lovely."

Katra sat down opposite him and watched him eat. "Good trip?" she asked.

"Rushed as usual," he said. "I'll be working in London starting next week, probably be there for a few weeks."

"Liam will be disappointed," she said.

"There's not much I can do about that," said Shepherd. "It's the job."

"He was hoping you'd be able to watch him play football. The school team plays every Saturday."

"I can watch this week for sure," said Shepherd, "and I'll try to get back next weekend. "How's Lady?"

Katra grinned. "Behaving herself," she said. "But she knows that you're the head of the house. As soon as you were out of the door she was up on the sofa."

"You kicked her off, I hope."

Katra laughed. "Liam did. Then he took her into the garden for an hour's training before supper." She looked at her watch. "Time I was in bed," she said.

"You don't have to stay up for me. I'll load the dishwasher."

"Thanks, Dan." She flashed him a smile and headed upstairs.

Shepherd finished his meal, drained his glass, and made himself a mug of coffee. He took it through to the sitting room and dropped onto the sofa. Liam's phone was on the coffee-table. Shepherd picked it up and scrolled through the Gallery, looking for the video he'd taken of Liam trying to walk the dog. He found it and watched it, chuckling at his son's attempts to stop the dog jumping up.

There were a dozen other videos of Liam trying to teach the dog tricks. The beagle could just about obey the "sit" command but clearly didn't understand "stay" and would only stare at Liam, bemused, as he tried to teach her to offer her paw. Liam was good with her, though, never raising his voice, talking to her patiently and quietly as he explained what he wanted her to do. Shepherd smiled and put down the phone. He tried watching an old movie on Channel 4 but he was too tired to concentrate so he switched off the television and the lights and went upstairs.

His son's bedroom door was ajar and Shepherd peeped in. Liam was fast asleep, lying on his back. The beagle was lying next to him, her head on the pillow. They were both snoring softly. Shepherd gently closed the door.

Gerry McElroy carried his mug of coffee into the sitting room and sat on the sofa facing the big-screen LCD television. It was nine o'clock in the morning but McElroy had been up since five. He rarely slept more than a few hours. The coffee was all he would have for breakfast. He couldn't face food, not since his daughter had died. He couldn't sleep, he couldn't eat, he couldn't concentrate on anything except that Debbie was dead.

He fought back the tears and sipped his coffee. Nothing had any taste now. His wife said he had to eat, he had to keep his strength up, but he was never hungry. Every evening when she came home from work she'd cook him a meal and he'd have a few mouthfuls. Then he'd put down his fork and shake his head. He didn't want food. He didn't want anything. He just wanted his darling Debbie back and that was the one thing he'd never have.

To the left of the television there was a set of shelves. He'd put them up himself, a couple of months after they'd moved into the house. Debbie had been two years old; she was walking but not talking, other than to say "Mum" and "Dad" and "Milk", but she had sat on the sofa and watched as he'd cut the wood, sanded it, and screwed the brackets to the wall; she'd watched him as if he was the most important thing in her life.

On the third shelf down there were half a dozen framed photographs. Three were of Debbie on her own, and had been taken at school. One was from the day she was born. It had been a long birth and a difficult one, and the strain was written on his wife's face, but she smiled proudly at the camera, which had been held by a nurse, clasping the tiny bundle that was Debbie to her cheek while he looked on, tears in his eyes.

The largest picture was a family group, snapped one Christmas when his in-laws had come to stay. Their neighbour had popped around for a drink and she had taken the photograph. His wife's parents were so happy to have a grandchild. Their daughter was an only child, and you could see the joy in the faces. Debbie had been three, blonde-haired and blue-eyed, with a face that always seemed to be smiling. They had known there would be no more grandchildren for them. The obstetrician had said McElroy's wife's womb had been damaged by the birth and she wouldn't be able to have any more children. It hadn't mattered then because Debbie was the perfect child.

A tear ran down McElroy's cheek and he wiped it away with the back of his hand. He cried every day. Every day and every night. His wife was so much stronger than he was. Maybe it was because she was an A and E nurse so she saw death on a regular basis. Maybe it was because she was just tougher than he was. She never cried in front of him, hadn't even at the funeral, but sometimes late at night she'd lock the bathroom door and he'd hear her sobbing inside.

His wife had gone back to work the day after the funeral. McElroy had stayed at home. He couldn't face leaving the house. He owned a small printing company and his partner had told him to take off as much time as he wanted. There would never be enough time, McElroy knew. Time wasn't helping, and it wasn't healing. He missed Debbie as much that day as he did the day that she died. He spent most of his time lying on the single bed in his daughter's room. Everything was exactly the same as the day she'd left for school. He could still smell her on the pillow, and if he lay there long enough he could sometimes imagine that she would be home at any moment, throwing her school bag on the floor, hugging him and telling him she'd missed him so much.

Tears streamed down his face and he blinked, trying to clear his eyes. He put down his coffee, went into the kitchen and pulled several sheets of paper towel off the roll. Debbie's homework schedule was still on the fridge: Wednesday, Maths and Literacy. McElroy jumped as the doorbell rang. He tossed the wad of kitchen towel into the rubbish bin and walked slowly along the hallway. He made out two blue uniforms through the frosted-glass window. Police. McElroy stopped. He didn't want to talk to the police. There was nothing he wanted to say to them any more, and every time they turned up on his doorstep they only had bad news for him. He turned to go back to the sitting room, but then one of his visitors knocked. "Gerry, it's the police. We need to talk to you."

"I've nothing to say to you," said McElroy. "Just leave me alone. Come back when my wife's here. She'll talk to you. She likes to talk, my wife."

"We don't want to talk to your wife, Gerry. We want to talk to you. That's why we waited until she went to work."

"What do you want?" said McElroy.

"We want a chat, Gerry. Trust me, you'll want to hear what we have to say."

McElroy opened the front door. There were two men, in uniform. He didn't recognise them, but in the weeks following his daughter's death there had been dozens of uniforms in his house, all of them sympathetic, all of them powerless to get him the one thing he wanted — justice. One was wearing a fluorescent jacket over his uniform. He was the younger of the two. His colleague was in his late thirties, bigger and stronger. They both removed their hats as they stepped across the threshold.

A grey police van was parked outside. A uniformed driver was looking in their direction. He put his hand to his forehead and saluted McElroy. Then Fluorescent Jacket closed the door behind them.

The constable walked through to the sitting room. McElroy got the feeling that it wasn't the man's first time in the house, but he couldn't remember his face. He was sure that he hadn't seen the policeman in the fluorescent jacket before, though. "What did you say your name was?" he asked him.

"I didn't," said the policeman. "Can we sit down? Have a chat?" He walked past McElroy into the sitting room and sat next to the constable.

McElroy stood facing them, his arms folded.

"You were heard talking in the pub, Mr McElroy," said the policeman. "Talking about the man who killed your daughter."

McElroy said nothing but stared sullenly at the two men.

"You've been saying things, Mr McElroy . . . saying that you wanted al-Najafi dead, that you wanted to do to him what he did to your daughter."

"That's what this is about, is it?" McElroy snarled. "That piece of shit comes to my country, drives around without a licence and without insurance, kills my little girl, gets out of prison on bail so that he can apply for asylum, and I get my nuts kicked for saying it's not right. Fuck this country. Fuck England and fuck you." He pointed his finger at them. "Get the fuck out of my house or I swear to God I'll kill you."

92

Fluorescent Jacket put up his hands, smiling. "Easy, Gerry," he said softly. "We're not here to give you a hard time. We're on your side. We're here to help."

McElroy lowered his finger, frowning. "Help? How can you help me?"

The policeman pointed at the armchair by the fireplace. "Sit down, Gerry, and I'll explain."

The van came to a halt and McElroy felt a hand on his shoulder. "You can lift your head now, sir," said the policeman in the fluorescent jacket. "We're here."

McElroy looked up. They had stopped in front of a metal-sided industrial unit. There was a for-rent sign on the front door. They had driven for almost thirty minutes and for most of that time McElroy had had his head down so he had no idea of where they were.

Fluorescent Jacket opened the side door of the van, climbed out and waved for McElroy to follow him. He took a key from his coat pocket and used it to unlock the door. He pushed it open and nodded for McElroy to go through.

The industrial unit was empty, stripped of whatever machinery it had once contained. There were oil stains on the wall and a metallic smell in the air. Mohammed Hussein al-Najafi was standing on an oil barrel in the centre of the building, his hands bound behind his back with duct tape. There was more tape around his mouth. He was standing as erect as he could to ease the pressure on his neck caused by a chain that ran over a metal girder in the roof. If he stood perfectly straight the chain was tight but he could still just about breathe.

Al-Najafi was wearing dirty blue jeans and a blue and grey checked shirt with dark sweat patches under the arms. It was a cold day but he was sweating a lot, sweating like a man who knew that he was in a lot of trouble. He was in his early forties, his skin leathered from years in the hot sun, his hair black and glossy, flecked with dandruff.

McElroy would never forget the Iraqi's face. He had been to all three of his court appearances and had stared at the man, wishing he was dead, wishing he'd had a loaded gun in his hands. Al-Najafi had never once expressed remorse, never said he was sorry, never even admitted his guilt. He hadn't spoken a single word in court: a solicitor in an expensive suit with a Louis Vuitton briefcase had done all the talking for him.

"What's happening?" said McElroy. "Why's he up there?"

"Because we're granting your wish, Mr McElroy," said Fluorescent Jacket. "This is the man who killed your little girl. Killed her and ran away. We know that the system has failed you. He's out on bail now and that's not fair and even if the courts do find him guilty then the most he'll get is five years and that's not enough. An eye for an eye, that's what we believe in. And that's what you want, too."

"But . . . how . . ." McElroy was unable to believe what he was seeing or hearing. A sudden thought struck him: maybe it was a trap. Maybe the police were testing him. A second officer, a large West Indian with massive forearms and legs that looked as if they were bowing under the weight of his huge torso, walked into the unit.

94

Fluorescent Jacket put a hand on McElroy's shoulder. "We're taking a risk letting you do this, Mr McElroy. But we think you deserve it."

"But you're the police . . ."

"It's because we're the police that we're doing this," said the officer. "We're sick of seeing scum like him walk free. He killed your daughter and hasn't even had the decency to admit what he did. He's playing the system, Mr McElroy. First, he said it wasn't him driving. Then, when the forensic evidence and witnesses showed he was lying, his defence team came up with a new strategy, that he was so traumatised by what had happened in Iraq that his first thought was to run. He might get away with it, too. It wouldn't be the first time that a sympathetic jury let an asylum seeker get away with murder."

McElroy frowned. "Is that true?"

"As true as I'm standing here," said the policeman. "The CPS is spitting feathers but there's nothing they can do. This is England, and under English law he can put forward any defence he wants. He'll say that he's been having flashbacks to being tortured by the police in Iraq so his first thought when he hit your daughter was to run away. Then his brief will say that he's stricken with grief but that it wasn't really his fault and so on and so on."

"And he'll get off?"

"He might go down for dangerous driving, but if they make it careless driving he might not even go to prison."

"That's . . ." He shook his head, unable to find the right word.

"Unfair? I'm afraid that's the way it is, these days, Mr McElroy. The entire criminal justice system is slanted towards the criminals. And, make no mistake, that's what this scumbag is. A criminal."

Fluorescent Jacket nodded at his colleague and the big policeman walked over to a metal crowbar that was leaning against one of the walls. He picked it up and gave it to Fluorescent Jacket, then headed towards the exit.

"I'm going to leave you alone now," said the policeman. He handed the crowbar to McElroy. "Do whatever you want," he said. "We'll clean up the mess."

McElroy stared at the crowbar. Then he looked up at al-Najafi. The Iraqi was struggling to stand on the tips of his toes to ease the pressure on his neck.

"Are you okay, Mr McElroy?"

McElroy nodded but didn't say anything.

"It's justice, Mr McElroy," said the policeman. "It's what you deserve."

The phone rang and Katra answered it. She waved the receiver at Shepherd. "Caroline Stockmann," she said.

Shepherd grimaced. Stockmann was the undercover unit's resident psychologist and he had already missed two appointments to see her.

Katra saw his discomfort and put her hand over the receiver. "Shall I say you're not here?" she asked.

"I'd better take it," said Shepherd. "I can't avoid her for ever." He took the receiver. "Caroline, sorry I missed our last session," he said brightly. "I was away on a job."

"So I gather," said Stockmann.

"I'm going to be in London on another operation, so we could do it next week," he said.

"I thought we could do the Mohammed-mountain thing again," she said. "Remember that pub where we met last time I was in your neck of the woods?"

"Yes," said Shepherd. It was just half a mile from his house.

"I'm there now," she said. "Can you pop around?"

"Are you stalking me, Caroline?"

"Only in the nicest possible way," she said. "Your biannual is way overdue and if we leave it any longer the paperwork gets complicated."

"Give me fifteen minutes," said Shepherd.

"No rush," said the psychologist. "They serve a very good pint here."

The policeman in the fluorescent jacket smoked a cigarette as he paced up and down alongside the police van. He looked at his watch. McElroy had been in the industrial unit for almost ten minutes.

"Here he comes," said the driver. McElroy was walking out of the door, head down, hands at his side.

The policeman stubbed out his cigarette on the ground and pocketed the butt. He knew better than to leave forensic evidence at the scene, even if they planned to dispose of the Iraqi's body miles from it.

As McElroy got closer, the policeman could see that his cheeks were wet with tears.

"I can't," said McElroy. "I'm sorry, I can't do it."

The policeman put his arm around McElroy's shoulders. "It's okay," he said.

"It's not okay," said McElroy. "That bastard deserves to die. I want him dead. It's just . . ." He sniffed and wiped his nose with the back of his hand.

"It's just you can't do it, right?"

"I know I should — he killed my Debbie — but . . ."

"It's nothing to be ashamed of, sir," said the policeman. He opened the side door of the van. The burly West Indian constable helped McElroy into the van.

"I'm sorry," said McElroy. Tears ran down his face.

"You don't have to apologise for anything, sir," said Fluorescent Jacket. "I can take care of this for you," he said quietly. "If that's what you want."

McElroy wiped his eyes. "Yes," he said. "That's what I want."

Fluorescent Jacket smiled. "That's what we're here for," he said. He closed the van door. "I won't be long," he told the driver, and walked back to the warehouse.

Caroline Stockmann was sitting at a table by the window with a half-full pint of bitter in front of her. She smiled and waved at Shepherd when she saw him walk into the pub. Shepherd went over to her, unsure how he should greet her. The meeting was official but she was dressed casually in a padded skiing jacket and blue jeans so a handshake seemed over-formal. However, she was the SOCA psychologist responsible for assessing his mental health every six months so a kiss on the cheek seemed equally out of place. She solved the conundrum for him by standing up and proffering her hand. "Dan, good to see you again," she said.

"I wasn't avoiding you, honestly," he said, as he shook it.

"I didn't mean to imply that you were," she said. "I was visiting your old Regiment and thought I might kill two birds with one stone."

"The SAS is being psychologically assessed?" he said. "I thought being slightly loopy was in the job description."

Stockmann sat down and adjusted her square-framed spectacles. "Post-traumatic stress disorder," she said. "Some of the guys are coming back from Iraq and Afghanistan a bit worse for wear so we're putting together a therapy programme."

Shepherd grinned. "Therapy? How's that working out?"

"You might laugh, but the suicide rate among former SAS troopers is about twelve times the national average, and it looks as if PTSD is one of the major causes." She glanced at the bar. "Can I get you a drink?"

"I'll get it," said Shepherd. "Can I get you anything?"

She raised her glass. "I'm fine with this, and I've got my car outside," she said.

Shepherd went to the bar, paid for a Jameson's and soda with ice, and returned to her table. "It's funny being with a civilian," he said. "Normally I'd never be sitting at a window."

"This is your home turf, so I didn't think tradecraft would apply," she said. "Would you be happier at a corner table with your back to a wall?" She took a leather-bound notebook and a pen from her pocket.

Shepherd wagged a finger at her. "Now you've got me thinking that you deliberately chose this table to put me off balance."

"Maybe I did," she said, deadpan. She sipped some beer. "You feel more secure with your back to a wall?"

"Everyone does," he said. "And windows make you vulnerable. You can be seen from outside, or worse."

"So the best place to be would be where?" asked the psychologist.

Shepherd was a regular visitor to the pub so he answered immediately: "The table over there, next to the booths."

"Not in a booth? That one in the corner seems perfect."

"The tables are fixed in booths," said Shepherd. "You can get trapped in a booth. But tables can be pushed out of the way. That table over there gives you a view of the main entrance, the bar, and the door to the toilets."

"Plus you can sit with your back to the wall."

"Exactly," said Shepherd.

Stockmann's eyes sparkled with amusement. "I have to say that I did some research which suggests you might be better rethinking that," she said. "I looked at over two hundred killings where the victim was sitting in a restaurant or a bar and where the killer came in from the outside."

"And?"

"And in the vast majority of cases, more than ninety-five per cent in fact, the victim was shot in the face or the chest. Rarely in the back."

Shepherd frowned. "That surprises me," he said.

"It's counter-intuitive," she said, opening her notebook. "But it's a fact, all the same. Assassins shoot their victims from the front, not the back. So in theory you'd be safer facing a wall."

"That wouldn't be much good if you were on surveillance," said Shepherd.

"Agreed," said Stockmann. "And undercover cops are rarely murdered in public places. It usually takes place in private."

"You've researched that too?"

Stockmann smiled coyly. "You'd be amazed at the things I'm asked to look at," she said. "So, how's life?"

Shepherd shrugged. "Just adopted a stray dog," he said.

"I wouldn't have put you down as a dog lover," said Stockmann.

"My son's been asking for one for years." Shepherd frowned. "Why wouldn't I like dogs?"

"I didn't say you didn't like them but I wouldn't think you'd necessarily want one in your home. You're not a pack animal, Dan. You know how to operate in a pack but that's part of your skill as an undercover agent. Some men feel the need to have a dog, to have power over another living thing, but I never got the impression that was an issue with you."

"You're probably right," admitted Shepherd.

"I should hope so," said Stockmann. "SOCA pays me very well for my impressions."

"And are you staying with SOCA?" asked Shepherd. He watched her carefully over the top of his glass.

"Why wouldn't I be?"

"Because Charlie Button brought you in. I thought you might be going back to Five with her."

Stockmann sipped some more beer and carefully placed her glass on the mat. "I still do work for Five from time to time — I'm a freelance when all is said and done. Have gun, will travel."

"Did she tell you she was going back to Five?"

Stockmann nodded. "You seem unsettled by the fact that she's moving on."

Shepherd sighed. "It's an important relationship, an undercover agent and the handler. You have to have complete trust because without that you're always looking over your shoulder."

"And you're worried that Charlotte's replacement won't inspire the same level of trust?"

Shepherd stretched out his legs. "I'm not resistant to change, if that's what you're implying."

"I'm not implying anything, Dan. I do understand how important Charlotte is to you, but no one stays in the same job for ever. If she didn't go this year she'd go next year or the year after. So at some stage you're going to have to deal with that."

"I can deal with it," said Shepherd, then winced as he realised how defensive he'd sounded. "That came out wrong," he said. "I think I'm just worried about having to break in a new boss, that's all. If I was still a cop, it wouldn't be such a worry, but SOCA is civil service and the last thing I want is some career civil servant making life-and-death decisions on my behalf."

"I'm sensing some resentment about SOCA."

"Will that go on my file?"

Stockmann chuckled. "You are sensitive today," she said.

"And you're being evasive."

She raised her glass to him. "Fair point," she said. "I'm here to assess your mental health, nothing else. Your opinions on SOCA are just between us. Unless, of course, you tell me that you're planning to go postal."

"There's no chance of that," said Shepherd. He drank some whiskey and soda as he gathered his thoughts. "I guess the problem is that SOCA is an amalgamation of several organisations. It was formed by bringing together policemen, spies, Customs officers, accountants, lawyers, scientists and making them all equal. We're all now civil servants, and that means I'm never sure of the background of the person I'm dealing with. When I was a cop, if you met an inspector you had a rough idea of what experience he had, and how he'd be different from a chief superintendent or a commander. You can't do that with the SOCA staff. A guy at the same level in the organisation as me might have spent ten years just shuffling papers in an office somewhere. Or stood at an airport checking passports, or checking white vans for booze on the cross-Channel ferries."

"And that's a problem?"

"Damn right that's a problem," said Shepherd, quickly. Too quickly, he realised. He raised his glass. "Sorry," he said.

Stockmann smiled. "I want you to express your feelings, Dan, not hide them. That's what I'm here for. Better you talk things through with me than explode while you're on a job."

"I'm not the exploding type, Caroline."

"Everybody has his breaking point," she said. She wrote something in her notebook.

"This isn't about breaking points," said Shepherd. "It's about trusting the people you work with. In the army, you can trust the men either side of you because you've all been through the same basic training. More so with the Regiment. Even with the police, there are standards, even if the powers-that-be seemed to be determined to drop those standards day by day. SOCA doesn't have that. Every time you come up against another SOCA face, you have to start from scratch. Does he know what he's doing?" He smiled thinly. "He or she, I should say. Does he or she know what they're doing? Can they be trusted? Will they watch your back or cover their own arse? Can they fire a gun, and if they can, will they hit what they're shooting at?" He caught her looking at the plaster on his forehead. "You're so sharp," he said.

"No, you're just hyper-sensitive," she replied. "I wasn't thinking about the fact that you were shot."

"Grazed rather than shot," he said.

"I really wasn't thinking that. I just happened to glance at the plaster. Cross my heart."

"It barely touched me," said Shepherd. He frowned. "You knew I'd been shot?" He shook his head. "Of course you did, that's why you're here."

"You're due a psychological review, Dan. That's why I'm here." She grinned. "Don't start getting paranoid on me. I'm on your side."

"Until the day when you think I'm not capable of doing the job. Then you can end my career."

"Do you think you'll be working under cover your whole life?"

"I hope not," said Shepherd. He sipped his whiskey slowly, playing for time as he got his thoughts in order. Chatting with Caroline Stockmann, as pleasant an experience as that could be, was often the equivalent of tiptoeing through a minefield. He smiled at her as he put his glass back on the table. "You know what's funny? I had a similar conversation with Razor a few days ago."

"Razor?"

"Jimmy Sharpe."

"Ah, yes. How is he?"

"Infiltrating racists, as we speak," said Shepherd. "I was telling him that no one stays in the same job for ever."

"Which is very true."

"Yeah, but I'd rather choose when I leave. I wouldn't want to be sent packing because of a negative psychological evaluation."

"That's understandable," said Stockmann. She had another mouthful of beer and smacked her lips. "This is a good pint," she said. "I should come to Hereford more often." She gestured at the plaster. "So, tell me about the graze."

"Friendly fire," he said. "The Swedey, with guns."

"The Swedey?"

"Avon and Somerset's armed-police unit," he said. "Shoot first and ask questions maybe at some undetermined point in the future."

"You're not serious?"

Shepherd pulled a face. "They came charging in, yelled that they were armed police and before I could drop my weapon one of them fired."

"They didn't know you were one of the good guys?"

"I was wearing a ski-mask, but even so they wouldn't have known that I was with SOCA. But that's not the point. You don't shoot anyone, villains, cops or civilians, without giving them a chance to surrender. I tell you, Caroline, I could easily have died. One inch to the left and it would have blown away a good chunk of my skull."

"You were lucky."

"Yeah, that's what they said the first time I was shot. I always say that if I was really lucky I wouldn't have been shot in the first place."

"And I gather that you came close to being shot by one of the robbers, too?"

Shepherd narrowed his eyes. "You're well informed."

"It's my job, Dan. Can you tell me what happened?"

"I had to get heavy with two of the guys. One was going to rape an underage girl, the other guy, the boss, was going to let it happen."

"There was a Mexican standoff?"

"There were no Mexicans there but, yeah, it turned into one of those if-you-shoot-me-I'll-shoot-him scenarios."

"Very Tarantino-esque." She scribbled in her notebook but Shepherd couldn't see what she was writing.

"Is that a word?" he asked.

"I gather," said Stockmann. "So you were pointing your gun at . . .?"

"Grimshaw, his name was. Lex Grimshaw."

"So you had your gun pointed at Grimshaw while the would-be rapist . . ."

"Maloney," said Shepherd.

"While Maloney had his gun pointed at you. Not a pleasant situation to be in."

"I'm never comfortable when it's two against one," said Shepherd.

"And it was unavoidable?"

Shepherd frowned. "What do you mean?"

"Was there anything you could have done to avoid getting into that situation?"

"You think I was being reckless?"

"It was two armed men against one."

"I had a shotgun."

"So size is important?"

Shepherd chuckled. "I think so, in this case, yes."

"You took a big risk, Dan. It paid off and you walked away, but it could have gone terribly wrong. Yet you seem to be more angry at the police officer who accidentally shot you than the career criminal who threatened to kill you."

"I'm not sure it was an accident," said Shepherd. "The cop was trigger-happy — he fired without giving me the chance to comply."

"When you thought that Maloney might pull the trigger, were you scared?"

"Not scared, no."

"So describe how it felt."

"Is that what this is about? My feelings?"

"It's about the situation you were in and how you reacted to it. It gives me an insight into how you deal with these stressful situations."

"I've been shot before," said Shepherd. "It's no big thing."

Stockmann smiled. "We both know that's not true, Dan," she said. "There's no need to play the tough guy with me. I've spoken to a lot of guys, and women, who've been shot over the years and it is a big thing."

Shepherd sighed. "I'm sorry, it's just that whenever anyone starts probing too deep my defences go up."

"It happens with everybody, nothing to be ashamed of. There are times when your defence mechanisms can save your life. But, like I said, I'm on your side."

"I wasn't scared. I was apprehensive. But no more so than a chess player who isn't quite sure what his opponent is going to do next. Or a poker player who has a good hand but isn't certain how good."

"It was that cerebral?"

"My heart was pounding and the adrenalin was pumping but, yeah, my mind was taking it calmly enough. He had options, so did I."

"You called his bluff, to use your poker analogy?"

Shepherd shook his head. "I wasn't bluffing."

"You would have shot Grimshaw, even if it had meant that Maloney would shoot you?"

"For sure. Caroline — Maloney was going to rape a young girl. I couldn't stand by and let that happen." He paused. "Do you think I put myself in harm's way for the fun of it?"

"You're over-thinking what's going on here, Dan," she said. "We're chatting, I'm just trying to get a feel for your state of mind. But it's interesting that you would think that."

"I don't think that. I just got the feeling that was the way your questions were going." He forced himself to relax, or at least to appear relaxed. "I was in a no-win situation, Caroline. I couldn't let Maloney attack the girl, and I couldn't shoot them first. I fired into the ceiling for the shock value."

"Plus, of course, you knew that the cavalry was on its way."

Shepherd nodded. "I'd sent Charlie a text message saying we were going in, and they had a GPS fix on my mobile, but we were in the middle of nowhere so I wasn't sure when they'd get there." His hand moved up to touch the plaster on his forehead but he fought the impulse and picked up his whiskey instead. "Anyway, all's well that ends well, right?"

"Exactly," said the psychologist.

"So I'm sane? Fit for work?"

"As always."

Shepherd sipped his whiskey. "Can I ask you a question?"

"I can't promise you an answer, but fire away."

"You assess all the SOCA operatives, right?"

"Not just me," she said, "but I do my fair share."

"Do you ever fail anyone?"

Stockmann laughed. "You make me sound like a school-teacher," she said.

"But it is a pass or fail, isn't it? I'm either fit for work or I'm not."

"It's not as clear cut as that. Part of what I do is to spot trends, and hopefully nip any negative ones in the bud before they become a problem."

"But there comes a point when there is a problem and you have to have them removed from duty?"

Stockmann tapped her fingers on her notebook. "If an operative isn't following advice and if he or she is no longer fit to carry out the role he or she has been assigned, then, yes, they might be offered an alternative posting."

"And that happens?"

"Sometimes."

Shepherd nodded thoughtfully. "And what sort of problems are we talking about?"

"Stress, mainly," said Stockmann. "But it's the manifestation of stress that causes the problems. We've spoken about this before. You're a runner and that's one way of dealing with the stress you face."

Shepherd grinned. "By running away from my problems, you mean?"

"By exercising. That's a healthy response to stress. Others deal with it by drinking too much or by taking drugs. Some don't deal with it at all. I'd say you have one of the healthier approaches. You don't need me to tell you how stressful your job is, Dan. You lie and befriend people only to betray them. You're working in an environment where one wrong word can be literally fatal. Very few people are geared up to deal with that sort of stress for long periods, yet you've been working under cover pretty much since you left the SAS, which was — what? Nine years ago?"

"Going on for that, yes."

"Not everyone deals with it as well as you do," said Stockmann. "Most would move on from undercover work after five years or so. Not many go beyond ten."

"It's not the easiest of jobs," agreed Shepherd. "Long spells away from home, not being able to tell your family what you're doing, having to remember who you are and who you're not."

"A lot of undercover operatives end up separated or divorced," agreed Stockmann. "They're not the easiest people to live with."

"Liam would probably agree with you on that," said Shepherd.

"It can't be easy being a single parent," she said, closing her notebook.

Shepherd smiled. "You know, it's probably easier being a single parent than a husband. My wife was always nagging me to spend more time at home. That's the reason I left the SAS when I did. Neither of us realised it'd be out of the frying-pan and into the fire. I don't think Sue would have been happy with all the hours I'm working now."

"Liam's doing well at school?"

"Really well."

"He seems to have coped well with his mum's death. It can't have been easy for either of you."

"We're getting through it," said Shepherd. "We talk about her a lot. That helps."

"How does Liam handle your absences?"

"He's generally okay about it."

"Was that why you got the dog?"

Shepherd sat back in his seat. "You're good," he said. "You don't let anything get by, do you?"

"You mentioned that you'd got a dog, and if you feel guilty . . ." She shrugged. "Elementary, my dear Watson."

"I guess there might have been an element of guilt involved," admitted Shepherd. "It's certainly true that he gets more than his fair share of presents whenever I get back."

"He's, what, twelve now?"

"Going on thirteen." Shepherd shook his head. "I can't believe he'll be a teenager. The years just fly by."

"Children have that effect on you," said Stockmann. "But he's a good kid?"

"The best," said Shepherd. "Doesn't seem to have any bad habits, he's doing well at school, enjoys sport . . . hasn't really put a foot wrong." He smiled. "I have to nag him to tidy his room, but that's par for the course, I gather. So, yes, he's a good kid."

"Anything else I should know about?"

"Everything's fine," he said. "Fine and dandy."

Fluorescent Jacket walked into the warehouse. He grinned at al-Najafi. "Don't you always hate that bit in

112

the movies when the villain has the hero in his power and then he spends ages telling the hero how clever he is, and he spends so much time talking that the hero gets away?" he said. "Monologuing, they call it, I think. Or grandstanding. But that's not what's happening here." He took out a pack of Rothmans, put a cigarette into his mouth and lit it with a cheap disposable lighter. He waited until he'd blown smoke up at the roof before speaking again. "Mind you, I'm the hero in this and you're the villain, so maybe a bit of monologuing or grandstanding is allowed. Either way, you're going to have to listen to what I have to say because it's not very often that I get to talk to one of the bad guys and tell them what I really think of them." He walked slowly around the barrel. The Iraqi tried to speak but the duct tape around his mouth muffled the sound to a dull growl. His eyes were wide and pleading and he was close to tears.

"When we arrest someone, these days, it's all covered by PACE, the Police and Criminal Evidence Act, which means you get a lawyer and can just keep saying, 'No comment', if that's what you want, and the interview will probably be recorded and there's a whole raft of regulations that we have to follow. Then, if it gets to court, a CPS solicitor will present the case and, again, he's bound by all sorts of rules, whereas you can lie all you want, and keep denying that you did what you did right up until the moment that a jury decides you're guilty. Then you can suddenly change your mind and say you're really sorry and throw yourself on the mercy of the judge. At no point are we the police allowed to

113

give our view. We're the so-called guardians of law and order but we're muzzled, pretty much. Or castrated."

Fluorescent Jacket took a long drag on his cigarette. "Thing is, Mohammed, you'd never have been treated that well back in Iraq, would you? The cops would put your balls in a vice or a cattle prod up your arse, then shove you in a dark hole and throw away the key, wouldn't they? Especially with you being a Kurd." He smiled without warmth. "Except we both know that you're not a Kurd, don't we? You were one of Saddam's élite troops, weren't you? You probably gassed the odd Kurdish village for sport, and I'm damn sure that you shot a few. But a story like that's not going to get you asylum, is it? So you spin the old victim story and you get an Amnesty International lawyer on your case and the next thing you know you're being fast-tracked to British citizenship."

He took a long drag on his cigarette and blew smoke at the Iraqi.

"But that wasn't good enough for you, was it? You started driving around in a second-hand car, moonlighting as a minicab driver even though you weren't supposed to be working — and despite the fact that you didn't have a licence or insurance. Got caught, too, didn't you, and got a slap on the wrist from the local magistrate? I don't understand that, Mohammed, I really don't. You ran a red light and hit another car and put the driver in hospital and you didn't do a day in prison. Do you remember that teacher in Dubai or Saudi or wherever it was? They had a class mascot, a teddy bear, and the teacher asked the kids what they

114

should name it. They decided on Mohammed — your name, right? Most popular name with Arabs so that's what they called the bear. Then one of the parents complains and the teacher's banged up in jail for blasphemy or whatever, then deported. She went to prison for naming a bear — but you, you come to our country and break God knows how many of our laws, and we do nothing. Why is that? Are we a soft touch, like they say?"

He smoked his cigarette as he walked around the barrel. Al-Najafi was struggling to keep the chain from strangling him.

"Then what do you do? You carry on driving your minicab, still without any tax or insurance or a driving licence, while the asylum bandwagon rolls on, the taxpayer paying all your legal bills. I never understand that, Mohammed — why my country allows scumbags like you to become citizens. But despite all we've done for you, you decide to take a shortcut that involves driving over a pavement and you run down ten-year-old Debbie McElroy. You don't kill her, mind. You stop while she's under the wheels and you hear her screams and you see the blood, and what do you do? Do you help her? Do you call for an ambulance like a good citizen? No, Mohammed, you run away. You run away and leave her to die. The coroner reckons it took her a good five minutes to bleed to death. Five minutes, Mohammed. She was probably begging for her mum and dad to help her. But they weren't there, were they? So she died alone, under the wheels of your car. And then what did you do? You ran home and when the cops came around you lied. You lied, Mohammed. Not you, you weren't there, your car was stolen, even though yours were the only prints on the wheel and there were two witnesses saw you hit Debbie. Still pleading not guilty, aren't you, still hoping that the British legal system will give you a break? And then what happens? Your high-powered brief stands up in court and says that you shouldn't be held on remand because that would jeopardise your asylum appeal, so the judge says you should get bail. And then what do you? You go back to driving your minicab." He shook his head. "I don't get it, Mohammed. I don't understand my country any more."

He stepped forward and stubbed out what was left of the cigarette on the barrel, then put the butt in his coat pocket.

"It ends here, Mohammed. We've had enough, my friends and I, so it ends here."

Al-Najafi tried to talk. The duct tape pulsed in and out but it muffled his words.

"The system's failed and it's beyond fixing now. The courts, the criminal justice system, the whole bloody shebang is weighted towards the criminal, towards scumbags like you. But we're taking back the power, Mohammed, my friends and I. We're showing the way, we're showing what can be done, and before long we'll turn the tide. We really will."

He smiled and nodded. "You know what, Mohammed? That felt good. There really is something to grandstanding. But I think I've said pretty much everything I want to say."

116

Sweat was pouring down al-Najafi's face and his whole body was trembling.

"This is for Debbie McElroy," Fluorescent Jacket said, staring at al-Najafi's face. "This is for the little girl that you killed, that you ran over and left to die under the wheels of your car."

He put his foot up against the top of the barrel and grunted as he pushed. It scraped across the concrete floor, then tipped over. For a second or two, al-Najafi scrabbled to keep his balance but the barrel fell and the chain snapped around his neck. The barrel crashed to the floor as al-Najafi's legs kicked and his body bucked. A wet stain spread around his groin.

Fluorescent Jacket didn't stay to watch al-Najafi die: he turned and walked out of the building.

As he climbed into the van, he found Gerry McElroy slumped forward in his seat, his head in his hands. "Are you okay there, Mr McElroy?" he asked.

"Is it done?" McElroy asked.

"It's done."

McElroy nodded. "Thank you," he said softly, his voice little more than a whisper.

On Friday Shepherd got up at four o'clock in the morning and drove to Gatwick Airport to pick up Martin O'Brien, who was flying over from Dublin. O'Brien was one of Shepherd's oldest friends, a former Irish Ranger who now ran his own security company. They stopped off for breakfast at a truckers' café, then drove east to Rotherfield, about six miles south-west of Tunbridge Wells.

The church where Tommy Gannon's funeral was due to be held was St Denys, built of sandstone that had weathered over the centuries, with a towering spire and arched stained-glass windows. Half a dozen young men with short haircuts, wearing cheap suits and well-polished shoes, were standing at the gate, smoking and talking quietly.

"Hi, lads," said Shepherd, as he climbed out of his BMW X3.

The men looked at him. None of them knew him but they all recognised a former soldier when they saw one. "Sir," muttered a couple.

"No need for the 'sir', lads, I was in Civvy Street long before you joined up." O'Brien got out and Shepherd locked the car.

"Were you in the Sass with Tommy's uncle?" asked one, a lanky lad with acne across his forehead.

Like most of the men who served with the Regiment, Shepherd generally didn't admit to having been in the SAS, but this was different. These guys had served with Tommy Gannon and had made the effort to come to his funeral. "Yeah," he said.

The men visibly stood to attention and there was new respect in their eyes. Shepherd and O'Brien shook hands with them all. "You guys are on your way to Afghanistan, right?" asked Shepherd.

"Yes, sir," said the lanky soldier, running a hand through his unruly hair. "We were supposed to be out this week but they let us stay back to come here. We're on a flight on Monday."

"You be careful out there," said Shepherd.

"You've been, sir?" asked a slightly overweight teenager with greasy brown hair.

Shepherd nodded. "Yeah, a few years back. It wasn't pleasant then and I don't think it's much better now. Just watch each other's backs and you'll be fine."

"We should be in Northern Ireland, tracking down the bastards that killed Tommy, not shooting ragheads in the sandbox," said the overweight teenager.

"Yours not to reason why," said Shepherd.

"You know what I mean," he said. "Who are the enemy? The Afghans never did anything to us, not even the Taliban. It's the bloody IRA, they're the enemy. They're the ones we should be fighting."

"The cops will be on the case," said Shepherd.

"Yeah, well, we can all sleep easy in our beds knowing that." The teenager shrugged. "I'm sorry, sir, I just . . ." He shook his head.

Shepherd put a hand on his shoulder. "Hey, I understand," he said. "But they won't get away with it. You've got to think about the job in hand, and that's Afghanistan. When you're over there you've got to be totally in the zone because you lose concentration for one second and you can be in deep shit."

"That's the truth," said the lanky soldier. He took a drag on his cigarette, cupping it in his hand as if he was doing it on the sly. "What's the story with the uniforms, sir? We were just told we weren't to wear them."

Shepherd turned to the church. Major Gannon was standing at the entrance with his brother. They were both big men and clearly brothers, with the same big chins and piercing eyes, but while the Major had been toughened by years in the SAS, two decades' working in the City had softened Henry Gannon, added inches to his waistline and thinned his hair. He wore black-framed spectacles and had a thick gold ring on his wedding finger. They were both wearing black overcoats over dark suits.

"Tommy's dad over there wasn't too happy at his son being career army," said Shepherd. "We're respecting his wishes."

"Tommy was a great soldier — his dad should be proud of him."

"He is," said Shepherd. "It's complicated."

He beckoned O'Brien and the two of them walked through the gate towards the church. "You been here before?" asked O'Brien.

"Henry's daughter was married here a couple of years back," said Shepherd.

"Nice church."

"More than a thousand years old," said Shepherd. "Sort of puts things in perspective." He gestured at the steeple. "The first steeple was put up in the fifteenth century, but the storms of 1987 blew it down. They used a helicopter to put that one up."

"Your trick memory is a thing of beauty," said O'Brien. "You don't forget anything, do you?"

"You're telling me that I'm a mine of useless information, aren't you?"

"You're too sensitive," said O'Brien.

"You're not the first person to have remarked on that," said Shepherd.

They reached the Gannons and shook hands with both men. "Spider, Martin, thanks for coming," said the Major.

"I'm sorry about your loss," said Shepherd to Henry Gannon. The words meant nothing, but they had to be said. He knew how he'd feel if anything ever happened to Liam.

"I remember the away-day Al organised for my bank," Henry said. "A day with the SAS. I think he took a particular delight in terrorising men who earn a million quid a year."

"Martin O'Brien," said O'Brien. "I met your boy a couple of times. He was a good lad, he'll be missed."

Henry nodded. "Al tells me you're based in Dublin, these days. Thanks for coming over."

"Least I could do," said O'Brien. "Tommy was a nice guy, and a great soldier. You should be proud of him."

Shepherd saw Henry's jaw tense at the word "soldier", but he forced a smile. "We'll all miss him," he said.

The Major gestured at the door. "Sit anywhere, lads, but the first two rows are for family."

Shepherd and O'Brien went into the church and sat in a pew close to the back. There were more than a hundred people and a buzz of whispered conversations. The coffin was to the left of a gleaming lectern, topped by two wreaths. A few minutes after they had taken their seats, two men in dark suits walked in. They were in their early thirties, a couple of inches taller than Shepherd with broad shoulders and wavy brown hair. Other than their choice of footwear, they were identical.

Jack Bradford was wearing gleaming black loafers while his twin brother Billy had on black Nike training shoes.

They grinned when they saw Shepherd and O'Brien, and sat down in the same pew.

"Long time no see," said Shepherd. "Where are you guys these days? Still in Iraq?"

"Most of the time, but we're back in the UK for the next few weeks, interviewing and hiring," said Jack. "There's more work than ever, what with the troops pulling out."

"But every man and his dog is out there so rates are coming down," added Billy.

"We've got some good clients, though, so we're doing okay," said Jack. "You still with SOCA?"

"Yeah," said Shepherd.

"What does that pay?" asked Billy.

"We don't do it for the money," said Shepherd.

The Bradford brothers laughed. A couple of mourners in the front pews looked around. The brothers quietened and waved an apology.

"I'm serious," said Shepherd. "I want to stay in the UK to be near my boy, and there's a pension. Regular holidays."

"And overtime?" asked Billy.

Shepherd grinned. "Yeah, lots of overtime."

"What about you, Martin?" asked Jack. "What are you up to?"

O'Brien lowered his voice to a whisper. "It's Secret Squirrel," he said. "I could tell you but then I'd have to kill you."

Jack chuckled under his breath. "Still got your sense of humour," he said. "Did you ever do that desert marathon thing?"

"Had to cry off — got snowed under at work. Next year, maybe."

The congregation fell silent as the priest walked to the altar. Shepherd settled into his seat. He didn't like funerals, but he knew that part of life was saying goodbye to the dead.

Ronnie Duncan stretched out his legs and used his remote to flick through the channels on the flat-screen television. "Why can't we get Sky Plus?" he asked.

His two minders treated the question as rhetorical. Neither had joined the Metropolitan Police to babysit a convicted child-killer. "I had more channels in prison," moaned Duncan. "Where's the sport? I want to watch the football."

"Two more days and you'll be out of here," said the senior of his minders, a sergeant in his forties. He had taken off his tunic and rolled up the sleeves of his shirt. Paul Prentice had been a policeman for almost twenty years and had accepted that he would never go any higher in the Met. He had also grown to accept that more often than not he'd end up doing unpleasant jobs, and jobs didn't come much more unpleasant than looking after a scumbag like Ronnie Duncan.

"Won't be soon enough for me, I can tell you," said Duncan. "You ever been to Toronto?" He scratched his spreading beer gut.

"Never been to Canada, never wanted to go," said the sergeant.

"What about you, John?" asked Duncan.

John Flowers shook his head. He was in his late twenties, a trainee detective in CID, and he'd been given the task of protecting Duncan because he'd messed up an arson investigation. He hated having to be in the same room as the man but he had to take his punishment if he was to have any hope of continuing his career with CID.

"How about pizza tonight?" said Duncan. "Domino's?"

"We had pizza last night," said the sergeant.

"I like pizza, and my lawyer said I can order what I want," said Duncan. "I'm the one whose life's under threat. I'm the one in the witness-protection scheme."

"You're not a witness, as it happens," said the sergeant. "You're getting a new identity because there are plenty of people out there who'd happily see you dead for what you did."

"Yeah, whatever," said Duncan. "But I'm the one who's having to start again in Canada."

"I don't see why that's such a hardship," said Flowers. "You get a new identity, you get a place to live and the Canadians are going to find you a job."

"You think I want to leave England? This is my home, mate. I'm only going because my life's in danger if I stay here because all the papers published my picture and that."

"You did kill a child," said the sergeant, quietly.

"And I admitted that and I pleaded guilty and I served my time," said Duncan. "Got all my remission

124

for good behaviour, never put a foot wrong while I was inside."

"Well done you," said the sergeant, sourly.

"What's your problem?"

The sergeant shook his head. "It doesn't matter."

Duncan sat up. "No, come on, if there's something on your mind, spit it out."

"I'm just here to babysit you until you're on the plane. It doesn't matter what I think."

"I served my time. I put my hand up to what I did and I did my porridge."

"You killed a five-year-old boy," said the sergeant. "You picked him up and you threw him against a wall and broke his neck."

"I didn't mean to kill him. I lost my temper."

"Yeah, and little Timmy lost his life. And you tried to get his mother to lie about what happened."

"Yeah, well, she didn't lie, did she? And I got sent down."

"You served six years," said the sergeant. "For killing a child."

The case had been on the front pages of all the national newspapers. Duncan had been living with Timmy Murphy's mother. Both were alcoholics and drug addicts and regularly smoked crack while the little boy was in the house. The mother had been unconscious when little Timmy had gone into the bedroom to ask Duncan for something to eat. Seconds later he was dead. Duncan had claimed that he was out of his head on drugs and alcohol when he killed the little boy, but he had been sober enough to carry the child to the stairs and stage a fall, and to convince the mother to lie to the police and tell them that little Timmy had tripped. The mother had backed up Duncan's story at first but it hadn't taken the detectives on the case long to get the truth out of her. She'd ended up with a two-year suspended sentence and, after pleading guilty to manslaughter, Duncan was given twelve years. The boy's father had been in court: when he'd heard the sentence he had stood up and screamed that he'd kill Duncan when he got out. He was a member of a north London drug-dealing family and his three brothers had been equally vocal about what they wanted to do to Duncan. The threats had continued throughout Duncan's time in prison and he was badly beaten up twice before applying to be kept in segregation.

Duncan had been smuggled out of prison two weeks before his official release date and taken to the safe-house. The Canadian government had agreed to take him, and the British government had agreed to pay for his new identity and relocation expenses. As soon as the Canadians came up with the passport, Duncan would be escorted out of the country. In all, his relocation would cost the British taxpayer in excess of three hundred thousand pounds.

"I did my time," said Duncan again.

"I'll order that pizza," said Flowers. He could see that Sergeant Prentice was gearing up for an argument. Prentice had made it clear from the start that he resented having to babysit a convicted child-killer but had managed to bite his tongue for most of the two weeks he'd been with Duncan. "Pepperoni, yeah? And extra cheese?"

"And garlic bread," said Duncan. "Don't forget the garlic bread." He lay down on the sofa and resumed flicking through the channels.

"Just pick something to watch," said the sergeant. "Anything. You're getting on my nerves."

"Yeah, well, your whining's getting on mine."

Prentice stood up. "Yeah?"

Duncan pointed the remote control at the sergeant. "You're just a hired hand, mate, so sit down and shut the fuck up. This isn't about you, it's about me."

"Yeah, well, I've just about —" The shrill shriek of an alarm stopped him in mid-flow. He looked at the window. "Is that my car?"

Flowers hurried over to the window and peered through the blinds. It was early afternoon but they were closed twenty-four hours a day. Across the road, smoke was pouring from the bonnet of Prentice's Ford Mondeo. "It's on fire, Sarge," he said.

"Don't piss around, John, I'm not in the mood."

"I'm serious, Sarge. Your car, it's on fire!"

Prentice rushed over to join Flowers. A housewife with a pushchair was hurrying away from the burning Mondeo.

"There's a fire extinguisher in the kitchen," said Flowers. He rushed off to get it while Prentice headed for the front door.

"What about my pizza?" shouted Duncan.

Flowers dashed out of the kitchen holding a small red object. "You stay there," he said to Duncan from the hallway. "And don't let anyone in." He hurried out of the front door and slammed it behind him.

Duncan sneered and carried on flicking through the channels. A uniformed constable appeared at the sitting-room doorway. He was dressed in what looked like riot gear, with black overalls, a bulletproof vest and a blue helmet with the visor up. "You have to come with me, Mr Duncan," he said.

"What?"

"We have to go out the back way now. We don't have time to argue."

A second policeman appeared, also wearing riot gear. "What's the hold-up?" he asked.

"What's going on?" asked Duncan. "I ain't going nowhere."

"We've received intel that this safe-house has been compromised," said the second policeman. "There's a contract out on you and the killer has this address." He gestured at the window. "That's what's going on outside, we think."

Duncan jumped off the sofa. "Why didn't you say so?" he said. "What do we do? Where do we go? You've got guns, haven't you?"

"We just need to get you out of here," said the first officer, putting a gloved hand on Duncan's shoulder. "We've got another safe-house ready for you and we'll have your passport this evening. You're on the first flight to Toronto tomorrow morning."

"Business class, right?" said Duncan. "My lawyer said I had to go business class or first."

128

"We can talk about that later," said the policeman, as he guided Duncan into the hallway and towards the kitchen. A third, also in riot gear, was holding the door open. "Let's get moving — the guy after you means business."

The three policemen kept close to Duncan as they took him across the paved backyard that led to an alley behind the row of terraced houses. A grey van was parked there with protective mesh over the windows. A fourth policeman had the side door open. "Where are we going?" asked Duncan.

"Need to know, Mr Duncan," said one of the officers. "And you don't need to know."

"Come on, come on," said the officer holding the door open. "We haven't got all day."

They bundled Duncan into the van. One of them pulled a blanket over his head. "Hey, what's going on?" Duncan protested.

"We don't want anyone to see you, Mr Duncan. Just sit quietly, and everything will be all right."

Duncan relaxed. The van moved as the policemen climbed in, then the doors slammed.

"You can get me a pizza, right?" asked Duncan. "At the new safe-house? Domino's pizza?"

"Whatever you want, Mr Duncan," said an officer. The van lurched forward.

The Major picked up his pint and raised it in salute. "Thanks for coming, lads," he said. They were sitting in a pub in the High Street, a short walk from the cemetery. Shepherd and O'Brien had walked there with the Major, and the Bradford brothers had joined them soon afterwards. The men raised their glasses. Shepherd was drinking coffee because he had a long drive ahead of him. He wanted to spend the rest of the weekend with Liam in Hereford, and he had agreed to drop O'Brien off at Gatwick Airport on the way back.

"It was a good turnout," said O'Brien.

"Yeah, Tommy was well liked," said the Major.

"He was a first-class soldier," said Shepherd. "Could have walked through Selection, if he'd wanted."

"Said he enjoyed real soldiering." The Major grinned. "That's what he called it. Real soldiering. Two tours in Afghanistan and one in Iraq. He couldn't wait to get back." He shook his head. "Three tours in war zones and not a scratch. Then he gets gunned down in a Chinese restaurant in Downpatrick. Bastards."

"Do they know who did it?" asked Jack Bradford.

The Major nodded. "A pal in Five's tipped me the wink." He drank some beer.

"So what happens now?" asked Billy Bradford.

The Major shrugged. "That remains to be seen."

"Have Five got a case?" asked Shepherd.

"What they've got is an informer in Newry, owns a pub in the Republican heartland. A couple of brothers were in the bar and they were boasting to the barmaid about what they'd done. She's the wife of the landlord."

"So it's just intel?" said Shepherd.

"It's intel from the horse's mouth," said the Major, "and with these guys it's all we're going to get. There's no CCTV, no forensics, and no one's going to stand up in court and give evidence against them."

"So what's their plan?" asked O'Brien.

"The spooks? They're going to watch and wait," said the Major. "Softly softly, catchee monkey."

"That's bollocks," said Jack Bradford.

"Took the words right out of my mouth," said his brother.

"It's the way the world works now," said the Major. "They'll gather evidence and they'll file reports and if and when they make a case they'll pass it to the CPS, and if they think they can win it then they'll go to court."

"And then there'll be another Peace Process and the bastards will be set free," said Jack. "They'll end up like Martin and Gerry, collecting their MP salary and pocketing half a million quid in second-home allowance."

"Not this time," said the Major, quietly.

"What are you thinking?" asked Shepherd.

"We'll see," the Major said.

O'Brien picked up Jack's pack of cigarettes. "I need a smoke," he said.

"Yeah, I'll second that." Jack raised an eyebrow at his brother. "Smoke?"

The three men headed for the door.

"Alone at last," said Shepherd.

"Did you plan it that way, Spider?" asked the Major.

Shepherd grinned. "I'm not that devious, boss."

"You've changed since you left the Regiment."

"That's to be expected," said Shepherd. "SOCA isn't the SAS."

"You don't wear balaclavas for one thing."

"And we don't solve our problems with guns, either."

The Major's eyes hardened. "They killed Tommy, Spider. They riddled him with twenty rounds while he was eating chicken fried rice with his mates. He wasn't in uniform, he didn't have a weapon, he was just getting some chow before heading off to Afghanistan to put his life on the line again."

"I'm not arguing, boss," said Shepherd.

"And you're not going to talk me out of doing what I have to do."

"It's your call," said Shepherd. "Whatever you decide, I'll back you one hundred per cent, and whatever you need, I'm there for you."

"Thanks."

"No thanks necessary, boss, I'm just stating a fact. But it's also a fact that if you go charging in now you're going to bring down a whole load of trouble on your shoulders."

"And if I don't, how can I look my brother in the eye again?" He leaned close to Shepherd. "I owe it to my brother, and I owe it to Tommy. I will do what I have to do, Spider. End of story. And nothing you can do or say is going to change that."

Shepherd sipped his coffee. "These brothers, what intel do you have?"

"Padraig and Sean Fox. Padraig's forty-seven, his brother's a couple of years younger. They live just outside Newry. They're terrorists and gangsters — they made a small fortune running fuel over the border, then turned it into a big fortune investing in property in Dublin and Belfast. Lately they've been running cigarettes in from Panama through Miami. They joined the IRA in their teens and both spent time in Long Kesh. They fell out with the Provos in the nineties and joined the Real IRA. My contact at Five says that the Foxes were both involved in the Omagh bombing."

"Involved how?"

"They're supposed to have stored the explosives and provided the detonators. They came very close to being sued in a civil case but there wasn't enough evidence."

"How good's that intel?"

"From an informer. Too sensitive to be used in court."

"Not the landlord?"

The Major shook his head. "No, someone very high up in Sinn Fein. The Foxes are as guilty as sin, Spider. They were complicit in the deaths of twenty-nine civilians in Omagh and they killed Tommy and his mates."

"They were the triggermen?"

"From the horse's mouth," said the Major.

Shepherd nodded slowly. He drained his coffee and put down the cup. "Okay," he said. "Do what has to be done. But not now. You have to choose your moment."

"Revenge is a dish best served cold? That's crap, Spider."

"It's not about revenge, it's about what will happen after the Foxes are dead," said Shepherd. "And now I am talking as a law-enforcement official. The way the world is now, the murder of the Foxes will be investigated with exactly the same vigour as the PSNI investigates the killings of the soldiers. I'm sorry, but that's a fact. And it's going to be a lot easier for the cops to nail you than it would be for them to nail the Foxes. The Foxes covered their tracks and made sure there were no forensics. They'll have alibis fixed up, they'll have long since got rid of the guns, and I'm damn sure there'll be nothing that ties them to Downpatrick."

"And your point is?"

"My point, boss, is that if you fly over to the north, everyone will know. If anything happens to the Foxes while you're there, it won't take an Einstein to add one and one and make two. Motive and opportunity are there for everyone to see. And even if you make sure the weapon is never found, the cops will keep after you. You make one mistake, one small bit of forensic, and you'll be done for."

"I plan to be careful, Spider. Trust me on that."

"I do, boss. But what I'm saying, you should stay on the mainland, leave it a while, and then go over under the radar."

The Major considered what he'd said. "You talk a lot of sense."

"And I'll go with you."

"You don't have to. It's not your fight."

"I don't have to. I want to."

"You're sure?"

"You need someone who knows investigative procedure so that you can cover your tracks," said Shepherd. "And I can do that better than anyone."

The van came to a stop. "Guys, I can hardly breathe under this blanket," said Ronnie Duncan. "Where are we?"

134

"Almost there."

"Why've I got to keep this bloody blanket over my head?"

"Because we don't want anyone to see you," said the same voice. "If word gets out where you are the press will be here, and if they find out you're going to Canada then that'll be the end of that."

Duncan cursed under his breath. His lawyer had already explained that his relocation to Canada had to remain a secret. The Canadians had agreed to take him but only if the British government covered all the costs and the relocation wasn't publicised. "I'm bloody suffocating here," he muttered.

A hand clapped on his shoulder. "Soon be over, mate," said a different voice.

Duncan frowned, not sure what the policeman meant. He heard a gate rattle open and then the van moved forward slowly. It stopped again and the front passenger door opened, then slammed shut. Duncan heard footsteps, then the sound of a metal door being pulled open. "Where are we?" he asked. "What's going on?" The van moved forward again for a few seconds and stopped. The side door opened and Duncan was bundled out. "What's happening?"

The blanket was pulled off his head and he shook his head, blinking. The policemen stepped away from him. Duncan saw they had lowered their visors. And for the first time he noticed that they didn't have any identification numbers.

He looked around, his heart pounding. Something was wrong — something was very wrong. He was in a warehouse with metal walls and a roof high overhead that was crisscrossed with metal girders. "Where are we?" he said. "This isn't a bloody safe-house." There were four men standing at the far end. They were wearing overalls and holding crowbars. He recognised one. He had seen him at each of his court appearances. He was little Timmy's father.

The four men began to walk towards him, swinging their crowbars. Duncan turned and ran but the five police officers had formed a wall between him and the exit and they pushed him back. "You can't do this!" he screamed. "You're cops!" One policeman was grinning behind his visor. "What are you doing? What's this about?"

"It's about justice. Justice for what you did."

Duncan ran at them but they pushed him back again. He stumbled and fell to the floor. The officers moved back as the men with crowbars rushed towards him.

The father took the first swing, slamming his crowbar against Duncan's leg. The kneecap cracked and Duncan screamed. The father's brothers took turns in hitting him, battering his legs and arms.

The policemen stood and watched as the beating continued. After a while Duncan stopped screaming. He curled up into a foetal ball with his hands covering his face as the blows continued to rain down. Eventually the brothers stopped. They stood looking down at Duncan's broken body. They were all breathing heavily, their overalls flecked with blood. They looked at the father and, one by one, they nodded at him.

He held his crowbar with both hands, his eyes wide and staring, his lips drawn back in a savage snarl. He looked at the policemen. They were standing with their arms folded, watching to see what he would do next. He could see his reflection in their visors. He looked down at Duncan, the bastard who had killed his son. He raised the crowbar above his head and brought it crashing down on Duncan's skull. Blood and brain matter splattered across the concrete floor.

Shepherd drove Martin O'Brien back to Gatwick to catch his flight to Dublin. They arrived at the airport a good two hours before the Aer Lingus flight was due to leave so Shepherd parked his BMW X3 in the short-term car park and they went for a coffee in the departures area. O'Brien commandeered a table while Shepherd went to the self-service counter.

"Thanks for leaving me alone with the Major when you did," said Shepherd, carrying over two coffees. "Back there at the pub."

"I figured someone had to find out what he was going to do, and you're the best man for the job, being a cop and all."

"I'm a civil servant now, remember," said Shepherd. "SOCA employees aren't cops. We're not even agents. In fact, no one's sure what we are. When we introduce ourselves we normally say we work for the Home Office."

"I thought you were supposed to be the British FBI."

"Yeah, well, it's not worked out that way," said Shepherd. "Most of the time we're treated like CSOs."

"CSO?"

"Community Support Officers. The wannabe cops who tell you not to drop litter."

O'Brien chuckled. "So how did you know I was leaving you alone?"

"Because you gave up smoking two years ago, you daft sod."

"Did it work?"

"Yeah, it worked."

"Well," said O'Brien, "I'm not so daft, then. So, what's he going to do?"

"What do you think?"

"What we all think," said O'Brien.

"Then you'd be right," said Shepherd.

"When?"

"He was all for going over with guns blazing there and then, but I think I've managed to persuade him to hold off for a while."

O'Brien sighed and folded his arms. "You can see it from his point of view," he said. "The Northern Irish cops won't be able to do anything. They were bugger-all use during the Troubles and even less effective now."

"You're preaching to the converted, Martin."

"Do you think the spooks will do anything?"

"I think they'll collate very large files and spend an awful lot of money on surveillance, but in terms of taking action, I don't think they'll do a bloody thing," said Shepherd. "The army will increase security at the barracks in the North and I doubt that squaddies will be allowed to pop into their local Chinese again, but other than that, I think they're just going to leave it up to the PSNI. They don't want troops back on the streets, that's for sure."

"So the bastards will get away with it?"

"For the moment," said Shepherd. "It'll be treated like a regular murder inquiry. It'll be investigated by detectives — they'll take statements, they'll look at what forensics they have, and if and when they can make a case, they'll prosecute."

"So there'll be no stopping him, then?"

Shepherd shook his head. "He said he wouldn't go right over, but he won't wait for ever. He wants revenge, and no one's going to talk him out of it."

"What do you think?"

"Do I think he's doing the right thing?" Shepherd shrugged. "Who knows? If a member of my family was murdered . . . I just don't know."

"I'm with the boss," said O'Brien. "Someone hurts your family, you lash out. You don't wait for the cops to sort it."

"Maybe," said Shepherd.

"You've gone soft," said O'Brien, and Shepherd could tell that he was only half joking.

"I'm in the law-enforcement business, Martin. I can't choose which laws I uphold."

"This isn't about breaking the speed limit, is it? It's about a couple of Irish gangsters letting rip with Kalashnikovs in a Chinese restaurant. I tell you, Spider, if it had been my nephew they'd killed I wouldn't think twice."

"I'm not arguing with you," said Shepherd. "And I've not gone soft. Trust me on that."

O'Brien grinned. "That struck home, did it?"

"Just because I work for SOCA doesn't mean I don't put friends and family first. I'll do what has to be done."

"You're going with him?"

"I don't see that I've any choice, Martin. I owe him."

"We all do," said O'Brien. "You can count me in."

"Too many cooks."

"Fuck the cooks," said O'Brien. "You're not doing it without me."

"Martin . . ."

O'Brien pointed a finger at Shepherd's face. "I'm in," he said, "and that's the end of it. And Jack and Billy will want to be part of it, too."

"Okay," said Shepherd.

"I'm serious, Spider," said O'Brien. "Don't even think about flying solo on this."

"I won't," said Shepherd.

O'Brien looked at the departures screen. "I should go," he said. "Just about time for a full cavity search. I ask you, do I look like an al-Qaeda terrorist?"

"Everyone has to be treated the same," said Shepherd. "Racial profiling is a big no-no, these days."

"It's bloody madness," said O'Brien. He grabbed his holdall and stood up. "I knew it wasn't over, the Irish thing," he said. "When they announced the first ceasefire, I didn't think it would last. And when they started power sharing and the Belfast Agreement, I knew it was only a matter of time before the killings started again. Do you know when it'll be over, Spider?"

Shepherd shook his head. "When hell freezes over," said O'Brien. "That's when."

Shepherd had plenty of time to think on the drive back to Hereford. What the Major wanted to do was wrong, legally and morally, but at the same time Shepherd knew that killing the Fox brothers was the right thing to do. It wasn't about politics, or law, or morality, it was something that had to be done, like putting down a mad dog. By their actions the Foxes had shown they had no respect for the law or for human life. They had behaved like rabid animals, and that was the way they deserved to be treated. Shepherd had killed before: he'd killed in combat and he'd killed in the line of duty, and once he'd killed a man who was trying to kill Charlotte Button, but he'd never before sat down and planned the assassination of another human being. It would be a first for him, and it wasn't something he would do lightly.

Shepherd knew that, whether he helped him or not, the Major would kill the Fox brothers. But the Major was a soldier, and getting away with murder required a familiarity with forensic techniques and police procedure. Shepherd could help, and he would. He'd do whatever was necessary to make sure that the Major got his revenge, even if it meant pulling the trigger himself. He'd met Tommy Gannon and liked him, and no man deserved to be mown down in a hail of bullets for no other reason than that he fought for his country.

As Shepherd reached the outskirts of Hereford, his mobile rang. It was Charlotte Button. "You're driving," she said. "I'll call you back."

"It's okay," he said. "I'm on hands-free." He pulled up at a red light. "And I'm stuck at traffic-lights."

"You're all set for Monday?"

"All good," said Shepherd. "I'll be seeing Jenny on Sunday at the house she's fixed up for me and I'll spend the night there so I can be at Paddington Green first thing Monday morning."

"And you're fully up to speed on TSG procedure?"

"It's all pretty basic stuff," said Shepherd.

"There's a couple of things you need to be aware of," said Button. "A child-killer was snatched from police custody today. Guy by the name of Ronnie Duncan. It's almost certainly the work of our vigilante cops. He was in a safe-house in Hounslow prior to being sent to Canada."

Shepherd frowned. "We're sending our murderers to Canada, these days, are we, instead of prison?"

"He'd served his sentence, and the Canadians were giving him a new identity. He was due to fly out the day after tomorrow. He was being held in a safe-house and someone broke him out."

"Not that safe, then," said Shepherd, drily.

"It's not funny, Spider."

"Why do you think it was the TSG vigilantes?"

"Only someone within the Met would have known where he was being kept," said Button. "He'd been taken out of prison early and kept well away from his old haunts. It had to be an inside job."

"But no sign of a body?"

"Not yet," said Button. "And there's been another killing that might be down to them, an Iraqi asylum seeker by the name of Mohammed Hussein al-Najafi. He was found hanging in an abandoned warehouse."

"But not suicide?"

"It was made to look like he'd killed himself but there were traces of adhesive around his mouth so he was gagged at some point. He'd killed a schoolgirl in a hit-and-run."

"I remember the case — it was in the papers." The red light went to green and Shepherd started driving again.

"Well, so far his death hasn't been picked up by the press," said Button, "but I've no doubt it will be. We're going to push out the line that he killed himself because he was overcome by grief, but the real story is that someone killed him and it was professionally done."

"There's no direct link between these two cases and the TSG, though?"

"They fit the profile," said Button. "And if it is them, they're upping their strike rate. It's as if they're gaining confidence."

"Because they're getting away with it?"

"Exactly. Hopefully that'll lead to overconfidence."

"And we'll put them behind bars and the capital's criminals will be able to sleep soundly in their beds once more."

"Your cynicism's showing," said Button.

"I just think there are better uses of SOCA resources than hunting down guys who seem to be doing a pretty good job of cutting the capital's crime rate."

"Ronnie Duncan was a drug addict and alcoholic rather than a career criminal."

"He killed a child, you said, and as part of his punishment he was going to get a new life in Canada. Forgive me if I don't shed any tears if the vigilantes have done what our criminal justice system should have done in the first place."

"I hope you're in a better mood on Monday, that's all I can say."

Shepherd sighed. "I'm sorry, Charlie," he said. "I was at a funeral this afternoon."

"Oh, I'm sorry," she said. "You should have said. Someone close?"

Shepherd cursed under his breath. He didn't want to tell Button that it had been the Major's nephew, but neither did he want to lie to his boss. "Army buddy," he said. "I'll be fine on Monday, Charlie, firing on all cylinders. How's Razor?"

"He's got a meet with a Met undercover operative who can get him close to Dawson, the TSG sergeant."

"How's that going to work?"

"The cop's been infiltrating various football gangs over the past year and as part of that investigation he's attended a few England First meetings. He came across Gary Dawson and has spoken to him once. He's going to introduce Razor and leave him to it."

"Anything else on Dawson other than his England First membership?"

144

"Nothing known," said Button.

"You know I'm not going into the same Serial as Dawson?"

"There wasn't a vacancy," said Button. "And, besides, Dawson's Serial didn't have access to the van that was seen near where the paedophile was found."

"So Dawson could be a red herring?"

"Or there could be cops from several Serials involved," said Button. "I'll see you during the week, see how things are progressing."

"Any news yet of when you'll be leaving?"

"Still up in the air," said Button. "As soon as I know, you'll know, I promise." She ended the call.

Five minutes later he pulled up outside his house. The CRV that Katra used was in the driveway. Shepherd parked. He heard Liam's voice from the back garden so he walked around the side of the house. His son was there with Lady. He looked up when he saw Shepherd. "Dad!" he shouted, and Lady barked. Boy and dog ran across the lawn. Liam hugged his father while the beagle jumped up and yelped.

"I've only been gone a day," said Shepherd. "I said I'd be back this evening."

"Yeah, but I thought you'd be working."

"Nothing would keep me from watching you play football tomorrow," said Shepherd.

"Really? You'll come to the game?"

"Wild horses wouldn't keep me from it," said Shepherd. "Why don't you get the football and see if you can get any past me?"

"A pound a goal?"

Shepherd laughed. "Ten pence," he said. "I think I'm being hustled."

Jimmy Sharpe bought a pint of lager at the bar and took it over to a corner table. Various items of Millwall FC memorabilia were displayed on the walls, including a signed first-team shirt and a shield with the club's lion emblem and motto beneath it. "We Fear No Foe Where E'er We Go". It was supposed to apply to the club's players but it was equally applicable to the Millwall fans, who had a fearsome reputation the length and breadth of the country.

Most of the pub's clientele looked as if they'd walked off the remand wing of a Category A prison — shaved heads, tattooed arms, branded sportswear and gleaming white training shoes. There was a good sprinkling of Millwall shirts, along with thick gold chains and sovereign rings. Sharpe had dressed to blend in, with new Nikes, Adidas tracksuit bottoms and a Lacoste polo shirt. An Asian woman smiled at him, revealing a gold tooth at the front of her mouth, and held open a holdall to show him the dozens of DVDs inside. "Five for twenty pounds," she said. She took out a handful and he flicked through them.

"Pirate movies, yeah?" said Sharpe.

She nodded enthusiastically. "*Pirates of the Caribbean*," she said. "Johnny Depp." She rummaged around in the holdall, muttering to herself.

"I meant . . . Never mind," said Sharpe. He pulled out a Hollywood blockbuster that hadn't yet been released in the UK. "Is this a good copy?"

"Perfect."

"Because I don't want any of that camera-in-the-cinema crap with heads bobbing around."

"Copy perfect," said the woman.

"Six for twenty quid?"

"Okay," said the woman, flashing her gold tooth again.

Sharpe chose six movies and gave her twenty pounds. As she headed for a group of Millwall fans at the bar, a young man in a leather jacket walked over holding a pint of lager. He had MILL tattooed on the knuckles of his right hand and WALL on the left, his head was shaved and he was wearing red Doc Marten boots. He nodded at Sharpe and sat down. "How's it going?" he asked.

"That seat's taken," snapped Sharpe.

"Yeah, by me," said the man.

"What's your fucking problem?" growled Sharpe.

The man leaned forward. "You're Brian Parker, right?"

That was the undercover name he was using. "Bloody hell, you're Ray Henby?"

The man winked. "In the flesh." He swigged his pint.

"How old are you?"

"Why?"

"Because you look like a bloody teenager, that's why," said Sharpe.

"I'm twenty-two," said Henby.

"How long have you been in the Met?"

"Joined two years ago. You're not in Human Resources, are you? If I'd known this was a job interview I'd have brought my CV with me."

Sharpe ignored the sarcasm. "I thought you had to do at least three years as a beat cop before they'd consider you for specialist ops."

"They made an exception with me. And a dozen or so others. We got pulled out of Hendon and put into the Football Intelligence Unit. They figured getting us in young was more important than having us walk around the streets in a pointy hat. Do I pass muster?"

Sharpe grinned. "Pass muster?"

"Look, mate, I'm doing you a favour by bringing you in. I don't know you, you don't know me, but I'm the one whose balls will be on the line if anything goes wrong. I've spent months easing myself into England First and I don't want all that work to be pissed away." He raised his glass. "Okay?"

Sharpe nodded. "No offence meant. I just wanted to know who I was going to be riding with, that's all."

"Well, now you know, so can I start the briefing — or do you want to tell me what it was like pounding a beat in Ballykissangel?"

"Glasgow," said Sharpe.

"Wherever."

"And Ballykissangel is in Ireland. I'm Scottish."

"Ballykissangel is the figment of some screenwriter's imagination," said Henby. "But I take your point. So, are you ready?"

"I'm all ears."

"You know about England First, right?"

"Offshoot of the old National Front. The British National Party became the political wing, the hard nuts split off into England First. Skinheads, racists, football hooligans, hang the Jews, send the Pakis back home."

"That's it pretty much," said Henby. "The BNP puts up candidates for the various elections and provides the talking heads for TV and the press, but England First provides the storm-troopers when they need something heavy doing."

"I've read the police intel on the group, but there isn't much in the media."

Henby nodded. "They're low profile. No slogans, the membership list is secret, so is their funding. I've been going to meetings for the past six months and I only know three of the top guys."

"What — it's run the like the Masons, is it? Secret handshakes and that?"

Henby grinned. "No secret handshakes, but you have to be invited to join, and even if you do, you'll only know the members of your cell. They're using the IRA model, keeping lots of small groups with only one point of contact, so if you get a mole in a cell the mole can only damage the cell, not the organisation."

"How deep in are you?"

"I'm not," said Henby. "My main function is to provide intel on the Millwall supporters, tip off our guys when there's going to be trouble, identify troublemakers, help with CCTV identification. I'm on the periphery of England First, that's all. My boss asked me to take a look at Gary Dawson when his mobile number came up on a membership list."

"Yeah, it seemed a bit tenuous, that," said Sharpe. "All they had was a phone number, right?"

"Yeah, but you can understand why Dawson would be careful. The BNP is a political organisation but membership alone is reason enough to be thrown out of the Met. England First is a hardcore racist organisation. He'd lose everything."

"You've met him, yeah?"

"Once I was given his details, I started looking out for him," said Henby. "I saw him a few times at various England First meetings, and one of my contacts introduced me but I didn't get a chance to talk to him."

Sharpe rubbed his chin. "I was hoping you could introduce me, get me up close and personal," he said.

"Dawson's twenty years or so older than me and he's not into football, so there was no connection," said Henby. "If I'd tried to force it, it would have set alarm bells ringing. I couldn't take the risk."

"Okay," said Sharpe, but there was no hiding his disappointment.

"What I can do is take you to an England First meeting where Dawson will probably be," said Henby. "There's one on Sunday night but I haven't been told where it is yet. My contact will be there — he's an okay guy and he knows Dawson. You're all about the same age so you can hopefully take a walk down Memory Lane and forge your own links. I'll introduce you and make myself scarce."

"What's your contact's name?"

"Lenny Brennan — he's a Millwall fan but he doesn't get involved much in the hooligan side, these days. Did three years for GBH a while back and prison

150

was a bit of a shock. He's been on the straight and narrow since."

"Racist?"

"Everyone at England First is racist one way or another," said Henby. "But I'd say that Brennan was more political than violent. He works for Westminster City Council, though, so he has to keep his membership a secret. Figured I might be able to use that as leverage at some point." He shrugged. "I don't know, he's actually a nice guy."

"For a racist?"

"If I was black or Asian I've no doubt he'd treat me differently, but I am what I am and he's a good guy to me. Like a big brother, you know? I have to force myself to remember that I'm a cop and he's one of the guys I'm investigating."

Sharpe sipped his lager. "Can I offer you some advice, Ray?"

"Knock yourself out," said Henby.

"If I sound patronising tell me, but you're hellish young to be working under cover. I've been doing it for more than ten years and I find it stressful — it's the toughest thing in the world to live a life pretending to be someone else."

Henby frowned. "So?"

"So I wouldn't do it for too long. I've seen young guys working under cover go off the rails. Drugs, booze, hookers. It fucks with your psyche, and one of the first signs is when you start to empathise with the guys you're investigating. If I were you I'd start looking for a move back into regular policing."

Henby nodded. "You're right," he said.

Sharpe grinned.

"You do sound patronising," continued Henby. "I'm not an amateur. I know what I'm doing."

Sharpe's grin vanished. "No offence," he said. "I just . . ." He put up a hand. "Sorry, forget it."

"It's okay," said Henby.

"I shouldn't be offering anyone advice," said Sharpe. He raised his pint. "It's not as if I'm without vices of my own."

"Ten years under cover?"

"Yeah, pretty much."

"Had a few hairy moments?"

"More than my fair share," Sharpe said. "Especially since I moved to SOCA. Bigger villains. Most of the time, anyway."

"And this empathy thing, it happens to you?"

"It happens to everybody, sooner or later. That's one of the reasons we have the six-monthly psychological evaluations."

"The what?" said Henby.

"The chats with the unit psychologist. We had them when we were with the Met and SOCA does them too." He leaned forward. "Are you saying you don't?"

"I'm not with an undercover unit, I'm attached to Football Intelligence."

"That's not right," said Sharpe. "Do you have a handler?"

"I report to a chief inspector. I call him whenever I've got anything. And he calls me if there's something he needs doing, like checking up on Dawson."

"And what about back-up?"

"I've not needed it so far," Henby said. "I'm in an intelligence role, basically."

"Bloody hell, lad," said Sharpe. "You need to get your act together. You can't do undercover work by the seat of your pants."

"It's been okay so far," said Henby. "Did you work under cover with the Met before you joined SOCA?"

"It was a police undercover unit, but we were available to any force in the country," said Sharpe. He smiled. "Back in the day when they were forces and not services. Then we got swallowed up by SOCA."

"And part of your brief is to investigate cops?"

Sharpe drank his lager and wiped his mouth. "I'm not happy about it either," he said. "But we don't get to pick and choose our cases."

"I'm being treated a bit like a mushroom on this," said Henby. "My governor tells me he wants me to get you close to Dawson, but he doesn't say why."

"Need to know," said Sharpe.

"And I don't?"

"We're in the same boat, Ray," said Sharpe. "What happens to Dawson is nothing to do with me. My boss tells me nothing. All I know is that Dawson's a cop and my boss wants to know what he's up to."

"With a view to getting him sacked?"

"Maybe," said Sharpe. "Or maybe turning him. Maybe see if he's giving them intel, access to the PNC, that sort of bollocks."

"So he might be prosecuted?"

Sharpe shrugged. "I wouldn't know, Ray, honest. I'm on a very low rung of the totem pole."

"I don't think totem poles have rungs, but I get your drift," said Henby. "Just do me a favour and give me a heads-up if you decide to pull him in."

"It won't be my decision, but sure, I'll call you if I hear anything."

"Dawson won't know you're under cover, will he? Because if he connects me to you then I'll be in the shit."

"We don't work that way, Ray," said Sharpe. "I'll be long gone before he gets a tug and we don't give evidence in court."

Henby raised his glass. "I'll hold you to that, Brian," he said.

Sharpe clinked his glass against Henby's. "You know that Brian Parker's my cover name, right?"

"They just said I was to meet a Brian Parker from SOCA."

"Okay, well, here's the scoop. Brian Parker works for SOCA, in admin. A desk job. Divorced, two kids he never sees, alimony payments he can barely meet. I won't tell Dawson that I work for SOCA but it won't take much digging for him to find out. If I can convince him that I'm of the same political persuasion, he might figure that I'll be a good source of intel for his England First mates."

"Isn't that acting as an *agent provocateur*?" Henby grinned. "Pardon my French."

"I won't be entrapping him," said Sharpe. "He'll see what's on offer and it's up to him to make the approach. One step at a time. Now, what's our back story?"

Henby frowned. "Back story?"

"How did we meet? How do you know me? What's our connection?"

Henby exhaled through pursed lips. "I hadn't thought about that."

"You've got to have the back story prepared," said Sharpe. "If someone asks and you stand there scratching your balls they'll smell a rat."

"Football?"

"I'm a Rangers fan and you support Millwall. How would that have happened?"

Henby looked crestfallen and Sharpe chuckled at the younger man's obvious discomfort. "Tell you what, the old betting shop is a safe bet. Where do you live?"

"Clerkenwell."

"You bet the horses?"

Henby shook his head.

"Okay, so you went in to bet on a game. There's plenty of bookies in Clerkenwell, you can be vague about that. I was in putting money on the horses and I gave you a sure thing. A twelve to one shot at Newton Abbot. I convinced you to put a bet on and you gambled twenty quid and won two hundred and forty. That's the sort of thing to forge a friendship, right?"

"Name of the horse?"

"Say it was Missie something. You're not a horse nut so why would you remember? I've given you a few other tips since and we've had a few drinks in the pub."

"Which pub?"

"What's your local in Clerkenwell?"

"The White Hart. And the Slug and Lettuce."

"Okay, both of them, and here. But we're mainly betting-shop buddies. During one of our pub chats I passed a racist comment or two so you asked me if I wanted to come along to an England First meeting."

Henby nodded. "Sounds good."

"If in doubt, keep it vague," said Sharpe. "Most people have pretty crap memories, but if you tell a lie it can come back to haunt you."

"Got it," said Henby. He looked at his watch. "I've got to go," he said. "I'll pick you up outside the pub tomorrow. Anything else before I head off?"

"Just one more question?"

"Fire away."

Sharpe jerked a thumb at Henby's hands. "The tattoos? They real?"

Henby held up his right hand and bunched it into a fist. He grinned at the blue letters on his knuckles. "Yeah. Of course."

"Bloody hell," said Sharpe. "Talk about deep cover."

"They'll come off," said Henby. "The new inks don't go too deep, a couple of laser treatments and they'll be gone."

"Even so, that shows . . . commitment."

"You have to if you want to get close to these guys," said Henby. He drained his glass. "They don't take prisoners — if your cover does get blown they'll put you in ICU before you can say, 'I'm a Celebrity, Get Me Out of Here.' That's if you're lucky. They killed an undercover cop last year. Kicked him to death. These

156

aren't criminals you're dealing with, they're fanatics. They don't care about the consequences of what they do. They really believe that they're part of the master race and that down the line they'll be ruling the world. Killing a cop, even a white cop, wouldn't worry them in the slightest." He stood up. "See ya tomorrow night, yeah? I'll pick you up outside. And wear a decent shirt."

"This is a Lacoste," said Sharpe.

"It's a fake Lacoste," said Henby. "And these guys can spot a phoney a mile off."

Shepherd left Hereford after lunch on Sunday. Liam had been subdued as he always was when his father was about to leave on an assignment. Saturday had been more relaxed. Shepherd had gone to see Liam play football: his son's team had won 3-1 and Liam had come close to scoring twice. Shepherd had shouted himself hoarse and afterwards they had celebrated at Burger King. In the evening they had gone into town to watch a movie that Liam wanted to see. Shepherd had enjoyed spending time with his son — it was a rare treat — but he was all too well aware that he was packing in as much as he could because he was going away for weeks, possibly longer.

Sunday was different, because Liam knew that his father would be leaving, so there had been tension in the air. They'd kicked around a football in the garden, eaten lasagne prepared by Katra and afterwards taken Lady for a walk, but they'd both been aware of the clock ticking in the background. Liam had played with his Wii while Shepherd had packed his bag, and he had walked with him to the BMW. Shepherd had given Liam a hug and promised to phone as soon as he got to London. Liam put on a brave face but there was no hiding the fact that he wasn't happy his father was leaving. He had gone back into the house before Shepherd had driven off.

Shepherd's mobile rang when he was an hour outside London. He took the call on hands-free. "How's it going?" asked Sharpe.

"I'm on my way to London," said Shepherd. "I start with the TSG tomorrow."

"Yeah, well, don't crack too many skulls."

"It's not like that any more," said Shepherd. "It's about controlling situations, not about breaking heads."

"You don't want to put too much store by the manual," said Sharpe. "They killed a guy at the G20 demos, remember?"

"He had a heart-attack," said Shepherd. "What do you want, Razor?"

"Just calling to let you know that I'm off to an England First meeting tonight. Hopefully I'll be meeting up with Dawson. Are you around for a drink later?"

"Maybe during the week. Let me settle in."

Shepherd ended the call. He drove through north London, using his sat-nav system to guide him to the house that Charlotte Button had fixed up for him. It was a two-bedroom end-of-terrace in a run-down part of Kilburn. To the right there was a wooden gate that had been sprayed with graffiti. He parked in front of the house, picked up his bag and rang the doorbell.

Seconds later a woman with curly blonde hair, wearing blue jeans and a blue denim shirt, opened the front door. It was Jenny Lock. It had been a good six months since he'd last seen her so he gave her a hug and a peck on the cheek. "Welcome to your new home," she said.

"Salubrious," said Shepherd, as he walked into a cramped hall that smelt of damp. The wallpaper was basic woodchip that had been painted with pale green emulsion. A bare light bulb hung from the ceiling.

"It's what you'd be able to afford as a single cop," she said. "Met officers get a hefty London allowance but it doesn't go far. Even after the slump, property still isn't cheap here. This is about right for your pay scale." She showed him through to a small sitting room where there was a fake leather sofa and a chunky television set.

"I don't even get an LCD?"

"The set comes with the flat," said Lock. "The sort of rent you're paying, you're not going to get top-of-the-range appliances."

"Couldn't you fix me up with a pretty barrister wife and a house in Mayfair?"

Lock laughed. "That's funny."

"I'm serious." He smiled. "Sort of."

"I'm not sure that Charlie would run to another operative," she said. She handed him a rental contract. "The name and phone number of the landlord and the agent are on our database, so leave this around if you have visitors. You've got a year's lease, paid monthly from a Barclays account in your name." She handed him an envelope. "A Barclaycard in the name of Terry

Halligan, and an ATM card. You'll need to put your signature on them both, and sign the rental contract. And there's a warrant card, too."

"Passport?"

"If you think you'll need to travel, let me know and I'll get you one within six hours. But there's a driving licence in there. Now, so far as your work legend goes, we've used your army background and given you five years with the Paras. Then you joined West Mercia Police."

"My local force," said Shepherd. "That's convenient."

"I don't just throw these things together," said Lock, primly. "They cover the fourth largest geographical area in England and Wales and they only have two and a half thousand officers so they're pretty spread out. We've put you based in Hereford because you've got local knowledge, but our main reason for choosing West Mercia is that no one in the TSG has ever worked for them."

"And why am I transferring to the Met?"

Lock smiled. "That's where we've been clever," she said. "We've given you a disciplinary caution for slapping around a drug-dealer. We've used another SOCA operative as the dealer so it'll stand up if anyone ever follows it up, and it's down on your record. You tell everyone that you wanted to try big-city police work but if anyone checks up they'll get the real reason you wanted to leave West Mercia."

"Nice," said Shepherd.

"We aim to please," she said. "Now, choice of vehicle. You've got a motorcycle licence and we thought we might make use of that, get a man-of-action thing going. We've put a BMW bike in your name since 2008. Did you see the side gate as you came in?"

Shepherd nodded.

"I've a key for that. It leads to the yard at the back of the house where you can leave it. We've kept it registered to an address in Hereford so if anyone runs it through DVLA at Swansea it'll check out. Ditto with your licence. We've given you a speeding conviction on the bike — you were caught doing sixty in a forty area, snapped by a speed camera outside Hereford. It's an HP2 Sport, fourteen and a half grand new but you bought it for ten grand when it was a year old."

"I don't have a car?"

"We thought a bike fitted the profile better. Single, never married, heavy into sports and bikes — makes you one of the lads right from the start. Plus one of the TSG sergeants at Paddington Green is a bike nut, which will give you an in with him. What are you planning to do with your car?"

"I'm not sure," said Shepherd. "I don't fancy taking the bike to Hereford so I'm going to need it."

"You can get the Tube to Paddington and the train from there to Hereford," said Lock. "But if you wanted to keep your car here I'd suggest you keep it some distance away. I could see about arranging a lock-up if that would help."

"Let's see how I get on," said Shepherd. "I might end up leaving the car in Hereford and using the train like you say. So, what hobbies have you given me? Do I support a football team?"

"I've left that up to you," said Lock. "Come on, I'll show you around the bedrooms." She went up the stairs and Shepherd followed her. There was a large bedroom and a smaller one, separated by a small bathroom. "I've put an exercise bike and a rowing machine in the spare room," she said.

"I'm more of a runner."

"I doubt you'll be doing much running around Kilburn," said Lock. "There's not much green space nearby and it's not the safest of areas. Anyone running in Kilburn is probably being pursued by a policeman. But it's more to add to your image if you have visitors." She went into the main bedroom. There was a framed photograph of a couple in their sixties on the dressing-table, "I gave you a mum and dad, but no siblings."

"Pretty accurate," said Shepherd.

There was a wardrobe with a mirrored sliding door. She opened it. There were a dozen shirts, half polos and half long-sleeved, and several pairs of jeans and chinos on hangers. "I bought most of the clothes from stores in Hereford and had them washed a couple of times. There's two suits and a couple of sports jackets, with a Hereford tailor's labels in them. Your motorcycle gear is downstairs in the kitchen. Leathers from a bike shop in Hereford."

"You don't think the Hereford connection is going to start alarm bells ringing?"

"Your SAS background? I don't think so. You're quite an exception, going from the SAS to SOCA. And

162

we did think we had to choose a place that you're very familiar with."

They went downstairs and back into the sitting room. Shepherd went over to a cheap pine bookcase filled with paperbacks, mainly well-thumbed thrillers and crime novels. There were a couple of framed photographs of Shepherd in desert camouflage gear, one of him standing in front of a tank, the other in a group of soldiers. "These are good," he said, picking up the group picture.

"We've a girl who's a wizard at faking them," said Lock. "It all adds to the legend, gives you an opportunity to tell a few war stories if you want."

"We're really pushing the action-man image, aren't we?"

"If these are vigilante cops, they're not going to be drawn to shrinking violets," said Lock. "We haven't faked up any police pictures — we thought that might be pushing our luck. But we have got you on the West Mercia Police staff list and you're hidden-flagged so we'll know if anyone goes looking for you."

"It all sounds great, Jenny, as always."

She smiled. "It's funny, but you do look like a Terry," she said. "I never saw you as an Eddie, but Terry definitely suits you." She went over to the dining-table where she'd left her briefcase and took out a Nokia N95 mobile. "This is registered in the Terry Halligan name and goes back two years. It's a Vodafone contract, still registered to the Hereford address. We've set up a complete false record of calls, all to numbers in our database, including text messages. If anyone does check up on your number it'll all look kosher but, more importantly, we'll know immediately that someone has been looking at you." She gave the phone to him. "There's a GPS tracker in there, but no eavesdropping facility."

"There are no microphones in the house?"

"Charlotte didn't think it was necessary," she said. "I gather the intention is to catch them in the act rather than to inveigle a confession."

"That's a pity because I'm good at inveigling."

"So I hear." She looked around the room. "I think we're all set," she said. "Can you think of anything else?"

"Nothing I can think of," said Shepherd.

"I'll be off, then. If anything springs to mind, give me a call. I know how difficult it can be investigating cops, so I'm there when you need me, whatever it is."

Jimmy Sharpe turned up the collar of his coat and stamped his feet. There was a chill in the air and Ray Henby was already fifteen minutes late. Two men with shaved heads and diamond earrings, wearing Millwall shirts under denim jackets, walked into the pub. The sound of men drinking and laughing billowed out and just as quickly died as the door closed behind them. A car horn sounded off to his right. It was Henby in a blue Vauxhall Astra. Sharpe jogged over and climbed in. "Sorry I'm late," said Henby. He was chewing gum and offered Sharpe his pack of Wrigley's.

Sharpe took a piece, unwrapped it and popped it into his mouth. "So, where are we going?" he asked.

"Pub in Tower Hamlets," said Henby. "They don't tell you where the meetings are until a few hours before because if the lefties find out there'll be pickets and the cops will turn up and it all turns to shit."

"There's a lot of that goes on, yeah?"

"Yeah — the Searchlight people keep trying to get spies into England First but they usually get rooted out. They want confrontations because it's good for raising their profile. The cops turn up supposedly to keep the peace but really they're there to show that they're politically correct. They protect Searchlight and the Socialist Workers Party and intimidate England First. Tonight is a fund-raising event and they don't want a confrontation so we call a special number a few hours before the off and we're given the address."

"Like with raves," said Sharpe.

"Yeah, I guess that's where they got the idea from, but there'll be no Ecstasy there tonight. Just booze and fags and racist banter."

"Sounds like a good night out," said Sharpe. "You go to a lot of them?"

"Only since I was asked to look at Dawson," said Henby. "To be honest, the football hooligans aren't that into the racism thing. You hear the chants and that at matches but it's more to do with taking the piss out of the team. They're not into firebombing immigrant families or beating up asylum seekers — they're more interested in kicking the shit out of other fans, no matter what colour they are. Lenny Brennan took me to my first meeting. He's a computer whiz and helps them with their website."

"He'll be there tonight, yeah?"

"Definitely. He wants to talk about the Millwall match next week."

"Will Dawson be there?"

"I guess so — he goes to most of the fund-raisers. I'll introduce you to Brennan and if you stick with him he should introduce you to Dawson. Then it's up to you."

"Sounds good, Ray. Thanks."

"Now it's my turn to give you some advice," said Henby. "Don't go overboard on the racial thing. Agree with what you hear but don't start throwing in 'kill all Pakis' or anything like that. That's how the infiltrators give themselves away. Too enthusiastic. You'll hear some pretty outrageous stuff but don't join in, not until you've been accepted."

"Less is more?"

"Pretty much, until you've been accepted. Just nod and smile and throw a few quid into the bucket when it gets passed around. You'll be fine."

"I appreciate your confidence," said Sharpe.

The pub was on the edge of a low-rise housing estate with graffiti-covered buildings and a children's play area with brightly painted climbing bars, a set of swings and a slide. Three young Asians in parkas sat on a bench sharing a cigarette and looking in their direction as Henby parked the Astra. Two more Asians on BMX bikes were also watching them from the far side of the playground and there were two more at the entrance to one of the blocks.

"I hope they're drug-dealers and not car thieves," said Sharpe, as he got out.

"That's racial profiling if ever I heard it," said Henby.

"They're not there for the swings," said Sharpe. "If there's so many Asians around, why choose to come here for the meeting?"

"Estates like this are the bedrock of support for groups like England First," said Henby. "The immigrants move in and the whites that can't get out resent the newcomers. The local politicians don't help — they're more concerned about getting the immigrant vote, so the locals feel increasingly disenfranchised. That's when the BNP start knocking on doors."

There were two big men with shaved heads and spider-web tattoos on their necks standing at the entrance to the pub, their hands in the pockets of their black bomber jackets. Henby nodded at them. "Hi, guys," he said.

They nodded back impassively as he and Sharpe walked into the pub. "We'll grab a drink and take it upstairs," said Henby. "What do you want?"

"I'll get it," said Sharpe. He forced his way to the bar. The pub was packed. A jukebox in the corner was playing a Rod Stewart song but it was almost drowned by the buzz of masculine conversation. There was only a handful of female customers, though most of the serving staff were middle-aged women. The bar was so busy that it took Sharpe almost ten minutes to get served. Two men next to him were deep in conversation about the best way of moving from Jobseeker's Allowance to Incapacity Benefit, and on the other side two teenagers were arguing about which was funnier, *Little Britain* or *Shameless*.

Sharpe carried the pint glasses over to Henby, who indicated a flight of stairs at the far end of the pub. Two more heavies stood there, wearing the same shiny bomber jackets as the men at the door. They moved apart to allow Henby and Sharpe to go upstairs. At the top they were met by yet another heavy, this one with a clipboard. "Ray Henby," said Henby.

The heavy wrinkled his nose as he scrutinised a list of names on his clipboard, then nodded and looked at Sharpe expectantly. "This is Brian Parker. He's with me," said Henby.

"No problem," said the heavy, adding the name to the list.

"What time's the man here?" asked Henby.

"On his way," replied the heavy. He opened the door for them to go through.

The room was almost as big as the bar downstairs, with more than a dozen tables facing a makeshift stage on which a lectern had been set up in front of a huge red and white flag of St George. The air was thick with cigarette smoke and the smell of stale sweat. Most of the people there were male, though there were two heavy-set middle-aged women with dyed blonde hair and matching tattoos sitting at one table. There were a couple of dozen skinheads in tight white T-shirts, blue jeans and cherry red Dr Marten boots, drinking bottles of beer, but there were plenty of men in suits who wouldn't have looked out of place in a bank or an estate agent's.

"How come they're smoking?" asked Sharpe.

Henby shrugged. "I think they can do pretty much anything they want," he said. He lowered his voice and put his mouth close to Sharpe's ear. "The two guys downstairs are both in Combat 18. They used to handle security for the BNP until they figured the BNP was going soft. You've heard about Combat 18, right?"

"Eighteen because the one and the eight stand for the first and the eighth letters of the alphabet," said Sharpe. "Adolf Hitler's initials. It's a Trivial Pursuit question, I think."

Henby chuckled. "Yeah, they're pretty much the armed wing of the British neo-Nazi movement. Carried out a fair amount of arson and assaults in the nineties but they've gone quieter now. There's Brennan." He indicated a table in the middle of the room. An overweight man in his forties was sitting on his own with a pint of bitter in front of him. He was wearing a denim jacket and had a Millwall scarf around his neck. He blinked through square-framed spectacles as Henby walked up. "Lenny, hey," said Henby. "This is my mate, Brian."

Sharpe offered his hand and Brennan shook it. His hand was large but there was little or no strength in the grip. The two men sat down and Henby was soon deep in conversation with Brennan about Millwall FC. Sharpe sipped his lager and looked around. People were still arriving. Most of the tables were full but there was plenty of room to stand. He did a rough head count. There were more than a hundred men, with a lot of handshaking and back-slapping going on.

Sharpe felt a nudge in his ribs. He looked across at Henby, who nodded towards the door. A man in his mid-forties had just walked into the room. Sharpe recognised him from the photographs that Charlotte Button had given him. It was Gary Dawson. He was wearing a dark blue blazer and black trousers and holding a half-pint glass of beer. He was deep in conversation with a man who had a shaved head and a small diamond earring. The pair went to the back of the room, still talking.

A few minutes later the door opened again and two big men in black leather bomber jackets and black jeans, wearing impenetrable sunglasses, escorted a man in his thirties to the stage. He was good-looking with chestnut hair that he kept brushing away from his eyes, a dimple in the centre of his chin, and a tan that came from lying under a foreign sun, rather than a bottle or a tanning centre. He was wearing an expensive double-breasted suit, and a sovereign ring glinted on his right hand. Heads turned to watch as he climbed onto the stage and the two heavies took up position at either side, their arms folded.

"That's Simon Page," whispered Henby. "He's number two in England First, deputy chairman. He's in charge of finances, fund-raising and the like."

"Did you know he'd be here?" asked Sharpe.

Henby shook his head. "They tend not to announce in advance who'll be speaking in case word gets out. I knew it'd be a big shot, but I didn't know that Page would be putting in an appearance."

Brennan leaned over the table. "Have you heard him speak before?" he asked.

"Never," said Sharpe.

Brennan nodded sagely. "You're in for a treat," he said.

Page picked the microphone off its stand and walked around it, like a stand-up comedian preparing to warm up his audience. "I don't know if any of you got a chance to see the news before you came out, but there was a big fire on Friday afternoon, not far from here." He pointed off to the right. "It was a four-storey house that had been divided up into four flats. Probably in the old days it would have been home to one extended family but those days are long gone. On the ground floor was a family of Nigerians. Turns out they were con artists, sending out emails promising to transfer money into bank accounts and then ripping people off. Oh, and they were all claiming benefit, too. There were six men in the flat and they all died."

There were cheers from the audience but Page quietened them with his hand. "This is serious. People died in that fire. A lot of people died. On the first floor there were seven asylum seekers from Afghanistan. They were all on benefits too. They died in the fire."

"Bloody Taliban!" shouted a skinhead at the front.

"Well, yes, actually, three of them were former Taliban fighters," said Page. "But because the Taliban are being hunted down and killed in Afghanistan, they're able to claim asylum here."

There were shouts of derision from the crowd and Page quietened them again. "I know, I know," he said.

"It's not fair that men who kill and maim our troops out in Afghanistan can claim asylum here in the United Kingdom, but that's the way it is. But seven of them died. There were asylum seekers on the second floor, all from Albania. They were on state benefits, too, even though they were criminals who had jumped bail and fled Albania. The council paid for the flat and had been looking for a house for them. There were five in the flat and they all burned to death."

There were more jeers from the audience and Page waited before continuing. "There were two survivors, though. The English couple who lived on the top floor were totally unscathed."

The audience cheered. Several skinheads stood up and began to chant "ENGER-LUND, ENGER-LUND!" Henby leaned over to whisper into Sharpe's ear: "The skinheads are QPR Casuals. Hardcore hooligans."

"Well, there was a right furore, I can tell you," continued Page. "The Commission for Racial Equality was up in arms and the British Islamic Council demanded an inquiry. Half the black pressure groups in London were threatening legal action. They can't understand why the blacks and the Muslims all died and the English couple didn't get so much as a scratch. There were questions asked in the House of Commons and the pressure groups demanded that the mayor explain why only the English couple survived. Anyway, just before I left the house the BBC had managed to get the fire chief on camera. The interviewer asked him why the English couple had survived while the Africans,

Muslims and Albanians had burned to death. Why had only the white couple not died? Was it because the Fire Brigade, like most of the country's institutions, was inherently racist? The interviewer demanded to know why the white couple weren't killed in the fire. Well, the fire chief took off his helmet and looked straight at the camera. 'Because they were at work,' he said."

Page stood ramrod straight, his chin up, as his audience erupted. There were cheers and yells and clapping, and half a dozen skinheads were stamping on the floor. Despite himself, Sharpe found himself laughing with them. Page let them cheer for a full thirty seconds before quietening them. "All right, that's a joke," he said. "And maybe not a good one. But it's a joke based on what's really happening to our country. We're becoming the sort of country where the English worker has to bust his gut and pay taxes to support a flood of foreign so-called asylum seekers and spongers, people who've never lifted a finger to help this country."

The crowd cheered. Sharpe joined in the clapping. He looked over his shoulder at Gary Dawson. He was cheering and punching the air.

Page spoke for more than an hour. It was a clever mix of anecdotes, jokes and serious political points. He was careful not to be overtly racist but several times he strayed into what Part Three of the Public Order Act of 1986 defined as "racial hatred", an offence that could have earned him seven years in prison. England First leaflets were being passed around to push home the

173

message, and the printed material was considerably more inflammatory than Page's words.

Sharpe smiled to himself: simply being in possession of the leaflet was an offence under the Act. He could see that Page had charisma, and he certainly knew how to work a crowd. He finished his speech with a rousing call for funds, telling the audience they should dig deep into their pockets so that England First could fight the rising tide of immigration. Then, as suddenly as he had appeared, Page was hustled off the stage and through the door.

"The guy talks a lot of sense," Sharpe said to Brennan.

"If he was a Labour or Conservative politician he'd be prime minister now," said Brennan. "He's as sharp as a knife, he's got a mind like a steel trap, and he listens to what people want. He's got that boyish Blair thing going but he's a leader like Thatcher was. I'd vote for him tomorrow if I had the chance."

The heavy at the door had swapped his clipboard for a red plastic bucket on which had been painted a cross of St George. As people left they were dropping money into it and by the time Henby and Sharpe got to the door it was half full of coins and notes. Sharpe took out his wallet and dropped in a fifty-pound note. The heavy noticed and nodded his thanks. Henby threw in a twenty.

"Want one for the road, Lenny?" asked Sharpe, as they walked down the stairs.

"Yeah, why not?" said Brennan. "About time I had a day on the sick."

"Bitter?"

"Yeah. Thanks."

"Ray?"

"I've got to head off, Brian," said Henby. He patted Sharpe on the back.

"Hot date?" said Sharpe.

"Chance'd be a fine thing." Henby waved goodbye to Brennan and headed for the exit.

As Sharpe was about to make for the bar, Dawson came down the stairs and called out to Brennan: "Lenny, how's it going?" He came over and shook his hand.

"I'm in the chair," Sharpe said to Dawson. "What can I get you?"

Dawson frowned, so Sharpe quickly held out his hand. "Brian," he said. "Brian Parker."

"Mate of Ray's," said Brennan, by way of introduction.

Dawson smiled and shook Sharpe's hand. "Gary," he said. "Gin and tonic, please."

Sharpe winked and went over to the bar, waving a twenty-pound note to attract a barmaid's attention.

A few moments later he carried the drinks back to Brennan and Dawson. They were standing in a corner. After they'd thanked him, Dawson said, "Haven't seen you around."

"First meeting I've been to," said Sharpe. "Ray thought I might like what I heard, and he was right. That guy Page talks a lot of sense."

"Doesn't he?" said Brennan.

"Why isn't he standing as an MP somewhere?" asked Sharpe. "He's got that star quality, hasn't he? Charisma."

"Because he tells it like it is, and the major political parties aren't prepared to do that," said Brennan. "They want to convince us that multiculturalism is a good thing, rather than the cancer that's eating away at our society."

"So he could stand for the BNP or something. UKIP, maybe."

"The UK Independence Party isn't much different from the rest of them," said Dawson. "They'll talk big about us leaving Europe but they're not prepared to do what's necessary to make this country great again."

"So, BNP, then," said Sharpe.

"The media would eat him alive," said Dawson. "They'd see him as a real threat so they'd bring out the big guns. The papers hate the BNP. They'd dig into everything he's ever done, every skeleton in every closet."

"Do you think he's got skeletons in his closet?" asked Sharpe.

"Who hasn't?" said Dawson. He sipped his gin and tonic, watching Sharpe over the top of his glass.

Sharpe smiled amiably. "Yeah, I guess so."

"Gary's right," said Brennan. "The media hates us because we don't swallow the bullshit they feed us. Anyone who stands up and tells the truth gets cut down."

"That's why all the secrecy, yeah?"

176

Dawson nodded. "If Searchlight or any of the other leftie groups found out that Simon was appearing, there'd be demonstrations like you wouldn't believe."

"Yeah," agreed Brennan. "They talk about free speech but we're not allowed to tell the truth. And they can say whatever they want about us, but if you start saying that darkies are responsible for most of the problems this country has, they put you in prison."

Sharpe drank some beer.

"So what do you do, Brian?" asked Dawson.

"I'm a book-keeper," said Sharpe. "Accounts and stuff. You?"

"Insurance," said Dawson. "How's business?"

"Suffering like everyone else," said Sharpe. "Bloody economy."

"We'd be in a lot better shape if we didn't have so many immigrants sponging off the system," said Brennan.

"That's the truth," agreed Sharpe. "But what can we do?"

"Send the bastards home," said Brennan. "Pay those that want to go, then force the rest of them out. It's like Simon was saying — why the hell are we letting Taliban fighters live here? They kill our boys and then we give them a house and a TV. The world's gone mad."

"Not the world, Lenny," said Dawson. "Just this country."

"So what's the answer?" asked Sharpe. "How do we stop the rot? How do we turn back the clock?"

"We stand and fight," said Dawson. "We fight for what's ours."

★　★　★

177

Shepherd set his alarm for seven o'clock on Monday morning and did thirty minutes on his exercise bike before shaving and showering. He put on his black police-issue trousers, long-sleeved white shirt and black tie, then fixed his black epaulettes with his police number; the U prefix showed he was with the TSG. He made himself a coffee and a bacon sandwich, then hauled on his motorcycle leathers over his uniform and put his police boots into a backpack.

Paddington Green police station was just fifteen minutes' drive from the house, and it had just turned eight thirty when Shepherd indicated and drove off Edgware Road down the side street that led to the rear of the station. He pulled up next to a wooden shed at the entrance and showed his Terry Halligan warrant card to a civilian guard who was reading a copy of the *Daily Mirror*. "PC Terry Halligan," he said. "I'm reporting for duty with the TSG."

The guard squinted at the card and handed it back. "So?"

Shepherd pointed at the metal shutters that led to the car park. "Can I leave my bike in there?"

The guard shook his head. "Work vehicles only."

"Where's the nearest place I can park, do you know?"

The guard shrugged. "There's pay-and-display the other side of Edgware Road."

"Not sure I want to leave the bike on the street."

The guard shrugged again. "Hyde Park's your best bet, then," he said. "Down to Marble Arch — you'll see the signs." He went back to studying his paper.

178

Shepherd flicked the visor of his helmet down and drove back around the police station and along Edgware Road to Hyde Park Corner, where he left the bike in the NCP underground car park. By the time he'd walked back to the station it was twenty past nine. He went in through the main entrance and asked a couple of Community Support Officers where he'd find the TSG offices. He followed their directions and found himself in a corridor on the first floor with several teak-effect doors. Each had a small plastic sign denoting the occupant and Shepherd knocked on the door belonging to Inspector Phillip Smith. "Come in," said a clipped voice.

Shepherd opened the door. Smith was in uniform, sitting behind a desk piled high with files. He was slightly plump with thinning blond hair.

"PC Terry Halligan," said Shepherd, as he stepped into the office.

"We were expecting you at nine o'clock," said Smith, looking up at a clock on the wall.

"I'm sorry about that, sir, I had trouble parking my bike." He held up his helmet. "Wasn't allowed to park it on the premises."

"We don't have the space for private vehicles," said Smith. "Make sure you're on time in future."

"I will do, sir. Sorry."

"You were told that you were going to Gravesend. Your Serial is up for its training day."

"Yes, sir, sorry."

"The bus is waiting for you so get a move on." Smith waved him away with a languid hand.

A uniformed sergeant holding a clipboard appeared in the doorway and grinned at Shepherd. "Ah, the late Terry Halligan, I presume." He held out his hand. "Roy Fogg, Sarge or Skip on the bus, Foggy in the pub. Welcome aboard." The sergeant looked older than he had appeared in the picture Shepherd had seen, and he was a few kilos heavier. He was Shepherd's height with a rapidly receding hairline and deep worry lines across his forehead.

Shepherd shook his hand. "Yeah, sorry I was late, Sarge. I had to find somewhere to park my bike."

"Parking's a nightmare here," said Fogg. He smiled at the inspector. "Can I take him now, sir?"

"You'll be in Sergeant Fogg's bus," Smith said to Shepherd. "You'd better get a move on."

"Yes, sir," said Shepherd. He followed Fogg out of the inspector's office and closed the door behind him.

"What sort of bike have you got?" asked Fogg.

"A BMW HP2 Sport."

"Nice," said Fogg. "I've got a Ducati Streetfighter. Where did you park?"

Shepherd pulled a face. "Miles away. Hyde Park Corner."

"Let me have a word with Robin Potter. He's a sergeant with Traffic and a bike nut. He's tight with the PC in Admin who assigns parking spaces and he arranged for me to park in the bike area. You might have to let him borrow it now and again."

"It'd be worth it."

"Probably won't be able to do it until tomorrow. Okay, let's get you your gear and then get on the bus.

180

The team's in the canteen. I'll introduce you first. They're a good bunch." Fogg ignored the lifts and took Shepherd up the stairs and through double doors into the canteen. A group of community support officers were sitting at a table close to the doors, tucking into fried breakfasts. One looked up. "Newbie's arrived, huh?" he asked the sergeant.

"How's it going, Ross?" said Fogg, ignoring the man's question. He walked by the table towards some officers wearing long-sleeved shirts and black ties, sitting with cups of coffee and tea in front of them. One spotted him and said something, and they all turned to look at Shepherd.

"Right, lads, listen up," said Fogg. "This is the man we've been waiting for. Terry Halligan. From sheep-shagging country, but don't hold that against him."

Shepherd raised his hand in greeting. "Hi, guys," he said. Then he realised that one of the officers at the table was female. "And lady." He had recognised her from Button's file: Carolyn Castle.

One of the men laughed. "Watch it, Pelican, he's got a hard-on for you already."

"The comedian there is Lurpak," said Fogg. "Known to his mother as Nick."

He stood up and shook Shepherd's hand. "Welcome aboard," he said. "Nick Coker."

Fogg continued the introductions. "The more feminine side of our team is represented by . . ." He started to point at Castle, but then jabbed a finger at another man. "KFC over there, Barry Kelly."

Kelly laughed. His hair seemed a brighter shade of red than it had been in his file picture, and the freckles across his nose were more pronounced.

"Before anyone gives me a crap introduction, I'm Carolyn Castle," said the female officer. When she shook Shepherd's hand, her grip was as firm as a man's. "Though these buggers insist on calling me Pelican." She was prettier than she'd appeared in the photograph, blonde hair tied up at the back and amused green eyes.

"The big man is Carpets," said Fogg. "Richard Parry."

Parry was a huge West Indian with massive forearms and a shaved head. His hand was about twice the size of Shepherd's but he didn't squeeze hard. "Good to meet you," he growled.

The man next to Parry introduced himself. "Darren Simmons," he said. He was the youngest of the group, with a cleft chin. "Glad I'm not the newbie any more," he said.

"Known to us as Nipple," said Kelly, "because, to be honest, he can be a bit of a tit."

Fogg nodded at the last member of the group. "This is Angus Turnbull, a.k.a. Colgate. He's our driver today."

Turnbull grinned, revealing perfect gleaming white teeth. "Glad to have you aboard," he said.

"I'll get Terry sorted with his kit," said Fogg. "On the bus in fifteen, right?"

Fogg took Shepherd back down to the first floor and showed him the team room where they could relax when they weren't working and then a large briefing room. Then he led him along a corridor to a room lined with lockers. "Take this one," he said, pointing. "I've put a kitbag there. Overalls, pads, gloves, everything's in it. The only thing I haven't got is boots. You've got them, right?"

Shepherd held up his backpack. "Sorted," he said.

"Dump your gear and let's go, then."

Shepherd put his motorcycle helmet into the locker and stripped off his motorcycle leathers. He sat down, took off his motorcycle boots and put them in the bottom of the locker, then pulled on his work boots.

"Let's go — we've got to be at Gravesend by eleven," said Fogg.

Shepherd picked up the black kitbag, which had METROPOLITAN POLICE SERVICE along the side in white letters, then followed the sergeant along a corridor, down the stairs and through a set of double doors to the underground car park where a grey Mercedes van with empty parking spaces either side of it was waiting. Above the front windscreen there was a black wire mesh shield that could be pulled down when needed. "That's our bus," said Fogg. "You stow your gear and I'll chase up the team."

Shepherd climbed into the van. There were eight seats and, behind them, racks on either side that were already filled with kitbags. At the back there was a row of long riot shields. Shepherd pushed his kitbag onto the rack on the left, then sat down by the side door. A hand sanitiser was fitted to the bulkhead. A rack above the seats opposite contained bags of forms, police tape and a first-aid kit.

An unmarked police car drove slowly by, heading for the exit. The driver nodded at Shepherd, who nodded back.

"Bloody hell, the newbie's nabbed the jump seat," said a voice. It was Kelly, heading towards the van while he munched a ham roll. Behind him were Castle and Turnbull.

"That's where Carpets sits," said Castle. "He always likes to be first off the bus."

"Right," said Shepherd. He stood up — there was at least a couple of inches of space above his head — and went to sit down at the rear on the driver's side.

"Whoa, Lurpak always has the bingo seat," said Kelly.

"Bingo?" said Shepherd.

"Boxed In, Not Getting Out," said Castle. She dropped onto the seat directly behind the driver. "Or Bollocks, I'm Not Getting Out," she added. "Depends who you ask. Lurpak likes it because it gives him a good view of traffic."

"Why don't you just tell me where to park my arse?" Shepherd said to Kelly.

"Take the prisoner seat," said Kelly, pointing to a single seat behind Castle. "That's always free until we haul in a slag."

Turnbull climbed into the driver's seat and Kelly opened the front passenger door. As he got in, Fogg hurried across the car park with Parry, Coker and Simmons. They filed onto the van. Simmons sat next to

184

Castle, Coker walked to the back and sat in the bingo seat while Fogg went to the back on the passenger side. Parry sat by the door and grunted as he pulled it shut. "Are we there yet?" asked Coker.

The rest of the team groaned. It was obviously a standard joke. Turnbull started the engine and Kelly switched on the radios. The van edged forwards, heading for the exit. "How did you find the inspector?" asked Kelly, looking over his shoulder.

"He was in his office," said Shepherd, "so it was easy. Just opened the door and he was there."

Castle laughed. "He got you there, KFC," she said.

"Hey, Terry, did you have a nickname at West Mercia?" asked Coker.

"Yeah, but I'm not telling you what it was," said Shepherd.

"That bad?"

"I'm just not saying," said Shepherd, folding his arms.

"Defensive," said Parry.

"We could call him that," said Coker. "Defensive."

"Nah," said Castle. "Too obvious. Let's see how he gets on today before we name him." She twisted in her seat and winked at Shepherd. "Everyone gets a nickname," she said.

"How did you get yours?" Shepherd asked.

The men laughed. "Dictionary definition of a pelican," said Kelly. "A bird with a big mouth."

"Shall I tell him why we call you KFC?" Castle asked Kelly.

Kelly laughed. "Do I care?"

Castle grinned at Shepherd. "He used to be called Chicken because of his small cock," she said.

"That's not true," said Kelly. "I happen to be fond of fast food, that's all."

Fogg shook his head. "I'm afraid not, KFC," he said. "It's your tiny cock."

"Thanks for your support, Sarge," said Kelly.

Shepherd looked over at Parry. "And Carpets?"

"Because when he walks he looks like he's carrying a roll of carpet under each arm," said Simmons.

Parry's mobile phone rang and he answered it. He listened for a few seconds, then cursed. "No, I don't have a bloody Alsatian puppy!" he shouted, and ended the call.

Kelly, Turnbull and Simmons began to bark and he flashed them the finger. "Bastards," he said.

"What's the problem?" asked Shepherd.

"One of these bastards set me up," said Parry, "and when I find out who it was I'll have their balls."

"Lets me off, then," said Castle.

"Not necessarily," said Coker.

"I left my warrant card in the canteen and someone swiped it and photocopied it," said Parry.

"And that leads to Alsatians how?" asked Shepherd.

"If you want to put a classified ad into *The Job*, you have to send a copy of your warrant card," explained Parry. "Whoever photocopied mine put an ad in saying that I'm in K9 and that I've got Alsatian pups free to good homes. My phone hasn't stopped ringing."

Parry's phone rang again. "Fuck off!" he screamed into it. Kelly, Turnbull and Simmons began to bark again.

According to the file that Shepherd had read, the Metropolitan Police Specialist Training Centre on the east side of Gravesend was a sprawling £55 million development off Mark Lane, close to the Thames Estuary. It was opened in 2003 with the aim of teaching the capital's police officers the finer points of public-order policing and the use of firearms. It was next to the National Sea Training College and every member of the TSG went over for a day's training every five weeks.

There wasn't much to see from the road, just a wire fence, a lot of parked cars and a featureless residential block. They drove onto the site, parked the van and hurried to the main block. Fogg led them to a classroom on the second floor, where an instructor from the Met's CO12 branch had already started the briefing. Two dozen TSG officers were sitting on chairs in a semicircle facing the screen.

"Area One, last on the scene as usual," someone shouted.

The instructor, a sergeant in his thirties, looked up from his PowerPoint presentation, which was being projected onto a large screen. Fogg apologised for being late as his team found places to sit.

"No problem, Foggy," said the instructor. "You missed a video presentation of various stadium disturbances and I was just about to explain what we'll be doing out in the practice stadium after lunch. With the Olympics coming up, we've got to get everyone up to speed on the various potential threats. We're going to start off with extracting drunks, then we'll move on to organised demonstrations, and we'll finish off with a suicide bomber."

"Going out with a bang?" asked Kelly.

"To be honest, the suicide bomber's the easiest of the lot," said the instructor. "We all hang back and send in CO19 to put six bullets in the bastard's head." He tapped on the keyboard, and a schematic of an athletics stadium flashed onto the screen. "Right, eyes down for a full house," he said. "Let's start with the basics."

Shepherd's buttocks were aching by the time the instructor had finished his presentation. It had been a long time since he had sat on a hard wooden chair and been lectured to. Kelly clapped him on the shoulder as they walked along a corridor towards the canteen. "Bet you didn't expect to be back in school on your first day, did you?" he asked.

"Hopefully the practical will be more fun than the theory," said Shepherd.

Fogg caught up with them. "You all right, Terry? Thought you were dozing off in there."

"Sorry, Sarge," said Shepherd. "Most of that was pretty straightforward."

"Yeah, but it's got to be done," said Fogg. "And we've got to get it right. The whole world's going to be watching the Olympics so we're going to have to be on our best behaviour."

"Even if it's a suicide bomber?"

"With any luck they'll be caught before they get anywhere near a stadium," said Fogg. "Much more

188

likely we'll see the Tibet sympathisers kicking off when China competes, and with all the TV cameras on us we don't want to be getting out the Tasers."

They picked up trays and joined the queue for food. "Did the inspector mention the secret shopper that phoned in last week?" asked Fogg.

Shepherd frowned, confused. "Secret what?"

"Someone from Professional Standards or the Anti-Racism Unit pretending to be you."

"I'm sorry, what are you talking about, Sarge?"

Parry and Castle joined the queue. As he put down his tray, Parry's mobile rang and he answered. After a few seconds he began cursing and switched it off. He pointed at Kelly. "If I find out it was you that put the advert in *The Job*, I'll swing for you, I really will."

"Wasn't me, Carpets," said Kelly. "I think it's an outrageous way to treat a colleague."

Fogg grinned at Shepherd. "Don't leave your warrant card around anywhere," he warned. "Keep it in your pocket."

"Gotcha, Sarge," said Shepherd. "What were you saying about the secret shopper?"

Fogg shrugged. "Nothing to worry about," he said. "It happens all the time. Someone rang up, said they were starting next week and wanted to know where was a good place to live. Colgate answered the phone and he's no fool so it worked out all right. He spotted it right away. He said that anywhere around Bayswater or Paddington or Kilburn was okay, or anywhere on the Circle or Bakerloo line."

"So?"

"So then the secret shopper asks what Bayswater's like, whether or not it's a bit ethnic because he doesn't want trouble with the neighbours."

"You're not serious?"

"As a heart-attack," said Fogg. "The Met's been proactive on the racism front for a few years now. I guess you didn't have it with West Mercia, but it's a bloody nightmare here. Colgate was in a no-win situation. If he gives any indication that Bayswater's multicultural mix is anything but a positive thing, then he's screwed. If he suggests a white middle-class area, he's screwed. If he doesn't report the caller for racism, he's also screwed. But if he does report it, he gets labelled as a stool-pigeon for ever more."

"So either way, he's screwed."

"Pretty much." They reached the front of the queue. Fogg ordered fish, chips and baked beans. Shepherd said he would have the same. Behind him, Kelly ordered two steak and kidney pies and double chips.

"So what did he do?" Shepherd asked Fogg, as they walked together to a table.

"He said that the line was breaking up and put the phone down. Told everyone else not to answer the phones for the next hour. That pretty much sorted it." Fogg laughed. "Those bastards in their ivory towers haven't a clue what real policing is about."

Shepherd spent the afternoon in a mock-stadium in the training centre, running through all the various scenarios that had been outlined in the classroom. It was tiring and he was exhausted by the time the session

190

was over. They had to wear the full protective riot gear: the helmet, with visor, was stifling and the fireproof overalls kept in most of his body heat, which meant he was sweating constantly.

When the CO12 instructor announced that they were done for the day, a cheer went up from the entire team. Shepherd took off his helmet and grinned at Fogg. "You think we'll be doing it for real in 2012, Sarge?"

"They wouldn't be making us do this if they didn't think it was odds-on," said Fogg. "That was my first thought when they announced that London was going to host the Olympics. I mean, didn't the powers-that-be realise we're setting the capital up as the ultimate target?"

"I guess they didn't think it through."

"As usual," said Fogg. "They forget we're not China — we can barely keep track of who comes in and out, never mind what they're doing while they're here. The Chinese threw all the dissidents in prison for the duration of the Olympics and didn't allow anyone in that they thought might be a threat. We can't do that."

"So what do you think will happen, Sarge?"

"I think we'll have demonstrations, for sure, but I wouldn't be surprised if we get a spectacular. I'd bet you anything you want here and now that, as we speak, there's dozens of Muslim groups planning all sorts of mischief, from suicide bombers to anthrax attacks to dirty bombs. And it just needs one of them to be lucky. We can train all we want but our expertise is all after the event. We just have to hope that MI5 and Special

Branch do their job properly, because if they don't it's going to end in tears."

"You're a bit of a pessimist, then, Sarge," said Shepherd.

"How can you do this job and not be?" said Fogg. "It's not as if we see the best in people, is it?" Shepherd watched him walk away. He knew what the sergeant meant. It was difficult to work in any branch of law enforcement without becoming cynical.

Kelly and Coker came up behind him, removing their helmets. "Bet you haven't got anything like this in Wales," said Kelly.

"Hereford isn't in Wales," said Shepherd.

"It's not really England, though, is it?" said Kelly. He winked at Coker. "We could call him Taff. What do you think?"

"Yeah, or Taffy," said Coker.

"I give up," said Shepherd. "Call me what the hell you want."

Kelly grinned. "He's getting upset, Lurpak."

"I'm not getting upset," said Shepherd.

"Do you want a quick tour, Taff?" asked Coker.

Shepherd winced.

"He doesn't like being called Taff, does he?" said Coker.

"It's the Welsh in him," said Kelly. "I still think we should go for Sheepshagger."

"I'll take the tour," said Shepherd. "Anything to shut you up."

Kelly and Coker took Shepherd down a road lined on one side with breezeblock house frontages. On the

192

other there was a mock-up of a council multi-storey building with common walkways. "This is where we practise public-order stuff," said Kelly. He pointed at the multi-storey. "The flats there are kitted out for real with furniture, TVs, the works. There's an angry-man suite, all lined with padding, so that we can practise dealing with nutters."

"That'd be your role, yeah?" asked Shepherd.

"We take it in turns," said Kelly. "It's quite therapeutic — you put the protective gear on and get stuck in."

"We get to throw petrol bombs and wooden blocks at each other," said Coker. "And we get paid for it."

They took him down an alley that led to a mock-up of an Underground station, complete with two carriages. "This is where we practise shooting innocent members of the public," said Coker.

"Subtle," said Shepherd.

Kelly and Coker walked him around the mock town, pointing out the various buildings and locations, then headed for the car park. As they walked together towards their van, Kelly spotted another grey Mercedes van parked near the gates. "Here's something you won't have seen before, Terry," said Kelly. "Official bloody secret, this is."

It was a regular grey Sprinter, the same as the ones that the TSG drove around in, but there were no POLICE markings on the outside. Kelly tried the side door and grinned when he realised it wasn't locked. "Have a look — see if you can guess what it is?" He opened the door.

Shepherd climbed in and looked around. There were fewer seats than there had been in the van he'd driven in to the centre, and a plastic curtain divided off the rear of the vehicle. He pulled it back. Instead of the racks where the TSG stored their gear, there was a metal gurney, a shower attachment and a large metal barrel with a hazardous-waste symbol on it.

Shepherd turned to see Coker and Kelly at the door, grinning at him.

"Well?" said Kelly.

"Portable shower?"

"It's the Queen's decontamination bus," Kelly said. "Whenever she's out in public, this bus is within a hundred yards of her. On board are two firearms officers with MP5s, a paramedic and two of our CBRN guys. If anyone throws a liquid or powder anywhere near Her Majesty, our two guys go rushing over to her with a stretcher and bring her onto the bus. As the bus is driven to the nearest medical facility, our guys cut off her clothing and douse her with water while the paramedic does the triage."

"No way," said Shepherd.

"God's truth," said Kelly. "Her Majesty's been briefed on what'll happen and she's apparently okay with it. There's another bus designated for the prime minister."

"That's amazing," said Shepherd, climbing out.

"You know what's amazing?" said Kelly, slamming the door shut. "That we live in a country where something like this is necessary. That's what's amazing." He patted Shepherd on the back. "Come on, let's hit the road. We don't get overtime for training."

Shepherd arrived home at just after eight o'clock in the evening. He parked his bike at the rear of the house and let himself in at the front. As he was making himself a cup of coffee, his mobile phone rang. It was Button. "Not got me under observation, have you?" he asked. "I've only just walked in."

"I know," she said. "We've got cameras in all the light fittings."

Shepherd looked up at the fluorescent light in the ceiling and heard her chuckle. "I bet I made you look," she said.

"You did," he said.

"Just checking to see that all went well," she said.

"No problems," he said. "It was a training day so it gave me the chance to settle in."

"Okay. Well, keep your head down," she said. "Call me if anything happens but I guess it'll take a while."

"How's Razor getting on?"

"Loving it, apparently," she said. "He's already Dawson's new best friend. You take care now."

"I will," said Shepherd, and ended the call. He took his coffee through to the sitting room and sat on the sofa. He switched on the television, then phoned Liam's mobile. His son sounded distracted when he answered. "What are you doing?" asked Shepherd.

"Teaching Lady to roll over."

"Why?"

"It's a trick."

"How about teaching her to tidy your room?"

"Dad . . ."

"Or cut the grass?"

"You know that sarcasm is the lowest form of wit?" said Liam.

"I heard that," said Shepherd. "Have you done your homework?"

"Most of it."

"Make sure it's all done. What did Katra cook for tea?"

"Cheesy scrambled eggs."

"That's what you have for breakfast."

"I just felt like it again."

"Vegetables?"

"Do chips count?"

"Just about."

"So, yeah, I had vegetables. Lady, stay!"

"She's not sleeping on your bed at night, is she?" asked Shepherd.

"No," said Liam.

"I should tell you that I've got this phone hooked up to the latest police lie detector and a red light flashed when you said that."

"I don't believe you."

"Flashed again."

"You're joking."

"Another red light."

"Dad, stop it . . . It's not funny."

"Okay, but don't let her sleep in your room, it's not healthy," said Shepherd. "I'll be back in Hereford on

Friday night. Tell Katra I called and that everything's okay."

"I will," said Liam.

"Good night," said Shepherd. "I love you."

"I love you too, Dad."

Shepherd ended the call. He plumped up a cushion and swung his legs up onto the sofa. They ached from all the running he'd done and his left arm was sore from carrying the full-length shield. He hadn't realised how tired he was until he'd taken the weight off his feet, and within seconds he was fast asleep.

Tuesday was Shepherd's first day on the job proper. He gave himself plenty of time to park the bike and walk to the police station, and he arrived half an hour before his shift was due to start. When he went into the team room, only Carolyn Castle was there. "Do you sleep here?" asked Shepherd.

"I was lucky with the traffic," she said, looking up from the magazine she was reading.

"Where do you park?"

She grinned. "I don't have to," she said. "My boyfriend drives. Parking's his problem."

"Is he in the job?"

"I'd never date a cop," she said. "He's a doctor at St Mary's. What about you?"

"Yeah, I'd never date a cop either. Though Colgate's quite the cutie."

"Who's a cutie?" asked a voice at the door. It was Turnbull.

"You," said Castle.

"I was joking," said Shepherd.

"I'm flattered," said Turnbull.

"I was definitely joking," said Shepherd.

Coker and Kelly appeared behind Turnbull. "What's going on?"

"Terry fancies me," said Turnbull.

"Great! We haven't had a gay on the bus for years," said Kelly. "Helps with our diversity quota. We've got Carpets, Pelican and now Gaylord. That's all our bases covered."

"I am not answering to Gaylord," said Shepherd.

Turnbull punched him on the shoulder. "Not so bloody cute now, am I?" he said. "Who wants coffee?" There was a kettle, jars of Maxwell House and Coffee Mate, and a tray of mugs on a table by the door. Turnbull switched on the kettle and spooned coffee into the mugs.

Coker and Kelly dropped on the sofa next to Castle. "Did you get laid last night, Pelican?" asked Kelly, patting her knee.

"Three times," she said, smiling sweetly and removing his hand. "Which I'm guessing is three times more than you, right?"

Fogg stuck his head around the door. "Bring your coffees into the briefing room," he said. "Two sugars in mine."

By the time the team had filed in, Fogg was already standing at a podium on which a laptop was hooked up to a projector. "Nothing special today," he said. "The borough commander wants us in the Wembley area where they've seen a rise in street robberies, mainly schoolkids being relieved of their mobiles. We've got descriptions but as usual they're not much help — young, black, BMX bikes, baseball caps. The descriptions vary from witness to witness but we're pretty sure it's the same gang. Up to six or seven at a time. So, eyes peeled for a group of young black males acting suspiciously."

Kelly laughed and Fogg flashed him a withering look. "Sorry, Skip."

Fogg held up a bundle of printed sheets. "I've got an intel briefing here on vehicles we need to look out for, and a few addresses that we need to swing by. But most of the shift we'll be flying the flag, showing the good people of Wembley that the police are in control."

They took their mugs back to the team room and headed out to the van. Turnbull was driving again and everyone sat in the seats they'd had the previous day.

They drove north to Wembley and spent the shift driving around the suburb. Turnbull mainly drove where he pleased, though occasionally Fogg would suggest that he visited a particular street or shopping centre. From his place in the bingo seat, Coker called out the registration numbers of any vehicles he felt were suspicious, and Kelly would enter them into the mobile data terminal on the dashboard. Up would come information on the vehicle, whether or not it was stolen, if its tax and insurance were in order, who the registered keeper was and whether he was of interest to the police. The information was also shown on a screen on the bulkhead behind the operator so that everyone on the van could see it. The terminal also had access to the Police National Computer and several other government databases.

If the MDT showed that there was anything wrong with the vehicle or the driver, they would pull it over. If the driver was alone, just two officers would get out and talk to him or her. Sometimes a simple conversation would be the end of it. The MDT wasn't always accurate and sometimes showed a car as not being taxed or insured when it was, and the information on the PNC wasn't always up to date. But if the information was valid or if the officers noticed anything untoward, the driver and any passengers would be asked to get out and would be questioned and searched, ideally in full public view. A search was as much about demonstrating a police presence as catching villains. More often than not it produced nothing more serious than a small amount of cannabis, in which case a verbal warning would be given, but if a serious quantity of drugs or a weapon was found, the person would be arrested and taken to the nearest police station to be charged and processed.

The final part of a search was the completion of a Form 5090, the fifty-ninety. It explained why the person had been stopped and who had stopped them, where the search had taken place and what, if anything, had been found. The form also contained the details of the person being searched, including their name, address, date of birth and description, their clothing and details of their vehicle. All the information was entered into the PNC at the end of the shift, and a copy was given to the person being searched. The form also outlined a complaints procedure whereby anyone who felt that they had been treated unfairly could contact a senior officer at the local police station, the Police Complaints Commission, the Citizens Advice Bureau or the Metropolitan Police Authority. From what Shepherd saw on his first day, almost everyone stopped felt that they had been treated unfairly but none would bother to make a complaint.

Each officer had a pad of fifty-nineties and there were extra supplies in the van. There was no quota to be achieved, but Headquarters could use them to monitor the officers' performance.

Most of the stop-and-searches involved vehicles, but Parry kept a wary eye out for suspicious pedestrians when he wasn't dealing with calls on his mobile about the non-existent Alsatian puppies. The reasons for a stop-and-search were spelled out on the fifty-ninety. Strictly speaking, the police could only stop someone if they had reasonable grounds to suspect that they were carrying stolen goods, a knife, burglary equipment, guns, controlled drugs, or they looked as if they might be terrorists. The power came from four Acts of Parliament — Police and Criminal Evidence, 1984; Misuse of Drugs, 1971; Firearms 1968; and Terrorism, 2000. But the truth of the matter was that the TSG stopped anyone they felt was acting suspiciously either behind the wheel of a car or on the pavements. A driver who visibly tensed or hid his roll-up, or who made a sudden turn when he saw the police van in his rear-view mirror, would have his details run through the MDT. Pedestrians who suddenly looked away, glared with undisguised hostility or tried to hide something behind their backs warranted a second look.

Shepherd was surprised by how easily people gave themselves away. Most people just ignored the van or, if they made accidental eye-contact, would smile or nod, If they were driving they would slow down and move to the side to allow the van to pass. But those with something to hide behaved in a completely different manner, either by tensing up, making a sudden turn or hunching over the steering-wheel as if they were trying to make themselves invisible — after only a few hours Shepherd could spot the signs for himself.

A lot of the people they stopped had been stopped before, and well over half had criminal convictions, usually drugs-related. Most accepted the stop-and-search with grim resignation, knowing that the quicker they complied, the sooner it would be over. Occasionally someone who had been stopped would argue that their rights were being infringed, but the officers had heard it all before and would listen patiently, usually with their arms folded and a look of bored indifference on their faces until the complainant had run out of steam.

The team wore their game faces whenever they left the van. In the van they laughed and joked and teased each other, but as soon as they moved outside their faces hardened and everything about their body language suggested they weren't to be messed around. They always put on their hats as they got out, and while they were polite when they spoke to the public, they always stood with their legs firmly apart, backs ramrod straight, and maintained a rigid eye-contact with whoever they were addressing. There was no doubting their alpha-male status and generally they were treated accordingly. Castle was no different, and while she was several inches shorter than the men and her blonde hair was tied back in a ponytail, she had no problem in asserting her authority. Shepherd noticed that her voice changed whenever she was carrying out a search: it dropped an octave and her accent became more of a south-London drawl.

At just after one o'clock Fogg told Turnbull to drive to Wembley police station in Harrow Road. They parked on double yellow lines and went inside to the canteen. Shepherd followed Kelly to the line for food. Kelly ordered double cod and chips, Shepherd asked for ham and eggs and chips. They carried their trays over to the table where Simmons had already started eating. He had brought a salad from home, layers of lettuce, tomato, cucumber and asparagus, with what looked like smoked salmon on the top.

"You make that yourself?" asked Shepherd, as he sat down opposite him.

"His mum does it for him," said Kelly, reaching across for a bottle of HP sauce.

Fogg sat down with a plate of pie and chips. "She takes good care of him — does his laundry, combs his hair . . ."

"Hey, I've got a good deal going there," said Simmons. "My mum's a great cook, my room's en-suite, and she's got a massive LCD TV that she never watches. Why would I want to move out?"

"Sex?" said Turnbull, sitting down at the table. He had a Tupperware container filled with sandwiches.

"I have sex," said Simmons.

"I meant regular sex," said Turnbull. "Between a man and a woman. Ideally not a relative."

"I do all right," said Simmons, spearing a tomato slice with his fork.

"Who's talking about sex?" said Coker, as he and Parry joined them. They had both chosen lasagne and chips.

"No one," said Simmons.

"Nipple not getting any?"

"I'm getting plenty," said Simmons, his face reddening. "I just don't shout about it."

"What about you, Terry?" asked Parry. "You married?"

"Nah," said Shepherd.

"Divorced? Separated? Living in sin?"

"None of the above," said Shepherd.

"Girlfriend?" asked Coker.

"Like Darren, I do okay."

Kelly snorted. "Nipple doesn't do okay," he said. "He's still a virgin."

"Yeah, right," said Simmons.

"Who's a virgin?" said Castle, joining the table and sitting next to Fogg.

"Guess," said Parry.

"Nipple?"

"Got it in one," said Coker. Simmons leaned over and stabbed his fork into Coker's chips. "Help yourself," said Coker.

As they sat and ate Shepherd saw several local police officers come in. They lined up for food and looked over at the TSG's table. For a brief moment Shepherd saw the same expression on their faces that he'd noticed in the faces on the streets, as if they resented the TSG being there. He'd seen it when he was in the SAS and had worked in close proximity with regular soldiers. The SAS were an élite, and while the average squaddies respected the skills of the SAS troopers there was always an air of resentment when they were around. The fact that the TSG were in their police station was an unspoken admission that they weren't up to the job, that crime had reached an unsatisfactory level and that only the TSG could bring it under control.

Fogg and his team seemed unaware of the reaction they were causing as they tucked into their food. They joked and teased each other incessantly, but it was always good-natured and done with affection. Again, it reminded Shepherd of his days in the SAS. There was no more professional a soldier than a member of the Special Air Service, but when they were between tasks there would be endless banter and mindless horseplay. It was an easy familiarity that had grown out of trust and respect and Shepherd knew that he was privileged to have been so readily accepted by the TSG team. He tried not to think about the fact that everything he had told them about himself had been a lie and that his ultimate aim was to find out who the bad apples were and put them behind bars.

They finished their meals, had a cup of coffee, then headed back to the van.

Half an hour after they had left the canteen, Castle spotted a group of black teenagers wearing baseball caps sitting on BMX bicycles outside a betting shop. "Have a look at our two o'clock, Skip," she said. "Could be our most wanted."

All heads turned to the right. There were six teenagers, all wearing expensive Nike trainers, dark blue New York Yankees baseball caps and gold necklaces. One was talking into a mobile.

"Let's give them a spin," said Fogg. Turnbull pulled over to the side of the road. As Parry opened the side door, one of the teenagers saw the van, shouted something, and they scattered. Parry jumped out and ran towards them, closely followed by Simmons and Castle.

Parry managed to grab one of the boys by the scruff of his neck but the rest pedalled off. Simmons lashed out at the back wheel of a bike as it passed him and the teenager lost control. The handlebars wobbled as if they had a life of their own but then the rider regained his balance and sped off. Simmons tore after him.

By the time Shepherd was out of the van the teenagers were all heading off in different directions, except for the one Parry had grabbed and now pushed up against the window of the betting shop. Shepherd saw one youth, tall and gangly, wearing a baggy black sweatshirt and a Nike backpack, pedalling against the traffic on the main road. He gave chase. The teenager kept glancing over his shoulder but when he saw Shepherd was on his tail he bent low over the handlebars and pedalled for all he was worth. After sprinting for a hundred yards Shepherd began to tire but he gritted his teeth and kept up the pace, his boots slapping on the pavement.

The teenager tried to cut across the oncoming traffic but a bus driver pounded on his horn and he swerved onto the crowded pavement instead to weave in and out of the afternoon shoppers, shouting and cursing. Shepherd's arms pumped back and forth and he could feel his lungs burning. He ran at least three times a week but he was a distance runner, not a sprinter, and he knew he wouldn't be able to keep up the pace for much longer. He didn't have the breath to shout, "Stop, police!" but he doubted that the words would have any effect. The only way to stop the teenager was to catch him, and with every passing second that was becoming increasingly unlikely.

Ahead of him Shepherd saw a man holding a wooden sign on the end of a pole, advertising a sale at a nearby sporting-goods store. He was wearing headphones, nodding to whatever tune he was listening to, and eating a slice of pizza with his free hand. As he reached the man, Shepherd grabbed the sign from him and threw it like a javelin. It spun through the air and clipped the back wheel of the bike. The edge of the sign caught in the spokes, the wheel locked and the bike skidded. It slammed into a phone box and the teenager went over the handlebars and hit the ground hard.

Shepherd reached the boy just as he was getting to his knees. He grabbed him by the arm and helped him up. "Are you okay?"

The teenager nodded. His right hand was grazed and there was dirt along his sleeve but there was no real damage.

"Have you got any ID on you?" Shepherd asked.

The boy ignored him. He looked around, still shaken from the tumble he'd taken. The man who had been holding the sign walked up, still listening to music on his headphones. He picked up the sign, pulled a face as he examined it, and walked back to where he'd been standing.

"What's your name?" asked Shepherd.

"I don't have to tell you nuffink," said the teenager.

"Have you got any ID?"

"I ain't got nuffink."

"What's in the backpack?" asked Shepherd.

"Nuffink."

"You won't mind me having a look, then, will you?"

"You need a warrant," said the boy.

"You've been watching too much TV," said Shepherd. "The fact that you did a runner means I've got every reason to suspect that there's something in there you don't want me to see." He turned the teenager around and unzipped the top of the backpack. Inside were half a dozen mobile phones and several wallets. Shepherd took out one of the phones and held it in front of the boy's face. "This yours?"

"Yeah."

Shepherd scrolled through the phone's address book. "So if I phone Mum, it'll be your old lady, will it?"

"Yeah."

Shepherd called the number. After a few seconds a woman answered. Shepherd told her who he was but before he could explain why he was calling the woman interrupted and said that her son had been mugged that morning by a group of youths who had stolen his phone after kicking him so badly that he was now in intensive care. Shepherd promised to call her back later. He dropped the phone into the backpack and zipped it up.

The teenager stared at the pavement and mumbled something about police harassment, but Shepherd was no longer interested in anything he had to say. He slapped handcuffs on the boy's wrists and marched him towards the van. "What about my bike?" asked the teenager.

"You can come back and get it later," said Shepherd.

"It'll get nicked."

"Do you think?"

By the time he reached the team, Parry and Simmons had put the other lad in the van and had taken off his trainers and socks. He was wearing two pairs of socks and between them were dozens of small twists of foil, which Simmons was laying out on one of the seats.

Fogg grinned when he saw Shepherd walk up with his prisoner. "Nice one, Terry," he said. He gestured at the boy in the van. "We've got cannabis and a fair amount of crack. He's coming in for dealing."

"It's personal use, innit?" said the teenager, sulkily.

"Plus he doesn't want to tell us who is he is," said Fogg.

"I don't have to tell you nuffink. I know my rights."

"What about yours?" Fogg asked Shepherd.

"Doesn't want to tell me who he is, but he's got a bag full of stolen phones. I spoke to the mum of one of the victims and he was badly beaten up earlier today. He's in hospital, intensive care."

"Someone gave me the phones. Dunno where he got them from," said Shepherd's prisoner, still staring at the pavement.

"There's cash in the bag, too," said Shepherd. "And some wallets."

"I found them," said the teenager. "I was gonna hand them in." He looked at Fogg. "He assaulted me, he did," he said, jerking his chin at Shepherd. "Hit me with a sign, he did."

"You should have stopped," said Shepherd.

"You can't go around knocking people off their bikes," said the boy. "And that's another thing. He left me bike back there. It's gonna get nicked."

"No problem," said Fogg. "Just take a receipt or proof of purchase to any police station. They'll get you sorted. Course, if you nicked the bike in the first place then it'd be a different story, wouldn't it?" He nodded at Shepherd. "In the bus with him," he said.

Shepherd helped the boy into the van and put him in the bingo seat. "I want to call my lawyer," he said.

"When you get to the station," said Shepherd.

Parry and Simmons finished searching their prisoner, then told him to put his socks and trainers back on. The drugs went into a plastic evidence bag.

210

Shepherd sat opposite his prisoner, who stared sullenly out of the window, muttering to himself.

"Nice one, Terry," said Castle, as she climbed in. "You went after him like a bat out of hell."

"What about the others?"

"Lurpak had a go but the buggers were just too quick. They'll be known to us, for sure — we'll get them sooner or later."

They drove the two teenagers to Wembley police station and went in through the rear entrance to the custody suite, where Fogg explained why the pair had been arrested and that they had refused to identify themselves. The custody officer smiled like a benevolent uncle and asked the two boys for their names and addresses. The smile didn't fade in the slightest when they told him to go screw himself. He sighed, tapped away on his computer, then asked Fogg if he'd take their prints through the automated Livescan inkless fingerprinting system. The pair were marched over to the machine where the fingers and palms of both hands were scanned and transferred to the IDENT1 database. Then they were propelled to a row of seats and told to sit down. In less than ten minutes IDENT1 had provided the names and addresses of both, along with a list of convictions for street robberies and possession of stolen goods.

The still-smiling custody officer finished completing the necessary documentation, then told them they would be held in custody until a detective could be found to conduct a tape-recorded interview. The teenagers began to protest but two constables seized them by the arms and took them along to the cells, removed their expensive training shoes and locked them in.

Fogg looked at his watch. "Let's call it a day," he said. "Traffic the way it is we'll get back to Paddington bang on the end of our shift."

Denzel Holmes liked white girls. He didn't know why but, given the choice, he'd always go for a girl with white skin rather than a girl with skin as dark as his own. Getting white girls was easy because Holmes was a drug-dealer and Harlesden was full of white girls who'd do anything for crack or heroin. If a girl was white and pretty then Holmes was happy enough to give her a free sample or two, but as soon as she was hooked she had to do more than just smile sweetly if she wanted to score.

The girl lying next to him was twenty-one, three years older than him. She had long blonde hair, a cute arse and the best breasts he'd seen in a long time. She was a student but since Holmes had introduced her to cocaine she had pretty much given up her studies. She'd said that her dad was a local magistrate, and he found that a turn-on. He'd met her at a club in Harlesden. She'd been there with her whiter-than-white friends, slumming it. He'd offered her a drink and she'd said she could buy her own. He'd offered her a line and given her two in the toilets along with his phone number. The next day she'd called him, asking if he had any more coke, and three days later she was in his bed, doing whatever he asked. Now he banged her two or three times a week but he was starting to get bored and he was planning to pass her on to his crew. After a few months with his boys she'd be ready to put to work on the streets.

She was snoring softly, her long blonde hair over the pillow. Holmes loved blonde hair, the longer the better. He liked the feel of it, the smell of it and the contrast between it and his almost black skin. He nudged her. "Hey, bitch, get me a beer from the fridge."

"I'm sleeping," she murmured.

"Fuck you, bitch, I'll give you sleeping." He put his foot against her stomach and pushed her out of bed. She yelped as she hit the floor. "Get me a bloody beer and then give me a blow-job."

She rubbed her nose with the back of her hand. "Have you got any more coke?"

Holmes grinned. "Yeah, baby, I've got what you need. Now go down and get me a beer."

She pouted, pulled on a bathrobe and left the room. Holmes rolled over, grabbed his cigarettes and lit one. He lay back and blew smoke up at the ceiling. It was just after one o'clock in the morning. He had two hours to kill before he had to be in west London to pick up a kilo of cocaine he'd arranged to buy from a Jamaican importer. It should already have arrived on a commercial flight from Kingston, smuggled in by a Jamaican minister and his wife. The dog collar and the overweight woman in her hat covered with flowers made four trips a year to London, ostensibly to conduct Bible study groups, and they had never yet been stopped by Customs.

"Come on, bitch, where's my beer?" he shouted. There was no answer. "Cow," muttered Holmes. He tried blowing a smoke-ring but it didn't hold together for more than a second. He coughed and tried again.

He heard footsteps on the stairs. "About bloody time," he said. A man appeared at the doorway. Holmes was so surprised that he yelped and pulled the quilt around him, but the man was smiling, he wasn't holding a weapon and he was white, so he wasn't there to shoot him. He was wearing a bright yellow fluorescent jacket over a white shirt and black trousers and Holmes realised he was a cop, even though he hadn't identified himself. A second man appeared behind him, a big West Indian wearing a bulky black jacket over his uniform.

"Who the fuck are you?" said Holmes, regaining his composure. They weren't from the local Drugs Squad and he was pretty sure they weren't Operation Trident.

"Police," said the man in the fluorescent jacket. "We sent your girlfriend home — hope you don't mind. There was some cash on the table so we gave her that for a taxi."

"Whatever," said Holmes, running a hand through his hair. "You got a warrant?"

"Why would we need a warrant?"

"You're wasting your time, Five-O, because there's nothing here. No guns, no drugs, no nothing. I never keep nothing in my crib."

Fluorescent Jacket shrugged. "Do I look like I care, Denzel?"

"I've got no court appearances due, no fines that need paying. I ain't done nothing wrong."

"Well, now, there's that for a start," said the West Indian. He nodded at the small mirror on the bedside table. "That white powder would be what, Denzel? Talc?"

"That bitch you threw out brought it with her. It ain't mine," said Holmes.

"You're a drug-dealer, Denzel. Of course it's your gear."

"Her fingerprints on it. Charge her. Maybe her dad can get her off." Holmes grinned. "Her old man's a magistrate — how about that?" He sat up and stubbed out his cigarette on the mirror. "Test my blood if you want. I don't use. Only losers take drugs."

"And winners sell them. Is that the theory?" asked the West Indian.

"I don't use drugs," said Holmes, flatly.

"You know how I know that you're lying?" said the West Indian. "Because your lips are moving."

A third man walked into the bedroom as if he owned the place. He was wearing a long-sleeved fleece over his uniform. He grinned at Holmes, revealing slab-like gleaming white teeth, and held up a large plastic bottle of Pepsi.

"Did you get that from my fridge?" asked Holmes. "What are you doing, going through my fridge? That's theft, that."

The policeman unscrewed the top off the bottle and slowly poured it onto the carpet.

"That's shag pile, that!" shouted Holmes. "I'll sue you for that. I'll sue you for a new carpet."

"So, were you named after the actor, Denzel?" asked Fluorescent Jacket.

"What actor?"

"Tom Cruise, you dipshit. What actor do you think? Denzel Washington. Was your mum a fan? Did she have the hots for him, is that it?"

"It's my grandad's name. I was named after him. What's my name got to do with anything?"

"I was just curious."

"Yeah, well, curiosity killed the cat, didn't it? Now I'm through pissing about, I want my phone call and I want my lawyer."

"You don't have a lawyer, Denzel. Whenever you're in trouble you get legal aid, paid for by us taxpayers. When did you last pay tax, Denzel? Did you ever pay tax?"

"What is this? Are you Five-O or the taxman?"

"Oh, we're Five-O, Denzel. We're most definitely Five-O."

"So why don't you get on with policing so we can all head off home?"

"Because we've got something to take care of first," said Fluorescent Jacket.

"Yeah, well, I want to see warrant cards because I want your names, man. I'm gonna complain loud and long about what you're doing here. You ain't got no cause and you ain't got no warrant and you ain't read me my rights."

216

"You haven't got any rights, Denzel," said the West Indian. "You gave up any rights you might have had when you started firing your gun in a crowded street."

"So what do you want?" asked Holmes. "What's so important that you come bursting into my crib at night?"

The West Indian grinned and cracked his knuckles. He was wearing the purple latex gloves that the cops used when they were doing searches, Holmes realised. He looked around. All three of the men were wearing gloves. He heard noises downstairs. Somebody moving around. "You'd better not be setting me up for nothing," he said.

"Like what?" asked Fluorescent Jacket.

"Like putting drugs somewhere and saying they're mine, which they're not, cos I never keep drugs in my crib and anyone who knows me knows that's the truth."

Fluorescent Jacket took out a semi-automatic. He pulled back the slide and a cartridge click-clacked into place.

"What's that?" asked Holmes.

"This?" said the policeman, holding up the gun. "You know what this is, Denzel. It's a gun. A firearm. Actually it's a Glock nine millimetre, which is what our armed boys use. And the gun of choice for many a gangbanger. No safety — you know that, right? No annoying safety to click on or off. It's got that trick trigger with its different bits so that it can't be pulled accidentally. Was that what you used in the drive-by in Harlesden when the little girl got shot? Or something bigger, something with a bit more kick? A Mac Ten, maybe. Or an Uzi?"

"I didn't shoot no little girl," snarled Holmes.

"No, you tried to shoot up the Lock City Crew and it was one of them who shot the little girl, but it's all cause and effect. And you were the cause of that little girl getting shot in the head."

"Yeah? So prove it."

"I don't have to prove anything, Denzel," said Fluorescent Jacket, sighting along the top of the gun. "This isn't a court. There's no high-priced lawyer paid for by the state, there's no jury of *Sun* readers who get their view of what's right and wrong from watching *Coronation Street* and *EastEnders*, there's no witnesses pulling out because you've threatened to burn down their houses. There's just you and me and these guys."

"So this is about what? This is about you trying to scare me into confessing, is that it? You wave your little gun around and I pee my pants and confess to something I didn't do?"

"You don't have to confess to anything, Denzel. This isn't about confessions, it's about justice. Justice and punishment."

"Fuck you," spat Holmes. "You're the police, you can't do nothing."

The policeman smiled. "You couldn't be more wrong, Denzel," he said. "It's because we're the police we can do what the hell we want." He held out his left hand and his colleague tossed the plastic bottle to him. "And what we want, Denzel, is for you to stop behaving like an arsehole."

218

"Fuck you, man."

"Here's the thing, Denzel. Generally if it walks like a duck and it quacks like a duck then it's a duck. You walk like a Yardie and you talk like a Yardie but you were born here and so were your parents, God rest their souls."

"What?"

"How do you think your mum and dad would feel if they knew how you'd turned out, Denzel? Dealing crack, firing guns in crowded streets, living the gangster life. Do you think they'd be proud of their little Denzel?"

"Leave my parents out of this, man," said Holmes. "Ain't nothing to do with them."

"Quite right, Denzel. You have to take responsibility for your actions. But my point is that you're British-born, which means we can hardly force you to go home because this is your home."

"That's right, man. I'm as British as you."

The policeman looked pained. "Two words, Denzel. Dog. Stable."

Holmes frowned. "Say what?"

"Just because a dog is born in a stable doesn't make it a horse."

The frown deepened. "What?"

"You're a Brit, Denzel, but you're not behaving like a citizen. You're behaving like an animal. And it's down to me and my friends here to stop you."

"What you gonna do, man? You gonna shoot me?"

"You must be psychic, because that's exactly what I'm going to do, Denzel."

"Bollocks! You the police — you can't shoot me."

"You've never been shot, have you, Denzel? You've never felt a bullet rip through your flesh, have you? You see, that's the problem. You've no real concept of the damage that a gun can do. The pain it can cause, the physical and psychological damage that someone goes through when they've been shot. The little girl that got hurt in Harlesden, she's never going to be the same again. Neither will her father. Can you imagine what it must have been like for him, cradling his little girl in the street, blood pouring from her head?"

"I told you already, it wasn't me what shot her."

"It's only the fact that the little girl didn't die that's keeping you alive, Denzel. I want you to remember that. And I want you to remember that if you ever carry a gun again, I'll come back and put a bullet in your head. And if you're seen with one gram of crack or smack or any other Class A drug, we'll kill you. You so much as get a speeding ticket and we'll be back."

For the first time Holmes realised that the men were serious. His hands began to shake and he pulled the quilt up around his neck even though he knew it wouldn't offer any protection against the Glock. "Look, man, you're cops, right? Cops can't do this."

The West Indian grabbed the bottom of the quilt and snatched it from Holmes.

Fluorescent Jacket pressed the top of the empty plastic Pepsi bottle against the barrel of the Glock and pulled the trigger. The makeshift silencer absorbed most of the explosion as the bullet ripped into Holmes's left knee. He screamed. Fluorescent Jacket fired again and the right kneecap shattered, blood splattering across the sheet.

Holmes collapsed back on the bed, his whole body in spasm.

"How's it feel, Denzel? How's it feel to be shot? Is it like it is in the movies?"

Holmes lay gasping for breath, his chest rising and falling as the blood soaked into the sheet he was lying on.

"If this was a movie you'd jump off that bed and karate-kick me into the middle of next week. Or jump out of the window and run down the street. But this isn't a movie and it hurts like hell, doesn't it? And it's going to be weeks before you heal, months before you can walk again."

Holmes closed his eyes.

"Are you passing out, Denzel? That's good because the next shot is really going to hurt. Then we'll call an ambulance. Get you to a hospital. The nurses who took care of that little girl might well be the ones who look after you. That'd be ironic, wouldn't it? And just so you know, Denzel, if you tell anyone who did this to you, we'll come back and finish the job." He put the plastic Pepsi bottle on the end of the barrel, aimed at Holmes's gut and pulled the trigger.

By Thursday Shepherd was able to operate as part of the TSG team almost on autopilot. He had developed the knack of spotting when a car was wrong or a pedestrian was acting suspiciously. He could pat down a man in less than thirty seconds and fill out a Form

5090 in a minute. A lot of time was spent sitting in the van, but there were spurts of adrenalin too, when Turnbull would have the lights and sirens on and they would chase after a car that refused to stop.

Although the Mercedes van was called a Sprinter, it wasn't designed for high-speed car chases, a fact that the city's drug-dealers and gangsters were all too well aware of. If they were in a crowded street, a driver would pull over because there was no place to run, but if they were on an open road and he or she had something to hide, it was worthwhile trying to get away. Twice on Thursday Turnbull had been given the slip by cars, in both cases small hatchbacks driven by black teenagers. They could zip around corners and along back-streets much faster than the lumbering van. But in both cases the registration numbers were noted and entered into the system. They'd be caught eventually, hopefully in traffic conditions that wouldn't allow them to get away.

Over the days Shepherd had found his attitude hardening. Most of the people they stopped, pedestrians and drivers, clearly resented being pulled up by the police and reacted accordingly. Because of the areas where they were working, the majority stopped were black or Asian, and most would claim that the stop was racially motivated. It wasn't, because the team only stopped people who were acting suspiciously or who were flagged up by the MDT. But after he had been accused a dozen or so times of being a racist, Shepherd stopped listening. He would stand tight-lipped until the complainant had run out of steam, then politely explain

222

why they had been searched and exactly what their rights were. Several times the police were accused of not doing their jobs and told that they should be out catching real criminals, not harassing innocent motorists, but the plain fact was that most of the motorists they stopped weren't innocent, which was why they had been stopped in the first place.

If the MDT showed that a car wasn't insured, and if the driver wasn't able to produce evidence that he did have insurance, the team had the right to seize the vehicle, which they did on Thursday morning. The car was a brand new Lexus SUV driven by a white teenager with half a dozen chunky gold chains hanging around his neck. And a New York Yankees baseball cap worn back to front. He claimed to have borrowed the car from a friend but he couldn't remember the friend's name or phone number or where he lived. The car wasn't insured or taxed but hadn't been reported stolen. Fogg tried to contact the registered owner but without success, so he seized the car and the driver walked off sullenly, a fifty-ninety in one hand and his mobile phone in the other, calling a friend to pick him up.

When vehicles were successfully stopped, more often than not it would be in full view of the public — by a bus queue or close to shops — to get the maximum publicity value. The man in the street might not want to be hauled out of his car and searched, but the fact that the TSG were out and about meant that villains were more likely to stay at home. Shepherd wasn't sure how effective the stop-and-search patrols were in keeping

223

down crime long term, but there was no doubting their value as a temporary deterrent.

Towards the end of the shift the van was heading back to Paddington Green when Sergeant Fogg got a call over his police radio. "Overtime, guys!" he shouted. Everyone on the van cheered. "Colgate, turn us around and head back up to Neasden. We've got intel that lefties are gonna lay siege to a pub where England First are having a meeting."

When the van pulled up outside the Duke of York in Neasden, there were already five TSG vans parked at the side of the road. "Commissioner's Reserve from Area Two," said Kelly, pointing out three of the vans to Shepherd. "They must be expecting something big to kick off." More than twenty demonstrators, half of them Asian, were gathered on the pavement on the opposite side of the road, facing the pub. Some were waving posters with "Nazi Scum!" and "Racist Pigs!" and pictures of Adolf Hitler with "BNP" superimposed across his chest. They were jeering and chanting slogans as vacuous as the ones on the posters. Twenty TSG officers in full riot gear and blue helmets with long shields were standing in the road in front of the demonstrators but the protesters made no move to get past them, seeming content simply to hurl abuse at the building.

Parry pulled open the side door and climbed out.

"Right, get your gear on while I talk to the inspector," said Fogg. He jumped out and hurried over to Inspector Smith, who was standing close by, talking to one of the Area Two sergeants.

Parry went around to the rear of the van with Kelly and began pulling out kitbags. The team put on their elbow, shoulder, thigh and knee protectors, then their fireproof overalls.

As they were pulling on their balaclavas, Inspector Smith strode over with Fogg at his heels. It was the first time that Shepherd had seen the inspector in riot gear. "There's an England First meeting going on upstairs in the pub," said Smith. "Probably fifty or so people, including a few well-known troublemakers. Most of the regular punters have already left so I need you lot to line up outside the door. We're not letting anyone out into the street until the demonstrators have dispersed. Keep them in a bubble, as long as it takes. And don't take any nonsense from them — give this lot an inch and they'll take a bloody mile." He turned on his heel and went back to the vans.

Fogg grabbed his kitbag. "Right, lads," he said. "Long shields and over to the pub. I'll catch up with you."

Parry and Kelly pulled the shields from the racks and handed them out. Shepherd snapped down the visor of his helmet. There was one entrance to the pub in the middle of the building, with double doors that opened into the main bar, which was almost empty. Shepherd looked up at the first-floor windows. Half a dozen skinheads were shouting at the demonstrators but the windows were closed so they couldn't be heard.

A bottle hurtled through the air above Shepherd's head and smashed into the pub door. He looked around and saw the TSG officers pushing the crowd back.

"Come on," said Parry, jogging towards the pub. Shepherd followed him with Kelly, Castle, Simmons and Coker close behind. They formed a semicircle around the double doors, slotting their shields together.

Through the glass-fronted door Shepherd could see three men in black bomber jackets coming down a flight of stairs. They all had close-cropped hair, tight blue jeans, Doc Marten boots and the overdeveloped arm muscles that went with hours in the gym and over-enthusiastic use of steroids. They walked up to the double doors and pulled them open. "What the fuck's going on?" asked one. "This is a private meeting, the room has been paid for, and no one's doing anything wrong." More men came down the stairs, including the skinheads.

Fogg walked up behind Shepherd. He had his helmet on but the visor up. He held up his hands to attract the attention of the men coming out of the pub. "Please stay where you are," he said. "No one can leave the premises at the moment. Bear with us and we'll soon be able to let you out."

"You can't keep us here!" shouted one of the skinheads. "It's a free country!"

Two more behind him punched the air. "Yeah, it's a free country!" yelled one.

"Free country or not, I'm of the opinion that if you leave the pub there is a good chance that a breach of

226

the peace will be committed!" shouted Fogg, fighting to be heard above the noise of the swelling crowd in the bar. "I need you all to stay put until we clear the demonstrators from across the road."

"We're not scared of no leftie scumbags!" shouted a skinhead, but Fogg had already turned his back on them and was jogging back to the inspector.

Shepherd scanned the faces of the England First supporters pushing to get out of the pub. Most were young and angry, eyes blazing with hatred, lips curled into snarls like dogs preparing to attack. A skinhead with a swastika tattooed across his neck spat at Shepherd and saliva splattered across his shield. Shepherd stared at the man, his face impassive. There was no point in taking it personally, he knew. The man wasn't angry with him, he was angry with the system. Maybe even the world. The saliva slid slowly down the Perspex screen.

More men were trying to get out of the pub, pushing those already outside against the shields. Shepherd's eyes narrowed as he saw someone he recognised. Gary Dawson. And, just behind him, Jimmy Sharpe.

"Bloody hell," said Parry. Shepherd looked at him. He was staring at Dawson. "You see that?" asked Parry.

"Yeah," said Shepherd. "What do we do?"

Parry looked over his shoulder. Fogg was talking to Inspector Smith by one of the vans. "Skip!" shouted Parry. Fogg looked across. "Over here, Skip!"

Fogg said something to the inspector, then jogged over to Parry. "What's the problem?" he asked. The skinhead spat again and Fogg lowered his visor.

Parry didn't say anything but he jutted his chin towards the pub door. Fogg looked at the men crowding in the doorway and cursed when he saw Dawson. They had eye-contact for less than a second before Dawson looked away.

"What do we do, Skip?" asked Shepherd.

"If we start taking names he's screwed," said Parry.

"I'm pretty sure that's what Smith intends," said Fogg. "He reckons there's a few in there with cases outstanding."

"He's not undercover, is he?" said Shepherd, out of the side of his mouth, playing the naïve newbie to the hilt.

"I bloody well hope so," said Fogg. He looked over his shoulder to where the inspector was talking into his radio. "Look, I'll distract Smithy. While I'm doing that let a few of them through. If there's repercussions, just say they breached the shields and you couldn't hold the bubble. It happens."

"Yeah, it happens to idiots," said Parry. "Thanks, Skip."

"I'll owe you one, Carpets," said Fogg. He went over to Smith and started talking to him, moving his body so that the inspector's back was towards the pub. Parry glanced over his shoulder and nodded at Shepherd. They moved their shields apart and created a gap a couple of feet wide. The skinhead who had spat at Shepherd's shield pushed through, and when his companions saw that no one was stopping him, they followed. Parry and Shepherd widened the gap and a dozen more men rushed through it, including the three

228

bodybuilders in bomber jackets. Dawson and Sharpe slipped by without a glimmer of recognition, and ran along the pavement. Shepherd and Parry forced their shields towards each other, trying to close the gap, but the men coming out were moving too quickly. A fist thumped into the side of Shepherd's helmet but it was a flailing limb rather than a deliberate punch. He grunted and shoved harder with the shield.

He heard shouts behind him. Three officers ran up, rammed their shields together and pushed up behind Parry and Shepherd. They moved aside, the shields slotted together and the gap was closed. The men trapped in the bubble screamed abuse and shook their fists but the shields held.

The inspector hurried over, his face hard. "What happened?" he shouted.

"Sorry, sir, I slipped," said Shepherd. "My fault."

"Get a grip, Terry. Now, keep those shields together and keep them up."

"Yes, sir," said Shepherd.

Fogg appeared behind the inspector. "Okay, sir?"

"Just don't let anyone else through," said Smith. He turned to Fogg. "Keep an eye on them, Sergeant," he said. "We'll wait for the lefties to calm down and then we'll let this lot go. Explain to them we'll be walking them down the road that way and if they make any attempt to go any other way they'll be back in a bubble until the early hours." He walked off, talking into his radio.

Fogg patted Shepherd on the shoulder. "Nice one, Terry. Thanks."

"Yeah, thanks for eating the shit sandwich," said Parry. "I owe you one."

Dawson jogged down a side-street, Sharpe following. They stopped behind a skip to catch their breath. "What just happened, Gary?" asked Sharpe.

"What do you mean?" asked Dawson.

"You know what I mean," said Sharpe. "Back there. The cops let us go. Why did they do that?"

"They made a mistake," said Dawson. "They screwed up."

Sharpe shook his head. "Like fuck," he said. "They knew you, didn't they?"

"Just forget it," said Dawson, walking away.

Sharpe hurried after him. "What's the story, Gary?" he asked. "Why won't you tell me?"

"There's nothing to tell," said Dawson.

Sharpe reached for Dawson's shoulder and pulled him back. "Are you with the lefties, is that it?"

"Don't be ridiculous," said Dawson.

"What, then?"

"I'm a cop," said Dawson. He glared at Sharpe. "There — are you happy now?"

"What — under cover?"

Dawson laughed. "No, just a cop. I'm with the TSG." He looked down the alley. "We can't talk here," he said. "Let's find a pub. I need a drink."

They walked down the alley and turned into a main street. A few yards down they found a pub and went inside. Dawson ordered the drinks and carried them over to a table next to a bleeping fruit machine. He raised his glass. "Cheers."

Sharpe returned the salutation. "You were joking about being with the heavy mob, right?"

"No. Been with the TSG for four years now. I'm a sergeant. I know those guys back there. That's why they let us go. Otherwise we could have been in the bubble all night."

"Bubble?"

"That's what they call it when they hold you in one place. The media calls it kettling but to us it's always been the bubble."

"You know what's funny?" asked Sharpe.

Dawson shook his head.

"We're sort of in the same line of business." He took out his wallet and showed him his Brian Parker SOCA identification.

Dawson laughed. "You're right, that is funny. I had no idea. You don't look like a cop."

"I'm not. I'm a civil servant," said Sharpe. "No powers of arrest, no blues and twos, no uniform. I shuffle papers, fill out expense sheets and that's it."

"Not very fulfilling, then?"

"Waste of bloody time, truth be told," said Sharpe. "I'm an accountant and that's as far as it goes."

"What did you do before SOCA?"

"Inland Revenue," said Sharpe. "Fraud. That's pretty much what I do with SOCA but I have to say I put more guys behind bars when I was a taxman. SOCA just doesn't get the job done, you know."

"Yeah, I heard it was for the chop," said Dawson. "Not fit for purpose, they say."

"It's certainly not putting the bad guys away like it was supposed to," said Sharpe. "Not like your mob. At least you get to make arrests. Where are you based?"

"Paddington Green," said Dawson.

"And you do the full bit with helmets and riot shields and batons?"

"Oh, yes," said Dawson. "Just like the guys back there at the pub."

"Wish they'd give me a baton," said Sharpe. "There's a fair few heads I wouldn't mind cracking." He wanted to give Dawson the chance to say something, anything, that suggested he, too, would relish the opportunity of righting a few wrongs, but Dawson just stared into his beer. "You're taking a risk, aren't you, Gary? Going to England First meetings? Wouldn't you lose your job?"

Dawson shrugged. "I'm not sure I care any more."

"Why's that?"

Dawson shrugged again. "I just hate what's happened to our country, Brian. I hate what we've become, and I hate the fact that no one seems to want to do anything about it."

"I hear that," said Sharpe.

"You know, my grandfather was born in the East End. He fought hand-to-hand against Mosley's Blackshirts. Had a scar on his chin from where he was hit by a docker's hook. Cut him right through to the bone. The Battle of Cable Street, they called it. And look at me now, going to meetings to cheer the men who are Mosley's descendants." He smiled ruefully. "My grandfather would be spinning in his grave."

"But they talk sense, right?"

"They're the only people who do, Brian. They're the only ones who care about our country and not themselves. See the way that Labour and the Conservatives were filling their boots with fake expenses, lying and cheating and stealing at the taxpayer's expense? They don't care about our country, they care about themselves. About feathering their own nests." He took a long drink of his lager. "People are fed up with being treated like third-class citizens in their own country. They're sick of seeing relatives pushed to the back of the housing queue or having to wait for medical treatment while asylum seekers are fast-tracked for whatever they want. You know why the Left hate the BNP and England First so much? Because when they enter into debates with the likes of Simon Page or Nick Griffin they get trounced. They talk sense, and that's why they have to throw eggs at them and scream, 'Nazi scum,' and accuse them of wanting a second Holocaust. That's not what they're about, Brian. They're talking a lot of sense."

He sat back and folded his arms. "It's the unfairness that gets me, Brian. Do you remember the anti-military march in Luton a while back? A load of Muslims got together to heckle the Royal Anglian Regiment when they got back from Iraq. Placards telling the squaddies to go to hell, all that sort of stuff."

"Yeah, I remember," said Sharpe.

"Ten people were arrested," said Dawson. "But it wasn't the Muslims who were arrested, it was locals who'd gone there to support the army. One of them was arrested for throwing a pack of streaky bacon. I kid you not."

Sharpe laughed. "That's funny."

"Yeah, it's funny, but at the same time it's not. Muslims can shout all sorts of shit at our troops who've been risking their lives in Iraq, but throw a pack of bacon at the Muslims and you're arrested. And what happens when left-wing activists hurl eggs at Nick Griffin? The cops do nothing. Now, you tell me what's going on there. Throwing bacon at a Muslim is an arrestable offence, but throwing eggs at an MEP is okay?"

"Either way it sounds like a waste of a good breakfast to me," said Sharpe.

"It's a serious point, Brian. We're all bending over to be politically correct while our country slides into anarchy. Someone has to stand up and fight for what's right."

"Can't we do something about it?" asked Sharpe.

"Like what?"

"I don't know. Hit the bad guys where it hurts? Be more proactive?"

Dawson shook his head. "It needs more than that. It needs political change. We need a party that can change the way our society operates."

"And you think England First can do that?"

"I hope so," said Dawson. He picked up his lager. "Because if something isn't done soon, our country's finished."

★ ★ ★

Shepherd and his team arrived back at Paddington Green just before midnight. It had taken the best part of three hours to disperse the protesters from the street outside the pub, and another hour to search and process the sixty-seven people who had attended the England First meeting. All were issued with Form 5090. No weapons or drugs were found during the searches but a quick look around the ground floor of the pub afterwards turned up three flick-knives, half a dozen brass knuckledusters and a considerable quantity of cannabis. "Nice bit of overtime," said Parry, as he climbed out of the van. "Soon have my kitchen paid for. The wife's going to love me."

"Carpets, Terry, KFC, can I have a quick word in the briefing room before you get changed?" said Fogg. Parry, Kelly and Shepherd followed him down the corridor. The sergeant waited until they were all inside and the door was closed before speaking. "I just wanted to clear the air about what happened in Neasden," he said. "You all saw Gary Dawson where he shouldn't be. I'll have a word with him, obviously, but so far as we're concerned it never happened, right?"

The three men nodded. "No problem, Skip," said Kelly.

"Anyone else see him or just you three?"

"Just us, I think," said Parry.

"Nipple? Pelican?"

"They were blindsided, Skip," said Parry.

"Okay. Don't mention it to them but if they bring it up then let me know ASAP, okay?"

The three men nodded again. "What do you think he was doing there, Sarge?" asked Shepherd. "Just wrong place, wrong time?"

Fogg looked pained. "Gary's a bit right-wing with his views, that's all," he said. "I was as surprised as you to see him there, though, and I'll make sure I explain the error of his ways to him. But we all know what would happen if Professional Standards found out, so mum's the word."

Shepherd was at Paddington Green early on Friday morning. As he walked into the locker room, Fogg was taking off his motorcycle gear. Shepherd put his helmet in his locker. "I just saw Robin Potter heading for the canteen," said the sergeant. "Let's swing by and ask him about your bike."

"Thanks, Sarge," said Shepherd. As soon as they had changed into their uniforms, they went along to the canteen. There was twenty minutes to go before their shift officially started so both men collected tea and bacon sandwiches. Shepherd paid, figuring it was the least he could do if Fogg would solve his parking problem. Potter was sitting with two other police motorcyclists, a plate of toast in front of him. He was wearing a bulky fluorescent jacket and his white full-face helmet was on the chair next to him. He was in his late thirties with a receding hairline and a sharp chin. Fogg sat down at the table and introduced Shepherd.

Potter shook his hand. "Foggy says you've got a decent bike."

"A BMW HP2 Sport."

"Nice," he said. "I'm a big fan of the BMWs, but I'm more a classic enthusiast. I've a couple of Vincents at home, a Black Shadow and a Rapide, and a couple of old Triumphs."

"And he rides a bike all day for a living," said Fogg. "He'd sleep on one if he could. Can you help Terry with a parking space, Robbo?"

Potter took out his notebook and passed it to Shepherd. "Write down your registration number and I'll talk to Frank in Admin. He'll get you put on the list. If there's a problem I'll call you but otherwise just tell the guy on the gate that Frank said it was okay. There are a dozen bikes over at the far end of the car park. Just pick a free space."

"Thanks," said Shepherd.

"You were in West Mercia, Foggy said."

"Yeah, for my sins," said Shepherd. He sipped his tea.

"What brings you to the Big Smoke?"

"Wanted a bit more excitement, I guess."

"Yeah, well, you'll get that in spades." He grinned at Fogg. "Are you allowed to say that, these days?"

"Probably not," said Fogg.

Potter finished his toast and stood up. "No rest for the wicked," he said. He nodded at Shepherd. "See you around, Terry." He picked up his helmet and headed out, followed by his two colleagues.

"Nice guy," said Shepherd.

"One of the best," said Fogg. "But crazy about bikes. He should be an inspector by now, maybe chief inspector, but he refuses to leave Traffic." He looked at his watch. "Come on, I've got a briefing to give."

Shepherd and his team spent the afternoon driving around north-west London, and in the afternoon they were called out to help search for a six-year-old girl who had gone missing. She had wandered out of her back garden while her mother was smoking crack cocaine in her bedroom. By the time the mother had woken up, the child was nowhere to be found, but two hours into the search she was discovered at a corner shop, trying to buy a bar of chocolate with play money. Mother and daughter were reunited and Shepherd's shift was over.

As he was stripping off his uniform in the locker room, his mobile beeped to show that he'd received a text message. It was from Charlotte Button: "Call me." He pulled on a pair of jeans and a polo shirt and went into the briefing room with his phone.

"How's it going?" she asked.

"Softly softly," he said.

"You still working?"

"Just finished."

"I think we need a strategy meeting."

"Charlie, I wanted to get back to Hereford tonight."

"What time's your last train?"

"Eight twenty."

"We can meet in the office in Praed Street. Seven. I won't keep you more than an hour. Razor will be there. You can swap notes."

"Okay," said Shepherd. He ended the call and went back into the locker room to get his sports jacket.

Simmons had finished changing into his civilian clothes. "You up for a pint?" he asked.

"Nah, I've got a date," said Shepherd.

"Anyone I know?"

"I hope not."

"Is she in the job?" Shepherd shook his head. "She local or from Hereford?"

Shepherd looked at him. "Bloody hell, Simmo, you bucking for CID?"

Simmons chuckled. "Just seems like you're not wasting any time — you've only been in the Big Smoke a week and already you're fixed up."

Shepherd put on his jacket. "Okay, she's a girl from Hereford. I'm going up to see her. Are you happy now?"

Simmons winced. "Long-distance relationships are difficult, mate."

"Tell me about it."

"I'm serious. Get her down here ASAP if you're serious about her. You need to keep a woman under lock and key or she'll stray, for sure."

Shepherd grinned. "Where the hell did you learn about relationships? From your mum?"

"I'm just saying, it's hard enough to keep a relationship going for the guys that live with their girls. If she's on the other side of the country, what hope do you have?"

Shepherd could see that the young constable meant well and he patted him on the back. "I'm a big boy, I can handle my women," he said.

"You know, the divorce rate in the TSG's more than fifty per cent," said Simmons. "Wives just don't get it, the job and what it means." Parry walked into the locker room, pulling off his stab vest. "Carpets here is one of the few to stick at it."

"Stick at what?" asked Parry, hanging up his vest.

"Marriage," said Simmons.

"Yeah, coming up for ten years," said Parry. "But my girl's one in a million."

"She'd have to be to put up with you," said Simmons.

Shepherd closed his locker and picked up his holdall. "I'm off," he said. "See you on Monday."

Outside he bumped into Robin Potter, who was smoking with two CSOs in fluorescent jackets. Potter made a gun with his gloved hand and pointed it at Shepherd. "Your bike's sorted," he said.

"Excellent," said Shepherd.

"You not riding tonight?"

Shepherd held up his holdall. "Weekend away," he said.

One of the CSOs held out his hand. "How are you doing?" he said. "Ross Mayhew. Saw you on your first day in the canteen."

Shepherd shook it. "Terry," he said. "Terry Halligan."

"Another bike nut, Robbo was saying," said Mayhew. He nodded at the other CSO, an Asian woman in her thirties. "This is Rhonda, my wing man."

Rhonda flashed Mayhew a tight smile. "Wing person," she said.

240

For a moment Shepherd thought she was joking, but the look on her face told him she wasn't. Mayhew shrugged and corrected himself. "Wing person."

"Nice to meet you both," Shepherd said, "but I've got to rush. See you around." He winked at Potter. "And thanks, Sarge, I owe you one."

"I might take you up on that one day, Terry," said Potter.

Shepherd crossed the road and headed towards Paddington station. He walked through the concourse, checking reflections in shop windows, went up the escalator to Starbucks, down the stairs and back along the concourse until he was sure he wasn't being followed. Then he walked on to Praed Street.

Jimmy Sharpe was already in the first-floor office with Charlotte Button and Amar Singh, one of SOCA's most innovative technicians. It had been more than six months since Shepherd had seen Singh and he shook his hand warmly. Singh was wearing a brown leather jacket that was stylish enough to be Armani, with Versace jeans. "Looking good, Amar," said Shepherd.

"I try to please," said Singh. "How's your boy?"

"He'll be a teenager soon — can't tell you how much I'm looking forward to that," he said, sitting down and putting his holdall beside his chair. "What's new?" he asked Button.

Sharpe passed Shepherd two photographs of a young black man covered with blood. "This happened two nights ago, a couple of miles north of your place in Kilburn," said Button.

"It wasn't me," said Shepherd, and grinned at Sharpe.

Button ignored his attempt at levity. "Name of Denzel Holmes, a member of the Much Love Crew. He was shot in the knees and the gut at close range. Someone called nine-nine-nine and an ambulance picked him up within eight minutes."

"Why do you think it was our guys?" asked Shepherd.

"The paramedics doped him up at the scene and while he was in A and E he was mumbling about being shot by cops. He changed his story when he woke up this morning and now claims it was other gangbangers. Operation Trident are investigating but I think his first accusation was the truth. I think he was shot by cops."

"What time did this happen?"

"Late," said Button. "One in the morning."

"Could have been anyone, then," said Shepherd. "Why isn't he dead? And who called the ambulance?"

"It was a man, his voice muffled, but he gave very clear, precise directions. He wanted him found and found quickly. And the front door was left on the latch."

"So they didn't want him dead."

"That's how I read it," said Button. "It was a punishment and a warning. Holmes was the drug-dealer that the Trident boys are sure was behind a drive-by shooting in Harlesden — the one last month where the little girl was hit in the crossfire."

Shepherd remembered the case. The little girl had been to the cinema with her father and two brothers, and a car had driven by spraying bullets at a group of youths standing on a street corner. They were with a gang called the Lock City Crew, mainly West Africans and Jamaicans. None of the youths had been hit but one had pulled out a gun of his own and started shooting back. The little girl had taken a bullet to the head and had spent two weeks in intensive care. The youth who had fired the shot was due to stand trial later in the year and his legal-aid lawyer had already announced that he would be pleading not guilty and that he had been acting in self-defence.

"There's fairness in what these guys are doing, isn't there?" said Sharpe.

"Excuse me?" said Button.

"Look, they shoot gun-wielding gangbangers in the gut, they kill killers, and they smash the hands of housebreakers. It's a sort of judgment of Solomon, isn't it?"

"It's nothing of the sort, Razor. If it is them, they shot a teenager at point-blank range."

"But they didn't kill him. And a lot of people might say he deserved it."

"And a lot of people might like to see adulterers walking around with a big red A on their chests."

Sharpe frowned. "Who's talking about adultery?" he said. "They're not hurting adulterers. They're hurting scum — scum that, if you were to ask me, deserve everything they get. That gangbanger had no qualms about firing guns in a crowded street, no compassion for the innocent passersby caught in the crossfire. So don't expect me to cry my eyes out because he took a gut shot."

Shepherd could see that Button was about to tear into Sharpe so he flashed him a warning look. "We are sure that the TSG were behind the shooting?"

"A ballistics check matched the bullets to a gun that belonged to a drug-dealer in Wembley. He was busted in a crack lab a year ago and he's just started a seven-year sentence. No gun was found when he was arrested."

"And what's the connection between the gun and the TSG?"

"Roy Fogg's Serial was part of the TSG team that went into the crack lab," said Button.

"Any connection between Gary Dawson and the gun?" asked Sharpe.

"He wasn't involved in the raid on the lab," said Button.

"So it's all circumstantial," said Shepherd.

"Agreed," said Button, "but circumstantial evidence is better than no evidence at all."

"But there's no evidence at all connecting Dawson to the vigilantes," said Sharpe.

"Except the fact that he's a racist, you mean?" said Button.

"Dawson's not a racist and I don't think he's a vigilante, either," said Sharpe.

"He's a member of a racist organisation," said Button.

"For political reasons, not racism," said Sharpe. "I've been at meetings with him and sat in the pub with him and nothing he says is racist. And he's had every chance to talk to me about vigilantes and he hasn't. I came pretty close to suggesting it myself and he's just not interested. Gary Dawson's a good cop who's just fed up with what's happening to this country. And I don't think he's alone on that score."

"He might just be being careful," said Button.

"I don't think so," said Sharpe. "He knows I'm with SOCA, he thinks I'm a kindred spirit. If he was going to confide in anyone it'd be me. I think he's straight. I certainly don't think he's going around kneecapping drug-dealers."

"He was lucky that the TSG were the ones keeping the demonstrators apart," said Button. "If they'd been regular cops and started taking names and addresses his career would have ended there and then."

"As opposed to a few months down the line, do you mean?" said Sharpe. "He's finished anyway, by the sound of it."

Button ignored the interruption. "When Fogg told you to let Dawson go, did you get the feeling it was anything more than just one cop helping out another?" she asked Shepherd.

"I don't follow you," said Shepherd.

"Is there some special connection between the two of them, do you think? Or was it a cop thing?"

"The latter, I reckon," said Shepherd.

"And who else spotted Dawson?"

"Parry. He was the one who called Fogg over. I got the impression that Parry wasn't going to breach the bubble off his own bat, but he was happy to do it once

Fogg had given him the go-ahead. Kelly definitely saw Dawson. Coker? I don't think so. Turnbull was in the van, and Castle couldn't see anything from where she was, ditto Simmons. Fogg called me, Parry and Kelly in to mark our cards, but that was all. And it wasn't discussed on the bus. So I think it was just Parry, Kelly, me and Fogg. Dawson was doing a good job of not drawing attention to himself. Razor, too."

"Yeah, well, I was just hoping that your buddies weren't going to start using their riot sticks," said Sharpe. "And those bloody shields hurt, you know. Do they teach you to slam them down on people's knees?"

"Actually they do," said Shepherd. "Where do we go from here?" he asked Button. "I assume we're going to need more. I've got to say, I don't know how likely it is that the vigilantes are going to sign me up."

"Well, something's cooking because you've both been checked up on," said Button. "I was just telling Razor that his name was put through the PNC yesterday."

"Was that Dawson?" asked Shepherd.

Button shook her head. "An intelligence officer at Paddington Green. It was one of a dozen names that were checked out, so it looks as if Dawson just slipped Razor's name into a list."

"And me?"

"You had the works two days ago," said Button. "PNC check, DVLA, and the West Mercia staff list was accessed."

"And again I suppose it's too much to hope that we know who was doing the looking?" said Shepherd.

246

"A civilian worker attached to CID was logged on to the computer, but it looks as if he just left the terminal without logging off. All the checks were done very quickly, and then the terminal was left on. Five minutes after the West Mercia database was accessed there were more PNC checks made and they're connected to cases that Paddington Green CID is working on."

"So the guy goes for a cigarette break and someone from TSG sits down at his desk," said Shepherd. "Risky."

"It was first thing in the morning, before your shift had started," said Button.

"Nothing they accessed would cause me any grief, right?"

"It's all good," said Button. "Everything backs up your legend. Nothing to worry about. The opposite, in fact. Whoever did the checking must now think you're vigilante material because your disciplinary file was accessed."

"We just don't know by who."

"Do you have any ideas who might be bad?" asked Button.

"Roy Fogg's well liked," said Shepherd. "If he's doing it, I think his guys would follow him. Nick Coker's a hard nut and there's a fair bit of resentment there. I could see him taking matters into his own hands. But others in the Serial are straight arrows, I'm sure of that." He stood up and went over to one of the whiteboards.

He tapped Carolyn Castle's picture. "Castle's as pure as the driven snow."

"Spider's got a girlfriend," said Sharpe, in a singsong voice.

Shepherd ignored him. He tapped the photograph of Darren Simmons. "Simmons will do whatever Fogg says, pretty much. Kelly, too." He pointed at the picture of Angus Turnbull. "He plays it by the book." He moved his finger along to Richard Parry's photograph. "Parry I'm not sure about." He grinned. "At the risk of being racist, I'd say he's a dark horse."

Sharpe laughed and Button shook her head.

Shepherd went to sit down again. "I can't see that the whole of Fogg's team can be in on it. Fogg maybe, Coker probably, Simmons if Fogg's involved, and maybe Kelly. That's four. The thing is, we have no idea how many have gone bad. He might even have been working on his own."

"That's doubtful," said Button. "Okay, one man could have shot Holmes, but I can't see that he could have spirited away Duncan on his own. Or crippled the Yardies. I think three, four, or maybe more."

"If it's more than four, he'll have to have picked his team from within the Serial as a whole. Maybe across Serials. And if that's the case, it's going to take for ever to identify them," said Shepherd.

"Not necessarily," said Button. "We can get taps on Fogg's phone, intercept his emails, put him under the microscope. But the key is going to be if you can infiltrate the group. You've got to start pushing yourself forward, Spider."

"They're cops," said Shepherd. "They're not stupid. What do you want me to do? Wander around saying,

'Wouldn't it be nice if we could kneecap drug-dealers?' and see if anyone bites?"

"Obviously not," said Button. "But maybe start acting a little more aggressively."

Shepherd put up his hands. "I'll try, but I'll tell you now, if I push it too hard I could blow the whole operation."

"They're checking up on you for a reason, Spider."

"Maybe, maybe not. They might just be curious. If I was given a new partner, I might well check them out."

"Is that what you did when I joined SOCA? Did you run my name through the PNC?"

"No, but I asked around," said Shepherd. "It's human nature. Just because they checked me out doesn't mean they're thinking of recruiting me."

"Just see what you can do," said Button. "Also, you need to look for the gun. If they were going to dump it they would have left it at the scene. So I'm guessing they're planning on using it again. Assuming it's Fogg, he might be keeping it at home or at the station. See if you can sniff around."

"Charlie, it's a high-security police station. I can't go breaking into lockers."

Button frowned. "I'm starting to feel that you're not fully committed to this investigation," she said quietly.

"It's not that," he said. "It's just that I'm in the lion's den. I'm not lying to drug-dealers or armed robbers, I'm lying to cops — and not just any cops. These are cops that might be committing murder."

"I'm watching your back, Spider."

Shepherd nodded, but he didn't feel reassured.

"There's something else I want to try," she said. She nodded at Singh and the technician picked up a briefcase. He placed it on a chair and opened it, then took out three small bubble-wrapped packages, each about the size of a pack of cigarettes.

"GPS transponder," said Singh, unwrapping one of the packages. "State-of-the-art, gives us a location to with ten feet or so, battery life of up to two weeks." He handed it to Shepherd. "Magnetic so you can slip it under a wheel arch and it'll stick like a limpet. The trick was getting the design right so that the magnets wouldn't interfere with the circuit."

Shepherd held the transponder in the palm of his hand. It was smooth and black except for one side which was grey metal. There was a single button on one end next to a tiny green light.

"When you're ready to place it, press the button once. You'll hear it click and the light will come on. Then place the grey side against metal. High up on the wheel arch will do, or inside the engine compartment."

"We need to know where those vans are next time there's an incident," said Button. "Can you get the transponders on the vans in your Serial on Monday?"

Shepherd slipped them into his pocket. "Shouldn't be a problem," he said. "And they call them buses, not vans."

"What about me?" asked Sharpe. "Do I keep hanging out with Dawson? Because I have to say, I've heard nothing that suggests he's a bad cop. His political views might not be to everyone's taste, but I've not picked up on anything that points to him being corrupt."

"Stick with him, Razor."

Sharpe sighed theatrically.

"Something you want to get off your chest?" asked Button.

"Dawson hasn't done anything wrong," said Sharpe. "The sort of things he says are just what you'd hear in any pub in the country over a pint or two, but because he's a cop he stands to lose everything."

"He knows what the rules are, Razor. No one's putting a gun to his head."

"I know." He held up his hands. "I'll stick with it."

"I'm so pleased," said Button, acidly.

Shepherd got to the station a good fifteen minutes before his train was due to leave so he bought himself a coffee and a chicken-salad sandwich from Caffè Ritazza to take with him. The carriage was almost empty and he dozed until his mobile rang. It was Major Gannon. "Where are you?"

"The train, heading home," said Shepherd.

"Excellent, I'm at Credenhill. I've some admin to sort out and I'm running a weapons test. Can you swing by the barracks tomorrow?"

"I'm watching Liam play football in the afternoon so I can do first thing or after five, whichever is best for you."

"Let's do morning, I'm heading back to London in the afternoon. I'll leave a pass at the gate."

"Fancy a run?" asked Shepherd.

"A run?"

"Yeah, let's do a few miles. Blow away the cobwebs."

"I'll have my gear ready," said the Major. "You still running with a bergen full of bricks?"

"Certainly am."

"You always were an over-achiever, Spider." The Major ended the call.

Shepherd dozed the rest of the way to Hereford. There were no cabs outside the station but his house was only a thirty-minute walk so he swung his holdall over his shoulder and strode quickly, his breath feathering in the night air. The house was in darkness when he got home and he let himself in and went straight upstairs. He eased open the door to his son's bedroom and crept over to the bed. Lady lifted her head off the pillow and woofed softly, her tail scratching across the quilt. "I can see you're being well trained," whispered Shepherd. Liam was fast asleep, snoring softly. Shepherd kissed his forehead. "Good night, kid." He slipped out of Liam's bedroom and went down the hallway to his room. He switched on the light and smiled when he saw a handwritten note on his pillow: "DAD — DON'T FORGET FOOTBALL TOMORROW!"

Shepherd woke just before eight o'clock. He showered and shaved, pulled on an old pair of tracksuit bottoms and a Reebok sweatshirt, then went downstairs. Katra was in the kitchen. "I must have been asleep when you got home last night," she said.

"I was kept late after school," said Shepherd, pouring himself a coffee from the cafetière.

"School?" said Katra, brushing a lock of blonde hair behind her ear. She had lived in England for more than five years, and while her English was close to perfect, Shepherd's sense of humour occasionally stumped her.

"My boss wanted to talk to me," he explained.

"But you're not working at a school, are you?"

"No," said Shepherd. "It's a joke, sort of."

"I don't understand," she said. "How's it a joke?"

"I guess 'joke' is stretching it a bit," said Shepherd. He gulped some coffee. "When you're a kid you might be late if your teacher kept you behind after school. So when you're an adult and you're late you say that and it sounds funny." He grinned. "Actually, now that I've explained it, it doesn't sound that funny. Forget I said it. Where's Liam?"

"Outside with Lady."

"I hope she's not making a mess in the house."

Katra shook her head. "She's been great," she said. "She makes this cute woofing noise when she wants to go out and if you don't open the door for her she scratches it." She stood up. "Do you want egg and bacon?" she asked. "And sausage? I have some of those Lincolnshire sausages that you like."

"Just a couple of slices of toast," said Shepherd. "I've got to go for a run this morning. I'll need the CRV, too, for a couple of hours." He went out into the back garden where Liam was trying to teach the dog to stay, apparently without much success.

"Dad, hi!" shouted Liam. Lady barked excitedly.

"How goes the training?"

"She's great, Dad! She'll sit and she'll fetch, but she doesn't quite get 'stay' yet." Liam ran over and gave Shepherd his mobile phone. "Can you video me?"

"Sure," said Shepherd. He put his mug on the grass and took a few steps back. He switched on the phone's video camera. "Okay, do your stuff!" he shouted.

Liam told Lady to sit and she obeyed immediately, her tongue lolling from the side of the mouth. Liam pointed at her nose. "Stay," he said firmly. The beagle panted happily. Liam took a step backwards, keeping his eyes on her. "Stay," he repeated. He took another. Then another. Shepherd kept the camera focused on the dog. "She's doing it!" said Liam excitedly. He took another step backwards but just as he did so she barked and ran towards him. "No, Lady!" shouted Liam, but it was too late: with two bounds she was at his feet, jumping up and yelping.

Shepherd smiled and stopped filming. "Looks like she needs a bit more training." He tossed the phone to his son. "And I said she wasn't to sleep in your room, remember? She's a dog, not a human. She can sleep in the kitchen."

"She gets lonely," said Liam.

"She's a dog, she'll get over it," said Shepherd.

"Dogs are pack animals, they have to sleep in groups," said Liam, folding his arms.

"Fine, you can sleep in the kitchen, too."

"Dad!"

"You're not going to win this one, Liam," said Shepherd, firmly. "She sleeps in the kitchen."

254

Liam bent down and patted his dog as Shepherd went back into the kitchen. Katra was buttering toast for him. He poured himself more coffee and drank it with his toast, then picked up the CRV keys and headed out. On the way he opened the cupboard underneath the stairs and took out his boots and rucksack. Liam came running after him. "Dad! You *are* coming to the football, right?"

"Sure," said Shepherd, sitting down to put on his boots. "Two o'clock, right?"

"Two o'clock kick-off. We should leave here about a quarter past one."

"I'll be back," said Shepherd, doing his best Arnold Schwarzenegger impersonation.

"And we can take Lady, right?"

"Can dogs play?" asked Shepherd, tying his bootlaces.

"To watch," said Liam. "It'll be good exercise."

"Providing she stays on the lead," said Shepherd. He stood up and shouldered his rucksack. "And clean your room before I get back."

Liam saluted. "Yes, sir," he said sarcastically.

Shepherd drove to the SAS barracks. He showed his SOCA identification to a uniformed guard, who checked his name against a printed list and waved him through. The Major's Jaguar was parked at the side of the indoor firing range. Shepherd left his rucksack on the passenger seat and pushed through the double doors. He flinched at the crack-crack-crack of a carbine. The Major had the weapon to his shoulder, aiming at a paper terrorist target. He fired another three quick shots and Shepherd wrinkled his nose at the acrid smell of cordite.

The Major lowered his weapon and faced Shepherd. He grinned as he took off his bright orange ear protectors. "Spider, good to see you."

"Good to see you too, boss," said Shepherd. The Major transferred the carbine to his left hand and the two men shook hands.

The Major was wearing a black Adidas tracksuit and well-worn Puma running shoes. He grinned when he saw Shepherd's boots. "Old habits die hard, huh?"

"I figure the times in my life when I've really needed to run I've always been wearing shoes or boots," said Shepherd. "Makes sense to train that way."

"Rather you than me," said the Major. He handed the carbine to Shepherd and picked up a similar one. "What do you think?" he asked.

Shepherd hefted the weapon. "Looks like an HK416," he said.

"Well spotted," said the Major. "But it's not out of Oberndorf. That's the MR556 made in Newington, New Hampshire."

"They're making Hecklers in the States now?"

"Have been since 2008," said the Major. "They started with the HK45 pistol but now they've moved into rifles." He gestured with the one he was holding. "This is the MR762, based on the HK417."

"Why would anyone want to buy guns like these?"

"Because civilians will soon be buying them in the good old U S of A, which means that before long the gangbangers over here will be waving them around.

256

The powers-that-be want a report, which, no doubt, will be filed away and forgotten about."

"Why would anyone want to buy an HK416?"

"For hunting, apparently."

Shepherd grinned. "Yeah, you'd want to go after deer with one of these. Don't they have enough guns in America?"

"Apparently not," said the Major. "At least it can't be fired on fully automatic. But as to them being manufactured in the States, it's only fair to point out that the HK416 was just an improved version of Colt's M4 carbine in the first place. Delta Force helped Heckler develop the new carbine and they were among the first to use it. The big difference between the HK416 and what you're holding is that the HK416 comes as a complete firearm or as an upper receiver kit that fits onto any AR-15 type lower receiver. The civilian version is only available as a complete weapon."

"Special Forces wannabes are going to be buying them, right?"

"And other assorted nutters," said the Major. "Do you want to fire off a few, tell me what you think?"

Shepherd nodded and pulled on a pair of ear protectors. He fired half a dozen shots at a paper terrorist target at the far end of the range. The Major monitored his progress through a pair of binoculars, and nodded his approval. "You're low and to the right but you could cover them with a coffee cup," he said.

"The sights are probably off," said Shepherd, removing his ear protectors and placing them on a metal table.

"Probably," agreed the Major.

"I wouldn't have thought the cops would be happy about villains getting hold of these."

"Not much they can do about it. As soon as they go on sale in the States some bright spark will find a way of getting them over here."

"I suppose their one saving grace is that they're so big they can't be hidden."

"Yeah, but imagine what would happen if a few Muslim hotheads got hold of them and laid siege to a shopping mall or a hotel. You could kill a lot of people with a weapon like this — in a very short space of time. Five reckon it's only a matter of time before we get a Mumbai situation in the UK." Shepherd made the weapon safe and placed it on the table next to the ear protectors. The Major did the same with his gun. "Ready for your run?" asked the Major.

"Sure," said Shepherd.

"Please don't tell me you brought your bricks with you," said the Major, as they walked outside.

Shepherd opened the CRV and picked up his rucksack. "Habit," he said. "Doesn't feel right without it."

"At my age, I'm happy enough to do a few miles without having a cardiac episode."

Shepherd grinned as he slung on the rucksack. The Major might be a decade older than himself, but he was still fitter than most men half his age. He slammed the car door. "Five miles?" he said. "Or ten?"

"How about I meet you halfway? Seven and a half." The Major winked and sprinted down the road towards the guardhouse. Shepherd hared after him. The Major vaulted over the red and white pole and headed to the right.

Shepherd ran around the pole and hurtled after him, running at full pelt. The rucksack banged against his back and he knew he wouldn't be able to catch up while the Major maintained his breakneck pace, so he settled down to match him stride for stride. After fifteen minutes the Major left the road, leaped over a ditch and raced through a patch of woodland. Shepherd followed. The Major glanced over his shoulder and grinned. Shepherd grinned back but his chest was aching and his feet were starting to hurt. He kept a close eye on the ground, knowing how easy it would be to trip over a root or slip on a patch of wet leaves. The sunlight flickered as he ran, and he ducked as a bumblebee flew close to his face. His feet crunched on twigs and he had to jump over a moss-covered log.

Shepherd increased the pace slightly and began to gain on the Major. He gritted his teeth and his arms powered back and forth, finding a rhythm that his body was happy with. Then they ran out of the trees and around the edge of a newly ploughed field. The rough soil made it hard going and both men slowed. The Major slipped and grunted as he regained his balance. "Careful you don't break a leg!" Shepherd shouted.

The Major slipped through a hedge and cut across a sloping grass field. He looked over his shoulder and slowed to a jog. Shepherd caught up with him and matched his pace. They jogged side by side for a while, until the Major started to walk. He was panting and his shirt was sweat-stained. He grinned at Shepherd, who had barely broken into a sweat. "I spend too much time at a desk, these days," he said.

"Stamina's just about putting in the miles," said Shepherd. "I'm probably only about half as fit as I used to be."

"We're getting older." He bent down and rubbed his right knee. "Remember when we'd do the Fan Dance, have a few hours' sleep and be raring to do it again? Now my knee's playing up after a few miles." The Fan Dance was how the SAS tested its recruits and involved running to the top of Pen y Fan, the tallest peak in the Brecon Beacons, fully loaded with kit and rifle, then down the other side, then back up and down again. Shepherd had no doubt that he could manage the Fan Dance, but it would probably take him at least twice as long as it had when he was twenty-five. "I'm going next week," said the Major. "To Ireland."

"How?" asked Shepherd.

"How?"

"If you're planning on flying, you have to know that you'll be tracked."

"I'll take the ferry."

Shepherd stopped walking. They were standing at the edge of a field of rape bordered by a thick hedgerow. "Using what vehicle?"

"What is this? A quiz?"

"I just want you to be aware of the pitfalls," said Shepherd. "If the Fox brothers are killed, the first thing the police'll do is draw up a list of everyone who wanted them dead and then they'll check the whereabouts of every person on that list at the time of death. If you're found to be in the North, it'll be open and shut."

"They'll need more than proximity, Spider."

"Once they have your name in the frame they'll keep on looking, and eventually they'll find something. And even if they don't, you'd be finished, you know that."

"So I'll rent a car."

"So you'll need a driver's licence and credit card in someone else's name. Can you get that sorted by next week?"

"Maybe." The Major started walking again.

Shepherd kept pace with him. "And what about a weapon?" he asked. "Are you planning to go over with one of the HK carbines?"

"Of course not."

"So what, then? Because if there's any way of linking the weapon to you, it'll all be over."

"I've access to untraceable weapons, Spider. You of all people know that."

"There's untraceable and there's untraceable," said Shepherd, patiently. "If you're thinking about using a gun souvenired from Iraq and Afghanistan, then forget it, because if there's any suggestion of a link to the armed forces they'll be looking at you. You need a gun that's either never been fired or points to someone else."

"Someone else?"

"You take a gun that's been used in another crime but one that isn't linked to you in any way. Say you can get a gun that was in the hands of the IRA. If that's the gun that's used to shoot the Foxes then suspicion will automatically fall on the boyos."

The Major's face broke into a grin. "I like that idea," he said.

"Let me talk to Martin," said Shepherd. "He knows people in the South so he might have an idea. But it's not just the weapon, it's everything. You have to have the Almighty with you at all times, right?"

Major Gannon ran the government's best-kept secret, the Increment. It was an ad-hoc group of highly trained special forces soldiers from the Special Air Service and Special Boat Service used on operations considered too dangerous for Britain's security services, MI5 and MI6. Wherever he went, he took with him a metal briefcase that contained the secure satellite phone they called the Almighty. The only people who had the number of the Almighty were the prime minister, the Cabinet Office, and the chiefs of MI5 and MI6. When they called, it was life and death and they expected the Major to answer immediately.

"That's true," he said. "But it can't go to Ireland with me because it's traceable."

"So is your mobile," said Shepherd.

"I could switch them off."

"You could, but that in itself will raise a red flag," said Shepherd. "They have to stay on and they have to stay in a place where you would normally be."

The Major nodded slowly. "You're right."

"Of course I'm right," said Shepherd. "It's my field of expertise, remember? This needs to be thought out, boss, and planned to the nth degree."

262

"Will you help?"

"Of course I will. But you have to let me take the lead — for the organising, at least. I need you to wait until all our ducks are in a row."

"You're a star, Spider. One in a million." He slapped Shepherd's rucksack and began to run. "Last one back's a cissy!" he shouted.

Shepherd laughed and gave chase.

On the way home, Shepherd pulled in next to a phone box. He dropped a pound coin into the slot and dialled the number of Martin O'Brien's Irish mobile. "Hey, it's me," he said, as soon as O'Brien answered. "Where are you?"

"Ireland," said O'Brien. "What's up?"

"Can you get to a landline?" said Shepherd. "A call box?"

"Give me two minutes," said O'Brien.

"Text me the number, I'll call you," said Shepherd.

He went back to his CRV and sat in it until his mobile phone beeped. It was a text message from O'Brien, a Dublin number. Shepherd went back to the call box, slotted in another pound coin and dialled. "Why the Secret Squirrel?" asked O'Brien.

"We're starting to move so I need a favour with the business in the North," said Shepherd.

"Name it."

"We need a short, ideally two, something that would point to our friends on one side or the other."

"He's going ahead?"

"It looks like it. And it would be easier if the short came from there."

"Muddy the waters?"

"He was all for taking something from home. And that would be a big mistake. Can you get me something?"

"Time frame?"

"The sooner the better."

"Yeah, I can get you a couple. Souvenired them from a cache we turned over in my Rangers days. Kept them for a rainy day."

"Where are they?"

"Outside Dublin. I can get them whenever you want."

"You're sure?"

"I don't check on them every week, but they're buried deep. And if they'd been found, I would have heard."

"Can you get them, check that they'll work, then send me a text letting me know that all's shipshape? We'll come over on the ferry."

"North or South?"

"If you're in Dublin, we'll come there, pick up the shorts and head North. That route will muddy the waters, too. And we'll need a vehicle. Something unremarkable but reliable, Irish plates, buy it for cash and don't register it. We'll drive up and down in it and torch it in the South."

"And the shorts?"

"We'll be leaving them at the scene. If that's okay with you. I don't want anything to tie us in to what's happened."

"Sounds like you've got it all planned out."

"Has to be that way — one wrong move and he'll lose everything."

"Yeah, but you can see his point, right?"

"No doubt about that," said Shepherd. "I just want to be sure that he doesn't get hurt, that's all."

"I could get the whole thing sorted this end, you know that. I'd do it myself if need be."

"I know. So does he. But it's personal."

"I hear you," said O'Brien, and ended the call.

Shepherd spent Saturday afternoon watching Liam play football with his school team. There were a couple of dozen other parents standing on the touchline, and several of the fathers seemed to be taking it as seriously as a cup final, screaming themselves hoarse, offering encouragement, advice and occasionally insulting the referee. Shepherd stood with Katra. She yelped with joy whenever Liam kicked the ball and jumped up and down and hugged Shepherd when he almost scored. She had Lady on a lead and the dog seemed as excited as she was. "He's good, isn't he?" said Shepherd, as he watched Liam dribble the ball past one of the opposition.

"He's got much better this year," said Katra. "He practises a lot in the garden."

"I wish he'd put as much effort into his homework," said Shepherd.

"Oh, Dan, he's doing fine at school. Really. You don't have to worry about Liam."

The referee blew his whistle and Liam's team cheered and punched the air. Two of the fathers started shouting insults at the referee but he was obviously well used to verbal abuse and ignored them as he jogged over to his car.

Liam came running up, his shirt splattered with mud. Lady made a big fuss of him, jumping up and adding to the stains. The boy bent down to kiss her and she licked him back.

"Liam, do you have any idea how many germs there are in a dog's mouth?"

"Same as a human's," said Liam, rubbing Lady behind the ears.

"Humans don't lick their own behinds," said Shepherd.

"Some of my friends do," said Liam. He laughed. "Joke."

Shepherd grabbed him by the back of the neck. "Come on, let's go home."

They climbed into the Honda CRV, Liam and the dog in the back, Katra and Shepherd in the front. When they got home Lady rushed into the garden and Liam hurried upstairs to shower. Katra began preparing vegetables while Shepherd made himself a cup of coffee. He carried his mug through to the sitting room and dropped down on one of the sofas. Liam's mobile was on the coffee-table and he picked it up. He looked through the Gallery at the videos Liam had taken of his attempts at dog-training and laughed as he watched Lady refuse to sit, confuse "stay" with "bark" and jump up to lick the lens at every opportunity.

Shepherd clicked on another video but his smile vanished when he saw what had been recorded. A boy of about Liam's age was being attacked by half a dozen teenagers. He was black, and howling as the larger boys kicked and punched him. The attackers were whooping like angry chimps and someone was filming the attack, urging them on. The video went on for a full ninety seconds and there was no let-up in the beating.

Shepherd sat back in his sofa and ran his hand over his face. It hadn't been horseplay: it had been a frenzied, vicious attack, and there was no doubt that the boy was hurt. He played the video again. The quality wasn't great but he could make out blood trickling from the victim's nose and hear the thuds of the kicks.

He sipped his coffee and played the video for a third time. The violence wasn't as shocking now, but it was still a horrific assault. Shepherd took the phone upstairs. Liam was in his bedroom. He'd showered and changed into a Pokémon T-shirt and blue jeans and was towelling his hair dry. He grinned when he saw Shepherd, but his face fell when he saw how angry he was. "What's wrong?" asked Liam. Then he saw the phone in Shepherd's hand. "What?" he repeated. "What is it, Dad?"

"The video — where did you get the video?"

"What video? What are you talking about?"

Shepherd held the screen towards Liam and pressed the button to play the clip. When the video finished, he glared at his son. "Well? What do you have to say for yourself?"

"What are you doing checking my phone?" protested Liam.

"Strictly speaking, as I pay the bill every month, it's my phone," said Shepherd.

"You were spying on me!"

"I was looking at the videos we took of Lady, but that's not the point. The point isn't what I was doing, the point is how did that video get on your phone? Did you take it?"

"Of course not," said Liam. He threw the towel onto the bed, picked up a comb and ran it through his hair. He turned his back on Shepherd so that he could look at his reflection in the dressing-table mirror.

"Liam, where did you get the video from?"

"Somebody Bluetoothed it to me."

"Who?"

"A boy. At school."

"Why?"

Liam sighed theatrically. "Everyone was getting it. It's nothing. Just a happy-slapping video."

"A what?"

"You know. Happy slapping. It's not serious."

"Liam, a boy was assaulted." He sat on the bed. Liam finished combing his hair and turned around. "Do you know who the boy is?" Liam shook his head. "He was bleeding, Liam. He was hurt."

"Dad, it's just a bit of fun. You see worse on TV all the time."

Shepherd held up the phone. "No. This isn't a clip of someone doing something stupid, this is an assault. A criminal assault."

Liam bit his lower lip. "I'm sorry."

"I need you to promise me that you weren't there when the boy was assaulted."

"I wasn't, Dad. I swear."

"Okay, I believe you," said Shepherd.

Liam held out his hand. "Can I have my phone back?"

"I'm going to need to hang on to it for a while."

"Am I in trouble?"

"You're not in trouble, Liam. But next time someone offers to send you a video of someone being hurt, I hope you'll do the sensible thing and say no. Okay?"

Liam nodded solemnly. "Okay."

Shepherd was up bright and early on Sunday morning. Liam and Katra were still asleep when he left for his run. Lady was lying in her basket and she wagged her tail hopefully when he went into the kitchen. He patted her, then went to get his rucksack from under the stairs. He ran for the best part of ninety minutes, alternating between fast sprints and steady jogs, breaking midway for twenty minutes of sit-ups and press-ups. He was bathed in sweat when he got back to the house and helped himself to a plastic bottle of Evian water. He gulped it down greedily. A phone tree for Liam's class was stuck to the fridge so that all parents could be contacted in the event of a school emergency. The name of the teacher, Miss Claire Tonkin, was at the top and the bottom. Liam's phone was where he'd left it on the kitchen table. He picked it up and tapped out Miss Tonkin's number. He half expected her to have switched the phone off because it was Sunday but it rang out.

"Miss Tonkin?" he said.

"Yes?" she said, her voice hesitant.

"I'm sorry to bother you on a Sunday. This is Dan Shepherd, Liam's father."

"Oh, hello, Mr Shepherd — Liam's okay, I hope?"

"He's fine, but there's something I'd like to talk to you about. I know it's Sunday but I have to go to London this evening and I won't be back until next weekend."

"What's the problem, Mr Shepherd?"

"I think I'll have to show you, Miss Tonkin. But it's about a possible assault on a pupil. You'll understand when you see what I have."

"This is very unusual, Mr Shepherd."

"I know, but it is important and I can't see any other way of bringing this to the school's attention. I really do have to be in London tonight."

The line went quiet. Shepherd paced around the kitchen. Lady whimpered and wagged her tail tentatively as if she sensed his unease. "If it's that important, then I suppose you could come around to my house. But it'll have to be in the next hour or so — I have to be somewhere for lunch."

She gave him her address and ended the call. Shepherd went upstairs, showered and changed into jeans and a black wool sweater. By the time he went downstairs again, Katra was in the kitchen.

"I have to go out for a while," he said, picking up Liam's phone. "I'll have breakfast when I get back."

270

He took the phone into the sitting room, removed its memory card and transferred the video of the boy being assaulted from the card to a thumb-drive. Then he drove to Claire Tonkin's house, which was in a neat terrace on the outskirts of the town. Liam's teacher wasn't anything like he'd imagined her to be from the voice on the phone. He'd expected a fifty-something spinster in tweeds but she was in her late twenties with shoulder-length blonde hair and a disarming smile. While she wore a conservative dark blue dress and a white linen jacket there was no hiding the fact that she had a figure to turn heads. She had a strong, confident handshake and she looked him in the eye, then took him through to her living room. It was pleasant, feminine, with a comfortable three-piece suite arranged around a Victorian fireplace. There was no television, Shepherd noticed, but several shelves packed with books, most of them hardbacks. "Please, sit down," she said, waving to the sofa. "I have to say it's a pleasure to finally meet you — you seem to have missed most of the parent-teacher evenings recently."

Shepherd grimaced as he sat down. "Actually, I've missed them all," he said. "I travel a lot for work."

"You're a policeman, Liam tells me."

"Sort of," said Shepherd. "I work for SOCA, the Serious Organised Crime Agency. We do investigative work but, strictly speaking, we're civil servants rather than police officers."

"But you do get to arrest the bad guys?" she said.

Shepherd grinned. "Occasionally."

271

"That's good to hear," she said. "So, how can I help you? You said something about a pupil being assaulted."

Shepherd took Liam's mobile from his pocket. "I found a disturbing video on his phone, a video of what looks like a boy being abused." He saw a look of revulsion flash across her face and held up a hand to reassure her. "Physically abused rather than sexually," he said. "It's what they call 'happy slapping'. A group of boys hitting another boy. But it's quite savage and the boy is obviously hurt."

"The boys in the video are from our school?" asked Miss Tonkin.

"Liam doesn't know. He says he doesn't recognise anyone in the video. It might not even be the school here, of course, but I wanted to check with you. Even if it happened somewhere else it still needs investigating."

"So Liam didn't film the attack?"

"Good Lord, no," said Shepherd. "A boy in his school Bluetoothed it to him a couple of days ago."

Miss Tonkin held out her hand. "May I?" she asked.

"Sure," said Shepherd. He called up the video and showed her how to start it. She watched it with a growing look of horror on her face. "This is awful," she said, when the video had finished. "Absolutely awful."

"Do you recognise the boy?"

"I'm afraid I don't," she said, "but it's a big school."

"Has a pupil been injured recently?"

She frowned. "I don't think so."

"It's hard to see on the video just how hurt the lad is," said Shepherd. "The resolution isn't great but it looks as if he's bleeding and there's a good chance that he'd have been taken to A and E. That's not rough-and-tumble, it was a real beating."

Miss Tonkin nodded. "You're absolutely right," she said. She watched the video again. When it had finished, she shook her head. "Terrible." She held up the phone. "Can I keep this?"

"I've made you a copy," said Shepherd, handing her the thumb-drive. She passed him back the phone. "What will you do?" he asked.

"I'll try to find out who the boy is, obviously. Then we'll take it from there. We have zero tolerance to bullying, I can tell you that much." She smiled. "I do appreciate you bringing this to my attention, Mr Shepherd." She stood up and extended her hand. "Rest assured, I'll deal with it. And I hope it won't be too long before we see you here again. At the parent-teacher evening next month, perhaps?"

"I'll do my best," said Shepherd. He couldn't help thinking that if he had known how attractive Liam's teacher was he would probably have made more of an effort to attend PTA events in the past. She showed him to the front door.

When Shepherd got back to the house, Liam was in the kitchen eating cheesy scrambled eggs. Shepherd sat down at the table and gave him his phone back. "I went to see Miss Tonkin," he said.

Liam put down his fork. "You did not," he said. "Why, Dad?" He put his head into his hands.

"She has to find out what happened to the boy in the video," said Shepherd. "He was hurt, Liam."

"But, Dad, everyone will think it was me that gave it to her."

"No, they won't. And if they do, just tell them it was your dad. Someone has to investigate what happened — that boy could have been seriously hurt."

Katra put a mug of coffee in front of Shepherd. "What do you want for breakfast, Dan?"

Shepherd gestured at his son's plate. "I'll have what he's having. With toast."

"Dad, am I going to be in trouble? Because of the video?"

"You weren't involved in beating up the boy, were you?"

Liam shook his head.

"And you weren't there when it happened?"

"I just got the video, Dad. I swear. I told you yesterday."

Shepherd smiled. "Then everything'll be fine," he said. "You didn't do anything wrong."

"But I don't understand why you had to talk to Miss Tonkin."

"Because that boy was hurt," said Shepherd. "It wasn't horseplay, it was a savage beating. You're *sure* you don't know him?"

Liam shook his head. "It was just a funny video, that's all. Like you see on TV."

"Well, next time I hope you'll realise that it isn't funny when someone gets hurt," said Shepherd.

Shepherd got back to London late on Sunday night. First thing Monday morning he took the Tube to

274

Paddington Green, picked up his leathers and motorcycle helmet and went along to collect his bike from the Hyde Park car park. As he drove it back to the police station, he felt his phone vibrate to let him know he'd received a text message. He showed his warrant card to the guard at the entrance to the police car park and, after the man had checked a list on a clipboard, the metal gate rattled up and he drove in.

After he'd parked next to two Traffic bikes, he took out his phone. The message was from Martin O'Brien. "All sorted. Ready when you are." Shepherd smiled and put the phone back in his pocket.

There were two CCTV cameras covering the level he was on, one pointing at the exit, another in a corner giving a general view of the parking spaces. He took off his helmet and walked slowly towards the TSG's vans. He put his right hand into his jacket and took out one of the transponders Singh had given him.

The vans used by his Serial were the seventh, eighth and ninth in the line. He glanced over his shoulder, checking the position of the CCTV camera behind him. When he reached the first van he moved to the right and bent down as he reached the offside rear wheel arch. He pressed the button at the end of the transponder and the green light winked on. He slipped the transponder under the wheel arch and felt it fasten itself under the rim. He straightened up and walked around the rear of the van, close to the wall. He stopped and listened but there was nobody else in the parking area. He took the second transponder from his jacket pocket, switched it on, and walked behind the next van. He slid the transponder under the rear nearside wheel arch and felt it click into place.

He took out the last transponder as he walked to the third van. Once he had slotted it under the wheel arch, he went to the locker room, swinging his helmet.

While he was changing into his uniform, Nick Coker and Barry Kelly arrived. "You're in early, Terry," said Coker.

Shepherd looked at his watch. There were fifteen minutes to go before his shift started. He'd wanted to get in early to attach the transponders. "Yeah, traffic was light."

"Didn't think traffic worried you Hell's Angels," said Kelly. "And you can use bus lanes now, right?"

"Wouldn't catch me on a bike," said Coker. "Half the drivers in London don't have a licence."

"That's a fact, is it?" asked Shepherd, taking off his polo shirt and hanging it in his locker.

"You should talk to Traffic," said Coker. "It's a bloody nightmare out there. You think the illegals bother with licences — never mind tax, insurance and MOT?"

"I guess not," said Shepherd, taking his police shirt from the locker.

"Damn right," said Coker. "If one of them knocks you off your Harley he won't be hanging around, that's for sure. Off like the bloody wind."

"It's not a Harley, it's a BMW," said Shepherd.

"Bloody hell, mate, what's that?" asked Kelly, pointing at the mass of scar tissue just below Shepherd's right shoulder.

"What do you think it is?" Shepherd turned to face him, his hands on his hips.

Kelly bent forward to get a closer look at the scar. "It's a bullet wound, right? You were shot?"

"You ought to be a detective," said Shepherd, drily.

Kelly straightened. "I didn't think there was much gun crime in West Mercia. I thought sheep rustling was as bad as it got."

"Happened in Afghanistan," said Shepherd. "I was in the Paras before I became a cop."

"A raghead did that?" asked Kelly.

Shepherd grinned. "Nah, friendly fire," he joked. "Of course it was an Afghan."

"How did it happen?" asked Coker. "Firefight?"

"Sniper."

Coker took a closer look at the wound. Then he walked around to look at Shepherd's back. "There's no exit wound," he said. "Is the bullet still in there?"

"They dug it out from the front," said Shepherd. "It hit the bone and went down, just missed an artery."

"You were lucky."

"Yeah, well, I always say that if I was really lucky I wouldn't have been shot in the first place."

"What sort of gun was it, do you know?"

Shepherd turned to put on his uniform shirt. "It was a 5.45 millimetre round, fired from an AK-74," he said.

"AK-47, you mean?" said Coker.

Shepherd shook his head. "AK-74," he repeated. "It's a small-calibre version of the AK-47. The Russians manufactured it for their parachute troops, but it was so good they made it the standard Soviet infantry rifle."

277

"You know a lot about guns, yeah?" asked Kelly.

"Just the one that shot me," said Shepherd.

"Did it hurt?"

"Bloody hell, KFC, you don't half ask some stupid questions," said Coker. "Of course it bloody well hurt."

"Actually, not as much as you'd think," said Shepherd. "The body kicks in with its endorphins, natural painkillers, so immediately after the impact you don't feel much. But afterwards, yeah, it hurt like hell." He put on his tie and took out his stab vest.

"You're a war hero," said Kelly.

"I got shot," said Shepherd. "That doesn't make me a hero." He closed the door to his locker. "Any idea what we're doing today?"

"Winning friends and influencing people," said Coker. "Same old, same old."

After he had finished his shift on Wednesday evening, Shepherd drove his bike over to Chelsea where the Major lived in a three-storey mews house in a quiet side-street. There was an integral garage to the left of the front door and beyond it a concrete tub containing a well-tended conifer. Shepherd swung the kickstand down, took off his helmet and pressed the doorbell, then smiled up at the CCTV camera that covered the front of the building. As he was taking off his backpack, he heard footsteps on stairs and the door opened. The Major was casually dressed in beige slacks and a salmon pink polo shirt. He ushered Shepherd into the hallway. There was a kitchen to the right and he nodded for Shepherd to go through as he closed the front door.

278

"I'll make coffee — or do you want something stronger?"

"Coffee's fine," said Shepherd. He held up his helmet. "I'm on the bike."

"Yeah, what's the story about that? Never had you down as a Hell's Angel."

"It's part of my cover," said Shepherd, putting the helmet and backpack on a chair. "I've got to look and act like an action man."

"Because?"

"Because then they'll invite me into their gang of vigilantes," said Shepherd. He held up his hands. "I know how stupid that sounds but it's the basic plan."

"And how's it working out?"

Shepherd shrugged. "Softy, softly," he said.

"Black, no sugar?" asked the Major, holding up a mug.

"Splash of milk," said Shepherd.

The Major took a jar of coffee beans down from a shelf and ground them by hand. "The rest of the guys will be here at seven thirty. I figured you and I could have a chat first," he said.

"Sounds good," said Shepherd, taking off his motorcycle jacket and sliding onto a wooden barstool next to a chest-level counter. The kitchen was spotless with white marble flooring, stainless-steel equipment and black marble worktops.

The Major spooned coffee into a stainless-steel cafetière and added boiling water. He gestured at an A4 manila envelope on the counter. "Intel's there," he said.

Shepherd opened the envelope and slid out two head-and-shoulders shots, half a dozen surveillance photographs, satellite photographs and a number of computer printouts, several of which were marked "SECRET". He flicked through the printouts. It was all detailed information about Padraig and Sean Fox, including RUC Special Branch reports, PSNI intel and MI5 briefing notes. "This is good stuff, boss."

"Yeah, I've got friends in low places," said the Major.

"It can't come back to haunt you, can it?"

"Not if you eat it after reading it," said the Major, pushing down the plunger of the cafetière.

"I'm serious, boss," said Shepherd. "This intel is gold — if something happens to the Fox brothers, whoever gave it to you is going to have a pretty good idea of what happened."

"I think they'll take the view that the murdering bastards got what was coming to them." The Major put the cafetière in front of Shepherd along with two mugs and a milk bottle. "There'll be no comeback, Spider. I promise."

Shepherd spread the three satellite photographs over the counter. "This is Newry, right?" he asked.

"South of the town," said the Major, sitting on the stool next to Shepherd. He tapped the middle photograph. "This is Sean's farm. It was the family farm, handed down from the father who died five years ago. The barn here has underground diesel tanks and they used to hide arms in the woodland here."

"He lives alone?"

"Wife and three kids, and his mother-in-law."

"Messy," said Shepherd.

"Sunday afternoon the brothers go fly fishing, then off to the pub."

"So we get them then?"

The Major poured the coffee. "Before we go any further, there's something we have to get straight."

"I'm listening," said Shepherd.

"This is my fight, Spider. I'm doing it. I appreciate your help, and there's no one I'd rather have watching my back, but when it comes to pulling the trigger, that's my job."

"However you want to play it is fine by me," said Shepherd.

"I'm serious about this," said the Major. "If anything goes wrong, I want you to be able to say you didn't kill the Foxes. I want you to be able to say that and to mean it."

"I have no problem with that," said Shepherd.

The Major gripped his shoulder. "Thanks, Spider."

"You don't have to thank me, boss. You'd do the same for me. For any of us."

The Major picked up his mug. "So, the Foxes fish the same river every Sunday this time of year, unless it's raining. The weather forecast for the weekend looks good. They finish at about five and get to the pub just before six. Then they have a few drinks and drive back to the farm where Sean's wife cooks whatever they've caught. They normally get to the river at about one o'clock. I reckon we pick them up when they arrive, take them into the hills and do it there."

"So we'd need to get over there on the Saturday. Back here Sunday night."

"And Martin's sorted?"

"He'll fix us up with transport and he's already got two shorts, throwaways that we can leave there. He wants to go up with us but I've made it clear it's just the two of us. If you want we can do it the weekend after next. It's your call, boss."

The Major looked at the watch on his wrist, a Rolex Daytona. "Let's head up to the sitting room," he said, gathering up the sheets of paper and photographs and putting them back in the envelope.

They took their coffees up a wooden staircase to the first floor where there was a spacious room with large windows overlooking the mews. There were two dark red chester-fields either side of a Victorian cast-iron fireplace and above it an oil painting of the Duke of Wellington on horseback. The Major dropped the envelope onto the large teak coffee-table and sat down on the sofa facing the window. Shepherd had brought his backpack with him and placed it by the side of the coffee-table before he sat down. There was a sideboard against one wall, topped by more than a dozen framed photographs in most of which the Major was holding a weapon of some sort.

"I was Tommy's godfather, you know that?" asked the Major.

"I didn't."

"I always wanted kids but never found a woman prepared to put up with me long enough to have one. Henry knew that, so he practically shared Tommy with me. Let me take him to football, teach him to shoot — I think it was because of me that he signed up." The Major put his head into his hands. "That's what screws me up about this, Spider. My brother works in the City, bloody good job with all the trimmings, but Tommy always looked up to me — you know? I was the action hero abseiling down mountains and jumping out of planes, shooting the bad guys. He was always asking for war stories and I was happy enough to tell them. Took him to Hereford for a few open days when he was a kid, let him fire Hecklers and play around with the gear. He loved it." The Major sighed and leaned back. "The only time Henry and I argued was when Tommy said he wanted to sign up. Henry hit the roof, and Tommy asked me to talk to him. Do the godfather thing. Henry didn't want Tommy in the army. Nothing to do with the danger, he just figured that Tommy would have a better life in the City."

"You've done all right, boss," said Shepherd, waving his arm around the room they were sitting in.

The Major laughed. "This?" he said. "You should see Henry's places. He's got a five-bedroom duplex in Clerkenwell with views over the City, a mansion in Sussex, a villa in Tuscany and a house in the Florida Keys. Money coming out of his ears. And he wanted his son to have the same life."

"But Tommy didn't?"

"Tommy wanted to be a soldier. That's all he wanted. He compromised eventually and agreed to go to university. Studied law at Durham. Henry figured that a few years as a student would get him out of the army thing, but it didn't. Soon as he graduated he signed up. Henry never really forgave me."

"He was doing what he wanted, and that's the best that any of us can ask from life," said Shepherd.

"I know, but I was his role model. If it wasn't for me . . ."

"If it wasn't for you he could have been a banker and got run over by a bus," said Shepherd. "There's no use in looking for someone to blame . . ." He tailed off, not wanting to finish the sentence because he knew he was wrong. There was someone to blame: the men who had pumped bullets into Tommy and his friends as they'd sat down to enjoy a Chinese meal. Shepherd threw up his hands. "You know what I mean, boss. You can't blame yourself."

The doorbell rang. Shepherd sipped his coffee as the Major went downstairs. He heard voices and stood up as the other man returned with Jack and Billy Bradford. They shook hands and sat down. "I'll get you guys coffee," said the Major, and headed for the kitchen.

"How's business?" Jack asked Shepherd.

"There's never any shortage of bad guys," said Shepherd.

"Where's Martin?" asked Billy.

"Ireland," said Shepherd. "I've already filled him in."

"Just the five of us?" asked Billy.

"It's all we need," said Shepherd.

Jack stood up, walked over to the windows and looked down into the mews. "Nice place, this. What do you reckon? A million? Million and a half?"

"That much?" said his brother, frowning.

"It's Chelsea," said Jack. "Chelsea's expensive, recession or not."

The Major came in with a tray that held the cafetière, a milk jug and two clean mugs. "I bought this place twenty years ago," he said. "Practically a shell when I got it. Rebuilt it myself pretty much."

"Never pictured you with a trowel in your hand, boss," said Jack, sitting down next to his brother and helping himself to coffee.

"My father taught me," said the Major. "He was a great one for DIY."

"So what's the story?" asked Billy.

"We're going over Saturday night. More accurately, Sunday morning, first thing," said Shepherd. "Weekend after next. We'll take the ferry to Dublin as foot passengers. There's a two-thirty Stena Line sailing that gets in at a quarter to six in the morning. Martin will fix us up with transport and a couple of shorts and he can collect us at the terminal. The boss and I will drive up to Newry and do what has to be done. We already have satellite photos of the area and intel on the occupants of all the houses in the vicinity. When it's done we drive back across the border. We torch the Irish vehicle and get the last ferry back to Holyhead on Sunday night. There's a nine-fifteen sailing that gets in at half past midnight but I'll also book us on the next day's two-fifteen as a fall-back. I'll drive us back to Hereford and if all goes to plan we'll all be at work Monday morning as if it never happened."

"Sounds like a plan," said Jack, rubbing his hands together.

"It'll just be me and Spider going over," said the Major.

"Come on, now," said Billy. "You need us watching your back, boss."

"We don't need to be mob-handed," said Shepherd.

"You're driving into bandit country," said Jack. "And after what those bastards did, they'll be on high alert."

"Which is why it's better that just the two of us go in," said the Major.

"Besides, we need you two guys in the UK," said Shepherd. "We need to establish alibis. I'm supposed to be in Hereford and the boss in London. We'll leave our mobiles with you and we need to set up a pattern of calls. Jack, if you could be in Hereford with my mobile, Billy can sit here. Jack, you call the Major's landline and, Billy, you answer. Two minutes and then hang up. A few hours later, Billy uses the Major's mobile to call my mobile. Another two-minute chat. We can work out the content later." Shepherd looked over at the Major's LCD television. "You've got a video recorder?"

The Major grinned. "State-of-the-art hard disk drive," he said.

"So Billy can record what's on TV the night we're away, ideally a live sporting event. You can watch it as soon as you get back. The one worry is the Almighty." Shepherd gestured at the metal satellite phone case by the door. "If it rings, we've got one hell of a problem. There's only half a dozen people who have that number and they all know the boss personally. There'll be hell to pay if it rings and isn't answered."

286

The Major raised a hand. "The chances of it ringing are slim at best," he said. "If the shit is going to hit the fan, I usually have wind that it's coming."

"And if there's even a chance of something brewing that requires the Increment, we call this off," said Shepherd. "But there's always the possibility that something might kick off while we're over the water. If it does ring, Billy's going to have to call the boss immediately, on a throwaway mobile. The boss can then call back and claim that the sat phone is kaput."

"They'll buy that?" asked Billy.

"If you call us in, then everything gets put on hold and we come straight back," said Shepherd. "If nothing happens, there'll be nothing to investigate. The worst possible scenario would be that we do what we have to do over there and then the Almighty rings. But the chances of that are so slim that we might as well all be buying lottery tickets."

Shepherd hefted his backpack onto the coffee-table and unzipped it. "I've got new Nokias for us all and put pay-as-you-go Sim cards in, each with fifty quid's worth of credit. I've pre-programmed with our numbers and used One to Five instead of our names." He began handing the boxes out. "So, One is the boss, I'm Two, Jack's Three, Billy's Four and Martin's Five. As soon as it's all done, destroy the Sim cards and the phones. Sim cards to be snapped, singed and flushed, the phones to be crushed. Any questions?"

"Why's he Three?" asked Billy, nodding at his brother. "Why's he Three and I'm Four?"

Shepherd frowned. "What?"

Billy grinned. "Joke," he said. "Trying to lighten the moment."

"Just don't screw up on the day," said Shepherd. "If the shit hits the fan down the line, the boss's alibi has to be watertight. The first thing they do is check his phone records so you have to make those calls and you have to make sure that the neighbours don't see you. As soon as we get back to Hereford, Jack can drive the boss to London. I'll follow first thing in the morning."

"I wish you'd rethink the number of bodies," said Jack. "They're hard as nails, those Newry boys."

Shepherd chuckled. "We're no pushovers ourselves, Jack."

Victor Mironescu flicked through the channels on his massive LCD TV but couldn't find anything to watch. On the roof of his detached house in St John's Wood he had a satellite dish the size of a small car and had access to more than a thousand channels but there was rarely anything that held his attention. He tossed the remote to the blonde girl who was sitting on the black leather sofa. "Watch what you want," he said. "I'm going to shower." The girl was sixteen and had just arrived from Romania. She was gorgeous with waist-length blonde hair and big blue eyes, and Mironescu was breaking her in before setting her to work for one of his escort agencies. Sarah had been trafficked into the country, but she had come willingly and knew exactly what she would be expected to do. She had arrived as a virgin, and Mironescu had been the first man to enter her. Over the next twelve months she would be entered by a thousand men, give or take, but first she had to be taught how to handle her customers. The first night in the house she'd had a list of things that she wouldn't do. She wouldn't do anal, she wouldn't do oral without a condom, she wouldn't swallow. It had taken half a bottle of vodka, a few slaps and a lit cigarette applied to her thigh but now she did everything that was asked of her.

The doorbell rang and the girl got up, but Mironescu waved her back. "I'll get it," he said. He walked down the hallway and opened the front door. Two men stood there, both holding up small black wallets.

"Police, Mr Mironescu," said the man on the right.

Mironescu leaned forward and peered at the card he was holding. He was wearing a bright yellow fluorescent jacket over his uniform. "What do you want?"

The two men put their warrant cards away. A third uniformed officer was standing behind them, a large black man with muscular forearms.

"We need to talk to you," said the policeman in the fluorescent jacket. "We can do it here or we can arrest you and take you to the station."

"Arrest me for what?" sneered the Romanian.

The policeman pushed past him and walked along the hallway. "You can't come in without a warrant," said Mironescu. "I know my rights."

"You don't have any rights," said the officer on the doorstep. He shoved Mironescu in the chest and the Romanian staggered back into the hall. "That's assault!" he shouted.

The policeman kicked Mironescu between the legs, hard. The Romanian howled and bent double as pain seared his groin.

"No," said the policeman. "That's assault." He grabbed Mironescu by the scruff of the neck and dragged him into the sitting room while his colleague closed the front door.

The girl got off the sofa, her hands covering her face. "It's all right, darling, we're the police," said Fluorescent Jacket. He gestured at Mironescu. "Do you work for him?"

The girl nodded fearfully.

"Not any more you don't." He jerked a thumb at the policeman in the doorway. "He'll take you to a place of safety."

"I don't want to go. I want to stay here."

"How old are you, darling?"

"Nineteen," she said.

He clicked his fingers at her. "Passport."

"It's upstairs."

Fluorescent Jacket gestured at the policeman in the doorway again. "He's going to go with you to get it, so you'd better tell me the truth. How old are you?"

"Sixteen," said the girl, in tears now.

"And where are your parents?"

She sniffed. "Romania. But they know I am here."

"You're not staying with this scumbag," said Fluorescent Jacket. "Go upstairs, pack your bag, and that officer'll take you to a safe place where there are people who can help you."

290

The girl went upstairs with the policeman. Fluorescent Jacket pointed at the sofa. "Sit down, Victor."

"He assaulted me," said Mironescu. "He kicked me."

"Don't be a baby, Victor. Sit the fuck down."

"I want to see your warrant," said Mironescu, still bent over and holding his groin. "You can't come into my house without a warrant."

The policeman seized him by the collar of his shirt and threw him onto the sofa. "Do as you're bloody well told," he said.

Mironescu glared at him but he stayed on the sofa, massaging his aching groin with both hands.

"What is it with you Romanians?" asked Fluorescent Jacket, lighting a cigarette.

"What do you mean?" said Mironescu.

"All we ever get over here are the bad ones," said the policeman. He took a long drag at his cigarette and blew smoke at Mironescu. "We get the pickpockets, the gypsy beggars, the hookers, and that's about it. Why do we never hear about Romanian doctors or Romanian engineers or even Romanian cockle pickers?"

Mironescu grimaced. "I don't understand."

"What I'm saying, Victor, is it seems that we only ever get Romanian pond scum. It can't be that your whole country is pond scum, can it?"

"Why are you here?" asked Mironescu. "What do you want?"

Fluorescent Jacket's mobile phone rang and he answered it. He listened and then walked to the far side of the room so that the Romanian couldn't hear what

291

he was saying. As he was talking on the phone, the girl and the policeman came back downstairs and went out of the front door.

"You brought her in, did you, Victor? Told her she was going to work as a waitress in a nice little restaurant and then you let guys pay to bang her?"

"She knows what she's doing," said the Romanian. "Came into it with her eyes open."

"Legs open, you mean," said the policeman. "Got a lot of sixteen-year-olds, have you, Victor?" The Romanian didn't reply. "You've got — what? Three Internet escort agencies? Each with thirty girls? Maybe more? Let's call it a round one hundred, shall we? And how often do they work in a day? Three times? Four?"

Mironescu shrugged. He worked his girls hard and complained if they didn't see at least five customers a day. If they did less than four they were doing something wrong and earned a beating. Nothing too severe, of course. Nothing that would mark the merchandise. But he had no intention of telling the cops how much his girls earned.

Fluorescent Jacket blew smoke up at the ceiling. "Let's say three times a day. And they charge a hundred and fifty pounds an hour, don't they?"

Mironescu didn't answer. A hundred and fifty pounds was the cheapest price. The prettiest, youngest girls could earn much more.

"So, each girl earns four hundred and fifty pounds a day. You keep half? A third? Let's be generous and say you only take a third. That's fifteen grand a day." He nodded enthusiastically. "That's bloody good money,

Victor. Fifteen grand a day — that's more than a hundred grand a week." He looked around the expensively decorated room. "Pays for this, I suppose."

Before he could say anything else the doorbell rang. The policeman went to open it. He returned a few seconds later with two more men in dark coats. With them was a figure that Mironescu recognised immediately: his friend and business partner Lucian Popescu. Popescu's right cheek was red and his eye was puffy. He was a strong man with a weightlifter's forearms but he stood meekly between the two men in dark coats.

"You know Poppy, of course." He grinned. "I guess you prefer Poppy to Lucy, right?"

"My name is Lucian," said Popescu.

"Sit down next to your partner in crime," said Fluorescent Jacket. He stubbed out the remains of his cigarette in an ashtray and pocketed the butt.

"What is this?" asked Popescu. "What is this about? What do you want?"

Fluorescent Jacket stepped forward. As he did so he removed a small Taser from his pocket, placed it against Popescu's neck and pulled the trigger. The two prongs sparked against the man's skin and his body went into a spasm. He collapsed onto the sofa. Mironescu shuffled away from him, his eyes wide with fright. "What are you doing?" he shouted. "What the fuck are you doing?"

Fluorescent Jacket put a finger against his lips. "Sssh," he said. "Or I'll give you some of the same, Mironescu." He frowned. "What is it with that -escu on the end of Romanian names? They almost all have it, don't they?"

"What?" said Mironescu. "What are you talking about? I don't understand."

"Your names, they all end in -escu, don't they? It must mean something, right?"

"It means 'from the family of' — it means that's who you belong to," said Mironescu.

"So you're from the family of Miron," said the policeman. "And Poppy's from the family of Pop?" He laughed. "I like that, the family of Pop. Pop goes the fucking weasel."

Popescu was starting to recover from the 50,000-volt jolt. He was looking around, still dazed.

"So, Poppy, Victor and I were just discussing all the money that you boys have been making from prostitution. Fifteen grand a day, we reckon."

"You want money?" asked Mironescu. "This is a shakedown, is it?"

"Where do you keep it, Victor?"

Mironescu folded his arms. "How much do you want? How much will it cost me to get you out of here?"

"Be nice, Victor, or you'll get a taste of what Poppy there got. Where's the money?"

"Fuck you!"

Fluorescent Jacket looked over Mironescu's shoulder, but before the Romanian could turn the man behind him had pressed the prongs of a Taser against his neck and pulled the trigger. The pain was incredible but Mironescu couldn't scream as every muscle in his body had gone into spasm. He couldn't scream, he couldn't breathe, he couldn't move, he just convulsed until the Taser was taken away.

The policemen watched as Mironescu started to breathe again. Popescu was sitting with hands on his chest as if checking that his heart was still beating.

"You . . . can't . . . do . . . this," panted Mironescu.

"Yes, we can, Victor. We can, and we will. Now, where do you keep your money?"

The Romanian took several deep breaths. His legs were trembling. "Not here . . . we take it . . . to the bank," he said.

Fluorescent Jacket nodded at the man standing by Mironescu but the Romanian threw up his hands. "Okay, okay!" he said. "In the master bedroom. The cupboard. The walk-in cupboard."

"Is there a safe?"

Mironescu shook his head.

Fluorescent Jacket looked over Mironescu's shoulder. "Take him upstairs," he said. "Poppy too."

"I told you, there's no safe," protested Mironescu.

"Be a good host and show us around, Victor," said Fluorescent Jacket, waving his Taser. "Or we'll zap you again."

Mironescu's arms were seized and they took him out of the sitting room and up the sprawling marble staircase. He nodded at the master bedroom. "There," he said.

They took him into the bedroom and sat him down in a green winged armchair. Fluorescent Jacket went over to the walk-in wardrobe and pulled open the doors. At the end there was a floor-to-ceiling mirror and, on either side, rows of suits on hangers. "Very stylish, Victor," he said. He took out one of the suits and admired it. "Hugo Boss, very nice," he said. "How much would a suit like this cost?"

"Two grand, maybe."

The policeman looked at his colleagues. "Hear that, lads? Two grand for a suit. Are we in the wrong job or what?"

The men laughed. "That's what my last car cost," said one.

He put the suit back on the rack. "I don't see any money here, Victor. You're not lying to me, are you?"

"On the floor," said Mironescu. "A black bag."

The policeman knelt down and moved the suits apart. He smiled when he saw the black Adidas holdall. He pulled it out, took it over to the bed and unzipped it. It was full of banknotes that had been bundled together with elastic bands. They were mainly twenties but several of the bundles contained fifties. "How much is there, Victor?" he asked.

"Forty thousand pounds, about."

"Nice," said the policeman, zipping the bag up.

"You can't take it all," said Mironescu.

"We can do what we want," said Fluorescent Jacket. He tossed the holdall to the uniformed policeman.

"You pigs, you're no different to me," said Victor. "You steal, you cheat, you lie."

"We're nothing like you, Victor, as you're about to find out. Take off your clothes."

"What?"

"Take off your clothes."

"Why?"

"If you don't take off your clothes we'll Taser you until you're unconscious and then we'll cut them off you."

Mironescu started to unbutton his shirt with trembling hands.

"You too, Poppy."

Popescu removed his jacket and gave it to one of the policemen. As the two men undressed, the policeman went into the wardrobe and pulled out a rack of ties. He selected eight and went back into the bedroom. The two Romanians were standing by the bed. Popescu was wearing red boxer shorts with white hearts on them and Mironescu had on tight zebra-patterned satin briefs. The policeman smiled at Mironescu's choice of underwear. Mironescu cupped his hands over his private parts. "Oh, come on, Victor, you can't be shy. Not with the number of teenage girls you've raped over the years."

Mironescu glared but didn't say anything.

"Take them off, Victor. Let's have you as naked as the day you were born. And you, Poppy."

Both men removed their underwear. They stood nervously hiding their groins with their hands.

"Lie on the bed, lads, make yourselves comfortable," said the policeman. Popescu looked across at Mironescu. "Don't look at Victor," said the policeman. "He can't help you." He held up the Taser and pulled the trigger. Sparks leaped between the prongs. The two men climbed onto the bed. "On your backs, boys," said the policeman.

They did as they were told. Fluorescent Jacket tossed the eight ties to one of the policemen and he in turn handed four to his companion. They tied Mironescu and Popescu, binding their wrists to the brass bedstead and their ankles to the bottom of the bed.

"This is crazy," said Mironescu. "Just take the money and go."

"All in good time," said the policeman. He went back into the wardrobe and returned with two more ties. He held them both up. One was dark blue with black stripes, the other pale yellow with brown dots. "Which do you want, Victor?"

"What?" said Mironescu.

"Do you want the blue or the yellow?"

"Fuck you," said the Romanian. "Fuck all of you."

"The yellow, I think," said the policeman. He walked over to the bed, pushed the tie between Mironescu's lips and then wound it around his head. He tied it tightly with a double knot, then stood back to admire his handiwork. Mironescu roared with rage but the gag reduced the sound to a loud grunt. "Shout all you want now, Victor," said the policeman. He walked around the bed and gagged Popescu with the second tie.

A uniformed policeman appeared at the bedroom door. In his gloved hand he held a large carving knife.

Mironescu's eyes widened when he saw the knife and he began to struggle. Popescu turned to see what he was looking at and the blood visibly drained from his

298

face. The policeman gave the knife to Fluorescent Jacket, who grinned at the two men on the bed. "Look at the way your dicks are shrinking," he said. "I guess that's the flight-or-fright response right there. Are you scared, Victor? Maybe now you're starting to understand how the girls you raped felt. Powerless, right? You know you're going to be hurt and you know there's nothing that you can do to stop it." He ran a gloved finger carefully along the length of the blade.

There was a hissing sound from the far side of the bedroom, then a click and a whoosh. Mironescu and Popescu's heads twisted to the right. The policeman in the dark coat was holding a cheap plastic cigarette lighter in one hand and a flaming butane blowtorch in the other. He put the lighter in his pocket and adjusted the flame until it was a tight blue arrow.

The two men on the bed jerked as if they'd been electrocuted and they thrashed around like stranded fish. Fluorescent Jacket walked over to the policeman with the blowtorch and took it from him, then turned to face the bed as he played the flame up and down the blade. He grinned at the terrified men. "Yeah, I think you're starting to feel it now, aren't you?" he said, raising his voice so that he could be heard over the noise of the blowtorch. "But it's not the pain that you're going to remember. The brain can't recall pain. It doesn't work like that. It's going to hurt like hell tonight and you're going to be in pain for weeks, but eventually the pain will fade. But you'll never forget what happened to you tonight. It'll be the last thing you'll think about when you go to sleep at night and the first thing you think about when you wake up. Every time you see a pretty girl, every time you think about sex, every time you take a piss, you'll remember what we did to you and why we did it."

Tears were streaming down Mironescu's face but the gag muffled his cries. His body was still thrashing up and down but he was getting tired. Popescu was just lying motionless, his eyes wide and staring.

Fluorescent Jacket continued to wave the roaring flame along the length of the blade. "You're not going to die," he said. "The hot metal will cauterise the wound so you'll bleed but you won't bleed to death. We'll call an ambulance and you'll be treated by the good old National Health and after a few weeks you'll be able to go home. And that's what you'll do, Victor. And you, too, Poppy. You're going to go back to your shit-hole of a country because if you don't the next time we pay a visit you'll lose your dicks as well."

He held up the blade. "I think we're ready now," he said. He smiled at Victor. "I'll do Poppy first, just so you get an idea of how much it's going to hurt."

He switched off the blowtorch and put it on the bedside table next to Mironescu. The Romanian was shaking his head from side to side and pulling hard at the ties but the knots were good and the silk ties were more than strong enough to hold him. Fluorescent Jacket walked slowly around the bed. Popescu was pushing himself hard down on the mattress as if he could disappear into it. He was trying to force his legs together but the ties held them wide open. He closed his eyes tightly and made small grunting noises like an animal in pain.

Mironescu watched in horror as the policeman sat on the edge of the bed. With his left gloved hand the policeman gingerly moved Popescu's penis. Mironescu closed his eyes and looked away.

"Oh, come on, Victor, you don't want to miss this. How often do you get to see a castration, close up?"

Popescu was shaking and tears were streaming down his face even though his eyes were tightly shut. The policeman slid the knife under Popescu's testicles and then pulled it up in one smooth movement. Popescu screamed and then almost immediately passed out. The hot knife stopped much of the bleeding but blood still pooled around the injured man's groin as the policeman stood up. "Let me just get the knife hot again and then I'll do you, Victor," he said.

At the end of the shift on Thursday, Coker and Kelly persuaded Shepherd to go for a drink with them at the Hilton Hotel, a short walk from the station. They all changed into civilian clothing and walked there together. The bar was quiet and most of the clientele were suited businessmen drinking on expense accounts. "What do you want, Terry?" asked Coker.

"Soda water," said Shepherd. "Ice and lemon."

"What?" said Coker. "Have a man's drink, mate."

"I'm on the bike, Nick. I never drink and drive."

"Goody Two Shoes, huh?"

"It's a powerful machine. You can't take any liberties with it."

"Leave him alone," Kelly said to Coker. "If he doesn't want to drink, he doesn't want to drink. Some people just can't handle their booze."

Shepherd sighed. "All right, put a whiskey in the soda. Jameson's if they've got it. I'll leave the bike in the factory and get the Tube."

Coker slapped him on the back. "I'll drive you home, mate. Kilburn's on my way."

Shepherd's mobile rang. It was Katra so he went over to a quiet part of the bar to take the call. "Dan, there are two policemen here. They want to talk to Liam. I said they had to talk to you first." She was breathing heavily, as if she was scared.

"It's okay, Katra," said Shepherd. "Calm down."

"They're detectives, Dan," she said. "They're not in uniforms."

"Let me talk to them, Katra," said Shepherd.

After a few seconds a male voice came on the line. "Mr Shepherd?"

"That's right, Dan Shepherd. Who are you?"

"I'm Detective Sergeant James Hollis from Hereford CID. We're here to talk to your son, Liam. Where are you, Mr Shepherd?"

"London," said Shepherd. "I'll be here for the rest of the week. Look, what's this about?"

"Your son had a video on his phone, a video of a boy being assaulted."

"That's right. I gave a copy to Liam's teacher, Miss Tonkin."

"The headmaster called us once he got to see the video," said Hollis. "We'd like to talk to your son and we're going to need his phone."

"Liam didn't take the video. A friend of his Bluetoothed it to him."

"That's not an issue, Mr Shepherd, but we will need your son's phone."

"Do you have a warrant?" asked Shepherd.

"Do I need one, Mr Shepherd?" said Hollis.

"It's my son's personal phone. I've already given a copy of the video to the school, I don't think you need the phone as well."

"We'd like our technical people to have a look at it," said Hollis. "If you're going to be difficult then I can get a warrant."

"I'm not being difficult, Detective Sergeant Hollis. I'm just asking that you respect my rights. I have the right to not hand over my son's personal property unless you have a warrant and I am asking you to respect that right. I also need you to acknowledge that my son is a minor and that you will not be questioning him until I am there."

"Obviously we won't be talking to Liam without a responsible adult present," said Hollis.

"I'll be back at the weekend," said Shepherd.

"We'd like to talk to him sooner than that," said Hollis. "Where is Mrs Shepherd?"

"She's dead," said Shepherd, flatly.

"What about the au pair? She can sit in on the interview."

"She's Slovenian so English isn't her first language and she doesn't know her rights. Can you wait for me to get back?"

"What exactly are you doing in London, Mr Shepherd?"

"Working," said Shepherd. "Look, it's Thursday, right? I can leave here Friday evening and see you at the station with Liam first thing Saturday morning."

"Saturday is my day off," said Hollis.

"Lucky you," said Shepherd. "Look, I'm not minded to allow you to take my son's phone without a warrant, and that means you're going to be looking for a judge to sign one out of hours. And I'm not prepared to allow you to interview him without my being there. I'm sorry if you think that means I'm being difficult but you have to understand that Liam is a child and I am his father and I'll do whatever I have to do to protect him."

"Okay, how about we compromise?" said Hollis. "You give me your permission to take away Liam's phone now, and we'll hold off interviewing him until you're back in Hereford. Can we agree to that?"

Shepherd wasn't happy about letting the detective take his son's phone but he knew that Hollis wouldn't find it too difficult to get a warrant, even out of regular office hours. "That sounds reasonable," he said. "Let me talk to Katra."

The detective handed the phone back to her. "What should I do, Dan?" she asked.

"Give them Liam's phone," he said. "And ask them to give you a receipt. Also, the detective I spoke to, Sergeant Hollis, ask him for a business card. And don't

304

let them ask Liam any questions. If they say anything to Liam, anything at all, tell him to go to his room and call me back straight away."

"I will, Dan. Is Liam in trouble?"

"No, it's nothing to do with him," said Shepherd. "Just let them have the phone. And tell Liam I'll call him back later for a chat so he's not to go anywhere."

Shepherd ended the call and went back to join his colleagues. "Problems?" asked Coker.

"Why do you ask?" said Shepherd, picking up his whiskey.

"Because you had a face like thunder, that's why," he said. "You were pacing up and down like you wanted to deck somebody."

Shepherd sipped his drink. It had been a mistake letting Coker see him on phone, but it was a mistake he could turn to his advantage if he played his cards right. "It's complicated," he said. "Involves a case I was working before I transferred to the Met."

Kelly and Coker leaned towards Shepherd as he lowered his voice. "Paedophile, nasty piece of work who'd already done six years for molesting a girl over in Ireland. He moved into our patch and was working in one of the local libraries. Wasn't on the Sex Offenders Register because he was done in Ireland, not the UK." He could see that he had their full attention. "Anyway, he starts hanging around one of the local primary schools." A look of disgust flashed across Kelly's face. "Yeah, he liked them really young. He was clever, though, and never too obvious. He managed to get invited into one of the schools so that he could talk about the library. Had a little act he did with a sock puppet. Had the kids eating out of his hand. You don't have to be an Einstein to work out what his MO was. He got them laughing at his puppet, got close to the ones he was attracted to, made sure they visited the library with their parents. Then he set up a reading group on Saturday mornings so that parents could drop their kids off while they went shopping."

"Bastard," said Coker.

"Yeah," said Shepherd, swirling his drink around his glass. "He assaulted two little girls before anyone knew what was happening. One of them started having nightmares, bed-wetting, all the signs. We had a really good female detective and she spent hours with the girls and got the full story from them. We arrested the guy and he was charged but he was clever. Guess he'd used his time inside to hone his craft — you know? Our technical boys went right through his computer and there was nothing. Same with his mobile phone. Nothing in his flat. Not a magazine, not a photograph, nothing. There was no DNA evidence, he didn't take any souvenirs."

"So it was all down to the witnesses," said Coker.

"Yeah," said Shepherd. "CID had him in for questioning for hours. He got himself a legal-aid brief and he just sat there with a smirk on his face and wouldn't say anything. Not a thing."

"How were you involved, Terry? You weren't CID?"

"I was there at the arrest, and I helped with the house search."

"And there was nothing there?" said Kelly.

306

"Like I said, he was clever. We reckoned he must have had a safety-deposit box or a lock-up somewhere but we never found it. We had nothing, just the word of the girls he'd abused. And that call was to tell me that the second one had just decided not to give evidence."

"Why's that?" asked Coker.

"The first girl, she was eight, her parents took her away. The mother was Australian and she said she couldn't stand to live in the UK after what happened. They left a month or so ago. Now the second girl has just pulled out — her parents don't want to put her through a court case." Shepherd shrugged. "You can understand why, can't you? She's nine. How can anyone expect her to sit in a witness box and talk about the scumbag who assaulted her when he's sitting across from her, smirking and licking his lips?" Shepherd shuddered. "I wish I could get five minutes alone with him."

"Yeah?" asked Kelly. "What would you do?"

Shepherd sneered. "What do you think?"

"You tell me, Terry."

"I'd kick the shit out of him," said Shepherd. "I'd show him what happens to scumbags who abuse children."

"And then what?" asked Kelly. "You get sent down for assault, and he'd get thousands in compensation."

"At least I'd feel better," said Shepherd. He finished his drink and banged his empty glass on the table. "My round," he said. "What's everyone having?"

★ ★ ★

Barry Kelly gave Shepherd a lift back to Kilburn in his car, a three-year-old Renault. "What you said, back there in the bar, about giving that paedophile a seeing-to, were you serious?" he asked as they pulled up at a red traffic-light.

"Maybe," Shepherd said.

"Not just the booze talking?"

"I'm not drunk, Barry. But you can't go around beating people up, even if they are scumbag paedophiles."

"Why not?"

Shepherd looked across at him. "Why not? Because we're cops, that's why not.

"But you don't want him to get away scot-free, right?"

"Of course not."

"So you think CID will get him?" The traffic-lights turned to green and Kelly drove off.

"I'm guessing not," said Shepherd. "There was no physical evidence and no confession, so without the victims giving testimony I don't see what they can do."

"You know what you should have done, Terry? Right at the start?"

"What?"

"When you went in on that initial search, you should have taken something with you."

Shepherd frowned. "What do you mean?"

"What's the reason he's going to walk? Lack of physical evidence. So you should have provided some."

"Forensics, you mean?"

308

"Not necessarily, but forensics would have done. I was thinking some kiddie porn, on a thumb-drive. Or a file of pictures. Hand them to him, get his prints on them. Sometimes you've got to be creative."

"Are you serious?"

Kelly smiled. "Maybe."

"Would you do that? Get creative to get a conviction?"

Kelly indicated and overtook a bus. "Maybe," he repeated.

"Maybe?"

Kelly's smile widened. "Maybe. Or maybe it's just the booze talking."

Shepherd spent most of Friday driving around north London, though in the late afternoon the Serial was called off patrol to help find witnesses to a shooting in Harlesden. No one was injured, but more than a dozen shots were fired between two rival gangs. Shepherd and the rest of the team were told to canvass a block of flats that overlooked the children's playground where the shoot-out had taken place. They paired off and knocked on every door, asking if the occupants had seen or heard anything. Half the doors they knocked on remained closed, even when they were sure that someone was at home. Of those who did answer, not one person could remember seeing or hearing anything. It was par for the course, said Fogg. The residents knew that if they offered themselves up as witnesses, they risked being in the firing line themselves next time.

Charlotte Button had asked for a meeting in the Praed Street safe-house before Shepherd left for Hereford. He got there a little after seven o'clock. Jimmy Sharpe was studying some new photographs that she had fixed to the whiteboard. Shepherd joined him. The additions were police mugshots of two middle-aged white men.

"Two Romanians. They're in ICU," said Button, behind them. "They've been castrated." Sharpe shuddered. "Names are Victor Mironescu and Lucian Popescu. Well known to the police as traffickers and pimps, but on a big scale. They've been bringing in girls from Central Europe for years and working them in walk-ups. Lately they'd moved into Internet escort agencies. A few girls who've escaped from their clutches have alleged rapes and beatings but the police have never managed to make a case against them."

"It's the judgment of Solomon again," said Sharpe.

"Sorry?" said Button.

"They were rapists, they got castrated. If there's a better case of the punishment fitting the crime, I'd like to know what it is."

"It would be nice if there was a trial and evidence somewhere in the process, though," said Button.

"You said the cops couldn't make a case," said Sharpe. "Probably because the girls were too scared to give evidence." He leaned forward. "Look, if you were to ask the average man in the street what should be done with rapists and kiddy-fiddlers, ninety-nine per cent would opt for castration. It's the perfect punishment. It hurts, it's a permanent reminder, and it stops you repeating the offence."

"Actually, Razor," said Shepherd, "and I don't know why I know this, but castration doesn't do away with the erection, just the sperm." He shrugged at Button. "Sorry."

"I'm sure Razor would prefer the death penalty because then there's no chance of repeat offending," she said.

"I'm not crying any spilt milk over two Romanian pimps and rapists who lose their nuts," said Razor. "I just hope they used a rusty knife."

"They're not going to die?" Shepherd asked Button.

"Question is, will they want to live without their knackers?" sniggered Sharpe.

"They'll live," said Button. "Between you and me, the Met's Clubs and Vice Unit cracked open a bottle of champagne last night." She sipped her tea. "Someone else was celebrating, too. A battered women's refuge in Harlesden found a holdall next to their back door this morning. It contained a shade under forty thousand pounds."

Shepherd raised his eyebrows. "Wow," he said.

"Exactly," said Button. "Wow."

"But there's no proof that the money came from the Romanians, is there?"

Button smiled. "Actually, there is," she said. "One of the vans that you put a transponder on was in Chelsea last night, which is where Popescu lives. It then drove to St John's Wood, which is where Mironescu lives." She sat back and waited until she was sure that she had their undivided attention. "It then drove to Harlesden, not far from the women's refuge. And from there to Paddington Green."

Shepherd nodded. "Open and shut, then."

"Not necessarily," she said.

"Come on, Charlie. CCTV should show when the van left Paddington Green, and when it was returned."

"As soon as we ask for the CCTV footage, they'll know we're on to them," said Button. "But if we get the CCTV footage, what do we have? Shots of a van leaving the station and returning."

"With the transponder showing where they went in between," said Shepherd. "Like I said, open and shut."

"Circumstantial," said Button. "And we won't know who was on board the van. Remember, Popescu and Mironescu are unlikely to say anything, and they've never left forensics behind before so I doubt they will have this time. They're cops so there's no way they'll break under questioning, so that doesn't leave us with much."

"So what's the plan?"

"The plan is the same as it's always been — you have to get closer to them. Ideally get them to take you along."

"Terrific," said Shepherd.

"Or find out who the next victim is and we can mount a surveillance operation," she said.

"That might be easier," said Shepherd.

"Keep your ear to the ground, see what gets them riled up," said Button. "If you can get a hint as to who they'd like to see taken out of commission, we can take it from there." She drank some more tea. "What are you doing over the weekend?"

"I'm heading straight back to Hereford after this," said Shepherd. "Liam's got a football match."

"You should think about boarding-school," said Button. "They really enjoy it when they get to their teens."

"I spend hardly enough time with him as it is," said Shepherd. "And I like hanging out with him. I figure it won't be long before he doesn't want me cheering on the sidelines so I might as well enjoy it while it lasts."

"What about you, Razor?"

"My new best friend Gary Dawson is taking me to a fund-raiser in south London," said Sharpe.

"I'd have thought that after his last brush with the TSG he'd have given it a miss," said Shepherd.

"It doesn't seem to have put him off," said Sharpe. "He rang me, asked if I wanted to go. I don't think he's trying to draw me into anything. Hardly ever talks about his work, or mine."

"So what do you guys talk about?" asked Button.

"This and that. Politics, sport. Guy stuff. But he's certainly not asking me to do any favours on the SOCA front. I think I'm wasting my time."

"Do we still think that Dawson is one of the vigilantes? I hardly ever see him talking to anyone in the Serial," said Shepherd. "He nods to Fogg but that's as far as I see him go."

"He might be careful," said Button.

"Or he might just be a cop who happens to have right-wing political views," said Shepherd.

"Right-wing racist views," said Button. "And that's not compatible with his job as a police officer."

Shepherd stood up. "You know, I never thought I'd be working for the thought police when I signed up for SOCA," he said. "Are we done? I've got a train to catch."

Shepherd woke up early on Saturday morning and went for a ten-mile run with his brick-filled rucksack. Liam was having breakfast with Katra when he got back. "Don't you eat anything other than cheesy scrambled eggs?" he asked.

"It's the breakfast of champions," said Liam.

Shepherd took a bottle of Evian from the fridge. "I'm going to shower, and then we've got to go and see the police about that video."

"Dad . . ." Liam moaned. "Do we have to?"

"Yes, we do," said Shepherd.

"Can we take Lady?"

"No, of course not," said Shepherd. He ruffled Liam's hair. "It'll be fine. Don't worry."

"I'm not in trouble, am I?"

"I told you already that you're not. Stop worrying." Shepherd went upstairs, showered, and put on a white shirt, dark blue tie and a grey suit.

Liam laughed when he walked back into the kitchen. "It's like you're dressed for a job interview."

"Yeah, well, it won't hurt to look respectable. The police often go by appearances. They shouldn't, but they do." He adjusted his tie.

"You look very nice," said Katra. "Like a businessman."

Shepherd grinned and picked up the keys to the CRV. "We won't be long," he said.

"And afterwards you'll come to the football match?"

"Sure," said Shepherd. He could see that his son was nervous, even though he hadn't done anything wrong. "There's no need to worry, Liam. Really. We're just going to have a chat with them, that's all."

Shepherd drove to Hereford police station and parked on the street close by. He walked with Liam into the main entrance, went up to the reception desk and told the middle-aged female sergeant behind the desk that he was there to see DS James Hollis. She asked them to sit on the orange plastic chairs below a line of posters warning of the dangers of drugs, rabid dogs and knives. Shepherd smiled to himself as he sat down. Terry Halligan had spent two years working at Hereford police station but this was the first time he had actually been inside.

"Why are you smiling?" asked Liam.

"Because I'm happy," said Shepherd.

"Are all police stations like this?"

Shepherd looked around. "Pretty much. Some are more modern, some are a bit older, but, yeah, this is where people come to talk to the police. The offices are through the door there. That's where the CID will be, and all the civilian staff who do the paperwork."

"And cells for prisoners?"

"Sure, there'll be cells. Probably close to the rear entrance so that prisoners can be brought in through the back."

315

"It doesn't look special, does it? It looks very ordinary."

"It is ordinary — it's just a building," said Shepherd. "And most of the work done here is pretty boring."

"You don't work in a police station, do you?"

"No, I don't have an office," said Shepherd. "I don't even have a desk."

"I don't think I'd like to work in a place like this," said Liam.

"Yeah, I know what you mean," agreed Shepherd.

A side door opened and a man in his late thirties smiled at Shepherd. "Dan Shepherd?" he asked.

Shepherd stood up. "That's me," he said. He put his hand on his son's shoulder. "And this is Liam."

"Thanks for dropping by," said Hollis. He had thinning hair and a spreading stomach and was wearing a tweed jacket with patches on the elbows that gave him the look of a college sociology lecturer. He held the door open. "Please, come on through."

Shepherd and Liam walked through the door into a cream-painted corridor. "Second door on the left, please," said Hollis, from behind them.

Shepherd and Liam walked along the corridor. Shepherd frowned when he saw the sign on the pine-effect door. "Interview Room". "This isn't a formal interview, is it?" he asked the detective.

"It's just a quiet place to talk, sir," said Hollis. "The CID room is a bit cramped." Shepherd pushed open the door. There was one table in the room, against the far wall, and above it, on a shelf, a double-tape-recording system. There were two CCTV cameras at

316

opposite ends of the room. The detective pointed to the chairs on the left. "Why don't you and your son sit there and I'll go and get my colleague?"

Shepherd and Liam sat down while Hollis closed the door. "Is this where they interrogate suspects?" asked Liam.

"I think question rather than interrogate," said Shepherd, "but, yes, this is where they do it." He nodded at the tape recorder. "These days they have to record every interview and the suspect gets a copy so both sides have a record of what's been said." He pointed up at the CCTV camera opposite them. "Usually they take a video as well."

"To stop the cops beating up the bad guys?"

Shepherd laughed. "Not exactly," he said.

The door opened and Hollis walked in, followed by a younger detective who was holding a briefcase. "This is my colleague, Detective Constable Graham Cooper."

Cooper shook hands with Shepherd and nodded at Liam, then sat down facing Shepherd. He was in his mid-twenties with square-framed spectacles and a receding hairline that suggested he would be completely bald before he reached middle age. "Thank you for coming in, Mr Shepherd," he said. He put the briefcase on the table, opened it, and took out a plastic evidence bag. Inside was Liam's Nokia phone. He put the phone on the table and the briefcase on the floor. "This is your phone, right, Liam?"

Liam nodded.

"Why the bag?" asked Shepherd.

Cooper pushed his spectacles further up his nose. "Sorry?" he said.

Shepherd pointed at the bag. "Why is my son's phone in an evidence bag?"

"Because it's evidence," Cooper said, speaking slowly and clearly, like a teacher explaining something to a particularly dull pupil.

"Evidence of what?" asked Shepherd. "I gave the video to Liam's teacher and presumably she gave it to you."

"The headmaster, Mr Edmunds, gave us the video," said Hollis. "We're now investigating the assault that took place."

"Fine, I understand that, but I still don't see why my son's phone is evidence. He didn't take part in the assault, he didn't film the assault. All that happened is that someone Bluetoothed the video to his phone."

"There's no reason to get upset, Mr Shepherd," said Cooper.

Shepherd sat back and placed his hands palms down on the table. "I'm not upset," he said calmly. "I simply asked you a question."

"Frankly, Mr Shepherd, you're here to answer questions, not ask them." He smiled and nodded as if he expected Shepherd to nod in agreement. Shepherd folded his arms and stared back at him. He was starting to get a bad feeling about the two detectives. Far from simply helping them with their inquiries, he felt that he and Liam were being treated as suspects.

"So, Liam, can you confirm that this is your telephone?" asked Cooper.

Liam looked fearfully at his father. Shepherd smiled encouragingly. "It's okay, Liam," he said.

Liam nodded at Cooper. "Yes, it's mine."

"And you had a video on the phone that you say was Bluetoothed to you? A video of a boy being assaulted?"

"Do you know who the boy is?" asked Shepherd.

Cooper held up a hand as if he was stopping traffic. "Please, Mr Shepherd. Can you allow your son to answer?"

"I don't appreciate the way you're treating us like suspects," said Shepherd.

"We need to know where Liam got the video from," said Cooper.

"I didn't film it," said Liam, quickly.

"It's okay, Liam," said Shepherd. "Let me handle this." He smiled at the detective. "I'm not sure that my son needs to be involved any more than he already is," he said. "I'm sure dozens of pupils got the video — it was probably passed from phone to phone."

"You're probably right," said Cooper. "But we still need Liam to confirm who gave it to him."

"Why?"

"Because we need to know who filmed the incident," said Cooper. "We know that Liam received the video via Bluetooth. And we know the number that it was Bluetoothed from, and we know who owned the phone that sent the video to the Liam's phone. But we need Liam to tell us who was using the phone at the time."

"Maybe I'm being obtuse, but if you already know who sent the video to Liam, why do you need him to tell you?"

Cooper leaned forward. "We know which phone the video came from, but we don't know who had the phone at the time," he explained patiently. "The last thing we want is to go and talk to the owner of the phone only to have him tell us that he didn't have the phone at the time, or it had been stolen, or any other nonsense."

"But Liam won't have to give a statement, or appear in court?"

Cooper sat back and clicked his pen. "All we're doing at the moment is conducting an inquiry, gathering information," he said.

"I understand, but I don't want Liam in court over this," said Shepherd.

"Mr Shepherd, as I've said several times now, we are just conducting an investigation. But if you continue to obstruct our inquiries, that most certainly would be an offence."

"Dad . . ." said Liam, his eyes wide.

"It's okay, Liam," said Shepherd.

"Why don't you tell them you're in the police?" whispered Liam.

Hollis raised his eyebrows. "You're in the job?" he asked Shepherd.

"SOCA," said Shepherd.

Hollis nodded. "Doing what?"

"I'm on the investigation side," said Shepherd. "Look, guys, I understand your concerns and I want to help. I was the one who reported the video in the first place, remember?"

320

"Then you'll have no problems in continuing to assist us with our inquiries," said Cooper.

"With a view to charging who, exactly?"

"The boys who carried out the assault, of course," said Cooper. "And there is something else." He reached down and opened his briefcase and took out a small DVD player. He put it on the table and switched it on. "We had our technical boys take a copy of the video off the phone to enhance the picture and sound. They've put it onto a disc so we can see it in more detail."

He pressed the play button. The DVD whirred and the screen flickered into life. The picture was bigger than it had been on the phone but the quality wasn't much better. They watched it in silence, though Liam looked away towards the end, when the boy was being kicked in the stomach.

"You've identified the boys carrying out the assault?" asked Shepherd.

"One of them is at your son's school," said Cooper. "We know who he is but we haven't spoken to him yet. We want to know who took the video."

"Why's that so important?" asked Shepherd.

Cooper pressed the stop button. "Listen to the soundtrack," he said. He pressed play again and boosted the volume. There were shouts and curses and the screams of the boy being attacked, but there was a single voice urging them on: "Go on, kick him, kick the bastard. Harder, go on, give it to him, kick the black bastard."

Now Shepherd understood why the police were so keen on identifying whoever had been filming the attack. It was racist and in the police's eyes that made the assault much more serious.

"You hear that?" asked the policeman.

"Yes," said Shepherd.

"So I'll ask you again, Liam. Who Bluetoothed you the video?"

Liam looked over at his father. Shepherd nodded. "You have to tell him, Liam."

"A boy in the year above me at school," said Liam.

"His name, Liam," pressed the detective. "What is his name?"

"Peter Talovic."

"Can you spell that for me, please?"

Liam hesitantly spelled out the name.

"Is that consistent with what you know?" asked Shepherd.

Cooper didn't answer but Hollis nodded.

"Talovic? Is that Serbian?"

"Bosnian," said Hollis. "The phone number is registered to the boy's father. Jorgji Talovic. He was a Bosnian refugee who fled the former Yugoslavia, but he's a naturalised British citizen now."

"But that's not relevant to our inquiries," said Cooper, clicking his ballpoint pen impatiently. "When was this?" he asked Liam. "When did Peter Talovic Bluetooth the video to you?"

"About two weeks ago."

"And where did this Bluetoothing take place?"

"What do you mean?" asked Liam.

"Where were you when you got the video?"

"At school. In the playground. He was giving it to anyone who wanted it. He said it was fun."

"And anyone who wanted it got it from Peter, did they?"

"Some kids got it from other kids. I Bluetoothed it to three or four kids."

"But Peter was the one who took the video, right?"

Liam nodded.

"Did you see him make the video?"

"No," said Liam.

"We've already agreed that Liam wasn't there when the attack took place," said Shepherd.

"Please allow your son to answer the question," said Cooper.

"You're trying to trip him up," said Shepherd. "You're asking the same question in a different way. He's already told you that he wasn't there when the attack took place. So he couldn't have been there when the video was made."

Cooper sat back in his chair and clicked his ballpoint pen. "If your son hasn't done anything wrong there's no question of tripping him up," he said.

"My son isn't here to be interrogated," said Shepherd.

"I was simply asking a question, Mr Shepherd. There's no need to be hostile."

Shepherd had a sudden urge to grab the detective and smash his face down onto the table, but he forced himself to smile. "I'm not being hostile, Detective Cooper," he said softly. "I'm simply looking after the interests of my son. We're happy to help you, and I would point out again that I was the one who first brought this to your attention."

"To the school's attention," corrected the detective.

Shepherd nodded, accepting the point.

Cooper leaned forward and smiled ingratiatingly at Liam. "So, Liam, when Peter Bluetoothed the video to you, did he say anything?"

Liam frowned. "Like what?"

Cooper shrugged. "Anything at all."

"He just said it was a cool video, a video of a boy being happy-slapped."

"But did he say anything of a racist nature?"

"Like what?" asked Liam.

"Did he, for instance, refer to the racial group to which the boy belonged?"

Liam looked at Shepherd. He was close to tears again.

"Look at me, Liam, not at your father," said Cooper.

"I don't understand the question," said Liam.

"Did he say that the boy in the video was black?"

"No."

"He didn't refer to the boy in a derogatory manner?"

Liam shook his head. "I don't think so."

"Is that yes or no?" asked Cooper, leaning forward.

"It's what he said," interjected Shepherd. "He doesn't know."

"He didn't say that he didn't know, Mr Shepherd. He said that he didn't think so."

"I don't remember," said Liam.

"There you are," said Shepherd. "He doesn't remember." He pushed back his chair and stood up so that he was looking down at the two detectives. "I think you have the information you need, detectives," he said. "I think we'll go now."

Hollis stood up. "Thank you for coming in, Mr Shepherd." He smiled at Liam. "And thank you, Liam, for being so helpful."

"Come on, Liam, let's go," said Shepherd. As Liam stood up, Shepherd pointed at the phone in the evidence bag. "Can we have Liam's phone back?" he asked Cooper.

"I'm afraid not. It's still evidence," said Cooper, putting his hand on it as if he thought Shepherd would try to take it.

"But you have the video, why do you need the phone as well?"

"Evidence," repeated Cooper. "You can have it back once the case is over."

"So there is a case?" said Shepherd.

"That depends on the results of our investigation," said Cooper, putting the phone and the DVD player back in his briefcase. "Well, thank you for coming in, Mr Shepherd." He smiled at Liam, but it was a fake baring of the teeth, like a shark preparing to bite. "And you too, young man."

Liam nodded but he still looked fearful. Shepherd put a hand on his shoulder. "Come on, Liam, let's get you ready for the football match." He shook hands with the two detectives. Hollis's hand was firm and strong, but Cooper's felt like a dead fish, limp and lifeless. "You guys have my mobile-phone number. Give me a call if you need anything else."

"We will, Mr Shepherd," said Hollis. He ushered Shepherd and Liam down the corridor and opened the door to Reception. "Really, we are grateful to you for coming in, and for bringing this to our attention. I'm sorry if it got a bit heated in there. My colleague can sometimes be a little over-enthusiastic."

"No problem," said Shepherd.

Hollis smiled down at Liam. "And don't worry, Liam, we'll take care of your phone and I'll make sure you get it back as soon as possible."

"Thank you," said Liam, quietly.

Shepherd and Liam went outside and climbed into the CRV. Liam sat in silence until Shepherd pulled up outside their house. "They were horrible, weren't they?" he said, in a small voice.

"Yeah," agreed Shepherd. "They weren't very helpful. The detective sergeant wasn't bad but that DC was behaving like an idiot."

"It was like they were blaming me. And I didn't do anything wrong, not really."

"I know, Liam. They were just doing their job."

"It didn't feel like that, Dad. They made it feel like you and me were criminals. And we're not." He looked at Shepherd. "Why didn't you tell them that you were an undercover policeman?"

"Because I'm not a policeman, not really," said Shepherd.

"But you were before you joined SOCA."

"That's right, but now I'm a civil servant, not a policeman."

"But you should have told them that you worked under cover, that you catch some of the biggest criminals in the country."

"It's not as easy as that, Liam."

"But you go after real villains, Dad, and they're just . . ."

"Just what?"

"It doesn't matter."

"No, tell me."

Liam sighed. "They're not important, Dad, and you are. And yet they were really horrible to you. You should have told them."

"Keeping a low profile is part of my job," said Shepherd. "It's best that people don't know that I work under cover. You're one of very few people who know what I do." He winked at Liam. "Come on, let's get you ready for football. Later I'll get you a new phone."

"Are you serious?"

"Sure. I told the detectives that they could have yours, so the least I can do is to get you a new one."

"Can I have an iPhone? Please?"

"Liam . . ."

"Dad, the iPhone is so cool. It's the coolest phone ever."

"Let me think about it," said Shepherd, climbing out of the CRV.

"Does that mean yes?"

"It means I'll think about it," said Shepherd.

It wasn't until his third week with the TSG that Shepherd got his nickname. He had arrived early on

Wednesday morning and parked his bike in the Paddington Green car park. Kelly and Coker were already in the team room. "Hey, Easy Rider, how's it going?" asked Kelly.

"Please don't tell me that's my nickname," said Shepherd.

"It's a work in progress," said Coker. "But we like the bike theme."

Castle and Simmons walked into the room. "I've just seen Foggy," said Castle. "We're in Harlesden today — the borough wants to do something about street robberies so it's a day of stop-and-search."

"There's an easy way of cutting down Harlesden's street crime," said Kelly. "Most of the muggings and car-jackings are down to the same six faces. Let's just pay them a visit."

"You know that's not gonna happen any time soon," said Castle. "Until then, we just drive around and fly the flag."

"Wanna game of snooker today?" asked Coker. "Make it more interesting?"

"Snooker?" asked Shepherd. "How does that work?"

"You've never played snooker?" said Kelly. "Great fun. Traffic do it all the time. First you stop a red car or a guy wearing red. That's one point. Then you go for a black car or black clothing. That's seven points. Or six if you get a pink, five for blue and so on. Then you go for another red. We try to get a hundred and forty-seven in a shift."

"The perfect break," said Castle.

328

"You're joking, right?" said Shepherd. "This is part of the newbie initiation, right? You get me stopping red cars all day?"

"He's sharp," Castle said to Coker.

"As a knife," said Kelly.

Fogg appeared at the door. "Briefing room in ten," he said. "Harlesden today."

"We know, Skip," said Kelly.

They spent the morning driving around the main streets of Harlesden. Simmons was driving, Coker was sitting in the operator's seat and Shepherd had taken Coker's place in the bingo seat.

Shepherd called out numbers of vehicles that he thought were suspicious. For the first couple of hours he worried about being accused of racial profiling so deliberately tried to find white or Asian drivers to check on rather than black but he soon realised it wasn't possible. Black drivers made up the majority and the simple fact was that their vehicles had the most issues that merited a stop-and-search. During the morning they found several small amounts of marijuana, a glove box full of crack pipes, and a carrier bag containing four thousand pounds that the driver claimed to have won at a betting shop and even had a receipt to back up his story. They seized one car that had no insurance, mainly because the driver had made a point of screaming abuse at Fogg.

They stopped at Harlesden police station for lunch and, again, Shepherd noticed looks of resentment from the local police. The TSG team sat at their own table and most of the locals studiously avoided eye-contact. Fogg gave them forty minutes to eat and then they piled back into the van. Within five minutes Shepherd spotted the driver of a red Polo hide a cigarette as they went by. He called out the registration number and the registered keeper of the car was a known drug-dealer. They did a stop-and-search and found a small amount of cannabis that merited a caution and nothing else. The driver was a middle-aged white man with a shaved head and the words LOVE and HATE tattooed across his knuckles. Despite his Neanderthal looks he was polite to the point of deference and called them all sir, even Castle.

Five minutes later Shepherd saw a black Series Seven BMW stop at the traffic-lights ahead of them. He scanned the number plate without thinking but realised immediately that it was one of the numbers on the borough's intelligence briefing notes they'd received that morning.

Coker was in the operator's seat, next to Simmons. "Hey, Lurpak, the BMW up ahead, it's red-flagged," said Shepherd.

"You're just trying to pot the black, aren't you?" said Kelly.

"I'm serious — it's on the intel sheet," said Shepherd. He read out the registration number and Coker tapped it into the MDT. The vehicle's data appeared on the screen as Fogg flipped through the briefing notes. The BMW was showing as uninsured.

"You've got a good memory," said Fogg, tapping the sheet. "Registered owner is Anthony Lambie, a.k.a.

Crazy Boy. Skipped his last court appearance. Usually rides with Ryan Roberts, a.k.a. Drive By."

"They put a lot of effort into their nicknames, don't they?" said Turnbull.

"There's three in the car, Skip," said Coker. "Three black males."

"Pull them over, Nipple," said Fogg, slipping his notes under his seat. "Everybody outside on this one."

Simmons edged the van forward. As the lights turned green and the BMW pulled away, he switched lanes and drove up behind it. Coker hit the siren and Simmons flashed the lights. "They'd better not run because we'll never catch a Series Seven," he said.

"We'd have trouble catching a number-seven bus with you driving," said Castle.

The BMW indicated left and pulled in at the side of the road. The two men in the front were talking or arguing.

"No insurance," said Coker.

"Let's do it," said Fogg. "And be careful."

Parry pulled open the side door and jumped out as Coker piled out of the front passenger door. Coker headed for the driver's side of the BMW while Parry walked quickly along the pavement, his arms swinging either side of his barrel chest.

Castle exited next and she hurried after Coker but stopped at the rear so that she could watch the passenger in the back of the BMW. Kelly moved up behind Parry so that he could watch the front passenger but also had the man in the back in sight.

Shepherd climbed out of the van, followed by Turnbull and Fogg. The sergeant held back so that he could see what was going on. Shepherd saw Simmons lean forward to switch on the video camera that covered the front of the van. Shepherd nodded at Turnbull and walked around to the front of the BMW.

The driver wound down the window. He was a big West Indian with a gold ingot hanging from a thick chain around his neck and a large diamond set into the lobe of each ear. "What seems to be the problem, Officer?" he drawled.

"Step out of the vehicle, please, sir," said Coker.

"Do you want to see my licence?" said the man, reaching into his trouser pocket.

"Keep your hands where I can see them and step out of the vehicle, please, sir," said Coker, with a harder edge to his voice.

"Okay, okay," said the man. He opened the door and grunted as he climbed out. He looked over at Parry and nodded in acknowledgement of the policeman's bulk. Parry nodded back, his face like stone. "So, what's the problem?" asked the man.

"Driving licence and insurance," said Coker, holding out his hand.

The man took out a Gucci wallet and found his licence. He gave it to Coker. The rear passenger climbed out of the car. Kelly took him by the arm and led him away from the vehicle. He asked the man for his name. It was Ryan Roberts. "What's occurring?" asked Roberts.

"Just wait until we've had time to question the driver," said Kelly. "Then we'll decide what's occurring."

There was a bus stop on the other side of the road and half a dozen passengers watched with undisguised curiosity. Cars were slowing as if passing the scene of an accident, and while pedestrians on their side of the road gave the police a wide berth, they still watched what was going on as if it was an episode of their favourite soap.

"Anthony Lambie?" said Coker.

"That's what the licence says."

"Insurance?"

"It's at home."

"Yeah, well, my computer tells me a different story, Mr Lambie. It tells me that this vehicle isn't insured."

"Computers make mistakes," said Lambie.

Coker waved him towards the pavement. "Step away from the traffic, Mr Lambie, while we just check that you're not carrying anything you shouldn't be carrying."

"This is BS," said Lambie. "You stopped me because I'm a black man in an expensive car."

"No," said Coker. "We stopped you because you're a black man in an expensive car without insurance. Now, please, onto the pavement. I'd hate to see you knocked over by a passing bus."

Lambie walked away from the car onto the pavement with Coker. Castle followed close behind and Shepherd and Turnbull moved to take up position next to Coker. "This is BS," repeated Lambie.

The front passenger got out of the car and Parry took him to the side and began patting him down.

Fogg walked over, holding the intelligence briefing. "You were supposed to appear at Harrow Magistrates Court two weeks ago," he said to Lambie.

"I was at a funeral. My brief's handled it."

"Not according to the information we've got," said Fogg.

"Yeah, well, your information's wrong," said Lambie. "Probably came from the same computer that told you I've got no insurance. My brief's got it sorted. I'm in court again next week. And it's a bullshit motoring offence, a fine at the most."

"You knocked a kid off his bike."

"Fool drove in front of me," said Lambie. "Cost me two grand to get the paintwork sorted."

"My heart bleeds," said Fogg. He nodded at Castle. "Put the cuffs on him, we're taking him in."

Castle took her Speedcuffs from their holster and stepped towards Lambie. "I don't want no bitch touching me," he said. "I'm a Muslim."

"She's only going to cuff you and pat you down," said Fogg.

"She ain't touching me," said Lambie.

"You don't have a choice," said Fogg. Castle took another step towards Lambie, holding out the cuffs.

"Fuck that!" shouted Lambie. "Ain't no female pig putting her hands on me."

Shepherd moved to stand next to Castle. "Don't give us a hard time, sir," he said. "Just put your hands behind your back and let us do our job."

Lambie lunged forward and hit Castle on the chest with both hands, pushing her back. She lost her balance, glared at him and moved forward again. Lambie raised his hands to hit her again, but Shepherd stepped forward and hit him on the side of the chin with a powerful uppercut. Lambie's legs folded and he slumped to the pavement.

"Bloody hell, Terry," said Fogg.

"Glass jaw," said Turnbull.

"The bigger they are, the harder they fall," said Castle.

"You hit him," shouted Roberts, pointing at Lambie, who was lying on his back, his eyes shut, breathing heavily through his nose. "You can't do that — you can't go around hitting people."

"We're the TSG, mate," said Kelly. "That's what we do. Now, stop jumping about or you'll get the same."

Fogg flashed Kelly a warning look. "It was necessary force to prevent him continuing a physical attack on our officer," he said. He nodded at Castle. "Cuff him and put him on the bus," he said.

Castle knelt down, rolled Lambie onto his front and put on the handcuffs. Lambie started to groan. Castle and Turnbull hauled him to his feet and dragged him towards the van.

"Right," said Fogg, putting his hands on his hips. "We're going to pat down the two of you, then we're going to search your vehicle. If you give me any problems, any lip, if you even so much as look at me wrong, you're going back to the station. Are we clear?"

Roberts and the other man nodded.

"And if we find drugs or weapons in the car, you're coming in."

"Ain't nothing in the car. We ain't stupid," said Roberts.

"Glad to hear it," said Fogg. He waved for Kelly and Coker to search the two men, who, without being asked, turned around, spread their legs and leaned against the wall with their hands above their heads. Fogg grinned at Shepherd. "That's TV for you," he said. "Our procedure is to search them standing up with their arms stretched out to the side, but these guys see so many movies and reality TV programmes that they automatically assume the position." He waved at the BMW. "Give Carpets a hand going over the car, see if they're hiding anything."

Kelly and Coker methodically searched the two men, from their collars down to their ankles, then made them remove their training shoes and socks. Shepherd opened the front passenger door of the BMW, checked the glove compartment and under the seats, examined the door panels to see if they'd been moved, then checked the back of the car. Parry went through the boot, removing the carpeted floor so that he could check the spare tyre and tool kit.

By the time they'd finished Kelly and Coker were filling out 5090s. "Car's clean, Skip," said Parry.

"Right, gentlemen," Fogg said, to the two men, who were bending down and tying their shoelaces. "Strictly speaking we can impound the car because it doesn't have insurance, but you've caught me on a good day so if you get in there and get it out of my sight within the next thirty seconds you can keep it."

"Okay, okay," said Roberts. He hurried over to the BMW, one of his shoelaces flapping, his copy of the 5090 in his hand. The other man got into the front passenger seat and they drove off. The team watched them go down the street and make a quick left turn.

"Bloody hell, Terry, you've got a bit of a short fuse there," said Fogg.

Kelly gripped Shepherd's shoulder. "Yeah, a short fuse," he said. "I think we've got Terry's nickname. Three-amp."

Parry chuckled. "Nice one," he said. "Three-amp it is."

"Don't I get a say in this?" asked Shepherd.

"No, Three-amp, you don't," said Coker.

"Careful, Lurpak, he might take a swing at you," said Kelly.

"It was a one-off, guys, it won't happen again," said Shepherd.

"The slag asked for it," said Kelly. "He had no right laying his hands on Pelican. If anyone's going to be touching her tits, it's us."

"What about the video camera in the bus?" asked Shepherd. "Is that going to be a problem?"

"It would if it had been on," said Fogg.

"I thought I saw Nipple switch it on when we stopped the car," said Shepherd.

"Yeah, but it'll have been off when you let fly," said Fogg. He grinned. "What can I say? We're always having technical hitches, aren't we, lads?"

"Always breaking down," agreed Kelly.

"Bloody nightmare," said Parry.

"Come on, lads, back on the bus," said Fogg. "Let's get Crazy processed and we can call it a day."

They piled into the van. Lambie was slumped in the prisoner's seat while Castle and Turnbull stood over him.

"What happened?" said Lambie, groggily.

"You fainted," said Castle.

Lambie groaned. "You hit me," he said. "My jaw hurts like hell."

"I'm a woman," said Castle. "I don't go around beating up men, it wouldn't be right."

"Someone hit me," said Lambie. "My mouth's bleeding. One of you bastards punched me."

"No, mate," said Turnbull. "You must have hit your chin on the ground when you fainted. Not an epileptic, are you? Maybe you should be wearing one of them padded helmets."

"You bastards," said Lambie. "Police brutality, that's what it is."

"Tell it to your solicitor when we get to the nick," said Fogg. "Until then, keep your mouth shut."

Lambie was taken to Harlesden police station to be processed. He made no mention of being hit and when the custody sergeant asked him how he had hurt his chin, Lambie said he'd cut himself shaving. Fogg told Turnbull and Coker to handle the paperwork while the rest of the team went to the canteen for coffee. There was less than an hour to go before the end of their shift and by the time Lambie had been fingerprinted and had had a DNA sample taken it would be time to head back to Paddington Green.

Shepherd took his coffee over to a corner table but he was intercepted by Castle. She didn't look happy. "What's up?" he asked.

She leaned towards him, keeping her voice low so that she couldn't be overheard by the rest of the team. "The thing is, Terry, it's hard enough being a woman in this unit without having you riding in as a white knight every time it gets a bit tough out there."

"What?" said Shepherd, genuinely confused by her reaction.

"You saw a punter getting heavy with me and you piled in like I was a little girlie out of my depth."

"Hey, Carolyn, it wasn't like that at all."

"That's what it looked like. And I can take care of myself. I've been with the TSG for four months. You're the newbie."

"Okay," said Shepherd. "I hear you. But hand on heart, what I did was nothing to do with you being a woman. I'd have done the same if it had been one of the guys who was in trouble."

"I wasn't in trouble, Terry. I was handling it."

"He hit you, Carolyn. The slag shouldn't have done that."

"Agreed. But it was up to me to give him tit-for-tat. I don't need a man to fight my battles."

Shepherd grinned. "Obviously," he said.

She grinned back. "Just so you know," she said. She punched him on the shoulder, hard enough for him to spill his coffee. "I'm sure your heart was in the right place."

After his shift finished on Friday evening, Shepherd drove his bike back to Kilburn and parked it in the yard behind the house, locking the rear wheel with a thick chain and pulling a grey cover over it. He showered and pulled on a clean polo shirt and jeans, then locked the house and walked to the car park, where he'd arranged a weekly rate to leave his BMW X3. There had been no vigilante incidents during the week and he had nothing to report so Button had decided that there was no need for an end-of-week debriefing. He called her on his hands-free as he drove out of London. "I did what you said and geared up the aggression," he said. "Decked a slag, as they say."

"They? Who says that outside of a Guy Ritchie movie?"

"There's a whole different language on the bus," said Shepherd. "I guess because they know they're among friends. Anyway, I knocked a guy out during a search."

"And?"

"And I'm not on report and they helped cover for me. Hear no evil, see no evil, speak no evil. And the van's CCTV coverage was blanked."

"Did Fogg say anything?"

"Basically that it wasn't a good idea to hit people on the street, but other than that there won't be any repercussions."

"Do you get the feeling that they're prone to violence?"

340

"They match force with force," said Shepherd. "They're careful to make sure any reaction is proportionate. They're certainly not going around bashing in heads."

"Not while they're on the job, anyway."

"Really, I don't think Fogg's the type to get involved in vigilantism. He's hard, but he's not violent. It's a job for him. I don't get the feeling that he's on a personal crusade."

"Someone has to be running the show," said Button. "A group of cops don't suddenly go maverick. They need convincing — they need to be led to it like horses to water."

"I know I keep saying this, but they're good cops, all of them. They laugh and joke and mess around but that's just a way of dealing with the stress. When it comes to the job they work hard and above all else they're fair."

"I hear what you're saying but, good cops or not, someone is still going around shooting, castrating and killing and we need to stop them."

"I guess so," said Shepherd.

"Please don't tell me you're going over to the dark side," said Button.

Shepherd laughed. "I'm fine," he said. "But I just wish we were putting as much effort into putting away real villains." He ended the call.

The traffic was heavy with commuters fleeing the city for the weekend and it was close to midnight when Shepherd arrived in Hereford. The house was in darkness so he let himself in quietly and went straight upstairs. He eased open Liam's bedroom door. His son was fast asleep and there was no sign of the dog. Shepherd tiptoed over to Liam's bed and placed a box on the bedside table. It was an iPhone that he'd bought during the week from a Carphone Warehouse shop in Praed Street.

He padded out and closed the door behind him, then went into his own bedroom, switched on the light and caught sight of his reflection in the dressing-table mirror. He looked tired — the result of a hard week's work followed by a long drive. But the week was far from over and Shepherd had his most difficult task ahead of him because this was the weekend that he and the Major had to take care of the Fox brothers in Ireland. He stared at himself and smiled slightly. He was more than capable of doing what had to be done, but that didn't mean he felt good about doing it. Killing was never to be done lightly, and it always came with consequences, no matter the motive or circumstances. He switched off the light, threw off his clothes and dived into bed. Within five minutes he was asleep.

Shepherd's alarm woke him at eight o'clock in the morning. He rolled out of bed, pulled on a sweatshirt and a pair of baggy tracksuit bottoms and went downstairs for his socks and boots. He retrieved his rucksack from the cupboard under the stairs and went for a brisk ten-mile run, not pushing himself too hard because he didn't want to risk straining a muscle. When he got back, Liam was in the kitchen, holding his new phone. "Dad, thanks — this is brilliant!"

342

Shepherd dropped his rucksack onto the kitchen floor. "Give me a hug, then," he said.

Liam rushed over and hugged him. Lady dashed out from under the table and jumped up at them both, her tongue lolling from the side of her mouth.

"I had to get you a new number and a new contract with O2," said Shepherd. "Internet access is free but you've got a thirty-five-pound limit for calls and texts every month and I don't want you going over that, okay?"

"Okay," said Liam.

"I mean it," said Shepherd. "I don't want any nasty surprises come the end of the month."

Katra was at the cooker making breakfast for Liam, his usual cheesy scrambled eggs on toast. She broke off from stirring the eggs to give Shepherd a mug of coffee and he thanked her. As he sipped it, the doorbell rang. "I'll get it," he said. He went to the front door and opened it. A man in his early fifties was standing on the doorstep, his arms folded across a barrel-shaped chest. He had greying curly hair, darkish skin that was mottled with old acne scars, and was wearing a black Umbro shell-suit.

"You're the father of Liam?" said the man. He had an accent, Central European maybe.

"Dan Shepherd, yes," said Shepherd, frowning. "And you are?"

"I am Peter's father."

"Peter?"

"Peter Talovic. He is at your son's school. You reported him to the police."

343

"I what?" said Shepherd, confused.

The man pushed Shepherd in the chest with the flat of his hand. "You told the police about my son," he said angrily.

"I don't know what you're talking about," said Shepherd. The man went to shove him again but Shepherd knocked his hand away. "You do that again and I'll hit you back," he warned. "Now, tell me what you're going on about."

"Your son told the police that my boy gave him a video. Now they want to arrest him."

Shepherd realised what the man was talking about. He held up his hands. "Look, my son didn't go to the police. I found a video of a child being assaulted on my son's phone. I took it to the school and they decided to go to the police."

"It wasn't your business," said the man.

"I'm afraid I don't agree with you," said Shepherd. "The boy in the video was being hurt — it wasn't horseplay. He was beaten, very badly."

"Now the police want to see my son in the police station. He might go to prison."

"That's really not my problem," said Shepherd. "I gave the video to the school, they called in the police. The police have decided to investigate. That's all there is to it."

"My son didn't beat anybody."

"Then he should tell that to the police."

"I do not want my son to go to prison," said Talovic. "I do not want my boy in trouble with the police."

344

"He's already in trouble, Mr Talovic. Your son made a video of a boy being assaulted. And from the sound of it, he made racist comments while he was doing it."

"Racist? What do you mean, racist?"

"Have you seen the video?" asked Shepherd.

Talovic nodded. "It's horseplay, that's all."

"It's more than horseplay," said Shepherd. "A boy is being assaulted, viciously, and someone is making racist comments while it's happening. That's why the police are investigating."

"You told them my son was a racist?"

Shepherd held up his hands again. "All I did was give the video to the school."

Talovic shook his head. "No, the police tell me that your son said Peter gave him the video. He has to tell them that is not true."

"You want my son to lie to the police?"

Talovic pointed at Shepherd's face. "Your son got Peter into trouble. I want him to tell the police that Peter wasn't involved."

"But he was involved," said Shepherd. "Your son Bluetoothed it to Liam."

Talovic's face screwed up into an angry frown. "Your son lied."

"No, he didn't," said Shepherd.

"Your son has to tell the police he got the video from someone else."

"Now you're being ridiculous," said Shepherd.

Talovic tried to push Shepherd in the chest again, but this time Shepherd grabbed the hand and twisted the man's arm behind his back. "I told you not to push me," said Shepherd. He increased the pressure on the arm and Talovic grunted. "Now, when I let you go, I want you to walk away from my house. If you try to hit me again I'll break your arm. Then I'll phone the police and I'll make sure that you spend the night in a police cell. Do you understand me?"

"Bastard!" Talovic hissed.

Shepherd twisted the arm further up the man's back and Talovic gasped. "I mean it," said Shepherd. "I'll break it." He pushed Talovic away from the door.

Talovic staggered forward, then turned around to glare at Shepherd. "I'll get you for this," he said.

"And if you threaten me again, I'll report you to the police," said Shepherd.

Talovic sneered at him. "You think I'm scared of the police?"

"I think you're angry and confused and I think you need to go home and calm down," said Shepherd. "If the police have a problem with your boy, go and talk to them." He went back inside and closed the door.

"Who was that?" asked Liam, as Shepherd went back into the kitchen.

"Peter Talovic's father," said Shepherd. He picked up his mug.

"What did he want?" asked Liam.

Shepherd didn't want to worry his son but he didn't want to lie to him. "He's not very happy about the police knowing about the video, that's all."

"So why did he come here?"

"He just wanted to talk to me," said Shepherd.

"What about?"

"His son."

"Peter?"

"He's upset that the police want to talk to Peter. But it's okay, he's gone now. He was just a bit upset — he'll calm down." Shepherd looked at his watch. "What time's football this afternoon?"

"Same as always, Dad, two o'clock start, but Mr Finch wants us there at one."

"Great," said Shepherd. "Gives us time to get some practice in. But just to let you know, I'll be out for a drink tonight with some friends from the SAS. And I'm going to be busy all day tomorrow."

"Work?"

"Sorry," said Shepherd.

"But it's Sunday."

"I'm sorry," said Shepherd again. "I'll be leaving really early, and I'm not sure when I'll be back. But this afternoon I'm all yours, okay?"

Liam shrugged. "Okay, no problem."

"I'll make it up to you," said Shepherd.

"Dad, it's okay," said Liam. "I'm not a kid any more."

"You're twelve."

"I'm almost thirteen and then I'll be a teenager."

"And I can't tell you how much I'm looking forward to that."

Katra put Liam's breakfast on the table. "What do you want, Dan?"

"I'll have a shower and then a bacon sandwich would be great. I don't know what time I'll be back tonight so don't wait up. And I'll be out first thing tomorrow morning. Busy all day."

"You work too hard," she said, opening the fridge and taking out a pack of best back bacon.

"And make sure he does his homework," said Shepherd.

"Dad . . ." moaned Liam.

"I will do, Dan," she said.

He picked up his wallet and took out the business card that Detective Sergeant Hollis had given him at Hereford police station. "Just in case that guy comes back when I'm not here, here's the number of the policeman I spoke to. Just call him."

Katra frowned. "Do you think he will?"

Shepherd shook his head. "It's just in case," he said. "I'm sure Mr Talovic'll calm down."

The Swan was on the outskirts of Hereford, well away from the Stirling Lines barracks and therefore not one of the watering holes that was generally frequented by the Regiment. It was a black and white building with a slate roof and a garden behind it, with a red-metal climbing frame and a set of swings. Shepherd parked his BMW X3 in the pub car park and walked in through the back door. It was just after six o'clock in the evening. The Major was sitting at a corner table with Jack Bradford. Shepherd ordered a black coffee. "Everything okay with Billy?" he asked.

"We left him with his feet up watching the footie," said Jack. "The boss has filled the fridge with lager so he's a happy bunny."

348

Shepherd looked at his watch. "We should eat now before we head off," he said. "It's an easy drive to Holyhead at this time so we've plenty of time. We can catch some sleep on the ferry."

"What have you told your boy?"

"I've said I'm popping out for a drink with friends and that I'll be back late. And that I'll be working all day tomorrow with an early start. There's nothing unusual in that. The au pair will take him over to see his grandparents."

"How is the lovely Katra?" asked Jack.

"She's fine," said Shepherd. "She asks about you all the time."

"Are you serious?"

"No, you moron," said Shepherd. "Why would she?"

"Because I'm the better-looking of the Bradford boys, always have been."

"You're identical," said Shepherd.

"Ah, but you've never seen us naked."

Shepherd rapped on the table with his knuckles. "And touch wood, I never will," he said. "Anyway, they're expecting me back late Sunday, which is fine. They'll both be asleep by the time I get in."

"Looks like we're all sorted," said the Major, picking up a menu. "Now, what's good here? I'm starving."

Shepherd left his car in a brightly lit side-street a fifteen-minute walk from the ferry terminal. He and the Major were carrying holdalls containing washbags and a change of clothes. They walked together through the streets of Holyhead. It was just after one o'clock in the morning and the pavements of the town were pretty much deserted, though a constant stream of cars and trucks headed towards the terminal. Holyhead didn't seem to have prospered from its association with the ferries: there were few restaurants and bars and the town had a dingy, depressing feel.

All Shepherd had to show at check-in was the computer printout of his on-line booking; they weren't asked to show identification and their belongings weren't searched. They waited with another two dozen or so foot passengers, most of whom appeared to be Polish construction workers. Shepherd and the Major had dressed to blend in and were wearing heavy workboots, faded jeans and donkey jackets. No one gave them a second look as they sat down in the waiting area and stretched out their legs.

"You've done the ferry a few times?" asked the Major.

"It's the easiest way into Ireland, North or South," said Shepherd. "There are no passport checks and Customs are more concerned about what's in the vehicles than what the passengers are carrying. Most of the drugs and arms brought into Ireland come through the ferries, and probably half the terrorists, too."

A group of Romanian gypsies walked into the waiting room, the men unshaven and wearing cheap suits, the women with gold hooped earrings and brightly coloured skirts, several holding small babies. They began talking in loud voices and two lit cigarettes, in defiance of a "No Smoking" sign behind them.

"Makes a change from flying in on a Hercules, which is how I did most of my trips to the North," said the Major.

A voice cut in over the Tannoy, informing the foot passengers that they could now board the ferry. The gypsies pushed their way to the front of the queue. Two of the Polish workers objected loudly, but the gypsies ignored them.

Shepherd and the Major joined the end of the queue and walked slowly onto the ferry. They found themselves a couple of seats near the cafeteria and made themselves comfortable. At exactly two thirty in the morning the ferry pulled out into the Irish Sea.

Shepherd woke to the sound of a male voice telling passengers with vehicles that they should make their way down to the parking levels as the ferry would shortly be arriving at the port of Dublin. He sat up. He had been lying across three seats, his head resting on his holdall, and had managed a couple of hours of fitful sleep. The Major was drinking a cup of coffee. "Didn't sleep?" Shepherd asked, wiping his face with his hands.

"Your snoring kept me awake." He nodded at a second cup on the table in front of Shepherd. "I got you a caffeine injection," he said.

Shepherd thanked him and sipped the coffee as he watched the ferry glide effortlessly into port.

By the time Shepherd and the Major were walking into the arrivals terminal, cars and trucks were already streaming off the ferry. There were no checks of any kind, immigration or Customs, and less than five minutes after the ferry had docked they were walking out into the cold Dublin air. Martin O'Brien was standing at the side of his Mercedes, the collar of his pea coat turned up against the wind. He shook hands with them both and opened the boot so that they could drop in their holdalls.

"Everything okay?" asked Shepherd, as he climbed into the front seat. The Major got into the back and slammed the door.

"All sorted," said O'Brien. He started the engine. "Do you want to eat?"

"I could eat," said Shepherd.

"There's a café that the market boys use," said O'Brien. "Full fry-up, plus they do booze in a teacup if you want."

"Fry-up sounds the business," said the Major.

O'Brien headed away from the terminal, joining a queue of horseboxes that had just driven off the ferry. "I got a Transit van, like you wanted," said O'Brien. "Five years old, Kerry plates — it's got a fair few miles on the clock but I've had it fully checked and serviced and it won't let you down."

"Where is it?"

"I've left in a lock-up, not far from the café we're going to. The stuff you wanted is in the back."

"Including the shorts?"

O'Brien nodded. "Two Glocks. I've cleaned them and test-fired them and they're as good as you'll get."

"What's their provenance?" asked the Major.

"They were in an IRA arms cache we came across when I was with the Rangers," said O'Brien. "We were a bit free and easy back then so me and a couple of the guys kept a few back for a rainy day. I had them wrapped in oilcloth and plastic under a few feet of earth."

"I hope the ammunition's fresh," asked Shepherd.

"It's fresh and untraceable," O'Brien said. "Mate of mine runs a logistics company, shipping gear to security contractors in Iraq. He gave me a box of nine mill ammo. I've put two clips with each gun." He grinned at Shepherd. "And before you get all forensic on me, I cleaned the cartridges and the clips."

"You're a star, Martin," said the Major. "Let me know how much I owe you."

O'Brien waved his hand dismissively. "It's on me, boss. Forget about it."

The Major leaned forward and patted O'Brien on the shoulder.

"Boss, I'm not happy about you and Spider going up North on your own," said O'Brien. "It's still bandit country around Newry."

"That's why it's better if it's just the two of us," said Shepherd. "Three men in a car are going to stick out."

"I could be close by, watching your back."

"We'll be okay, Martin," said the Major. "We'll be back tonight and then we're straight over the water."

O'Brien nodded. "Okay," he said, but he didn't sound convinced.

The café was a fifteen-minute drive from the port. It was a single-storey building with wire mesh over the windows and a dozen trucks and vans parked behind it. O'Brien locked the Mercedes and took them inside.

They ordered three full breakfasts but declined the elderly waitress's offer of whiskey in teacups and went for coffee instead. As she walked back to the kitchen, O'Brien leaned forward. "So, what's the story?" he asked.

"We'll be up and down today," said Shepherd. "We'll bury them up there and leave the shorts. We come back here for a full clean-up and we'll torch the van before catching one of the late ferries back. We need somewhere to burn the van, somewhere we won't attract any attention."

"I've got the perfect place for you. Old quarry, hasn't been used for years."

"When we're driving back from the North I'll call you to arrange the meet," said Shepherd.

O'Brien took them to the rear of the Transit van and unlocked the door. There was a green nylon sports bag on the floor of the van next to a tarpaulin. He took a pair of black leather gloves from the pocket of his coat and slipped them on, then unzipped the sports bag. He pulled out a plastic-wrapped bundle and unwrapped the plastic to reveal a piece of oilcloth. Inside it, there were two more cloth-wrapped packages.

Shepherd and the Major put on gloves and O'Brien handed them a package each. Both contained Glock semi-automatics. They checked the guns, and ejected the magazines. Both were fully loaded. The two men rewrapped the weapons and put them back in the sports bag.

"Everything you wanted is here," he said to Shepherd, and pushed aside the tarpaulin. "All the

354

fishing gear. I even got you the latest flies — the guy I got them from says the fish will snap them out of your hand."

Shepherd picked up two brand new spades and examined them.

"Bought them from a garden centre out in the sticks, no CCTV and I paid in cash," O'Brien told him. "Just like you said. You've got a criminal mind, Spider."

"Just making sure that we cover all our tracks," said Shepherd. He pulled the tarpaulin back into place and looked at his watch. "Speaking of which, tracks is what we've got to be making."

"And you're absolutely sure you don't want me as back-up? Just give me the word — you won't even know I'm there."

The Major punched him lightly on the shoulder. "You've done more than enough, Martin," he said. "We'll see you later tonight."

Shepherd climbed into the van's driver's seat and turned the ignition key. The engine kicked into life straight away. Shepherd listened to it idle. It sounded fine. O'Brien locked the rear door of the Transit while the Major climbed into the front passenger seat. Then he walked around to the driver's door. "You need anything, you call me," he said.

"Will do, Martin," said Shepherd. "But if all goes to plan, we'll be back here in a few hours." He drove off. In his wing mirror, he saw O'Brien waving goodbye.

It took less than an hour to reach the border, though there was nothing to mark that they had crossed from

Ireland into the United Kingdom. There were no barriers, no police or Customs, no CCTV cameras. The only indication that they had left Ireland was that the road signs were in miles and not kilometres. The Major had a map book open on his lap. "We're well ahead of schedule," he said.

"We've some digging to do first," said Shepherd.

The Major looked up from the map. "What?"

"We dig the hole first. It'll save time later. Plus, in the unlikely event that anyone sees us digging, we can spin them a line. That's a lot harder to do if we've two bodies in the van."

"I get the feeling you've done this before, Spider."

"I haven't, boss, but I've spent time with enough people who have to pick up a few of the tricks of the trade. And getting rid of bodies is an art."

"Where are we going to do it?"

"I spent a couple of hours on Google Earth and I've found a place about half an hour's drive from the river, farmland all around and not a house for miles."

"I envy you your trick memory," said the Major. He lifted the map book. "I'm pretty good at navigation but you only have to look at a map once."

"Just lucky," said Shepherd.

"Did anyone ever tell you why your memory works the way it does?"

Shepherd shrugged. "Never really talked about it with a doctor or anything," he said. "There's no real point. It's not like there's something wrong."

"What about at school? Didn't it give you an unfair advantage during exams?"

Shepherd chuckled. "To be honest, it wasn't that big a help. My memory's near enough infallible but that doesn't mean I understand what I remember. And it's no help for maths or English."

"Languages?"

"Yeah. I can remember vocabulary until the cows come home, but my French accent is appalling and the grammar has always defeated me."

"But navigation has always been a breeze?"

Shepherd laughed. "Yeah, I've never done a McNab and got lost in the desert, but just because I can memorise a map and a route doesn't always mean I know where I am. Where it does come in useful is working under cover because I can memorise files and photographs. The job I'm doing at the moment, I've been dropped into a group of more than a hundred cops. A few hours with the files and I know them all by face and name and their personal details."

"Investigating cops again?"

Shepherd wrinkled his nose. "Yeah, I hate doing it. That's not why I joined SOCA. There's a whole department geared up for investigating cops but they seem happier with outsiders doing it in this case."

"And I gather the lovely Charlotte is on her way out."

"What big ears you have, Grandma," said Shepherd, surprised that the Major knew that Button was leaving.

"I keep them to the ground. You always knew she'd go back to MI5, though."

"Yeah, just hoped she might stay a bit longer," said Shepherd.

"What about you? Will you stay?"

"Not if I get more jobs like the one I'm on now," said Shepherd.

"There's always a spot for you on the Directing Staff," said the Major. "The Regiment would have you back in a heartbeat."

"My fitness isn't what it was, boss."

"It's not about fitness," said the Major. "It's about technique, it's about skills, and you've got them in abundance."

"I'm not a teacher, I'm a doer," said Shepherd. "That's just the way it is. I want to be out there doing something, not teaching someone else."

He turned off the main highway and drove along a narrow road, barely wide enough for two vehicles. There was a farm off to the left, and a tractor was driving across a field followed by a flock of seagulls. The road wound around a hill and past a derelict cottage. The Major looked up from the map. "I'm lost," he admitted.

Shepherd grinned. "We're in the middle of nowhere," he said. "Bandit country. In the old days there'd be patrols out in those fields in deep cover and there'd be helicopters over-head. These days it's just farmland." He pointed at a clump of woodland off to their right. "That's the place," he said. "The nearest house is two miles away, and this is the only road that goes near it. And the river where the Foxes fish is ten minutes' drive."

The Major nodded. "Sounds good to me."

Shepherd slowed the van. "I figure if we can just get fifty feet or so into the woodland, no one will be able to see us from the road," he said. He spotted a gap in the trees up ahead. He checked the wing mirrors then turned off into it. The van bucked over the rough ground and he slowed to walking pace. He curved to the right behind a spreading beech tree. "What do you think?" he asked the Major.

The Major bent to squint into the wing mirror. "Bit further, maybe. I can still see the road."

Shepherd went forward another twenty feet and stopped. He switched off the engine and climbed out. The two men stood together, listening. The only sound was the click-click-click of the engine as it cooled. Shepherd went around to the back of the van. He opened the door, took out the two spades and tossed one to the Major. They walked away from the van and emerged into a small clearing. "This is good," said Shepherd. "There won't be so many tree roots. We can hide the disturbed soil with mulch when we've finished."

"How did you learn so much about disposing of bodies?" asked the Major.

"Hanging out with the wrong crowd," said Shepherd. "After a few days there'll be no sign that anyone was ever here." He started digging. The soil was rich and black and relatively free of stones so it was easy to move. The two men dug one hole, about six feet long and three feet wide. The deeper they went the harder the soil became, giving way to tough clay that soon had them sweating heavily. They stripped off their jackets, rolled up their sleeves and carried on. Once they were down three feet they took it in turns to stand in the hole and dig.

"How far down do we go?" asked the Major, as he watched Shepherd dig.

"At least four feet," said Shepherd. "Any less than that and there's a danger they'll rise to the surface. Five or six is better — let's see how we do for time."

The Major looked at his Rolex. "We're well ahead of the game," he said. He wiped his forehead with the back of his arm. "You're okay with this, Spider?"

"If I wasn't, I wouldn't be here," said Shepherd, as he continued to dig.

"It's a big thing, what you're doing."

"It needs to be done, boss. I understand that." He stopped digging and leaned on his spade. "I won't lose one second of sleep over this," he said. "There'll be no guilt, no recriminations. It's combat. They chose the field of battle — they went into a Chinese restaurant and gunned down unarmed lads. All we're doing is redressing the balance. In a better world we'd be facing each other over a killing ground and we'd all be wearing uniforms, but they made the decision to fight like terrorists so killing them like terrorists doesn't worry me at all." He started digging again. "But one thing's for sure. I won't be going to prison for them. We'll do this, and we'll do it right."

Padraig Fox pulled his hip flask out from the pocket of his waterproof Barbour jacket and held it out to his brother. Sean was at the wheel of the Range Rover but he grinned, took it and drank. "Twenty-year-old malt," said Padraig. "Got a dozen cases of it in last night," he said. "Couple of the guys did a warehouse in Belfast, and that's our taste."

"Excellent," said Sean, giving the flask back to his brother. "Are you gonna sell it or keep it?"

"What do you think?" laughed Padraig. "Too bloody good to sell on."

"Make sure six cases come my way, then," said Sean.

"Wouldn't have it any other way, little brother," said Padraig. He swigged from the flask, screwed the cap on and put it back into his pocket. "Hits the spot, all right," he said.

Padraig's phone rang and although the number was blocked he took the call. "The parcel's arriving on Wednesday," said a voice, then the line went dead. "The ciggies get to Dublin on Wednesday," he told his brother.

"Grand," said Sean. They had arranged for five million cigarettes from Panama to be shipped to Miami and from there to Dublin, hidden under the wooden flooring and insulation of an elderly freighter. They stood to make a profit of more than half a million pounds once they'd sold the cigarettes on to gangs in Ireland and the UK.

Sean slowed down, turned off the main road and drove along a narrow track that wound through a patch of woodland. Shadows flicked across the windscreen. "Did you hear they're planning peace marches in Belfast and Derry next weekend?" he asked.

"Are they now?" said his brother. "And who'll be doing the organising then?"

"Some women's group, Housewives For the Peace Process or something. They're talking about hundreds of thousands taking part. Martin and Gerry might be there."

"Like hell they will," sneered Padraig. "If they know what's good for them they'll keep well away." He scratched his chin. "We should put something together. Show those bitches that they'd be better off in the kitchen or the bedroom than walking the streets waving placards."

"Are you thinking what I'm thinking?"

"Be nice," said Padraig. "We've got the Semtex."

"Yeah, but do we have time to make a decent car bomb? And the cops will be on full alert for sure."

"Doesn't have to be in a car," said Padraig. "We could do an office or a shop on the route. I'll talk to a few people this evening, see if we can't get something going."

"Just like the old days," said Sean.

"The old days never went away just because some of the boys lost their fire," said Padraig. "But we'll show them what for."

Sean slowed the Range Rover, then headed down a muddy track past a wooden sign that read "Private Property". Off to the left was the farm owned by the man who had sold the Foxes the fishing rights to the river that ran through his land. The farmer was a Republican sympathiser and a long-time friend of the brothers, and throughout the Troubles he'd allowed them to use his land to store arms and equipment.

They drove around the copse. The track ended at a five-barred gate that led to a potato field. Sean switched to four-wheel drive and steered the Range Rover off the track and followed a thick hedge to the river. "Now, what the hell do they think they're doing?" asked Padraig, pointing at the two fly fishermen standing on the riverbank. "Don't they realise this is private property? Stupid bastards."

"They can't be locals — everyone around here knows that's our stretch," said Sean. "Probably tourists. Yanks, I bet."

"Well, they can sod off somewhere else and anything they've caught is ours," said Padraig.

Sean brought the Range Rover to a stop under a spreading beech tree and the two men climbed out. The sky was clear of clouds but there was still a chill in the air and Padraig zipped up his Barbour. "I've got a shotgun in the back," said Sean.

"Yeah, if they give us any lip we can spray their arses with buckshot," said Padraig. He took out his flask and drank from it while Sean opened the back of the Range Rover and pulled a double-barrelled shotgun from under a tartan blanket. He rummaged under the blanket for a box of shells and slotted two in, then handed the gun to his brother and slammed the door.

Padraig kept the gun broken over his left arm as they walked across the meadow to the river. The two fishermen didn't hear them coming and continued to flick their flies over the fast-running water. "Where's their car?" asked Padraig.

"Must be somewhere — they couldn't have walked from the village."

"Well, they're going to be walking back, that's for sure," said Padraig, clicking the shotgun closed and pulling back the hammers. "Good afternoon, gentlemen!" he shouted. "Do you realise you're on private property?"

The two men turned around. One was tall and broad-shouldered, a couple of inches over six feet with a wide chin and a nose that had been broken at least twice. He lowered his fishing rod and smiled amiably. He was wearing waders and a tweed jacket and had on a floppy cotton hat peppered with brightly coloured flies. "We thought this was a public river, didn't we now, Danny boy?"

The other man nodded. He was also wearing waders but had a green anorak with the hood up. He was younger than the first by a good ten years. "That we did," he said.

Padraig kept the shotgun pointed towards them. The older of the two fishermen had a Dublin accent but his companion was English.

"We're on holiday — I've brought Danny up for a spot of fly fishing, show him the ropes and all. Asked at the pub and they said the river was jumping with fish this time of year."

"They did, did they?" said Padraig. "They didn't happen to mention that the Fox brothers own the river, did they?"

364

"No, they didn't," said the man. "But it looks as if there's plenty to go around."

"Did you catch much?" asked Sean.

"Half a dozen big buggers," said the younger fisherman.

"You'll be leaving them with us," said Padraig.

"That's not fair," said the bigger man. "We caught them fair and square."

"The river's ours and so are the fish in it," said Padraig, gesturing with the shotgun.

"You shouldn't be waving that around now," said the older man, his eyes sparkling with amusement. "Someone could get hurt."

"Just give me the bloody fish and get the hell off our land," said Padraig.

The fisherman bent down and picked up a canvas shoulder bag.

"Come on, toss the bag over here," said Padraig.

"My father gave me this bag," said the man.

"Think of it as the fine you're paying for trespassing," said Padraig.

The man shrugged. "I don't want any trouble," he said.

Padraig smiled. The fisherman was a big man but even big men paled at the sight of a gun, especially a shotgun. "That's good to hear," he said. "Now sling the bag over here."

The man threw the bag into the air and it landed in the grass, just out of Padraig's reach. Padraig bent down to pick it up. The man moved so quickly that Padraig didn't have time to react and before he could straighten up he felt something hard press against his neck. "Now my gun's not as big as yours but if I pull the trigger it'll blow your brains right into your precious river," said the man, and now his accent was English, not Irish.

The younger man had also produced a gun. It was a Glock and it was pointed at Sean's chest.

"What the hell is this?" demanded Padraig.

"Drop the shotgun," said the man. "Drop it or so help me, God, I'll pull the trigger."

Padraig let the shotgun fall from his fingers and it thumped into the grass.

"Are we going to leave their car where it is?" asked the Major, checking the plastic ties that were binding Padraig Fox's wrists.

"No need to hide it," said Shepherd. "We'll be miles away before anyone knows that they're missing."

He used a short length of rope to tie Sean Fox's ankles. Both men were lying face down and sacks had been pulled over their heads. They had sworn and protested as they had been led to the van and bound, but they had gone quiet once the sacks had been put on.

The Major sat down between the two bound and hooded men, holding his Glock. "Let's be off, then," he said.

Shepherd slammed the rear doors and climbed into the driver's seat. He started the engine and drove slowly across the grass to the road. He glanced over his shoulder. "Okay?" he asked. The Major nodded. "Any problems, just put a bullet in their heads," he added, for the benefit of their two prisoners. He turned onto the road and headed west. He kept a careful eye on the road ahead and kept checking the rear-view mirror. He had already memorised the route, which avoided any traffic-lights or stop signs so that he could keep moving. There were no windows in the side or back of the van but someone could look through the windscreen, and there was a small chance that they might see what was going on, so he wanted to keep the vehicle moving. There were few cars on the road, but for several minutes he was forced to follow a mud-splattered tractor driven by an overweight farmer in a flat cap, who waved cheerily when he turned off into a field. A helicopter flew low overhead but it was a Robinson two-seater, not police or army. Judging from its erratic flight path there was a beginner at the controls.

The road ahead was clear and Shepherd accelerated up to sixty for a few minutes, then slowed, still watching his rear-view mirror, but there was no one following him. He patted the side pocket of his jacket and felt the reassuring hardness of the Glock.

He slowed the van as he got nearer the turn-off, but just as he was about to leave the road a saloon car towing a caravan came up behind him. Shepherd cursed under his breath. The car made no attempt to overtake him and he knew that if he slowed to make the turn, the car and caravan would almost certainly have to stop. If that happened there'd be an outside chance that the occupants would remember the van.

"What's wrong?" asked the Major.

"Bloody caravan behind us," said Shepherd. "I'm going to go on and do a U-turn." He accelerated and left the car and caravan behind. After a couple of miles he reached a crossroads. He turned left, did a quick three-point turn, then headed back the way he'd come. He passed the car and caravan. The car was being driven by an elderly man with thick-lensed glasses — he seemed to be more worried about the GPS unit on his dashboard than about the road ahead. The second time that Shepherd approached the turn-off the road was clear ahead and behind him. He turned off and drove slowly through the woodland, following the route he'd driven that morning.

He brought the van to a halt in the same place he'd parked the first time. There were deep tyre tracks in the mud. There was nothing they could do about them, but Shepherd wasn't concerned as they were going to torch the van anyway once they'd got it back to the Republic. He brought the van to a stop and switched off the engine. He climbed out and pulled open the rear door. The Major jumped out. He looked around the wooded area and cocked his head as he listened, but the only sound was the clicking of the engine as it cooled.

Shepherd untied Padraig Fox's legs while the Major freed his brother. Shepherd pulled out his Glock and tapped it against Padraig Fox's knee. "We're gonna help you out of the van and we're going to take a walk," he said. "You try anything, anything at all, and I'll put a bullet in your leg and we'll still make you walk."

"So it's the easy way or the hard way, is it?" said Padraig, his voice muffled by the sack. "Where'd you learn to do this? Watching old gangster movies, you thick Brit bastard?"

Shepherd slammed the butt of the Glock down on the man's knee. Fox grunted but didn't cry out. He was a hard man, all right, and Shepherd knew that hard men had to be dominated from the outset or things could go very badly wrong. "Next time it'll be a bullet," he said. "And we're miles from anywhere so there's no cavalry going to be riding to your rescue."

He grabbed the belt of the man's trousers and pulled him out of the van, then kept a tight grip on the collar of his jacket, keeping the muzzle of the gun pressed against the back of his neck. He manoeuvred him away from the van while the Major pulled Sean Fox out and steadied him.

Shepherd and the Major frogmarched the brothers through the undergrowth, issuing terse warnings when there was something in their way, roughly helping them over fallen branches and around bushes.

"Where are you taking us?" said Padraig Fox, limping from his injured knee.

"It's a mystery tour," said Shepherd. "And keep your mouth shut or I'll cripple your other leg."

"If you tell me what this is about, we can sort it out," said Padraig Fox.

Shepherd jerked the man's collar. "I told you already, keep it shut," he said.

They reached the clearing where they had dug the hole. A dozen starlings scattered from a tree, cawing as they flapped away. They settled in another tree further away and went silent.

"Kneel down," said the Major, pressing the barrel of his Glock against the back of Sean Fox's neck. He used his left hand to grip the shoulder of Fox's coat to keep him steady as he went down onto his knees.

"What's this about?" asked Padraig Fox. "What do you want?"

Shepherd tapped him on the side of the head with his gun. "We want you on your knees," he said.

"Please don't do this," said Sean Fox, his voice trembling.

"We just want to ask you some questions," said Shepherd.

"Whatever you want, whatever you need to know, we'll tell you, won't we, Padraig?"

"Be a man, Sean," said his brother. "Don't let the bastards hear you grovel."

"Just do as you're told and everything'll be all right," said Shepherd. He pushed Padraig Fox down onto his knees, keeping a tight grip on the collar of his jacket.

The Fox brothers were kneeling just inches from the hole. Shepherd looked over at the Major, waiting to see what he would do next. Off in the distance, a fox barked.

The Major took a deep breath. Then he slowly aimed his Glock at the back of Sean Fox's head. Shepherd thought he was going to say something but he just pressed his lips together and pulled the trigger, firing one shot, then stepping quickly to the side and putting a second bullet into Padraig Fox's head before his brother had even toppled forward into the grave.

370

The Major fired two more shots into Sean Fox's back and shot Padraig again.

The brothers twitched for a few seconds, and then were still, lying together in the pit.

The Major tossed his gun into the hole. Shepherd did the same. Then they picked up the spades and began shovelling earth on top of the bodies.

"There he is," said the Major, pointing at O'Brien's Mercedes. He had parked at an entrance to an abandoned limestone quarry some thirty miles outside Dublin. He already had the gate open for them and he flashed his lights to let them know to drive through. Then he followed them along the rutted track, past an abandoned prefabricated office, its windows smashed and graffiti spray-painted across the walls.

Shepherd parked the van in the middle of the quarry. The sky was starting to darken and stars to wink overhead. "Nice choice," said Shepherd.

"Can't be seen from the road and the nearest cops are ten miles away," said O'Brien. "We'll be well away before anyone knows what's going on."

Shepherd went around to the back of the van and took out a black garbage bag containing the two holdalls they had brought with them. He took them out and carried them over to O'Brien's Mercedes.

"How did it go?" asked O'Brien.

"Smooth as silk," said the Major.

O'Brien looked at Shepherd, who nodded. "Let's burn the van and get the hell out of Dodge," he said.

The Major and Shepherd stripped off their clothing and handed it to O'Brien. He threw everything into the back of the van, on top of the waders and fishing equipment. When they had stripped down to their underwear and socks, they walked over to the holdalls and changed into clean clothes and training shoes. O'Brien took a screwdriver and removed the registration plates from the vehicle, then pulled the tax disc off the window.

Shepherd quickly checked the Major, making sure that there was nothing on him that could transfer evidence. "That's the lot," he said to O'Brien.

O'Brien dropped the registration plates into the boot of his Mercedes and took out a red plastic can. He whistled to himself as he splashed petrol around the inside of the van.

Shepherd and the Major climbed into the Mercedes as O'Brien walked around the van, pouring petrol over the side and through the open windows. When he had finished, he tossed the can onto the front seat and stood back. He took a box of matches from his pocket, lit one and tossed it inside. There was a loud "whoosh" as the petrol ignited. He tossed in the box of matches, then took off his leather gloves and threw them into the flames too. He walked over to the Mercedes, got in and drove off. They were a good hundred yards away when the van's petrol tank exploded and it erupted into a ball of flame. "Just time for a coffee before you catch the ferry," said O'Brien. "And maybe a sandwich. I could murder a bacon sandwich."

★ ★ ★

Shepherd and the Major walked out of Holyhead ferry terminal and strolled through the town. It was as deserted as the last time they'd passed through, though once again the roads were busy with cars and trucks pouring off the ferry. Shepherd's BMW was where he'd left it, and they were soon driving across the bridge from Anglesey to the Welsh mainland. "I was waiting for you to try to talk me out of it," said the Major, as they drove along the A5 through the Snowdonia National Park, the Cambrian Mountains to their right.

"Did you want me to?" asked Shepherd. The Major shook his head. "So what would have been the point?"

"I just thought, you know . . . you being in law enforcement."

"That I might have a view? I already told you, boss, I know why you did what you did. I would probably have done the same myself if I was in your place. If things had worked out differently and I'd stayed in the Regiment, I could well have found myself up against the Fox boys with an MP5 in my hands. They were terrorists, they deserved what they got and I won't lose a wink of sleep over what I did today."

"Thanks, Spider."

"No thanks necessary, boss." It was one o'clock in the morning and there was little traffic on the A5 but Shepherd kept to just below the speed limit. "I did wonder why you didn't say anything to them," he said. "Before you . . ." He left the sentence unfinished.

"I was going to," said the Major. "I had it all planned out. I was going to tell them that I was Tommy's uncle, that he was a better man than they'd ever be, that they were murdering scum who deserved to die like dogs, but when they were kneeling there with the sacks over their heads I realised I didn't need to say anything. They didn't deserve to know who I was or why they were dying. I just wanted them dead. I know why I did it and Tommy's father will know, and if Tommy's up there looking down at us, he'll know, but so far as the Fox brothers are concerned, screw 'em. They're dead and that's all that matters. It's all the closure that I need."

Shepherd understood. "Just one thing," he said quietly.

"Sure. Anything."

"We don't mention it, ever again. Not ever."

"Like it never happened?"

Shepherd smiled ruefully. "No, it happened. We'll never forget what we did, but we don't talk about it. No one saw us, there's no forensics. Providing we never, ever talk about it, it'll never come back to haunt us."

"Deal," said the Major.

As they approached the outskirts of Hereford the Major used his throwaway Nokia to phone Jack Bradford and arranged to meet him in the car park at the Swan. Shepherd and he got there first and waited for five minutes until Jack pulled up behind them in his silver grey Audi. They climbed out of the BMW. Shepherd handed the Major his holdall and they walked together to the Audi. "Everything okay?" asked Jack.

"Couldn't have gone better," said the Major. He opened the rear door on the driver's side and tossed his holdall into the back.

374

"Give me the Nokias and I'll get rid of them," said Shepherd.

The Major took his from his jacket and handed it to him. Jack retrieved his from the unit on his dashboard and passed it through the window.

"Tell Billy to destroy the phone and the Sim card when you get back to London," Shepherd said to Jack.

"And I'll watch whatever he's recorded off the TV," said the Major. He stuck out his hand. "Job well done, Spider, thanks."

"No sweat, boss."

Shepherd flashed Jack a thumbs-up as the Major climbed into the front passenger seat, and he waved as the two men drove off towards London. He looked at his watch. If they made good time the Major would be home soon after dawn.

He climbed into his car and drove slowly back to his house. All the lights were off and he let himself in through the back door. Lady was in her basket and wagged her tail. "It's okay, Lady, go back to sleep," he whispered. He crept upstairs. Liam's bedroom door was closed so he decided not to disturb him and went to his own bedroom. He shaved and then showered, washing his hair thoroughly and using a nailbrush methodically, then towelled himself dry. He changed into clean clothes and went back downstairs. He made himself a cup of black coffee, sat down at the kitchen table and wrote a note to his son. "Liam — Sorry I got back too late to say goodnight. Have gone back to London. See you next weekend. I'll phone you. Love

Dad. PS Here's your pocket money!" He left the note and ten pounds underneath the salt cellar.

He was exhausted but he had to get to London in time for his shift with the TSG, so he poured some more coffee into a plastic cup to take with him. On the way to his car, he noticed that one of the rear tyres of the CRV had gone flat. He cursed and looked at his watch. He didn't want Katra to have to change it and she needed the car to get Liam to school. He'd have to do it himself. He went back inside the house to get the keys.

Shepherd arrived at Paddington Green on his bike just before half past eight. He hadn't slept and had had barely enough time to snatch a quick cup of coffee at his house in Kilburn. He'd phoned Katra as he drank his coffee and told her he'd changed the flat tyre for the spare. She promised to get it fixed after dropping Liam at school.

Kelly and Coker were in the team room watching television and Simmons and Parry were in the locker room changing into their uniforms. The Serial was starting a week on Commissioner's Reserve, which meant that the three vans could be sent anywhere in London, as and when they were needed. The Serials took it in turns to act as Commissioner's Reserve and it was generally more exciting than being tied to the borough.

"Good weekend, Three-amp?" asked Parry, as Shepherd walked in.

"That really is my nickname, then?" asked Shepherd, putting his helmet in the locker.

"If the cap fits," said Simmons. "Do you think I'm happy about being called Nipple?"

Shepherd laughed. The man had a point. He stripped off his motorcycle leathers.

Fogg appeared at the door to the locker room. "Briefing room in ten minutes, guys," he said. "We're heading for Trafalgar Square. The Tamils are kicking off again." He disappeared down the corridor.

"I don't get the Tamils," said Simmons. "They're terrorists, right?"

"The Tamil Tigers are the terrorists, but they're a spent force," said Shepherd.

"Yeah, but the guys who keep demonstrating, they must support them, right?"

"It's complicated," said Shepherd, and laughed. He realised that was what he always said to Liam when he came up with a difficult question.

"What's funny?" asked Simmons.

"I was just thinking what we'd be doing if al-Qaeda was out on the streets claiming that it was unfair what we were doing to their terrorists," lied Shepherd. "We'd probably be lined up to protect their right to free speech."

"Yeah, the world's gone mad," said Simmons. "Did you hear the latest bullshit from the government think-tank on drugs?"

Shepherd shook his head.

"They're saying we should follow the example of the cops in Boston. Apparently the cops did a deal with big drug-dealers, saying that they wouldn't arrest them for dealing if they stopped shooting each other. The murder rate went down and the cops are saying it's a brilliant scheme."

"Yeah, you're right," said Shepherd. "The world has gone mad."

"It's like telling burglars that we won't arrest them providing they don't damage anything."

"Yeah, if there's no deterrent, criminals are just gonna keep on breaking the law," said Shepherd. "You know what I'd do with burglars?"

"What?"

Shepherd made a chopping motion with his hand. "Do what the Saudis do," he said. "Chop off a bloody hand."

Simmons grinned. "You'd do that?"

"Just give me the axe, my son. And for rapists and the like . . ." He made a snipping motion with his fingers. "It'd stop them reoffending, if nothing else."

Castle appeared at the door. She was already dressed in riot gear. "Tamils are kicking off again," she said.

"Yeah, we heard," said Simmons.

"Good weekend, Three-amp?" she asked.

There was no way he could possibly tell her what he'd been up to over the previous forty-eight hours. "Quiet," he said.

"Well, the Tamils will liven it up for you," she said. "Word is that they're going to try to storm the Sri Lankan Embassy today."

Shepherd slammed his locker door. "Bring it on," he said.

★ ★ ★

Shepherd got home just after eight o'clock that evening. He was dog tired. It had been a hard day and towards the end of the shift he'd barely been able to keep his eyes open. He was hungry but he couldn't face cooking. He'd spent most of the day face-to-face with angry Tamils who didn't understand why they weren't allowed to throw bottles at the Sri Lankan Embassy. He had been sworn at and spat at, accused of being a racist, a bastard, a racist bastard and pretty much every other abusive name under the sun in several languages.

He flopped onto the sofa and switched on the television but within minutes he was snoring loudly, dead to the world. He was woken by the sound of his mobile ringing and he answered it, still half asleep. "Dan?" It was Katra.

"Hi, Katra, is everything okay?"

"Everything's fine. Liam did his homework and he's asleep now."

"What time is it?"

"Nine o'clock."

Shepherd groaned. He'd meant to phone his son when he got home. "Tell him I'll call him tomorrow," he said. "I had a really busy day."

"I took the car to get the tyre fixed," said Katra. "I used the credit card to pay for it."

"That's fine," said Shepherd.

"The thing is, Dan, the mechanic said he thought someone had done it deliberately."

"Done what?"

"Punctured the tyre," said Katra. "He said it looked like a knife had done it."

"It could have been a nail or anything," said Shepherd.

"No, he showed me the cut and it looked like someone had stuck a knife into it. He said it couldn't be repaired, he'd have to throw it away."

"Don't worry about it, Katra."

"I thought it might be that man, the one that came around to the house."

Shepherd shook his head, trying to clear his thoughts. She meant Jorgji Talovic. "I don't think that's likely," he said.

"Who, then?"

"If it was anyone it could have been kids but it's easy enough to get a nick in a tyre."

"Okay," she said, but he could tell she wasn't convinced.

"If it worries you, leave the car in the garage from now on," he said. "But, really, I don't think you need worry about it. If it was somebody with a grudge, they wouldn't just do one tyre, they'd do them all." Shepherd ended the call and put the phone on the floor. He closed his eyes and seconds later he was fast asleep. He woke up again in the small hours and groped his way upstairs to bed, where he fell asleep again, still fully clothed.

At seven thirty Shepherd was woken by his alarm clock. He sat up rubbing his face and wondering why there was such a bad taste in his mouth. Then he realised he was still wearing his clothes and that he hadn't cleaned his teeth the previous night.

380

He stripped off his clothes, brushed his teeth, then shaved and showered. He felt well rested, which was hardly surprising since he'd slept for almost twelve hours.

He watched Sky News as he ate a fried-egg sandwich and drank a cup of coffee. There was nothing about the Fox brothers, but that wasn't surprising. Shepherd doubted that their relatives would have gone running to the police when they didn't return from their fishing trip.

He drove his bike to Paddington Green. The security guard at the gate knew who he was now so there was no need for him to show his warrant card: he just nodded and the guard opened the gate. As he was parking his bike his mobile began to ring. He didn't recognise the number but he took the call. "You bastard! The police are still after my son!" a man shouted.

Shepherd took the phone away from his ear and looked at the number again. "Who is this?" he said.

"You know who I am. Peter's father. I told you, your boy has to tell the police my son had nothing to do with the video on his phone."

"And I told you, my son isn't going to lie to the police."

"You want a problem with me?" said Talovic. "Is that what you want? You want to fight with me?"

"I don't want to fight with anyone, Mr Talovic," said Shepherd. "The policemen I spoke to seemed reasonable. Just tell them your side of the story."

"You did talk to the police! I knew it!"

"They questioned my son," explained Shepherd, patiently. "They wanted to know where he got the video from. My son told them. If your son received the video from someone else, all he has to do is to explain that to the police."

"The police say my son made the video. They say he was there — they say he was encouraging them."

"Is that true?"

"I don't care if it's true or not true," said Talovic. "I don't want my son in trouble with the police."

"It sounds like he's in trouble already," said Shepherd. "Look, Mr Talovic, this is nothing to do with me."

"It's everything to do with you," said Talovic. "It's your fault. You have to fix it."

"I'm going to end this call now, Mr Talovic. I've nothing more to say to you."

A few seconds later, Shepherd's phone rang again. It was Talovic. Shepherd pressed the red button to reject the call. Talovic tried another three times before he gave up.

Shepherd paced up and down the car park, wondering what he should do. Talovic was becoming a nuisance and an aggressive one at that. He called SOCA's intelligence unit in a nondescript office building in Pimlico, central London. The woman who answered said only, "Hello." It was standard procedure for SOCA operatives, who were instructed never to identify their location or function. If Shepherd had asked if he was talking to SOCA or to Intel the woman would immediately have ended the call.

"Good morning, I need a mobile phone number checking, please," he said.

"Name, ID number and radio call sign?" asked the woman. Shepherd gave his full name and the two SOCA numbers. "And the number of the phone?" Shepherd gave her the number of the phone that Talovic had used to call him. "Please hold," said the woman. Shepherd heard her typing away on a computer terminal. There was a brief pause, then more tapping. "The phone is registered to a Mr Jorgji Talovic. I have an address in Hereford if you want it."

"Please," said Shepherd. "And while I'm on would you run a PNC check on him for me?"

"Hold the line," said the operator. This time the line was quiet for almost a full five minutes before the operator came back. "Nothing on the PNC," she said.

Shepherd thanked her and ended the call. As he turned he realised that Ross Mayhew was standing behind him. The CSO was wearing a fluorescent jacket and holding his cap. Mayhew grinned. "How's it going, Three-amp?"

"Same old," said Shepherd, wondering if the CSO had overheard his conversation. "You heard about my nickname, then?"

"It could have been worse."

"What about you? Did they give you one?"

"I'm only a bloody CSO, me," said Mayhew. "Nicknames are for the TSG."

"You heading out?" asked Shepherd, still trying to read the man's face, looking for any indication that he'd overheard the conversation.

"Time to walk the streets for a bit, fly the flag," said Mayhew. "The guys said you were former army."

Shepherd nodded. "Three Para."

"See much action?"

"Afghanistan. Just one tour."

"Heavy?" said Mayhew.

"Wasn't too bad," said Shepherd.

"I was in Iraq, did two tours, the last one in 2007," said Mayhew. "I was with the First Battalion, Royal Green Jackets but by the time I left it was Second Battalion, The Rifles."

Shepherd felt his pulse quicken. There were times in his undercover life when his legend collided with the real world, and they were the times when he was at his most vulnerable. Of all the battalions in the British Army, Ross Mayhew had served in the same one as Tommy Gannon. Shepherd instantly flashed back to Gannon's funeral but he was sure that Mayhew hadn't been at the service.

"Why did you leave?" he asked.

"Got fed up with the BS," he said. "Loved the action but back in the UK it was just square-bashing bollocks. You?"

Shepherd rubbed his shoulder. "Took a bullet," he said. "Didn't want to push my luck."

"Plenty of guns in London," said Mayhew.

"That's the truth," agreed Shepherd. He was watching Mayhew carefully for any sign that the CSO was anything other than just a chatty colleague. "How's the CSO thing working for you?"

Mayhew pulled a face. "It's a foot in the door," he said. "I really wanted to be a cop but I didn't fit the right ethnic profile."

"What?" Shepherd was confused.

Mayhew took a step closer to him and lowered his voice. "The Met doesn't want guys like me," he said. "They want the right ethnic mix, and that means blacks and Asians and women get priority."

"Are you serious?"

"Deadly," said Mayhew. He looked over his shoulder as if he was worried about being overheard. "Of course they can't say that, but I was told on the QT. A few years ago they'd have fallen over themselves to take me on, but it's all changed. Now the Met wants to show how diverse it is so Asians and blacks walk into the job but guys like me are shown the door. Still, can't complain. This pays okay and there's a fair amount of excitement. I'll stick it for a couple of years and then reapply."

"What is it you want to do? TSG?"

Mayhew shook his head. "Nah, CO19. Firearms. I was a good shot in the army, bloody good, in fact."

Shepherd turned to go. "Best of luck with it, anyway," he said.

"Did you hear about the Sikhs wanting to join CO19?" asked Mayhew. He looked around again but there was no one within earshot. "I'm not making this up. Sikhs have got to wear turbans, right? But in CO19 you have to wear helmets. So now they're insisting that the Met comes up with a bulletproof turban." He sneered. "A bulletproof turban. Can you believe that?"

"Sounds ridiculous," agreed Shepherd.

"It's a bloody travesty," said Mayhew. "Does that mean if they want to be police divers the Met has got to come up with a diving helmet to take their turbans? It's bollocks — it's political correctness gone mad and it's the likes of me that suffer. The Met should be hiring people because they're the right men for the job, not because of their bloody colour." He took a deep breath. "Sorry, didn't mean to blow my stack," he said.

"No problem," said Shepherd. "I can understand why you'd feel annoyed. But, like you said, you've got a foot in the door."

"How did you switch from the army to the cops so easily?" asked Mayhew.

"It wasn't that easy," said Shepherd. "There were plenty of interviews, the same sort of hoops that I'm sure they made you jump through. But I didn't apply to the Met. I got taken on by West Mercia. I think they're a bit less selective."

"Yeah, I know what you mean. Probably isn't a disadvantage to be white in Hereford. In London at the moment it's a positive disadvantage." He shrugged. "Anyway, can't say that, of course." He forced a smile. "I relish the opportunity to work in a diverse and multicultural society." He tapped the side of his nose. "I can talk the talk," he said, "and these days that's all that matters. See you around, Three-amp."

The team was called in to help with an evidence search in south London towards the end of their shift, so Shepherd didn't get back to Paddington Green until almost eight o'clock. No one seemed to mind working late as it meant more overtime. Shepherd was looking forward to an early night, but as he was changing into his civilian clothes Kelly came up to him. "Fancy a Spanish, Three-amp?" asked Kelly. "Some of the guys are going over the road to San Miguel — it's police friendly."

The last thing Shepherd wanted was a night out drinking, but he knew it was important that he appear to be one of the boys. "Sure, but I can't drink. I've got the bike."

"What is it with you and two wheels?" said Kelly. "You can just get the Tube back to Kilburn. Hell, you can almost walk it."

"You've talked me into it," said Shepherd. "I could do with a beer."

Simmons walked into the locker room and began stripping off his uniform. "Spanish, Nipple?" asked Kelly.

"Yeah, but lay off the *boquerones*, will you? Your breath always smells like a toilet the next day."

"Stop kissing me on the mouth, then," said Kelly.

"*Boquerones?*" said Shepherd.

"Tapas," said Kelly. "Marinated anchovies." He smacked his lips. "Lovely."

Shepherd pulled on a long-sleeved fleece. He walked out of the station with Kelly but Simmons and Castle caught up with them as they crossed Edgware Road. They went together down Chapel Street, opposite the Hilton Metropole, then passed a dry cleaner's and laundry. A doorway led to a flight of steps heading down into the basement. "San Miguel," said Castle. "Our home from home."

On the wall overlooking the stairs a sign said "OPEN" in red lights surrounded by flashing blue ones. "The blue lights are for us," said Kelly. "They like us here."

"Given the amount of money we spend, they should love us," said Castle.

The stairs opened out into a large room with a bar to the left and tables to the right. Several off-duty policemen were at the bar wearing waterproof jackets over their uniforms and drinking bottled beer. Shepherd saw Robin Potter sitting at a table with two Traffic cops and waved hello. Potter smiled back and raised his bottle in salute.

Castle headed over to a large circular table with six wooden chairs. Shepherd followed her. As they sat down Coker came down the stairs and joined them. An elderly waiter wearing a grubby apron came over to give them menus.

"Do you want a little wine, Three-amp?" asked Castle.

"Nah, I'm happy enough with my life," said Shepherd. "Nothing to whine about, really."

The men all laughed and Kelly banged the table. "He got you there, Pelican."

Castle ignored him and asked the waiter for two bottles of Rioja and two of sparkling water.

Kelly waved at the man. "*Boquerones al vinagre*," he said. "Two orders."

"Bastard," said Simmons.

"I told you, don't kiss me on the mouth and it'll be fine," said Kelly. "Veal casserole," he said to the waiter. "*Chorizo al vino* and mushrooms in garlic oil."

"Good choice," said Castle. "And I want balls."

"Of course you do, Pelican," said Coker. "That's why you joined the storm-troopers."

"Meatballs," she said to the waiter. She smiled sweetly. "Two orders."

"*Fabada*," said Simmons.

"What's *fabada*?" asked Shepherd.

"Bean stew," said Simmons.

"Yeah, I know it's been stew but what is it now?" asked Kelly. Simmons groaned but everyone else laughed. The waiter patiently wrote down the rest of the order, most of which came from Kelly. Then he shuffled off.

Shepherd looked at Coker. "You said we were storm-troopers, which I can't help thinking is a bit of a dangerous analogy."

"*Sieg Heil!*" said Kelly.

Coker grinned. "Okay, crack troops, then. When you've got a problem, send in the police. When the police have got a problem, who do they send in?"

"The Ghostbusters?" asked Castle.

Coker ignored her. "The bloody TSG, that's who," he said. "Who go into the places the borough are scared to go, and we deal with the scum that they're too frightened to go near."

"You've got a pretty low opinion of the rank-and-file cops, then?" asked Shepherd. Everyone at the table laughed.

"Let me tell you a story," said Kelly, leaning forward. "A few years ago I had a run-in with a very heavy drug-dealer. Nasty piece of work, East End boy made bad, was big into crack cocaine and heroin, selling it into some of the bigger housing estates. Got very heavy with late-payers, had no qualms about shooting his rivals, and killed at least three people to my knowledge. Ricky Wilkes, his name was."

"Yeah, good old Wilkesy," laughed Coker. "He's in Florida, right, doing life?"

"Yeah, he went over there to meet some Colombians and one of them was a DEA agent," said Kelly. "He was never the sharpest knife in the drawer. Anyway, when he was in London he was pretty much untouchable. Whenever the Drugs Squad got close he'd just buy off a few witnesses or pay someone to take the fall. He must have been responsible for twenty per cent of the drugs and half the assaults on our patch. Anyway, I decided to get him. I couldn't get him on drugs but I did pull him over once and got him fined a grand for driving without insurance. I used to do a stop-and-search whenever I saw him — must have given him a couple of dozen fifty-nines. Then finally I got him on a biggie. Found a young druggie Wilkes had knifed, nearly killed him. Had him charged with assault and almost got him but he paid off the victim, gave him five grand to forget what had happened. Anyway, that's when it starts to get a bit anti-woodentop because Wilkes found out who I was and got an address. My old address, as it happened, because I'd split from the missus and moved out. He got the old address and that means he got it from the book." He nodded enthusiastically. "And the only way he could have got my address from the book was if a bloody copper had given it to him. Some bent bastard taking a backhander."

Shepherd knew that every police station had a staff book: it listed all the officers, their next of kin, addresses and contact numbers. It was supposed to be highly confidential and only used in emergencies.

"Wilkes sends someone to cut the brake pipe of my car except of course it's not my car it's my missus's and she almost crashes," continued Kelly. "Luckily my kids weren't in it."

"Bastard," said Shepherd.

"It gets worse," said Kelly. "About a week later I take the kids shopping and we're in the Bluewater shopping centre. Wilkes had managed to track me there, don't ask me how, but he comes up to me bold as brass and right there and then threatens me and says he's going to put me in the ground. My kids started crying and, I tell you, if they hadn't been there I'd have done for him. Thing is I was off-duty so I couldn't do much even if the kids weren't there. Anyway, he says that he was sorry I wasn't in the car with the kids when it crashed but next time I wouldn't be so lucky. He went off with two of his mates. Just then a copper walks by, one of Kent's finest. So I tell him who I am and what happened and that I want to make a complaint and I want to get copies of any CCTV footage. You know what the woodentop does? He points and says there's a

391

station outside the shopping centre and that I should report it there."

"Moron," said Coker.

The waiter returned with their wine and water. Kelly waited until he had placed the bottles on the table and left before continuing his story.

"I thought maybe he didn't get what I was saying, so I took out my warrant card and said I was in the job, that I was with my kids and that I'd just been threatened by a big-time drug-dealer." He picked up one of the bottles of Rioja and sloshed wine into Shepherd's glass. "He couldn't have cared less, told me to go to the station and walked off like Dixon of fucking Dock Green. That's why I hate the woodentops, mate. Worse than useless."

"And what happened with Wilkes?" asked Shepherd. "Before he went tits up in Florida?"

Kelly carried on pouring wine for the rest of the team. "Why do you think something happened?"

Shepherd shrugged. "Because you don't look like the sort who'd let something like that drop," he said.

Kelly nodded. "Damn right," he said.

"You should have given the guy a good kicking," said Shepherd.

Kelly pulled a face. "Do that with a shit like Wilkes and he'd come back at you with a gun. Or petrol-bomb your house. Once he knew where my wife lived I was screwed. I backed off but tried to get him flagged with Intelligence. That's when I was told that SOCA were on to him and SOCA took precedence, so that was that."

"What did SOCA want him for?" asked Shepherd.

"They wouldn't say, but nothing ever came of it. Two years ago he went over to Florida and, by all accounts, he'll be inside for twenty years or so."

"So all's well that ends well," said Shepherd.

"I think you were right the first time," Coker told him. "Someone should have taken Wilkes down a dark alley and shown him the error of his ways. And screw SOCA for stopping you flagging him. Bigger waste of time than the woodentops, SOCA."

"I hear they're going to wind it up," said Kelly.

"SOCA? Where did you hear that?" asked Shepherd.

"Grapevine," said Kelly. "It's a waste of money. Too many highly paid cooks and not enough Indians." He grinned. "Spot the mixed metaphor."

"Yeah, it was supposed to be a British FBI but it's turned into as big a flop as the Child Support Agency," said Kelly. "Name me one major success they've had, one big bust. You can't, can you? We go into battle every day for no thanks, they get big salaries and company cars and do fuck-all."

Shepherd smiled and nodded. Kelly had a point, but he couldn't tell him so. The waiter came back with a tray of dishes and began placing them on the table. A waitress appeared with two baskets of French bread. Coker took a chunk before she had even put them on the table.

Shepherd stabbed his fork into a piece of chorizo and listened to the banter of the cops around him. They were totally relaxed with each other, friends as well as colleagues, and when they teased each other it was with affection and mutual respect. Yet again the bond between them reminded him of the relationship between the men in the SAS. They knew they could rely on each other, that there would always be someone there to watch their back, someone they could trust. Shepherd knew that he was well on his way to being part of that trust, that they liked Terry Halligan and respected him, but Terry Halligan didn't exist and the only reason he was trying to earn their trust was so that he could betray them. It wasn't the first time that Shepherd felt disgust at the job he was doing, and he was sure that it wouldn't be the last. It went with the turf.

Shepherd's alarm woke him at seven thirty and he groaned as he fumbled for the snooze button. He'd drunk six glasses of wine in the restaurant, which was well within his capacity but his body definitely needed more sleep. He waited until his alarm beeped again, then rolled out of bed, showered and shaved, then made himself a mug of coffee, still in his bathrobe.

Kelly had dropped Shepherd outside his house a little after midnight so he had to take the Tube to work. It was no great hardship but meant an extra fifteen minutes' travelling time. He sat down on the sofa, swung his feet up onto the coffee-table and phoned Charlotte Button.

"Good morning, you're up bright and early," she said. "How's it going?"

"All good," he said. "Had a night out with the boys and we're all getting on well. No one's asked me to castrate a rapist yet, but it's early days. Something I wanted to bounce off you. I had an interesting chat with a CSO at Paddington Green yesterday. Just chit-chat about making the transition from the army to the cops. He wants to be in CO19 but the best they would do is let him on litter patrol."

"And?"

"And I explained that I'd joined West Mercia Police and he jumped immediately to Hereford."

"Ah," said Button.

"Either he's very good at joining the dots, or he'd been sniffing around. And he knew about my nickname, which means he must be on friendly terms with someone on my team."

"You have a nickname? That's so sweet."

"Please don't do this," said Shepherd. "It's far too early in the morning for sarcasm."

"Come on, you have to tell me."

"No, I don't," said Shepherd.

"Pretty please?"

Shepherd sighed. "Three-amp."

"Three-amp? I don't get it."

"Good," said Shepherd. "Now, can we talk about this CSO?"

"I'll run a check on him," said Button. "What's his name?"

"Ross Mayhew. He was in Iraq, two tours." He decided not to mention that Mayhew had served with the Second Battalion, The Rifles. Button had never discussed the Real IRA attack on the Chinese restaurant but she must have known that Major

Gannon's godson was one of the men killed, and he didn't want her going along that train of thought.

"Anything else?" she asked.

"All quiet," he said. "How's Razor getting along?"

"Ticking over," said Button. "One thing for sure, Gary Dawson's going to be out of a job when this is all over."

"For his political beliefs?" asked Shepherd.

"For being a member of a racist organisation," said Button.

"From what I've seen, Dawson's more concerned about upholding the law than he is about race."

"We'll let the CPS sort that out," said Button.

"Any news of your successor?" asked Shepherd.

"Not yet," said Button. "Soon as I know, you'll know. I promise." She ended the call. Shepherd went upstairs to get dressed.

Working on the Commissioner's Reserve was more varied than being attached to the borough. The team could be sent anywhere in the capital and generally they went in larger groups, with up to fifteen vans turning up to some of the bigger incidents. On Wednesday they were on duty at Chelsea's Stamford Bridge stadium in west London, keeping the visiting Liverpool fans out of trouble. Despite football intelligence to the effect that a major fight between the rival fans was on the cards, the match went ahead peacefully and Shepherd and the team spent the best part of three hours sitting in the van in full riot gear, waiting for a call that never came. Not that anyone seemed upset at not seeing action — they were all happy enough to take the overtime. Shepherd's mobile rang three times while he was in the van. It was Katra, but he couldn't risk taking the call while surrounded by his colleagues so he switched off the mobile and didn't call her back until just after eleven o'clock at night.

She answered immediately and he could tell she had been crying. She sniffed and told him that someone had just thrown a brick through the sitting-room window. "Are yo —"

"We're both fine but there was a mess and I didn't know what to do," she said.

"A brick, you said?"

"Half a brick. Dan, do you think it was that man? The man who punctured the tyre?"

"I don't know, Katra. Did you see or hear anybody?"

"Liam and I were in the kitchen. He was doing his homework and I was ironing and helping him."

"Did you call the police?"

"I wanted to talk to you first. I called you but you didn't answer. I didn't know what to do, Dan — I'm sorry." She started crying again.

"No, I'm sorry, Katra, I was working, I couldn't answer the phone. Is Liam okay?"

She didn't answer and Shepherd pleaded with her to stop crying.

"He's asleep," she said eventually.

"Okay. What have you done about the window? It's not raining, is it?"

"No, the weather's fine. I picked up the glass and I've put a piece of cardboard over the hole."

"How big is the hole?"

"It went through the window that opens, on the left, and it's all smashed."

"Okay, here's what you do," he said. "In the left-hand drawer in the kitchen, where I keep all the receipts and handbooks and stuff, there's the business card of a glazier. They have a twenty-four-hour service so they'll come out tonight. If there's any problem call me."

"Do you want me to phone the police?"

"I don't think it's worth it, Katra. It's only vandalism so it'll be pretty low down their list of priorities."

"But it must be that man again," said Katra.

"We don't know that for sure," said Shepherd. "Did you see him?"

"No," she said.

"Then you're just guessing," said Shepherd. "The punctured tyre could have been kids messing around and so could the brick."

"I don't think so, Dan," she said.

Shepherd rubbed his face. Katra was almost certainly right: one act of vandalism might have been an unlucky break but two was almost certainly personal — and Shepherd didn't have any enemies in Hereford other than Talovic. And if it was someone he'd crossed in his undercover work they wouldn't be slashing tyres or throwing bricks through windows. But he didn't want Katra any more worried than she already was, and even if they did tell the police he doubted they would do much. "Let me deal with it when I come home, okay?"

"Okay," she said quietly.

"Katra, I'll take care of it, don't worry. Just get the window fixed tonight so that the house is secure."

"I will, Dan," she said, and ended the call.

Shepherd hadn't eaten since lunchtime but his stomach was churning and he didn't feel hungry. He made himself a cup of coffee, added a slug of Jameson's and sat in front of the television half watching Sky News until he fell asleep.

Shepherd's team spent Thursday providing extra security for the state visit of the President of France. The van was one of six that shadowed the presidential motorcade from Stansted airport, in Essex, to Downing Street and Buckingham Palace, then to the French Embassy in Knightsbridge. They had no time to stop anywhere for lunch but Fogg arranged for sandwiches to be delivered to them when they were parked at the rear of the embassy.

As Shepherd bit into a beef sandwich his phone rang. The caller had blocked the number but he climbed out of the van and took the call. "Have you told the police yet?" The caller was male, the voice gruff and aggressive.

"Who is this?" asked Shepherd. He turned to the van but no one was paying him any attention.

"You know who I am. Have you told the police yet? Have you told them my son is nothing to do with the video?"

"Mr Talovic?" He kept walking away from the van, still holding his sandwich in his right hand and the phone in his left.

"Have you told them?"

"Did you burst the tyre on my car? Did you throw a brick through my window?"

"Fuck you!"

"It was you, wasn't it?"

"You think a brick is something? I'll do worse than that — I'll burn your house down, I'll do whatever I have to do until you tell the police to back off."

Talovic began to swear effusively and Shepherd ended the call. Within seconds the phone was ringing again. Shepherd answered: "Look, I know that you punctured the tyre of my car and I know that you threw a brick through my window, and if you do anything else I'll report you to the police."

"I'm not scared of the police."

"That's clearly not the case, Mr Talovic, because if you weren't scared of them, you'd be talking to them instead of threatening me. There's nothing I can say to them that will make them stop their investigation. They already know that your son filmed the attack. All he has to do is to tell the police everything he knows."

"They will send my son to prison."

"He's under age," said Shepherd. "And he didn't actually hurt the kid. It's not your son they want, it's the boys that were doing the attacking."

"And if my son betrays them, what will they do to him?"

"He's not betraying anyone. He's just telling the truth."

"Your son has to tell the police that he got the video from someone else."

400

"I've already told you that he's not going to lie to the police. And if you do one more thing to my property or my family, I'll make sure that —"

"Fuck you!" shouted Talovic, and the line went dead.

Shepherd cursed and phoned Katra. He asked her where she was and she said she was at the supermarket. He asked her to make sure that the burglar alarm was set at night, and that all the windows and doors were locked.

"Is something wrong, Dan?" she asked.

"The father of the boy who gave Liam the video has been calling me. I don't think he'll do anything but I need you to keep an eye out for him. If you see anybody hanging around the house, call me straight away."

"Do you think he might do something?"

"He's just angry. I think he'll calm down eventually."

"So it was him that threw the brick at the window?"

"I don't know . . . maybe."

"Should I call the police?" Shepherd could hear the apprehension in her voice.

"Katra, it's okay. Just keep your eyes open, that's all. And when Liam's not at school make sure that he's in the house or the garden for the next few days. I'm sure there's nothing to worry about but it's better to be safe than sorry."

Shepherd put his phone away and walked back to the van. "Problem, Three-amp?" asked Kelly, as Shepherd climbed in.

"Nah, just someone trying to sell me a magazine subscription," said Shepherd. "Dunno how he got my number."

"Not *Amateur Asian Slappers*, is it?" said Kelly. "My subscription for that's almost up."

Shepherd faked a laugh. He continued to eat his sandwich but he couldn't taste anything: all he could think about was Talovic and his threats.

Jason Brownlee didn't hear the police van as it pulled up behind him, but he looked around as he heard the doors open. "We want a word with you, Jason," said a policeman, putting on his cap as he walked away from the Mercedes van. He was in his early thirties and wearing a fluorescent jacket over his uniform.

"I ain't done nuffink," said Brownlee, keeping his hands in the pockets of his khaki cargo pants.

"If I had a penny for every time I've heard that," said the policeman, amiably. "Let's see your ID."

"I don't have any," said Brownlee.

A second policeman climbed out of the van. He was in his mid-twenties but already his hair was starting to grey and there were dark patches under his eyes as if he hadn't slept well the previous night. "Not even a driving licence?" he said.

"I don't have a licence," mumbled Brownlee. "Failed my test, didn't I?"

"Doesn't stop you stealing cars, does it?" said the younger cop. "Three TWOCs last year, right?"

"No comment," said Brownlee. He had the hood of his sweatshirt pulled low over his face and he kept his head down.

"Let's have a look at your wallet, Jason," said Fluorescent Jacket.

Brownlee sniffed and handed it over. Fluorescent Jacket flicked through the thin wad of notes and pulled out a credit card. "This isn't yours," he said.

"Borrowed it from a friend," said Brownlee.

"I just bet you did," said the officer. He gave him the wallet back. "Date of birth, Jason?"

Brownlee mumbled it.

"Get in, Jason."

"Why? I ain't done nuffink," said Brownlee, shoving his hands back into his pockets. "You can't take me in if I ain't done nuffink."

"You've been taken in enough times to know that's not true," said Fluorescent Jacket, spinning Brownlee around. He pulled the man's hands from his pockets and handcuffed his wrists behind his back. Then the two policemen grabbed an arm each and marched him towards the van.

"I'm going to the doctor's," said Brownlee. "I'm on the sick."

The policemen ignored his protests and took him to the rear doors. They opened them. There were two uniformed constables in the back of the van and they moved to the front to allow Brownlee inside. The second policeman followed him in and pulled the doors shut while Fluorescent Jacket opened the front passenger door and sat next to the driver.

"Why are you mob-handed?" asked Brownlee. "Scared, yeah?"

"That's right," said the officer on his right. "Scared shitless."

The driver pulled away from the kerb. The officer on Brownlee's right pulled a black bag from under the seat in front of him. "What's that?" asked Brownlee.

"Trick or treat," said the officer. He grinned and pulled the bag down over Brownlee's head.

Brownlee began to protest but the officer on his right seized him by the throat with a gloved hand and hissed in his ear, "Keep your mouth shut or I'll Taser you, scumbag."

Brownlee went quiet. In his four-year career as a housebreaker and car-stealer he'd been arrested more than two dozen times, but he'd never been hooded. He wanted to ask them what was going on but he didn't think the Taser threat was an empty one.

The policemen started talking about the forthcoming Liverpool-Fulham match, joking and swearing like a group of guys down at the pub, but they weren't regular guys, they were policemen, and Brownlee didn't understand why they had hooded him or why they had turned up mobhanded. The van he was in wasn't the sort of van they used to hoover up drunks on a Saturday night — they always had a cage in the back with two bench seats. The van they were using was full of seats, and it didn't make sense to use it to pick up one person. Being mob-handed didn't make sense either because Brownlee never carried a weapon, not even a knife. But nothing about what had happened made sense to him so he sat with his head down and waited for it to end. The van made a series of turns and he soon lost all track of where he was. He tried counting off the seconds but he gave up after two hundred.

The policemen continued to laugh and joke as if they were alone in the van, though at one point one of them tapped Brownlee on the shoulder and asked him if he could breathe. Brownlee swore at him and was rewarded with a slap to the back of his head.

Eventually the van came to a halt. He heard doors open and shut and then the sound of a metal gate being pulled back. The van moved forward again, edged over a bump and came to a halt. Brownlee's heart was racing and his face was bathed in sweat. He had no idea where they had brought him, but he was sure of one thing: they weren't in a police station.

He heard the side door slide open, then hands grabbed him and he was hauled out. He was half dragged, half carried across a concrete floor and thrust onto a chair. The hood was ripped off his head. Brownlee looked around, panting. He was in an empty industrial unit with bare brick walls and metal girders overhead. Bare fluorescent tubes lit the interior and at the far end was a large air-conditioning unit.

The cop who had handcuffed him appeared in front of him, holding a sledgehammer. He had taken off his fluorescent jacket and rolled up his shirtsleeves. He grinned at Brownlee. "So, let me tell you exactly what's going to happen, Jason," he said. "We are bringing your career to a halt, here and now."

"What career?" said Brownlee, frowning. "I don't have no career." He heard a noise behind him and twisted around in his chair. The four other policemen were standing by the van, staring at him with hard eyes. Brownlee turned back to look at the cop in front of him.

"You're responsible for about ten per cent of all break-ins in the area where you live. Did you know that?" said the cop, swinging the sledgehammer. "Do you have any idea how much paperwork you generate?"

Brownlee said nothing and stared at the floor.

"Every time you break into a house, two officers have to go around to talk to the victim, then we have to fill out a crime report and that's a dozen pages right there. Then we have to do a follow-up visit and liaise with Neighbourhood Watch and send a report to Crime Prevention and all because you'd rather thieve than work for a living. If we can stop you thieving, I reckon we could save ourselves over a thousand man-hours every year." He let the handle of the sledgehammer slide through his fingers until the metal head hit the floor with a dull thud. "Do you know what they do to thieves in Saudi Arabia?" asked the cop.

Brownlee shook his head.

"They cut off their hands," said the cop. "Not both, just one. Unless they carry on stealing in which case they lop off the other. But you know what, Jason? You hardly ever see a thief missing both hands. And you know why that is?"

"This is bullshit!" shouted Brownlee.

"It's all about deterrence," said the cop, ignoring his outburst. "Chopping off a hand is a deterrent. A slap on the wrist by a well-meaning magistrate isn't. Which is why you've been running riot for the past four years, isn't it?"

Brownlee glared at the cop but didn't say anything.

"You see, what we can't understand is why the courts didn't put you behind bars years ago, Jason. You've been caught in the act, you've been caught with stolen goods, you've left footprints, fingerprints, and once you left a turd in the middle of a bed, didn't you?"

"This is bullshit," repeated Brownlee, quieter this time.

"But what really pissed us off was the old lady that you pushed down the stairs last month. She was in hospital for a month. A month, Jason."

"I didn't push nobody," said Brownlee.

"It was in your patch. You broke in through the patio window like you usually do, you cut the phone line and you unlocked the front door for a quick getaway. It had your MO all over it. You understand MO, right? *Modus operandi*. Your way of operating."

Brownlee didn't respond.

"But she came home early, didn't she? Mrs Wilkinson, her name is. Alice Wilkinson. She was a primary-school teacher for almost forty years — did you know that? Two children, but she outlived them both, and she has three grandkids in Australia. You couldn't meet a sweeter old lady. And what did you do? You pushed her downstairs, face first. Broke her jaw, fractured her arm."

"I didn't do nuffink," said Brownlee, though his voice lacked conviction.

"She'll be scarred for life, the doctors say. Not that she's much life left, but every time she looks into the mirror she's going to remember what you did to her."

Brownlee shook his head, even though he knew there was no point in denying it.

"Her memory isn't what it used to be so she couldn't identify you. But it was you, Jason. Without a shadow of a doubt."

He swung the sledgehammer, narrowly missing Brownlee's knee. Brownlee flinched and began to beg them to let him go.

"That's not going to happen," said the cop, "not until we've done what we're here to do."

"Please don't," whimpered Brownlee.

"Here's the thing," said the cop. "We thought about running you out of town, but then someone else will have to clean up your mess and that's just not fair. What we've got to do is to stop you reoffending." He nodded at two cops who had moved to stand behind Brownlee. One of them bent down and undid the handcuffs. Brownlee jumped up, but before he could run the two men grabbed an arm each. "We're not going to do what the Saudis do, but we are going to make sure that you can't use your right hand — not for a while anyway."

"You can't do this!"

"Yes, we can, Jason. And you're going to take it like a man. And when we've finished, we're going to drop you close to a hospital. Funnily enough, it'll be the hospital that treated Mrs Wilkinson. I suppose that's ironic, rather than funny, but you get my drift, right?"

The two policemen wrestled Brownlee to the ground. Another officer wrapped a piece of rope around the wrist above Brownlee's right hand and pulled it tight. A fourth grabbed his left arm and held it to his side.

"Please don't do it — I won't rob again," sobbed Brownlee. "I won't steal — I swear."

"That's the plan, Jason," said the cop, raising the sledge-hammer above his head. "But remember one thing, and remember it well. If you ever tell anybody what happened to you, we'll bring you back here and kill you. That's a promise."

Brownlee screamed as the cop brought the sledgehammer down on his hand. The bones splintered, blood splattered across the concrete and he passed out.

Friday was a relatively quiet day and Shepherd spent most of his shift sitting in the van around the corner from Trafalgar Square, where local-authority workers were demonstrating against plans to slash their pensions. Intelligence had suggested that a group of anarchists were planning to infiltrate the march but in the event it passed off peacefully and by six o'clock in the evening there were only tourists in the square.

Shepherd drove his bike back to Kilburn, collected his BMW and headed back to Hereford. He was just leaving London when his phone rang and he took the call using hands-free. It was Charlotte Button.

"On your way home?" she asked.

"Yeah, Liam's got a football match tomorrow."

"How is he?"

"Heading towards his teen years with a vengeance."

"Still at the local school?"

"Yeah, he's fine there. Our au pair takes good care of him and his grandparents are just down the road."

"There's a lot to be said for boarding," said Button.

"Nah, I like hanging with him at weekends," said Shepherd. "He's at the fun age, you know? Old enough to have a decent conversation with but he still thinks I'm wonderful."

"You are wonderful," said Button.

Shepherd laughed. "You've called me up to massage my ego, have you?"

"No — actually, I've called to fill you in on your CSO buddy, Ross Mayhew. Like you said, he was in Basra. That was his last tour, as a sergeant with the Second Battalion, The Rifles. I don't suppose you know why they changed their name from the Royal Green Jackets, do you?"

"They were amalgamating regiments, I think," said Shepherd. "Cost-saving. Some of the regiments had to go."

"And they moved their barracks to Northern Ireland. I guess part of the government's policy of decentralisation. Anyway, again like you said, he did two tours. Did he tell you he left as a sergeant?"

"We didn't have too deep a conversation," said Shepherd. "Though he could have been feeling me out."

"He joined from school, did ten years as a squaddie and was made up to sergeant before his second tour. Left the army when he got back from Afghanistan."

"That's a bit strange," said Shepherd. "He must have been career army to do that long. And getting his stripes suggested he was doing okay."

"He handed in his papers when he got back from Afghanistan and he was honourably discharged. But it's not easy getting information from the army. Other than that he was honourably discharged, I can't get a word out of them. But I can tell you why he didn't get taken on by the Met."

"He says because he didn't fit the right ethnic profile."

"I'm sorry, what?"

"Mayhew said the Met was more interested in recruiting blacks and Asians."

"And you believed that?"

"I've heard similar things from other cops," said Shepherd. "The Met wants its workforce to reflect the community it serves, and that means it needs more cops from the various ethnic groups."

"Well, I can tell you that Mayhew wasn't rejected because he was white," said Button. "Apparently there were psychological issues."

"Post-traumatic stress disorder?"

"Perhaps, but that's not what showed up in the tests that all entrants have to take," said Button. "It was more a question of anger-management issues. Aggression is a great thing in a soldier but it's not always helpful for a police officer."

"So he had the wrong temperament for the Met but he could join as a CSO?"

"The criteria are a lot less stringent for Community Support Officers than they are for the police," said Button. "I guess because they don't have the same powers or responsibilities."

"He wants to be in CO19," said Shepherd.

"I doubt they'll ever let him near a gun again," said Button. "Do you think he might be in on it?"

"I don't know," said Shepherd. "I've seen him talking to the Serial in the canteen, but I just had him down as a wannabe. But, yeah, if he's got his heart set on CO19 there'd be no point in him sucking up to the TSG. I'll keep an eye on him."

"Meanwhile I'll have a word with a friend of mine at the Ministry of Defence," said Button. "Everything else okay?"

"Yeah, I'm easing in," he said.

"Any problems?"

"It's fine," said Shepherd. "Just winning friends and influencing people, setting them up for the big betrayal." Button didn't say anything and Shepherd winced as he realised how that had sounded. "I've had a tough week, Charlie. These TSG guys work hard and play hard. They're a tight-knit team, and when I'm working I'm never alone so I'm constantly on my guard. There's no let-up, you know?"

"I know it's not easy," she said. "Would a chat with Caroline help?"

For a moment Shepherd thought she was talking about Carolyn Castle, then realised she meant the SOCA psychologist. He chuckled. "I'm under cover, tracking down killer cops, and you think therapy's the answer?"

"I was thinking that perhaps you could talk through your feelings with someone who might be able to help put them into context," said Button, patiently.

"I'll go for a run with a rucksack full of bricks instead," said Shepherd. "That usually does the trick."

"Sounds like a plan," said Button. "You have a good weekend."

Shepherd arrived home just after midnight. Lady came running from the kitchen when she heard him open the front door and jumped up, pawing at his legs and whimpering. He patted her and tickled her behind the ears. He went through to the sitting room. The glazier had done a good job: there was no sign that the window had ever been broken. He made himself a cup of coffee and took it upstairs. Lady tried to follow him but he made her stay in the kitchen. On the way to bed he popped into Liam's room but his son was fast asleep. As he went back into the hallway, Katra opened her door. "Hi," she said sleepily.

"Go back to bed," he said.

"I'm awake now," she said, rubbing her eyes.

"It's late," he said, "I'll talk to you in the morning." She nodded, went back into her room and closed the door.

Shepherd showered and fell into bed. He was asleep as soon as his head touched the pillow.

He woke to the sound of his phone ringing. He rolled over and looked at the alarm clock on his bedside table. It was eight o'clock. He groped for his mobile and squinted at the display. Talovic. Shepherd groaned and took the call.

"So you are back," said Talovic.

"What?" said Shepherd.

"You are in Hereford. Now you can talk to the police."

"If I talk to the police, Mr Talovic, it'll be to report you for vandalising my car and throwing a brick through my window." Shepherd sat up. "How did you know I was back? Are you spying on me?"

"You have to tell the police that my son had nothing to do with the video on your son's phone."

"I've already told you that's not going to happen. I'm not lying to the police and neither is Liam."

"You want a problem with me? Is that what you want?"

"Mr Talovic, it's obvious that I already have a major problem with you. The only question is, how do I deal with it?" Shepherd ended the call. Talovic rang back almost immediately and Shepherd switched off his phone. He got out of bed, shaved, showered and pulled on a pair of black jeans with a denim shirt.

Katra was already in the kitchen and had a mug of coffee ready for him. She asked him what he wanted for breakfast but Shepherd shook his head. "I'm going out for a while," he said. "I'll eat when I get back."

"For a run?"

"No. I'll take the car. I won't be long." He sipped his coffee. "That man, Talovic, he hasn't been phoning the house, has he?"

Katra leaned against the sink and folded her arms. "Somebody has been calling and hanging up. It might have been him. But they don't say anything. When they hear it's me they put down the phone."

"And you haven't seen him hanging around?"

"No," she said. She frowned. "Has something happened?"

"Nothing I can't handle," he said. "Don't worry about it." He went outside and drove to Talovic's house. It was a semi with a front garden that hadn't been mown for at least a year and was on an estate of similar council houses to the north of the town. There was a Sky satellite dish on the end wall and a rusting Honda Civic in the driveway. Shepherd was trying to work out what to say to the man. He had no doubt that Talovic had thrown the brick through his window and punctured the CRV's tyre, but no proof either.

The front door of the house opened and Talovic appeared on the step. He was wearing his Umbro shell-suit and holding a rolled-up newspaper, which he pointed at Shepherd. "I see you!" he shouted across the street. "I see you watching me!" He put his hands on his hips and stared defiantly at Shepherd, his chin up aggressively.

Shepherd climbed out of his car. He walked towards Talovic's house.

"I'm not scared of you!" Talovic yelled.

Shepherd saw the net curtains twitch at the sitting-room window and caught a glimpse of a grey-haired woman with a tight, pinched face before the curtain fell back into place. He walked past the

Honda Civic. The back seat was filled with old fast-food wrappers and screwed-up carrier bags. There was a scratch running down one side of the car and a wing mirror was cracked. He stopped beside it and stared at Talovic. "This has gone too far," said Shepherd. "You're going to war over nothing."

"War? What do you know about war?" snarled Talovic.

"I know you slashed my tyre and threw a brick through my window."

"Prove it," sneered Talovic.

"And you did it for nothing," said Shepherd.

"Nothing to you, maybe, but my son is in trouble with the police because of your son."

"Your son is in trouble because he filmed an assault," said Shepherd. "A racist assault."

"Your son gave the video to the police. He shouldn't have done that," said Talovic.

"My son did no such thing," said Shepherd. "I showed the video to his teacher and the school called in the police. But that's nothing to do with Liam or me."

Talovic jabbed his rolled-up newspaper at Shepherd's face. "It's everything to do with you. And you have to stop it. You have to stop it now." He took a step towards Shepherd.

"I can't do that. It's a police investigation. It's up to them."

"Your son can tell the police that he was mistaken, that somebody else gave him the video."

Shepherd shook his head angrily. "I keep telling you that's not going to happen. He's not going to lie to the police and neither am I."

416

Talovic prodded Shepherd in the chest with the newspaper. "If you know what's good for you, you'll do it."

"Are you threatening me?" said Shepherd.

"I'm telling you that if you don't want something bad to happen to you, you'll tell the police that your boy made a mistake."

Talovic went to prod him again but Shepherd slapped the newspaper away. It fell from Talovic's hand and landed on the uncut lawn. "Don't touch me," he said softly. "I came here to talk to you, not to start a fight."

"We're already fighting," said Talovic. "You are trying to destroy my life and so I will destroy yours."

"Now you're being ridiculous," said Shepherd. "This is an argument over nothing."

"Nothing? You report my son to the police and you say it's nothing!"

"It's something that you can easily sort out with them."

"You caused this problem, you can sort it out," said Talovic.

"That's not going to happen," said Shepherd, quietly.

"Then if it doesn't, I'll fuck with your life — I'll fuck with you so bad that you'll wish you'd never set eyes on me."

"What are you talking about?" said Shepherd.

"I'll kill your fucking son and I'll rape that pretty wife of yours and I'll kill her and then I'll kill you and I'll dance on your graves."

Shepherd couldn't believe what he was hearing. "What?" he said. He realised that Talovic thought Katra was his wife.

"You're deaf and stupid, are you?" said Talovic, taking a step towards him. His face was so close to Shepherd's that spittle peppered his chin. He pushed Shepherd in the chest with the palm of his hand. "You will tell the police you made a mistake or I will burn your fucking house down."

Shepherd was genuinely stunned by the man's outburst. He had stood face to face with some of the hardest criminals in the country but had never felt anything approaching the pure hatred that was pouring out of Talovic. "You can't threaten someone like that," he said. The net curtains twitched again but he ignored them.

"I can do what I want," said Talovic. "You think I am scared of you? You're nothing to me. You're not even shit on my shoe." He stabbed his finger at Shepherd's face but Shepherd grabbed his wrist and held it firm. He stared at Talovic, and as he looked into the man's eyes he realised there was no point in saying anything to him. Talovic was beyond reason. He wanted to hit the man, to scream at him to leave his family alone, that Katra was his au pair and not his wife, and that if he went anywhere near her or Liam then Shepherd would kill him, but he knew that the words would have no effect on a man like Talovic.

Talovic pulled his hand away. "You tell the police it was nothing to do with my boy, or you'll wish you were dead," he said.

418

Shepherd narrowed his eyes but said nothing.

"You think you're a hard man, do you?" asked Talovic. "You don't know what hard is. You don't scare a man by staring at him, you scare him by destroying the things he loves." He spat at Shepherd — phlegm splattered across his cheek — then went back into his house and slammed the door.

Shepherd walked quickly to his car. He kept a small pack of tissues in the glove compartment and used one to clean his face. He folded the tissue carefully, wrapped it in a second, and placed it in the glove compartment. He drove home. Katra was still in the kitchen. Shepherd asked her to make him a coffee, then fished two Ziploc bags from one of the kitchen cupboards and took them to the car. He used one of the bags to cover his hand as he collected the tissue from the glove compartment and placed it in the second bag. Then he took the bagged tissue back into the house and put it into his desk in the sitting room.

When he went back into the kitchen Katra was peeling potatoes. "Is everything all right?" she asked, clearly worried.

"Everything's fine. Are you coming to watch Liam play football?"

"Of course," she said. Lady ran over to her, tail wagging, as if she knew that a trip was on the cards.

Shepherd took his coffee into the sitting room. He sat down on the sofa and called Steve Renshaw, one of SOCA's best biometric laboratory officers. He was based at SOCA's forensics lab in Tamworth, fourteen miles north-east of Birmingham. Their paths had crossed on several high-profile SOCA cases and Shepherd had been impressed with the scientist's professionalism. He apologised for bothering Renshaw at the weekend.

"No problem. I'm in the lab," said Renshaw. "We're backed up like you wouldn't believe. I'm doing twelve-hour shifts during the week just to stand still, and this is my third weekend in a row. Still, can't complain — the overtime's paying for my new conservatory."

"Too busy to do me a favour?" asked Shepherd.

"Never too busy to help you, Spider," said Renshaw. "Ask and ye shall receive."

"If I send you a saliva sample can you do me a DNA analysis on it?"

"No problem."

"Then run it through as many DNA databases as you can, especially Europol?"

"Ask me something difficult," said Renshaw. "Might take a day or two. Are you in a rush?"

"A day or two will be fine, thanks."

"Have you got a case number?"

"It's not a case yet. This is more by way of an investigation," said Shepherd. "I'll courier it to you."

"Okay, but just so you know that the evidence won't be any good in court down the line, there'll be no chain of custody."

"It won't be evidence, Steve," promised Shepherd. "I just need to know who this guy is, if he's in the system or not. If it's any help he's a Bosnian, but now he's got British citizenship."

"I'll see what I can come up with," said Renshaw. "Gotta go. I've got three million quid in fifty-pound notes to fingerprint."

Shepherd thanked him and ended the call. He rang a local courier company but their phone went unanswered. At the second number he tried he spoke to a woman, who said she would have the package collected before noon. Shepherd wrote Renshaw's name and address on a large manila envelope and put the Ziploc bag inside. He left it on the hall table with his Visa card and went into the kitchen. Katra was now cutting up the potatoes and dropping them into a pan of water. "I'm doing shepherd's pie for dinner," she said.

"With real shepherds?"

"No, with . . ." she began, then realised he was joking. "You're teasing me." She stopped cutting the potatoes and looked at him with a worried frown. "Is everything okay with that man?"

"I think so," said Shepherd, hoping he sounded more confident than he felt. "Just make sure you keep the doors and windows locked at night. And set the burglar alarm."

"Do you think he might do something?" She brushed a lock of hair away from her eyes with the back of her hand.

"People who make threats usually don't carry them out," he said, and knew that much was true. "He's just angry, that's all. He wants to blame someone for what his son did and it's easier for him to blame me than it is to blame himself. He knows I know about him now so he'd be really stupid to do anything else." He looked at his wristwatch. "I'm going for a run," he said. "I've left a package and my credit card in the hall. A courier should be coming for it some time this morning."

He went back upstairs, changed into his running gear and collected his rucksack from the cupboard. He ran for the best part of an hour, hard and fast, and most of the time he thought about Talovic and what he was going to do about him.

It was Thursday when Renshaw got back to Shepherd with the results of the DNA analysis. Shepherd was just getting out of the van in the Paddington Green car park and asked him to hold while he walked over to his bike. The rest of the team followed Fogg inside. Shepherd put the phone to his ear. "Sorry, Steve, bit hectic at the moment," he said.

"I know what you mean," said Renshaw. "I've been snowed under myself."

Shepherd looked at his watch. It was just after seven. "Are you still in the lab?"

"We never close," said Renshaw. "Now, that sample you sent me. I got a match through the Europol database."

"Excellent," said Shepherd.

"I don't know who told you he's Bosnian but the guy is Imer Lekstakaj. He's an Albanian, wanted for rape and murder."

"No way," said Shepherd.

"Is that bad news?" asked Renshaw.

"It's . . ." Shepherd exhaled deeply. "It's unbelievable," he said. Lekstakaj had obviously been allowed into the country without the most basic checks being carried out. Every day Shepherd had phoned home first thing in the morning and last thing at night to check that Katra and Liam were okay, and as nothing untoward had happened he'd started to think that perhaps the threat had passed, but clearly Lekstakaj was more than just an angry parent.

"There's no doubt," said Renshaw. "Odds are the usual one in eight billion."

"Can you send me the file?"

"I'd rather not, unless you make an official request. I'd need a SOCA case number."

"It's not at that stage," said Shepherd.

"I can give you details over the phone," said Renshaw. "He's a nasty piece of work. The girls he raped were under age. One was twelve, the other fifteen. The twelve-year-old was scarred for life. He slashed her face with a box-cutter. When her father found out he confronted Lekstakaj and Lekstakaj shot him. The father lived long enough to tell the Albanian cops what had happened. Lekstakaj went on the run but raped again. This time he killed her afterwards but he didn't use a condom either time so they have his DNA on file. That was back in 1994. The Albanian cops have been after him since then but they don't know where he is now. Have you got a pen?"

Shepherd smiled. "Just tell me, Steve, my memory's pretty good," he said.

Shepherd got back to his house in Kilburn just after seven o'clock on Friday evening. It had been a tough week and he was dog tired but he wanted to get back to Hereford so he took a quick shower, gulped down a mug of black coffee and picked up his BMW X3. He was just leaving London when his mobile rang. It was Katra and he took the call on hands-free. "Dan . . ." she said, and started crying.

"What? What is it?" asked Shepherd.

"It's Lady," she said. "She's dead."

Shepherd braked to avoid a cyclist, an overweight woman who was wobbling from side to side as she tried to build up speed. "What happened?" The woman swore at him as he drove by, her face contorted into a snarl.

"The vet says she ate something she shouldn't have, but we didn't see her eating anything, Dan. She just got sick and started foaming at the mouth. We took her to the vet but she died."

"I'm sorry, Katra. Did the vet say what it was?"

"She said she didn't know but she said she could do an autopsy tomorrow and find out. Do you think we should do that?"

"Sure — we have to find out what happened. How's Liam taking it?"

"Oh, Dan, he's so upset. We came back from the vet and he went upstairs to his bedroom. He was crying, I think."

"Get him for me, Katra, I'll talk to him."

"He's locked the door," said Katra. "He won't open it."

"Okay, I'll call his mobile. I'm driving back now so I'll be there in a few hours. About midnight, probably.

And listen, Katra, I need you to make sure all the doors and windows are locked."

"It's that man, isn't it? Peter's father?"

"Let's wait until I'm home and we'll talk about it then," said Shepherd. He ended the call and tapped out Liam's number. The phone rang out but Liam didn't answer. Shepherd called Katra and asked her to go upstairs and tell Liam to answer his phone. He waited two minutes and called again. This time Liam answered. "Liam, I'm so sorry about what happened," said Shepherd.

"It was horrible, Dad, she was in so much pain."

"I'm sorry."

"She'd eaten something but I didn't give her anything, just a dog treat. She hadn't had her supper because we give her supper when we're eating."

"We'll get another dog," said Shepherd. He braked as he approached traffic-lights on red.

"I don't want another dog!" snapped Liam. "I want Lady!"

Shepherd grimaced. He'd said the wrong thing. "I know, I know . . . I'm sorry."

"She was really hurting, Dad, and there was nothing I could do. She was looking at me like she wanted me to help but I couldn't." He began to cry.

"Liam, I'm so sorry. I'll wake you up when I get home."

"I'm okay," said Liam, tearfully.

"You're not okay," said Shepherd. "But locking yourself in your room isn't the right way to go."

"I just want to be on my own."

"I understand that," said Shepherd. "But Katra's upset, too. She needs your support now. She really loved Lady, you know."

"I know," said Liam. He sniffed.

The lights turned green and Shepherd accelerated away. "Go down and make sure she's all right," he said. "I'll see you later."

"Okay, Dad, I'll take care of her," said Liam.

Shepherd arrived in Hereford just before midnight. There was no sign of the CRV, and for a moment his heart raced. Then he remembered that Katra had said she would park it in the garage after the damage to the tyre. As he walked up the path, she opened the front door for him. Her face was tearstained and her eyes were red from crying. "Dan, I'm so sorry," she said.

"It's not your fault," said Shepherd, hugging her.

"She was hurting so much," said Katra. She wiped her nose with the back of her hand. "I don't know what happened."

"I'll talk to the vet tomorrow. Is Liam okay?"

"He's sleeping, I think," she said.

Shepherd thanked her and hurried upstairs. He pushed open the door to Liam's bedroom. As the light from the hallway fell across the bed, Liam opened his eyes. "Dad," he said. Shepherd went over to him and sat down beside him. "What time is it?" asked Liam, rubbing his eyes.

"Late," said Shepherd. He bent down and kissed his son on the top of the head. He wrinkled his nose. "When was the last time you washed your hair?"

426

"Yesterday?"

"Are you sure?"

"Wednesday, maybe."

"Make sure you use shampoo after the match tomorrow."

"I don't want to play."

"You have to," said Shepherd. "You're on the team."

"They can play without me," he said.

"It'll take your mind off things," said Shepherd.

Liam sat up. "I don't want to take my mind off anything," he said.

"I just meant it's better to be doing something, that's all. If you don't want to play, that's fine, but I don't think you should let the team down."

"Okay, Dad."

"Are you okay?"

"What are we going to do about Lady?"

"What do you mean?"

"Do we bury her? Or do we cremate her? Do we go to a church?"

"I'll ask the vet tomorrow," said Shepherd.

"Can I come?"

"Best not," said Shepherd. He tucked the quilt around his son and sat with him until he was asleep.

Shepherd woke up at nine o'clock. Liam was still asleep but Katra was in the kitchen. She made him a cup of coffee and an omelette.

"I didn't want to wake Liam, I don't think he slept well last night," said Shepherd as he sat down with his breakfast.

427

"What are you going to do?"

"I'll talk to the vet," said Shepherd.

"I mean about that man."

"We don't know for sure that it was him," said Shepherd. "I want to find out what happened and then I'll know how to handle it."

"I thought things like this didn't happen in this country."

"They don't, usually," said Shepherd. "But there are bad people all over the world. But let's not jump to conclusions. Let me speak to the vet first."

He finished his breakfast and drove to the vet's surgery. Susan Heaton worked from home, a pretty, ivy-covered cottage with a garden that had been concreted over to make parking spaces for six cars. He pushed open the front door where a young Asian girl in a white coat smiled brightly at him. "I'm Dan Shepherd, here to see Miss Heaton," he said.

Before the receptionist could reply, the vet came out of her office. She was in her early thirties, with short blonde hair and pale blue eyes. Like the receptionist, she was wearing a long white coat but she had shapely legs and high heels. She was talking on a mobile phone but she ended the call and smiled sympathetically at Shepherd. "Mr Shepherd, I'm so sorry about what happened to Lady. She was such a sweet dog." She put the phone in the pocket of her coat and picked up a clipboard off the reception counter.

"Thank you," said Shepherd. "Do you have any idea what happened to her?"

428

She ushered him into her office. It was bright and airy with french windows looking out over her garden. Her degree was on the wall, along with framed photographs of several dozen cats, dogs and ponies, which Shepherd assumed were grateful patients. As she sat down, she put the clipboard on her desk. "There was some partially digested meat in Lady's stomach," said the vet. "Hot-dog sausage, I think. The rat poison was inside it."

"Liam didn't feed Lady yesterday," said Shepherd. "He just gave her a dog treat."

The vet nodded. "The dog treat was still in her stomach. Mr Shepherd, you do understand what I'm saying, don't you? The poison couldn't have got into the meat accidentally."

"I understand," said Shepherd. "Somebody deliberately poisoned Lady."

Heaton held up her hands. "No, I'm not saying that, Mr Shepherd. It could have just been someone with a grudge against dogs. Did Lady go out to the park, or anywhere else?"

"I'm pretty sure she was in the house or the garden at all times," he said.

"What about walking her on the lead? Did she eat anything, sniff around any rubbish, that sort of thing?"

"Liam says she was in the house or the garden all day."

Heaton grimaced. "Then I think you have to consider that someone did target her." She sighed. "That's horrible. I'm so sorry."

"In cases like this, do you have to notify the police?" asked Shepherd.

The vet shook her head. "No, but I suggest that you do," she said. "We can't have people throwing poisoned sausages around. A child could pick it up. Rat poison is deadly to animals and humans. Do you have any idea who might have done it?"

Shepherd had a pretty good idea who'd done it but he didn't want to tell the vet. "What happens now to Lady?" he asked.

"That's up to you," she said. "I can dispose of the remains if you want. Or there are places that can arrange burials. Or some people bury their pets in the garden. It's up to you."

"Can I talk to Liam and get back to you?" said Shepherd.

Heaton smiled. "Of course you can. There's no rush. We'll keep her refrigerated, so any time next week will be fine."

Shepherd stood up and offered his hand. She shook it. She wasn't wearing a wedding ring, he noticed. "And let me know what I owe you," he said.

"Sally can give you the bill on your way out," she said. "Look, I don't know how you feel about having another dog, but I've been taking care of one that's just given birth and I know her owners are looking for homes for the puppies. The mum's not pure-bred, like Lady, I'm afraid, so the pups are a bit of a mixture, but the mother has a lovely temperament."

"I'll ask Liam," said Shepherd. He thanked her again, then left her office. He paid the bill with his Visa card and got back into his car. He started the engine, but sat where he was for several minutes working out what he should do next.

Shepherd drove home and parked in the driveway. He looked up at Liam's bedroom window and saw his son standing there. He waved and Liam waved back half-heartedly. Shepherd went inside. Katra was in the kitchen, chopping onions. "Katra, you didn't give Lady any meat yesterday, did you? Hot dogs?"

"I didn't feed her at all," she said, brushing her hair from her eyes with the back of her hand. "Liam gave her some dog treats. He was training her to stay and he was giving her a tiny piece when she did what he wanted."

"So he was in the garden with her?"

Katra nodded. "For an hour after he got back from school."

"And did you see any meat or anything like that lying around?"

Katra frowned and brushed her hair away from her eyes again. Her eyes were watering and Shepherd wasn't sure if she was upset or if the onions were making her cry. "No," she said. "Definitely not."

Shepherd closed the door to the hallway to make sure Liam couldn't overhear them. "I don't want you to say anything to Liam, but the vet thinks Lady was deliberately poisoned."

Katra covered her mouth with her hand and whispered something in Slovenian.

"You mustn't tell Liam, okay?" said Shepherd.

Katra nodded. "Who could have done such a thing?"

"I don't know for sure," said Shepherd.

"The father of that boy in Liam's school," she said. "Maybe him? I told you I thought he burst the tyre. And what about the brick through the window? That was him, I'm sure."

Shepherd knew that Katra was right, but he wanted to downplay her fears. "Honestly, I don't know," he said. "We mustn't jump to conclusions. It might just be a random thing. Lady didn't bark, or bite anyone, while I was away, did she?"

"She was a sweet dog," said Katra. "As good as gold."

"Just don't say anything to Liam. I don't want him worrying about it," said Shepherd. He went out of the back door into the garden, stood on the lawn and looked around but didn't see anything out of the ordinary. He went over to the hedge and slowly walked around the perimeter of the garden, keeping his eyes on the ground. He spent a good ten minutes scouring the hedgerow and the lawn, but found nothing. Then he went to the side of the house where they kept the wheelie-bin and the hosepipe that he used to water the lawn during the summer months. He looked around but couldn't see anything unusual.

"What are you looking for, Dan?" asked Katra, behind him.

Shepherd jumped. "You could creep up on the devil." He laughed. "I was just checking to see if someone had tossed the poisoned meat into the

432

garden." He pushed the coiled hosepipe with his foot. "But there's nothing."

"Maybe Lady ate it all," said Katra.

"Maybe," said Shepherd. He grabbed the wheelie-bin and pushed it to the side. Katra gasped when she saw the hot-dog sausage lying on the ground. Shepherd bent down and picked it up.

"Be careful, if it's poisoned," said Katra.

"It's only dangerous if you ingest it," said Shepherd. Katra frowned and Shepherd realised she didn't understand the word. "Eat," he said. "It's only poisonous if you eat it. But I'll wash my hands, don't worry." He looked at the sausage in his palm. It seemed normal. He sniffed it, but it smelt exactly as he expected a hot-dog sausage to smell. He gripped it between both hands and twisted. It ruptured and Shepherd saw white granules inside. He cursed under his breath, then opened the top of the wheelie-bin and dropped it in.

"Is it poisoned?" asked Katra.

"I think so," said Shepherd, closing the lid.

"What are you going to do? Are you going to tell the police?"

"No," said Shepherd. "I'll take care of it." They went back inside. Shepherd shouted for Liam to come downstairs but there was no reply. He went up to Liam's bedroom and knocked on the door. There was no answer. "Liam, come on, I want to talk to you."

The door opened. "Hi, Dad," said Liam.

"Football today, right?"

"I guess."

"Are you going to be okay?"

"I'm sad about Lady."

"I'm sad about Lady too," said Shepherd. "I know it's maybe too soon to be thinking about another dog but the vet says she has some puppies that need homes and we could go and see them if you want."

Liam nodded. "Maybe," he said. "Are they beagles?"

"No, she said they're mongrels but they need good homes. Why don't you think about it?"

"Okay, I will," said Liam.

"And there's something else you have to think about," said Shepherd.

"What?"

"The vet wanted to know what to do with Lady. Whether you wanted to bury her or, you know . . ."

"Like a funeral?"

"We could have a funeral, if you wanted. We could bury her in the garden. Or there are pet graveyards. What do you think?"

"I dunno," said Liam. He rubbed his face. "I miss her so much."

"I know you do, and I'm sorry."

"She was such a sweet dog. She never hurt anybody, Dad. She didn't deserve to die like that."

"I know."

"She wanted me to help her but I couldn't. I couldn't do anything."

"You took her to the vet, and that was helping. So she knew that you loved her and that you wanted to help."

434

Liam wiped his eyes. "Did the vet say what it was?" He sniffed.

"She probably ate something that she shouldn't have," said Shepherd. "Try not to think about it. Just remember what a great dog she was and what a great time you had with her."

Liam nodded. "Okay."

"Good lad. And get yourself ready for football. Let's see you get some goals today." Then he hugged him. "I know it's hard, Liam. I know you miss her. You just have to get through it, and every day it'll hurt a bit less."

"Like with Mum, you mean?" he said. He was standing with his arms limp at his sides.

Shepherd put his hands on Liam's shoulders and looked into his tear-filled eyes. "Oh, Liam, it's nothing like your mum."

"Because I still miss Mum, every day, and that's not getting any better."

"I know. That's not what I meant. Of course we'll never stop missing your mum, and we'll never stop thinking about her."

"I do miss her." A tear rolled down his cheek.

"I miss her too."

"And I don't ever want another mum."

"Your mum will always be your mum, Liam. No one's ever going to take her place."

"And I don't want to get another dog. If we get another dog it's like we've forgotten all about Lady. Like she never existed."

"It's not about replacing Lady. It's about giving a home to a dog that needs one, that's all. But if you don't want to, that's all right. You don't have to decide now."

Liam nodded solemnly. "Okay," he said.

"Good boy," said Shepherd, and hugged him again. This time Liam hugged him back. "You make sure you're ready for the game, okay?"

"You're going to watch, right?"

"Of course — Katra, too. But I've got to go out for a while first."

Shepherd parked his BMW close to the police station and walked along the pavement to the entrance. The sun was shining and it was a warm day, but he was wearing a dark suit, shirt and tie. He walked into Reception and smiled at the female sergeant behind the counter. "I'm here to see DS James Hollis or DC Graham Cooper," said Shepherd. "They're expecting me."

The two detectives kept Shepherd waiting for thirty minutes. It was Hollis who opened the door to speak to him. He was wearing the same sports jacket with leather patches on the elbows that he'd had on the first time Shepherd had seen him. "Mr Shepherd, as I said on the phone, DC Cooper and I aren't actually on duty today. We're just in to catch up on some paperwork."

"Yeah, and I'm sure you're claiming overtime," said Shepherd. "I need to talk to you. That bastard has just killed my dog."

"What?"

"Talovic. He threw hot-dog sausages laced with rat poison into my garden."

"When was this, Mr Shepherd?"

"Yesterday. Look, I need to sit down and talk through something with you," he said. He looked over his shoulder. There were three teenagers sitting on the plastic chairs by the window, and an old married couple holding hands. "Can we have some privacy?"

"Come on through," said Hollis, holding the door open for him. He showed Shepherd along to one of the interview rooms. "If you wait there, Mr Shepherd, I'll get DC Cooper."

Shepherd waited for a further ten minutes before Hollis returned with his colleague. The two detectives sat down opposite him. Cooper flicked through his notebook and clicked his ballpoint pen before speaking. "You're here about Mr Talovic?" he said.

"He poisoned my dog yesterday," said Shepherd.

Cooper wrote in his notebook. "And why did he do that, do you think?"

"Because I reported the video on my son's phone," he said. "Prior to killing my dog he phoned me twice to threaten me, and he threw a brick through my window."

"A brick?" said Cooper.

"A house brick."

"And when was this?"

"Wednesday last week," said Shepherd. "And he punctured the tyre of my CRV."

"And did you report these incidents?" asked Cooper.

"That's what I'm doing now," said Shepherd.

"Why did you leave it so long, Mr Shepherd? It sounds as if it's been going on for some time."

"It has," said Shepherd. "He threatened me shortly after I came to see you with Liam. He's made intimidating phone calls, he tried to assault me, he's killed my dog, punctured the tyre of my car and thrown a brick through my window. I want him arrested and charged."

"When did the assault take place?" asked Cooper.

"Last Saturday. I went around to his house and he tried to hit me, then spat at me."

"And, again, you didn't report it at the time?"

"I'm reporting it now," said Shepherd.

"Why did you go around to his house?"

"Because he'd thrown a brick through my window."

"Do you have evidence of this?"

"He didn't deny it," said Shepherd. "And he assaulted me."

"Were you injured?" asked Cooper.

"No. I wasn't injured, but he attacked me. But that's not the reason I'm here. His name isn't really Jorgji Talovic, and he's not a Bosnian. He's Albanian. His real name is Imer Lekstakaj and there are outstanding warrants for rape and murder."

"What?" said Hollis, looking at Shepherd over the top of his spectacles.

"He used a false identity to claim asylum here. He was never a Bosnian refugee. He's a murderer and rapist on the run from the Albanian police."

"And you know this how?" asked Hollis.

"I know this because it's fact," said Shepherd. "So what I need is for you guys to get in touch with the cops in Albania and have him extradited as soon as possible."

"How do you spell his name?" asked Cooper.

Shepherd slowly spelled out Lekstakaj's name, then gave the policeman the man's date and place of birth. "Europol has a file on him."

"And how would you know all this, Mr Shepherd?" asked Cooper.

"Look, can we go off the record?"

Hollis and Cooper looked at each other. Hollis shrugged.

"What is it you want to tell us, Mr Shepherd?" asked Cooper.

"Off the record, right?"

"What exactly do you mean by 'off the record' — because it means different things to different people?" said Cooper. "We could hardly let you confess to a murder off the record, could we?"

"I just want to talk without anything getting written down," said Shepherd. "Just to let you know where I stand."

"Okay," said Cooper. "What is it you want to tell us?"

"Off the record?"

"Off the record," said Cooper, clicking his ballpoint home. Hollis frowned and pushed his spectacles higher up his nose.

"I told you I work for SOCA, right?" said Shepherd. "So I have access to forensics. I ran his DNA by them."

"You had his DNA analysed without his knowledge?" asked Cooper.

"He spat at me."

"And you had the saliva analysed by your colleagues?"

"Yes."

Cooper looked at Hollis. "And you then ran his DNA through the Europol database?"

"To see if he was who he said he was, yes."

Cooper grimaced. "Have you any idea how many laws you broke doing that?"

"I was investigating a crime," said Shepherd.

"You work for SOCA. I'd say that a dispute between parents is a bit out of your remit," said Cooper.

"Which is why I wanted this off the record, so I could tip you the wink and let you get on with it. It's got to be a feather in your cap if you arrest an Albanian murderer here in the UK, right?"

"It's more complicated than that, sir," said Cooper.

Shepherd didn't like the use of the honorific. It wasn't being used as a sign of respect but to put him in his place, a way of showing him that he wasn't part of the system. "I don't see why," he said. "He claimed to be a Bosnian refugee and on the back of that lie was granted British citizenship. A simple DNA test will establish his true identity, and he can then be extradited to Albania."

"First of all, there's no guarantee that he would be sent back to Albania," said Hollis.

"There's a Europol warrant out for his arrest on rape and murder charges."

440

"But he's British. That was one of the first checks we did after we'd interviewed him about the video on the phone. He's a full British citizen, has been for five years now. We tend not to extradite British citizens to places like Albania. There'll be appeals up to the House of Lords and then it'll be on to the European Court of Human Rights. He's married to a Brit and the father of a British child. It'll be in the courts for years and, frankly, I don't think he'll ever be sent back."

"He lied to get his citizenship," said Shepherd.

"Unfortunately it's a lot harder to take away British citizenship than it is to get it," said Hollis, pushing his spectacles higher up his nose again with the middle finger of his right hand. "There's a whole industry out there geared up to protecting the rights of asylum seekers."

"But he was never an asylum seeker. He was an Albanian murderer on the run." Shepherd gritted his teeth and tried to control his mounting anger. Hollis was acting like a social worker, not a policeman. He wanted to shout and bang the table and tell the detectives what idiots they were, but he knew there was nothing to be gained from losing his temper. "Okay, how about this?" he said quietly. "Why not contact Europol and ask for details of Imer Lekstakaj? Compare the photograph and fingerprints on their file with Talovic. Then contact the Albanian police and let them start extradition proceedings."

"I'm not sure that'll help," said Cooper.

"Why not?"

"Because at some point we'll be asked why we were interested in Lekstakaj. Either at primary disclosure or secondary disclosure the defence is going to be provided with all the evidence we have and that's going to include the fact that you sent off his DNA sample without authorisation."

"I told you that off the record," said Shepherd.

"Understood, but that doesn't mean I can forget what you said," said Cooper. "At some point we'll be asked what sparked off this investigation and why we suspected that Talovic isn't who he says he is. And the answer to that question is that you took it upon yourself to use SOCA facilities to carry out a personal investigation. And that is obviously going to weaken any case we have."

"That's ridiculous," snapped Shepherd.

"Is it?" said Cooper. "What if a judge decides that you acted unlawfully in taking a DNA sample from Talovic? If that were to happen, everything that followed would be inadmissible in court. And you'd be leaving yourself open to a civil action for compensation. For all we know, you could be the one ending up in the dock trying to explain why you acted the way you did."

"I didn't take a DNA sample, he spat at me," said Shepherd. "He spat at me after he'd threatened to kill my son and rape my au pair. I carried out a basic check on a man who I believe to be a danger to me and my family. You'd have done the same."

"Actually, sir, I wouldn't," said Cooper.

There was the honorific again. It was Cooper putting distance between himself and Shepherd.

442

"What would you have done?"

"When he spat at you? Phoned the police." Cooper put down his ballpoint pen, folded his arms and looked impassively at Shepherd.

"What — dialled nine-nine-nine?"

"Called us. Called the station."

"And what would you have done? Rushed around and arrested him for spitting?"

"We would have taken your statement and added it to our report," said Hollis.

"And what about my dog? He's killed my dog."

"Do you have any evidence that Mr Talovic poisoned your dog?"

Shepherd felt his pulse race. "Mr Talovic?" he said. "*Mr*? Suddenly he's Mr Talovic. He's an Albanian murderer and you're calling him Mr?"

"Actually, sir, that's racist," said Cooper.

"What?" said Shepherd.

"Calling him an Albanian murderer. You're using his nationality as a derogatory term and I'm afraid you can't do that."

"He's Albanian. And a murderer. I was stating a fact."

"It's down to tone, sir," said Cooper. "You have referred to Mr Talovic as an Albanian murderer several times now and that's a racist statement so I must ask you not to speak like that again."

"Or you'll arrest me?" said Shepherd.

"If you continue to make racist statements, yes," said Cooper.

Shepherd sat back in his chair and forced himself to smile. He knew there was no point in getting into a confrontation with a man who was clearly more interested in scoring points for political correctness than he was about fighting crime. "I apologise," said Shepherd. "I spoke without thinking. Perhaps you could tell me what the best course of action to take would be. Mr Talovic has threatened me and my family, and while there is no evidence to prove that he killed my dog, I do feel that the fact that it happened so quickly after him threatening my family suggests that he is probably involved. And there is no doubt that he spat at me and threatened me with bodily harm. So where do we go from here?"

Hollis sighed. "To be honest, sir, if you insist, we can charge Mr Talovic with threatening behaviour and possibly breach of the peace, but as no serious assault was actually committed he's unlikely to get more than a caution. But there is every likelihood that he will make a counter-allegation against you. And if, for example, he says that you assaulted him or made racist statements, then you will be facing more serious charges than him. Plus you will have to be put in the system. You will be charged, fingerprinted and a DNA sample will be taken, the facts will be presented to the Crown Prosecution Service and it will be up to them who is charged."

"So you're saying that if I do press charges against him, he could end up with a caution and I could end up in the dock?"

"I'm afraid so, yes," said Hollis.

444

"You realise that's crazy?"

Hollis sighed. "I'm just telling you the way things are, sir. My view on whether it's sensible or not is totally irrelevant. I just want you to understand that we have absolutely no discretion in the matter. We have to follow procedure to the letter. If Mr Talovic makes a counter-allegation against you, we have to treat that with the same degree of seriousness as we take your initial allegation."

Shepherd nodded slowly. "Okay," he said quietly. "So let's forget about going down that route. Mr Talovic is not who he says he is. He is not a Bosnian refugee, he is a criminal from Albania who is currently wanted by the Albanian police." He looked across at Cooper. "And I'm using Albanian there as an adjective rather than as a derogatory racist label."

Cooper nodded with no indication that he realised Shepherd was being sarcastic.

"So how do we go about bringing Mr Talovic, or Mr Lekstakaj, to their attention?"

"That's not really our problem, sir," said Cooper. "We're tasked with solving and preventing crime at a local level, not with the extradition of citizens who may or may not be the subject of investigations overseas."

Shepherd nodded slowly. "Terrific," he said.

Shepherd cursed under his breath as he walked over to his car and pressed the key fob to unlock the doors. He had used all his powers of self-control to prevent himself grabbing the two detectives and banging their heads together. He pulled open the door and heard a voice calling him. "Mr Shepherd! Hang on." He turned to see Hollis jogging along the pavement. "Hang on a minute."

"You're not going to charge me for having impure thoughts, are you?" asked Shepherd.

Hollis pulled a face as if he had a bad taste in his mouth. "I'm sorry about what happened back there," he said. He glanced over his shoulder as if he was worried about being overheard. "Cooper is a bit . . . Well, let's just say he's graduate entry and destined for bigger and better things. He wants to make commander by the time he's forty and he talks about one day running the Met." He took off his spectacles and began polishing them with a handkerchief. "Thing is, he'll probably end up doing it. He's a box-ticker, knows exactly what boxes to tick to move up, and he never puts a foot wrong. He goes by the book, and won't deviate from it for anything. And that whole PC thing, he means it. When he was in uniform they called him PCPC and behind his back now we call him PCDC. It's not going to have the same ring when he gets promoted, but within a year he'll be a DS for sure."

"So?" said Shepherd, gently pushing the car door closed.

"So he's a difficult guy to work with," said Hollis, putting his glasses back on. "He pulled me up in an interview last month because I said 'nitty gritty'. And he did it during a recorded interview so it's on the record."

Shepherd nodded. "I get it," he said.

"You know about 'nitty gritty', then? Because I didn't."

"It's what they used to call the detritus at the bottom of slave ships," said Shepherd. "It's now considered offensive to use it with black suspects."

"Well, you're better informed than I was," said Hollis. "We were interviewing two black teenagers about a few street robberies. Nothing major, they'd been stealing mobiles off schoolkids. The sort of thing that in the old days would have been sorted with a clip around the ear and a few harsh words. Nowadays, of course, it's all PACE and solicitors and social-worker reports. I told the lads that we wanted to get down to the 'nitty gritty' and before I know it PCDC is lecturing me on racist remarks. The two suspects loved it, of course. It's no wonder they don't respect the police, the way we act." He used the handkerchief to mop his brow. "Anyway, long story short, I just wanted to tip you the wink. Cooper is a master at covering his own arse and if any file on Talovic, or whatever his name is, goes across his desk, he'll tell all about the DNA test you did. He might even be putting it in the report now for all I know, along with a note that he had to pull you up on your racist remarks."

"He's an Albanian," said Shepherd.

Hollis held up his hands. "I'm not arguing with you, but PCDC will see things his own peculiar way and there's nothing you or I will be able to do to change that. I'm just saying that if you want to do anything about Talovic, I'd recommend that you give our station a body swerve. Try the Border Agency, maybe, and get him on his immigration status. Or, better still, see if you can get your mob on the case. Get a SOCA file started and leave out all the family stuff. Or find some way of getting the Albanians involved directly. Get them to approach the Home Office."

Shepherd nodded. He could see that the detective was only trying to help. "Okay, thanks."

Hollis took out his cigarettes and lit one. He offered the pack to Shepherd but he shook his head. "I shouldn't smoke either, but it helps the stress," said Hollis. "PCDC would report me if he ever saw me having a fag inside." He chuckled. "And he'd report me for using the word 'fag' as well, probably."

"Can't be easy," said Shepherd.

"It's a brave new world, that's for sure," said Hollis. "It's certainly not why I signed up to be a cop, but the likes of PCDC relish it. Ducks to water." He took a long drag on his cigarette.

"What's happening about the boy, Peter?" said Shepherd.

"Gone to ground," Hollis said. "Hasn't been at the school since we went around to the house. Father says he's gone somewhere with his mother but can't or won't say where they've gone."

"So what happens?"

Hollis shrugged. "We wait. Try again in a week or so. It's not as if we can force the father to give up his son."

"You've looked for relatives?"

"We ran his surname but didn't get any matches. Of course, now we know why." He blew smoke up at the sky. "You didn't say what you did with SOCA."

448

"I'm in a low-profile unit," said Shepherd.

"I'm Hereford born and bred, so I've got a feeling for the guys who are with the Regiment. I hope you don't mind me asking, but I get the feeling you're former SAS, right?"

"You've got a good eye," said Shepherd.

"It's the way you carry yourself," said Hollis. "And the way you kept yourself in hand when PCDC was handing you all that crap."

Shepherd grinned. "Yeah, it wasn't easy."

"You should try dealing with it on a daily basis," said Hollis. "It'd do your head in." He took another long drag on his cigarette. "Look, it's none of my business, but if I were you I'd sort this out yourself. The law just isn't geared up for handling situations like you're in. You want my advice, get a few of your Regiment mates and go around and show him the error of his ways." He smiled. "Just don't forget to wear your balaclavas."

Shepherd watched the detective walk away, then took out his mobile phone. He tapped out Jack Bradford's number. His friend answered almost immediately. "Jack, can you and Billy do me a favour?" he asked.

"Name it."

"I've got a problem in Hereford and I could do with a couple of friendly faces watching my back. If you and Billy could be around for a few days, it'd make me feel a hell of a lot easier."

"We'll be there tonight — is that soon enough?"

"I'm around over the weekend so tomorrow night will be fine."

"Do we need anything?"

Shepherd knew he meant guns but was being careful on an open line. "I don't think so, Jack. Just your good selves."

Jack Bradford was as good as his word: he and Billy had arrived in Hereford just before midnight on Sunday. Shepherd had slipped out of the house and briefed them on the problems he was having with Lekstakaj. He gave them the man's address and asked them to keep an eye on him and on his own house until the following weekend. He explained that he didn't want Katra or Liam worried, so while they were to keep the house under surveillance they were also to keep a low profile.

On Monday morning he left his motorbike at home and caught the Tube to Edgware Road, opposite the Paddington Green police station. Before he went inside the building he tapped out a number on his mobile. Kenny Mansfield answered. He sounded flustered, as if he was in the middle of something that required all his attention. "Yeah, what? Mansfield here, who's that?"

"Kenny, it's Dan Shepherd. SOCA. We met last year for the briefing on criminals in Pattaya."

"Sure, Dan. Look, can I call you back in about five minutes?"

"No sweat. Talk to you later."

There was a Costa coffee shop along the road so Shepherd went in and ordered a mocha from a pretty Polish girl. Just as she finished sprinkling chocolate on top, his mobile rang. It was Mansfield. There was the hum of traffic in the background. "Sorry about that, Dan — I had a DS breathing over my shoulder."

"Are you busy?"

"To be honest, I've just popped out for a fag, so you've my undivided attention for the next five minutes or so. How did the Thailand thing go, by the way?"

"Not as expected, but I was happy enough with the result," said Shepherd. "Look, I need a favour, Kenny. Can you put together a briefing on Albanian criminal activity for me?"

"Not a problem," said Mansfield. "I gave a couple of lectures on Balkan gangs at Hendon last year. What is it you need to know?"

"Who's doing what, and what we're doing about them. Just to get me up to speed."

"Have you got an active case?"

"It's a grey area," said Shepherd. "Can I pop around this evening? About seven thirty?"

"Sure, I'm usually in the office until nine," said Mansfield. "Are you bringing your Scottish mate with you?"

"Razor? No, he's got other fish to fry. Cheers, Kenny, catch you later. Oh, one more thing, when I pop around I'll be Terry Halligan. It'll make things easier."

Mansfield laughed. "I don't know how you can keep track of who you are," he said. "Doesn't it give you a headache, slipping in and out of legends?"

"Yeah — sometimes even I'm not sure who I'm supposed to be," said Shepherd. He ended the call and crossed the road to the station.

★ ★ ★

The team were heading for a drink in the Hilton Hotel after their shift finished but Shepherd told them he had a plumber coming around to the house to deal with a leaking toilet. He caught a Bakerloo line Tube train from Edgware Road to Charing Cross, then spent ten minutes moving between platforms checking that he wasn't being followed before catching a westbound Circle line train to St James's Park. After leaving the station he spent another fifteen minutes walking around the park before crossing the road and going into New Scotland Yard, under the watchful eyes of two uniformed officers in bulletproof vests cradling MP5 assault rifles. He showed his warrant card to a uniformed sergeant. "Terry Halligan," he said. "Here to see Kenneth Mansfield. He's expecting me."

The sergeant tapped Shepherd's name into a computer, then nodded at a row of seats and asked him to wait. He picked up a phone and a few minutes later Kenny Mansfield appeared in the lift lobby and waved for Shepherd to join him. He was just under thirty, tall and thin and wearing a cheap suit that barely covered his wrists and ankles. "Nice to see you again, Terry," said Mansfield. He smiled at Shepherd, revealing teeth that had yellowed from years of smoking. Shepherd placed his wallet, phone and keys in a plastic tray and stepped through an airport-style metal detector. Mansfield waited until he had retrieved his belongings before shaking his hand and leading him to the lifts. "Do you want a coffee?" he asked. "I know you don't like meeting us cops out in public so the best I can offer is the canteen dishwater."

"Yeah, let's give it a go," said Shepherd.

They got into the lift and the doors closed. "This is probably a stupid question, but Dan is your real name, isn't it? Or was that SOCA thing a legend too?"

"Dan Shepherd it is, but I'm under cover as Halligan so it was easier to show his warrant card at the door."

"Impersonating a police officer," said Mansfield. "You know you can get into trouble for that?"

Shepherd chuckled. "How's the family?" he asked. "Last time we met you had a kid on the way."

"She's six months old and as bright as a button," said Mansfield. He took out his wallet and pulled out two laminated photographs, one of a beaming baby, the other of a pretty brunette holding her. "Her name's Emily."

"Nice," said Shepherd, looking at the pictures. "I guess you're not getting much sleep."

"Nah, she's brilliant," said Mansfield. "Sleeps through the night mostly, hardly ever cries — she's the perfect baby."

Shepherd gave him back the pictures. They arrived at the fourth floor and Mansfield led the way to the canteen, which hadn't changed since the last time Shepherd had visited. The walls were painted a drab orange and most of the tables were occupied by overweight office workers who looked as if a brisk walk would kill them.

"Grab a seat," said Mansfield. "How do you take it?"

"Black and no sugar, thanks," said Shepherd. He sat down by the bombproof windows overlooking Victoria

Street and watched the traffic crawl by until Mansfield returned with their coffees in chipped white mugs.

"So, you wanted intel on our Albanian friends," said Mansfield, sitting down opposite Shepherd. "They're not the brightest of criminals, so it's mostly violence-led," he continued. "The Romanians have some pretty hi-tech ATM and credit-card frauds going but the Albanians prefer a sawn-off shotgun and a kick in the nuts. They started in London with armed robbery, prostitution, people-trafficking, and extorting money from their own people. They're nasty pieces of work, generally. It's that old truism that the men with the least to lose have the least to fear. Albania is one of the poorest countries in the world. Throw one of them into Pentonville prison and he'd think you've put him in a five-star hotel."

Shepherd sipped his coffee. It was bitter and tasted instant. "Drugs?"

Mansfield nodded. "Once they had money streams coming in from hookers and extortion, like all villains looking to grow they moved into drugs, mainly bringing them overland from Central Europe. Any opposition and they shoot first and ask questions later. You think the Yardies are bad, these Albanians kill without blinking an eye. Have you got an operation planned? Because if you have you're gonna have to watch your back, Dan."

"It's early stages," said Shepherd.

"They tend to bring drugs, guns and girls in by the same route, often packed into the back of containers. The girls are forced to work, beaten and raped until they can't fight back. Once they've broken the girls, they start to use them as mules, bringing drugs in internally. Swallowing them and suchlike."

"This is mainly a London problem, right?"

Mansfield shook his head. "Most of them are in London because that's where the money is, but we've got ethnic Albanian gangs operating right across the country, as high up as Glasgow and Edinburgh, as far west as Cardiff. We're watching gangs in Liverpool, Telford, Lancaster, Manchester, even sunny Brighton."

"What about Hereford?"

Mansfield frowned. "Never heard of anything in Hereford," he said. "That's where the SAS is based, isn't it? Not likely to be a hotbed of crime, I'd have thought."

"And what are we doing about it?" asked Shepherd. "Are there ongoing investigations?"

"Nothing specifically targeting Albanians," said Mansfield. "They'll get pulled in as part of a Drugs Squad bust or a Clubs and Vice investigation. To be honest, if anyone's worried about the Albanians here it's the Albanians back in Albania. They know there's a problem. Their chief of police has been pressing the Home Office to send back a hundred criminals, more than three-quarters of them murderers convicted in their absence. Most of them got into the UK pretending to be Kosovan refugees."

"So what's the hold-up?" asked Shepherd. "If the Albanians can identify them, why don't we just ship them back to Albania?"

"They fight like hell not to be sent back," said Mansfield. "They'll claim that they'll suffer human-rights abuses if they get sent back, or that their trials were rigged in their absence and that they weren't allowed to give their side. Albania's legal system doesn't have the best reputation and it wasn't long ago that they had the death penalty."

"Even if they're convicted murderers, we don't send them back?"

"Especially murderers," Mansfield said. "They can claim that they were caught up in the whole Yugoslavian thing and as a result got post-traumatic stress disorder so that if they did kill it was down to the PTSD. And then they claim that they won't be able to get the proper medical care back in Albania. There's loophole after loophole in the extradition laws and there's a whole legal-aid industry geared up to exploit them."

"It's no wonder this country's in the mess it is." Shepherd sighed.

"A lot of them marry as soon as they get here and once they've got British citizenship it gets very murky," Mansfield continued. "The 1988 Human Rights Act gives them protection because their family life would be disrupted. And once it goes all the way through the courts, which would take years, it's still down to the Home Secretary to make the final decision. And if the guy can get enough friendly faces waving placards to say what an asset he is to the UK and if enough people petition their MPs, he can make a political decision and allow him to stay."

456

Shepherd pulled a face. "So there's nothing we can do to make sure that someone gets sent back?"

"We can start the ball rolling," said Mansfield. "We can put a case together and pass it on to the CPS, but then it's out of our hands. If the CPS decide to prosecute, they wouldn't be looking for extradition, they'd just be looking for a conviction in a UK court. The judge might give a recommendation that the guy be considered for deportation after he'd served his sentence, but he'd have to do his time in a UK jail first. And, like I said, it's not definite that he would be deported."

"What if the Albanians applied for extradition?"

"Then they'd be dealing with the Home Office, and you know what a shower they are. They're even worse than the CPS — couldn't organise a piss-up in a brewery." Mansfield sat back in his chair and fiddled with a red disposable cigarette lighter. "Why don't you tell me what this is about, Dan?"

"What do you mean?"

Mansfield smiled. "The Met has its fair share of morons, but they don't put them in Intelligence, generally," he said. "The clue's right there in the name. Intelligence. If you need help, just tell me what you want. I know you're one of the good guys, Dan, so unless it means me losing my pension then I'm at your service."

"Like I said when I phoned you, Kenny, it's a grey area."

"Grey's my favourite colour."

457

Shepherd sipped his coffee and grimaced. It really did taste foul. He put down his mug and looked at the young intelligence officer. He instinctively trusted Mansfield, and had done the first time they'd met. And Mansfield was right: he was nobody's fool. "There's a man in Hereford wanted by the Albanians for rape and murder. He got British citizenship by marriage. Now he's making my life difficult."

"Difficult in what way?"

"He's thrown a brick through my window, killed my dog, and now he's threatening my kid."

"Because?"

"Over nothing. His son Bluetoothed a video to my son of a boy being assaulted. I told the school, the school called in the local cops and this guy has taken it into his head that I can get the whole thing stopped. Which I almost certainly can't. I've tried reasoning with him but he just keeps on crowding me and I'm pretty sure that if I don't do something he's going to cause me a lot of grief."

"You've spoken to the local cops about him?"

"They were as much use as the proverbial chocolate teapot," said Shepherd. "I need to know everything there is about this guy so that I can do something about him."

"What information have you got?" asked Mansfield.

"The name he's using is Jorgji Talovic and he claims to be a Bosnian. But I ran a DNA sample through the Europol database. He's Albanian, his name's Imer Lekstakaj and there are outstanding warrants for rape and murder."

458

"So I'm guessing you'd like a look at those warrants," said Mansfield.

"You read my mind, Kenny. I was going to go all around the houses with you, but you're right, I should have just asked you straight out. I'm sorry."

"No sweat," said Mansfield. He stood up. "Let's take a wander upstairs and see what we can dig up," he said.

They left the canteen and took the lift to Mansfield's office, a windowless box that was filled with stacks of reports, reference books and magazines, most of them dotted with bright yellow Post-it notes. "Whatever happened to the paperless office?" asked Shepherd.

"Went the same way as 'peace in our time', I think," said Mansfield. "Pretty much everything that goes across my desk has to be stamped and signed so emails just don't cut it. Mind you, the number of times our system crashes means I just don't trust anything I can't hold in my hand." He cleared a pile of files off a chrome and leather chair and waved for Shepherd to sit down while he went behind his desk. Two computer terminals stood on it, along with more stacks of paper and three wire in-trays stacked high with internal memos. "I've told them that when I die they're just to lay me down here and set fire to the office, Viking-style," he said.

"They wouldn't do that," said Shepherd. "It'd contravene too many health-and-safety regulations."

Mansfield chuckled as he dropped down onto his leather executive-style chair. "Spell the Albanian name for me," he said.

Shepherd did so and Mansfield tapped the keyboard of the terminal on his left.

"You won't get into trouble for this?" asked Shepherd.

"I've got pretty much free run of the Europol databases, and our investigations are so wide-ranging our fingerprints are everywhere," said Mansfield. "But all I'm doing here is checking the Europol arrest-warrant list and that's widely available." He sat back. "I can't let you take a hard copy, but I seem to remember that your memory is close to photographic, right?"

"It's never let me down yet," said Shepherd.

Mansfield pushed back his chair and stood up. "Look, I'm gasping for a fag. Why don't you make yourself at home while I hit the pavements?"

Shepherd moved over to Mansfield's side of the desk and sat down in his chair. There was a Europol file on the screen. "Cheers, Kenny. I owe you."

"Always useful to have a mate in SOCA who owes you a favour," said Mansfield. "You do fix parking tickets, right?"

Shepherd laughed. "Yeah, I wish."

Mansfield gestured at the monitor. "It's pretty self-explanatory," he said. "Anything sensitive is password protected so you can't get into trouble." He took a pack of Rothmans and his lighter from his pocket. "I'll be back in ten."

Mansfield left the office as Shepherd began to read the file on the screen. At the top left there was a police photograph, a head-and-shoulders shot, face on, and two side shots, with a full set of fingerprints. Lekstakaj had served time in prison twice, once as a teenager for rape and again as a twenty-five-year-old, for attempted murder. He had pleaded guilty to knifing a man in the chest during an argument over a parking space and served just six years.

In 1996 Lekstakaj had raped a twelve-year-old Muslim girl, Elira Halil. Steve Renshaw had already given Shepherd the bare details of the rape and assault, but the file had the full Albanian police report and an English translation. And there were photographs of the girl's face, showing the deep cuts Lekstakaj had inflicted with a Stanley knife. Shepherd grimaced as he studied the photographs. Only a psychopath could have inflicted those injuries on a young girl. She had told her father who had attacked her, and rather than going to the police, the father had confronted Lekstakaj at his home. Lekstakaj had produced a gun and shot the man in the chest, then fled his small village in the foothills of Mount Korab. He had moved to the Albanian capital, Tirana, where he had worked as a labourer and part-time enforcer for a local money-launderer for almost two years. Then he had pulled a teenage girl into an alley and raped her savagely. Her name was Zamira Lazami and she had been on her way home from school. This time Lekstakaj made sure the girl wasn't able to identify him. He strangled her and stabbed her with a hunting knife.

The police found the knife in a storm drain and matched the fingerprints on it to Lekstakaj, but despite an extensive manhunt he was never found and the police assumed he had left the country.

Lekstakaj had no family, and had apparently never married or had children. There was a report from a prison psychiatrist detailing his mental instability and his tendency to be violent. According to the psychiatrist, Lekstakaj's rapes were merely an expression of his anger rather than for any sexual gratification; he would always be a danger to society. At no point had he ever expressed remorse for his actions and, according to the psychiatrist, he was a textbook sociopath.

Shepherd scrolled back up the screen and looked at the police photograph. Lekstakaj was staring at the camera with a total lack of interest. There was no emotion at all: his face was a blank mask and his eyes were lifeless. There were more wrinkles now, and the man had less hair, but other than that he hadn't changed. Shepherd knew now that he wouldn't be able to talk any sense into Lekstakaj. He was a brutish, murderous thug and he would keep battering away at Shepherd until he got what he wanted. Or until he was stopped.

He went back through the police report, then reached a section that had been compiled by the Albanian police's Europol liaison officer. There was an appeal for information concerning the whereabouts of Lekstakaj, with the officer's email address and phone number.

He scrolled back up and read through the details of the rape and murder of the schoolgirl. It was a senseless assault, vicious and cruel, the work of a crazed animal rather than a human being. The girl's mother was dead, and she had been living with her father, Aleksander Lazami. Shepherd frowned as he realised that there was a Europol reference number next to the father's name. He used the mouse to click on it but nothing happened. He studied the screen and spotted a search button in the top left-hand corner. He cut and pasted the reference number into the search facility and hit enter.

He sat back as the screen changed. Aleksander Lazami was also on the Albanian police's "Most Wanted" list and an extradition warrant had already been served against him. As Shepherd read the details, he smiled slowly. "What a bloody small world," he muttered to himself. The Albanians had tracked Lazami down — he had changed his name to Jovan Bashich and was now living in north London. The file on Lazami had a photograph but no fingerprints as he had never been arrested in Albania, but there were details of a trial that had been held in his absence where he had been found guilty of extortion and fraud. It had taken place a year after his daughter was murdered. According to the prosecution statement, Lazami was believed to have bribed his way out of the country and crossed the border into Kosovo and from there travelled to England where he had claimed political asylum and was eventually granted British citizenship. The Albanians had applied to have him extradited and the case was now working its way through the appeals system. There were also charges of possessing a consignment of AK-47s and attempted murder awaiting him if he was ever returned to Albania.

Mansfield appeared at the door to the office. "Everything okay, Dan?" he asked.

Shepherd grinned. "Couldn't be better," he said.

"Anything else you need?"

"Can you run a PNC check for me? I need info on a Jovan Bashich in north London and I'd be happier doing it here rather than at my base." Shepherd stood up so that Mansfield could have his chair back.

"No problem," said Mansfield, sitting down. "I'm running a couple of hundred names through the computer today, so the more the merrier." He turned to his PNC terminal, tapped in the name and sat back. "There you go," he said. "Runs a minicab company in Stoke Newington. Few motoring offences but nothing else."

Shepherd studied the screen and effortlessly memorised the details. "You're a star, Kenny."

Shepherd caught a black cab from outside Scotland Yard and had it drop him around the corner from the offices of Lazami's minicab business. Speed-E-Cabs was above a fish-and-chip shop, its location promoted by a yellow flashing light above a doorway leading to a flight of bare wooden stairs. Shepherd headed up and pushed open a door, wrinkling his nose at the pungent smell of urine, stale beer and body odour. To his left was a wooden bench on which sat two middle-aged women in tarty clothes arguing over a bottle of vodka. When they saw Shepherd's police issue trousers and boots, they quietened and tried to sit up straight.

464

"Good evening, ladies," he said. They both studiously avoided eye-contact with him.

Two middle-aged men with greasy hair and pockmarked faces were behind a thick sheet of glass into which was set a small wire grille. One was talking on a headset while the other was sitting on a plastic chair reading the *Evening Standard*. Both were wearing scuffed leather jackets with the collars turned up. Pages cut from pornographic magazines were plastered over the walls. To the left of the window, a wooden door had been reinforced with a sheet of steel that was dented in several places.

Shepherd went over to the glass and leaned down to speak into the grille. "I want to see Jovan Bashich," he said.

"He's not here," said the man reading the newspaper, without looking up.

Shepherd held up his Terry Halligan warrant card and pressed it against the glass. "Tell him if he doesn't speak to me now, I'll be back with a dozen colleagues and we'll be going through the licences and immigration status of every single one of your drivers."

The man put down his paper and for the first time noticed Shepherd's white shirt and black tie under his fleece. He peered at the warrant card, then looked at the other man and nodded. The man with the headset tapped out a number and spoke in a guttural language that Shepherd assumed was Albanian, then said something to the man with the paper. "What's it about?" he asked Shepherd.

"It's about me not kicking that bloody door down and arresting you for obstruction," said Shepherd, putting away his warrant card.

The two men looked at each other again. Then the man with the paper sighed and pushed himself up out of his chair. He had a bunch of keys hanging from a chain on his belt and used one to open the door. He pointed at a flight of lino-covered stairs. "Up there," he said. As Shepherd started up it, the man pulled the door shut and locked it again. Shepherd could hear the two women disputing ownership of the vodka bottle as he reached the top. There were damp patches on the ceiling that had gone black with mould, and holes in the skirting-board. Facing him was a door with "OFFICE" painted on it in white letters. He pushed it open.

The man sitting behind a large wooden desk was a good ten years older than the one in the photograph he'd looked at in Kenny Mansfield's office, but it was definitely Jovan Bashich, a.k.a. Aleksander Lazami. Lazami was a big man, at least two hundred pounds, balding, with a grey moustache and watery brown eyes. He was wearing a brown suit and a black shirt that glistened with grease around the collar.

Shepherd stepped into the room and closed the door behind him. There was a wooden chair next to the desk and he sat on it and smiled amiably at Lazami. "Nice place you've got here," he said. "Very homely." There was a framed photograph on the desk next to a pile of timesheets. It was a formal picture, and in it Lazami was wearing a much better suit than he had on now, with a red and black striped tie. He had his arm around

466

a dumpy blonde woman with pearl earrings. Sitting on her lap was a young girl, seven or eight years old with a gap-toothed smile and ringlets. The Lazami in the picture was beaming with pride and wasn't sweating anywhere near as much as the man behind the desk.

Lazami frowned and tugged at his left ear. "What do you want?" he asked.

"A chat," said Shepherd.

"You want to shake me down, is that it? You want money?"

Shepherd chuckled. "You're not in Albania now, Aleksander," he said. "We don't work like that in England. Haven't you learned anything since you moved here?"

Lazami's frown deepened. "Albania? Why do you talk about Albania? I am from Kosovo. Refugee from Kosovo. Now I am British. British like you."

"I know who you are, Aleksander," said Shepherd. "Don't play the fool with me."

"My name is Jovan Bashich and I am from Kosovo."

"I know who you really are. And I know you're not Kosovan. Your name is Aleksander Lazami and you're an Albanian. You're wanted for extortion, possession of arms and attempted murder."

Lazami's eyes hardened. "What do you want?" he said. "You want to send me back?" He slapped his chest. "I am British now. I am as British as you. And nothing was ever proved. Nothing!"

"The Albanian government has started extradition proceedings, but you already know that."

"My solicitor says that the British government will never send me back," said Lazami. "There is no evidence against me. And I have a family here now. A wife and a son. They were born here. No one will send me back." He sneered at Shepherd. "If you want to talk to me, you can talk to my solicitor. I have nothing to say to you. You will go now. You will leave my office. I have rights here. If you want to talk to me my solicitor must be here to advise me."

"I'm not here to send you back. I'm just here to talk about what happened to your daughter."

Lazami's jaw dropped and he sagged in his chair as if he had been punched in the stomach. "What do you know about Zamira?" He mopped his brow with a grubby handkerchief.

"I know everything, Aleksander." Shepherd pointed at the framed family photograph. "Your family here, do they know about Zamira?"

"They know nothing about me, other than what I've told them," said Lazami. "They know me only as Jovan Bashich from Kosovo. My wife, she is from Wimbledon. She has never been outside England."

"You married her for a passport?"

"I married her because I needed a wife," he said. "After Zamira was killed, I had nobody. I had nothing." He stood up and went over to a rusting green-metal filing cabinet. He grunted as he bent down to pull open the bottom drawer from which he took out a bottle of slivovitz and a couple of greasy glasses. He put the glasses on the desk and kicked the drawer shut, then sat down and poured two slugs of the plum brandy. He pushed one across the desk towards Shepherd.

468

"I'm in uniform," said Shepherd, gesturing at his shirt and tie.

"You don't look like a man who cares about his uniform," said Lazami. He picked up one of the glasses, raised it in salute, then drained it. "He raped her, then killed her. He raped my angel and then butchered her. He strangled her with his bare hands and then gutted her like a fish. For what? So she wouldn't identify him? He left his semen inside her and even the Albanian cops know about DNA." He refilled his glass. "You know what Zamira means?" He shook his head. "Of course you don't. Why would you? It means 'good voice'. And she had the voice of an angel, my little Zamira. She was always singing and I swear she could sing before she could talk."

Shepherd picked up his glass and took a sip of the brandy. It slid easily down his throat and a warm glow spread through his chest.

"The one blessing, the only blessing, was that my beloved wife wasn't alive when it happened," said Lazami. "You British, you complain about your National Health Service, but you have never been at the mercy of Albanian doctors. If Elira had been in England, she would be alive now but she was in Albania and . . ." He shrugged, leaving the sentence unfinished. "After Zamira died, I knew that I couldn't live in Albania any more. I wanted a new life, and I found it here in England. Getting here was easy — refugees were flooding in from Yugoslavia, and I used the papers of a man that had been murdered outside Sarajevo."

"The man who killed your daughter, you know who he is?"

"I found out afterwards who he was. He had done it before, raped a girl. I paid the cops for a look at his file. But he's nowhere to be found. They think he left Albania after he killed her."

"Imer Lekstakaj?"

"Yes. May he burn in everlasting hell." Lazami banged his glass down on the desk, hard. "I call them even now but the case is cold. They don't know where he is."

"They don't know where he is, Aleksander. But I do." Shepherd took another sip of his brandy.

Lazami leaned forward. "Whatever you want, I will give it to you," he said, his eyes burning. "You want money? I will give everything I have. Just tell me where he is."

"I don't want your money. This isn't about money." He reached into his pocket and took out the three photographs that Kenny Mansfield had given him. He slid them across the desk one by one.

Lazami stared at the photographs but made no move to touch them. He nodded slowly. "That is him," he said, his voice a hoarse whisper. "That is the man who killed my daughter." He looked at Shepherd, his eyes watering. "You have to tell me where he is."

"That's why I'm here," said Shepherd.

First thing on Tuesday morning, Shepherd phoned Jack Bradford and told him to drop the surveillance on Lekstakaj and watch over Shepherd's house instead.

470

Jack hadn't asked for an explanation. Shepherd spent the day with his team, prowling around north-east London, breaking for lunch at Harlesden police station. He was called a racist at least half a dozen times. Shepherd no longer took the insults personally — no one wanted to be stopped and searched and it was natural to blow off a little steam. Like all the members of the team, he simply smiled and let the insults wash over him.

Back at Paddington Green at the end of his shift, he stripped off his stab vest and flopped onto one of the sofas. Kelly was making tea and he handed Shepherd a mug. "Okay, Three-amp?" he asked, sitting down next to him and swinging his feet onto the table.

"Do you ever get fed up with the abuse we get on the street?" asked Shepherd.

"Water off a duck's whatsit," said Kelly.

Richard Parry walked over with a mug. Kelly slid across the sofa to make room for him. "Carpets here gets called a racist as often as I do," he said. "It goes with the turf."

"We know we're not racist," said Parry. "That's all that matters."

"I don't care what colour the scumbags are," said Kelly. "Black, white, green with yellow spots, if they break the law they should get what's coming to them. We don't care what colour the victims are and we sure as hell don't care what colour the bad guys are."

Simmons walked over, biting into a ham sandwich he'd picked up from the canteen. "What's up?" he asked.

"Three-amp's fed up with being called a Klansman," said Parry.

"I'm okay," said Shepherd. "It just gets a bit old, being told I'm picking on minorities."

Simmons laughed. "Bloody hell — where we were today, we were the minority."

"You know what happens when we have a serial killer?" said Kelly. "Some talking head will appear on television telling us what we already know, that in all probability the killer is a white middle-aged male who used to set fire to pets when he was a kid."

"Because that's the profile," said Shepherd.

"Damn right it's the profile," said Kelly. "Serial killers are almost never young and black and they're as rare as hen's teeth. But what happens when we get a kid knifed in Brixton? Or a kid gets shot in Willesden? Suddenly we get all coy and we start talking about knife crime and gun crime and how something must be done and how society is falling apart when what we should be talking about is black crime. It's young black men who use knives and guns and the sooner we accept that and get it out into the open the better. But we can't because it's racist so we pretend it's not black crime and we talk in code. We say that the case is being investigated by Operation Trident, which is just a clever way of saying that the assailants are black. But every cop who has ever walked a beat knows that when it comes to knives and guns, it's young black males that are the problem. If you removed every young black male from the streets of London tomorrow there'd be no knife crime and no gun crime."

472

"You're not saying it's only blacks that carry knives and guns?" said Shepherd.

Kelly nodded enthusiastically. "I'd say seventy-five per cent of knives and guns that we find are in the hands of blacks," he said. "And the whites are carrying weapons because they're scared of the blacks. But do you know what would happen if I ever went public with those observations? Or mentioned it within earshot of a senior officer?"

"You'd be out," said Shepherd.

"Damn right I'd be out," said Kelly. "My feet wouldn't touch the ground. And that's the state we've reached. You can't speak the truth any more. You have to run everything you say through a PC bullshit filter."

"So what's the answer?" asked Shepherd.

Kelly shrugged. "We wait for the backlash, I guess."

"The backlash?"

"It's got to happen, sooner or later," said Simmons. "The system's a pendulum, taken over the long term. Swings and roundabouts." He took another mouthful of his sandwich.

"And what do you think will happen?" asked Shepherd.

"We'll start getting tough when it counts," said Kelly. "When we start putting people away for life, we'll mean life. When we catch a gangbanger with a gun, he'll go down for ten years and he'll stay behind bars for ten years. We'll stop putting pensioners in prison for not paying their council tax or overfilling their wheelie-bins and we'll only incarcerate the people that deserve to be incarcerated."

473

Shepherd grinned. "And when's that going to happen? The next millennium?"

"It can happen quickly, providing there's the will," said Parry. "We've got enough prisons, just filled them with the wrong people. We've more than enough cops, just got them in the wrong jobs. You know the Met's got more officers dealing with racial awareness than rape?"

Coker walked in with a carton of milk. He drank from it and wiped his mouth. "What are we talking about?" he asked, collapsing onto a chair.

"The unfairness of the criminal justice system," said Shepherd.

"Don't get KFC started," said Coker, waving his carton in the air. "He'd clear the prisons by bringing back capital punishment."

"Come on, we all know there are scumbags out there who'd be better off dead," said Kelly.

Parry laughed. "Strictly speaking, I think you mean that society would be better off. They wouldn't be better off — they'd be dead."

"I'm just saying that we need to get our courts working for the victims and not the criminals," said Kelly. "And if that means bringing back capital punishment for paedophiles, serial killers and terrorists, then so be it."

"I'm with KFC on this," said Simmons. "Everything's geared up to helping the criminals. No one gives a shit about their victims. Look at that Libyan, the one who brought down the Lockerbie plane. He kills two hundred and seventy people and does eight years in prison. Then the Jocks let him out because he's sick."

"I think the word is that he didn't do it," said Shepherd. "Our masters wanted him out of the country so he couldn't appeal his sentence."

"Maybe, but that's not the point," said Simmons. "The point is that a court found him guilty of mass murder but he was released after eight years. And look at those two kids in Edlington, the ones that tortured those other kids. Okay, they got sent down but as soon as they reach eighteen they'll be released and relocated at a cost of millions, same as those little shits that killed Jamie Bulger."

"Nipple's right," said Parry. "Everyone forgets about the victims and their relatives but they bend over backwards to help the criminals. The world's gone mad."

"So what's the solution?" asked Shepherd.

"It just needs someone at the top, someone who can lead, someone who can make changes," said Kelly. "Blair was too interested in his own future on the public-speaking circuit, Brown is a simpleton who couldn't even manage the economy, David Cameron is just Blair wearing a different hat. We need a leader, a leader with balls, a leader who isn't afraid to do what's necessary."

Shepherd grinned. "Boris Johnson?"

Kelly laughed and banged the table with the flat of his hand. "You know what we need? We need a Margaret Thatcher, that's what we need. She had balls."

"That much is true," agreed Shepherd. "Blair or Brown would never have fought for the Falklands."

"One day," said Simmons. "One day we'll have a leader who'll do what's necessary to let us take back the streets. Until then . . ."

He left the sentence unfinished. "Until then what?" asked Shepherd.

Simmons shrugged. "Until then we do the best we can," he said.

Fogg appeared at the door, with Castle at his shoulder. "Where's Colgate?" he asked, looking around the room.

"Canteen," said Coker. "He's on his way."

"Fill him in, will you? I'm heading home. We've got an early-morning rapid-entry to do for the borough," he said. "I want everyone in here at six sharp, no excuses. We'll be rolling out at six thirty." Kelly groaned. "Don't worry, KFC," said Fogg, "overtime's approved. Time and a third."

"That's more like it," said Kelly. "What's the story?"

"We won't know until tomorrow," said Fogg. "They're giving us the mushroom treatment. Last time the place was raided they were tipped off, so this time they're taking no chances. So tomorrow, six sharp."

Kelly raised his mug in salute. "We hear and obey, O Master."

Shepherd's alarm woke him at five o'clock on Wednesday morning and by six he was parking his bike next to Fogg's Ducati. He hurried upstairs to change into his uniform. Kelly and Coker were in the locker room, fastening their ties. "Still riding that death trap?" asked Kelly, as Shepherd took off his leathers.

476

"Yeah, I'm starting to think the same," said Shepherd. "I might come in on the Tube — that way at least I can drink after my shift without worrying how I'll get back." He hung up his jacket. "Any idea where we're off to?"

"Mum's the word," said Coker. "Foggy won't say."

"Does this Secret Squirrel stuff happen a lot?" asked Shepherd, pulling on his police boots.

"A fair amount," said Kelly. "Don't take it personal. The borough leaks, that's the problem. Drugs Squad have got their contacts, so have most of the CID, and they don't want their informants caught up in anything so they'll tip them the wink." He slapped Shepherd on the back as he went out.

Carolyn Castle rushed in, her kitbag on her shoulder. "Overslept," she said.

"Didn't your boyfriend give you a nudge?" asked Coker, as he headed for the door.

"He pulled an all-nighter," said Castle, opening her locker. She winked at Shepherd. "How's it going, Terry?"

Shepherd liked the way she used his name rather than his nickname, even though Terry was as contrived as Three-amp. Both were artificial, designed to conceal his true identity. Shepherd didn't mind deceiving criminals but he hated lying to cops. Especially pretty blonde ones with flashing green eyes. "All good, Carolyn," he said.

She put out a hand and he thought for a moment that she was going to brush his cheek, but at the last second she reached behind his back. She winked as she pulled a yellow Post-it off the back of his shirt. Written in black felt-tip capital letters was "KICK ME, I'M AN IDIOT".

Shepherd remembered the slap on the back from Kelly. He took the note from her. "KFC's little joke," he said.

"Little things amuse little minds," said Castle.

Shepherd went through to the briefing room. Kelly and Coker grinned at him from their seats at the back. Shepherd screwed the Post-it into a ball, flicked it at Kelly and mouthed, "Bastard," at him.

Kelly was about to retort but he closed his mouth when Inspector Smith appeared at the doorway in full riot gear, his helmet in his right hand. He was followed by a middle-aged man in a crumpled grey suit. "Heads up, everyone," said Smith. "For those of you who haven't met him already, this is Christopher Moore of the borough's intelligence unit. He'll brief you on the location and the targets, then I'll fill you in on the method of entry. Listen up because I want everyone on the road by six thirty." The clock on the wall said ten past.

Smith leaned against the wall as Moore went up to the lectern and tapped on the laptop there. A face flashed up onto the projection screen, a black man with an arrogant stare, his nose flared in contempt. "Jerome Alleyne, a Yardie and a nasty piece of work," said Moore. "He's shacked up in a terraced house in Harlesden." He tapped on the computer and the screen was filled with a surveillance photograph of Alleyne opening the front door of a shabby two-storey terraced house. "Alleyne was for several years a major player in the crack-cocaine market, but recently he's moved into the manufacture of methamphetamine, a.k.a. crank, ice, speed, wire, zip." He tapped the keyboard again and another surveillance picture filled the screen, this one of a pretty black girl laden with Primark carrier bags, two toddlers behind her, opening the front door of the house. "Alleyne has been living with this girl, Shayla Coltraine, for the past two years. The kids aren't his — she had them by two other men. The intel we have is that he's built a lab in the attic."

He tapped on the keyboard and a close-up of the roof showed a fully open window set among the tiles.

"For anyone who hasn't come across a methamphetamine lab before, I can tell you that they're dangerous places. Lots of flammable liquids and explosive components. The fumes alone can kill you,"

Kelly raised his hand. Moore sighed. "Yes?"

"I've never got the difference between flammable and inflammable," said Kelly. "Which one means they burn?"

"They both do," said Moore.

"How can that be?" asked Kelly. "Visible doesn't mean the same as invisible, does it?"

"Pipe down, KFC," said Smith.

Kelly shrugged apologetically.

"The crucial thing is to secure the lab," said Moore. "It's possible that Alleyne has rigged it so that he can torch the place if he's raided."

"You have definite intel on that?" asked Fogg.

"No, but it's not unknown so we have to assume it's a possibility," he said. "We need the lab secured so that the guys in the CBRN suits can go in." He pressed the mouse and two diagrams flashed onto the screen, a schematic of the ground floor on the left and the first floor on the right. The front door led into a hallway. To the left were the stairs, to the right a sitting room and behind it a kitchen. On the first floor there was a landing, a large bedroom, a small bedroom and a bathroom. A red cross was marked in the middle of the landing. "We haven't managed to gain access to the house but there is one for sale further down the terrace and we assume that the floor plan is the same," said Moore. He clicked the mouse and a photograph of the first-floor landing filled the screen. "Alleyne will almost certainly be in the main bedroom on the right, and the kids are in the smaller room on the left. In the ceiling between the two rooms is the hatch that leads to the attic, shown here by the red cross. There should be a fold-down ladder leading up to it. We don't know if the ladder will be up or down but with the kids around we assume it will be up and the hatch locked."

Moore clicked the mouse again and Alleyne's PNC details filled the screen. "Alleyne has convictions for violence and drug-dealing, but there's no intel to suggest that there are guns in the house. He's known as a night owl, generally sleeps until midday."

"And he's definitely in the house now?" asked the inspector.

"We have it under observation as we speak. He's in there."

Moore moved away from the podium and the inspector took his place. "Right, you heard the man," said Smith. "No guns, so we go in fast and hard, lots of noise, lots of aggression. I want the house totally dominated." He smiled. "But go easy on the kids. It's a densely populated neighbourhood so there'll be lots of eyes on us."

He tapped on the keyboard and a map of the area around the house flashed onto the screen. The target was marked with a red circle, and two streets away there was a black cross with the letters FRP. "We meet at the forward rendezvous point," said the inspector. "Foggy's group does the main entry, and Gary's will be at the back in case Alleyne legs it. There's an alley that runs behind the houses." Smith looked at the intelligence officer. "The gate to the alley is open, right?" he asked.

Moore nodded. "Never locked," he said.

"Gary, I need two of yours in full CBRN gear ready to go in as soon as we have the house secure," Smith continued. "If all goes to plan, Alleyne will go out the front with the woman and her kids. He will be brought here for questioning. Social Services will look after the woman and the kids until the house is clear, which could be a day or two. Once Alleyne's out we'll do a full search for drugs, money, ID, the works. We'll have a few CSOs on the site handing out leaflets explaining what's going on to keep the locals happy." He looked up at the clock on the wall. "Right, we've got time for a quick brew and then we're out of here."

★ ★ ★

Shepherd pulled protective pads over his knees and then fastened more over his thighs. Then he put on shoulder and elbow pads before pulling on the black flameproof overalls and zipping them up. Two CSOs walked up in fluorescent jackets, a man and an overweight West Indian woman. Shepherd realised that the man was Ross Mayhew. He was holding a handful of leaflets. "What's the story?" asked Shepherd.

The leaflets had the Met's crest at the top with a phone number and several paragraphs in large type. "It explains what we're doing," said Mayhew. "Once you guys go in, we start handing them out to anyone in the vicinity and shoving them through letterboxes. Hearts and minds, that's the theory. If we tell everyone what's going on and why, they're less likely to kick off." He nodded at his partner. "This is Daisy. She's my wingman today."

Daisy giggled girlishly and shook Shepherd's hand. Her hand was larger than his. "Terry," said Shepherd. He finished adjusting his stab vest.

"Not how I thought I'd spend my time when I left the army," said Mayhew. "Acting as a postman. Wish I was going in with you."

"You'll get there one day, I'm sure," said Shepherd.

"One day I'll tell you about the time we cleared a house in the centre of Basra," said Mayhew. "Took out three ragheads, bang, bang, bang. Got the third before the first hit the floor."

A look of horror flashed across Daisy's face and she gasped. "It was war, Daisy," said Mayhew. "Kill or be killed." Daisy waddled away, her large thighs whispering against each other with every step. Mayhew grinned at Shepherd. "Women," he said, and hurried after her.

Shepherd checked that his identification numbers were in place on his shoulder straps, then went to stand next to Coker and Kelly, who were already kitted up. The van was parked in front of an off-licence with posters in the window offering three cans of any beer or lager for the price of two.

There were few pedestrians around and those that there were hurried by, averting their eyes. It wasn't the sort of area where the police meant anything other than trouble.

Fogg was talking into his radio as he walked over to the van, where Castle was adjusting her stab vest. He patted her on the back. "Ready?" he asked.

She nodded and went to join Coker, Kelly and Shepherd. They were all holding their helmets but were already wearing their fireproof balaclavas. Parry, Simmons and Turnbull joined them. "Right, here's how we play it," said Fogg. "Carpets, you go in with the enforcer. Take care of the door, step aside. KFC and Colgate, straight in and up the stairs. Turn right and into the main bedroom and contain the target. Nipple, you go right in behind them, take care of the woman. Try not to get too physical."

"I'll talk to her nicely, Sarge," said Simmons.

"Pelican, you head up after them, peel left and keep the kids quiet. Keep them in the room. As soon as the target is outside, put the woman and the kids together in the kids' bedroom, then get them out of the house.

Three-amp, you go in after Pelican, stay on the landing and secure the hatch to the attic. No one goes up there before the CBRN boys have had a look. Lurpak, secure the bottom of the stairs just in case the target gets the jump on them."

"O ye of little faith," said Kelly.

"It wouldn't be the first time," said Fogg. "Is everyone clear on what they're doing?"

They all nodded.

"Remember, lots of noise, shout who we are and keep on shouting. We want total disorientation so that it's over before he has time to react." Fogg looked at his wristwatch, then at Gary Dawson, who was just finishing briefing his team, two of whom were kitted out in the bulky chemical-biological-radiological-nuclear suits. "Okay, Gary?" he asked.

"Ready when you are, Foggy," replied Dawson.

"Let's do it," said Fogg.

Dawson and his team jogged towards the alley that led to the rear of the terrace. Parry picked up the bright orange enforcer from the rear of the van and stood next to Fogg. The rest of the team lined up behind Parry in the order that they would be entering the house — Kelly, Turnbull, Simmons and Castle, with Shepherd and Coker bringing up the rear. They all put on their helmets, pulled down their visors and adjusted their gloves.

Shepherd found himself breathing heavily as his body geared up for the coming confrontation. Castle turned to him and winked. "No looking at my arse as we go up the stairs," she said.

484

"I promise," he said.

"In we go," said Fogg. Parry began to jog down the pavement, towards the house, holding the enforcer to his chest. As he got closer he increased the pace, and within seconds their boots were pounding in unison.

A VW Polo drove by and Shepherd caught a glimpse of a black woman glaring at them.

They reached the house. Everyone held back to give Parry room to swing the enforcer.

"I bet he does it in three," said Coker.

"Two," said Kelly.

"The door's probably reinforced," said Turnbull. "A tenner says it takes him four."

Parry grunted, swung back the enforcer and slammed it into the door, close to the lock. The wood splintered but the door held.

"One," said Coker.

"We can all count, Lurpak," muttered Kelly.

Parry grunted again, swayed back, then slammed the enforcer against the door a second time, a few inches higher. It caved in and one of the hinges ripped from the surround. Parry stepped to the side.

"I win," said Kelly. He kicked the door open and hurried over the threshold, his hands in fists, like a prize-fighter's. "Police!" he screamed. "Police! Stay where you are!"

He charged along the hallway, closely followed by Turnbull. By the time Shepherd was through what was left of the door, Kelly and Turnbull were already halfway up the stairs, shouting at the top of their voices.

Simmons hared up after them. "Armed police!" he screamed, which Shepherd knew wasn't exactly true.

Kelly and Turnbull reached the top of the stairs, still shouting, and turned right towards the main bedroom. Simmons peeled off to the right.

Shepherd's boot caught on a loose piece of carpet and he stumbled, his hands flailing for balance. He grabbed Castle's waist and she yelped.

"Sorry," he gasped.

"Stop trying to feel me up." She headed for the bedroom where the children were.

Shepherd reached the top of the stairs. The hatch leading into the attic was closed. He stayed where he was, his face bathed in sweat, breathing hard.

Coker was standing at the bottom of the stairs, looking up. He nodded at Shepherd. Parry stepped across the threshold and went into the sitting room, shouting. A few seconds later there was the sound of furniture being smashed and a crash that suggested that a television had been thrown across the room.

"We've got him!" shouted Kelly, from the main bedroom.

Simmons appeared at the door, holding a young black woman by the arm. She was wearing only a baggy T-shirt with a marijuana leaf in the colours of the Jamaican flag on it. "My kids!" she screamed. "Leave my kids alone!"

Simmons let go of her arm and she pushed Shepherd aside and ran to her children. He saw Castle standing by a bunk-bed talking to a little girl with dreadlocks. "Leave my fucking kids alone!" shrieked the woman.

486

Castle stood back as the woman grabbed the two children and hugged them. They were both crying.

Fogg came up the stairs. "Everything okay?" he asked Shepherd.

"Seems to be," said Shepherd.

"You're fucking animals, all of you! You should be ashamed of yourselves! You should be fucking ashamed of yourselves."

"Calm down," said Castle, raising her visor. "You're upsetting your children."

"I'm upsetting the children?" the woman yelled. "I'm upsetting the fucking children? You're the ones who came in like the fucking Gestapo." The children started to wail and she held them tighter. "See what you've done?" she shouted. "How would you like the Gestapo kicking your door down in the middle of the night?"

"We're not the Gestapo, it's seven o'clock in the morning, and it's your own fault for letting a drug-dealer live in your house," said Castle, patiently. "And if you thought anything of your kids you wouldn't let him put a meth lab in your attic. Do you know how dangerous that is? The whole house could go up in flames, or your kids could die from the fumes. We're doing you a favour here."

Kelly and Turnbull pulled Alleyne out of the main bedroom. He'd been handcuffed with his hands behind his back. "Fucking pigs," he shouted. "Where's your warrant?"

"Put him on the bus," said Fogg.

"I want to talk to who's in charge!" shouted Alleyne. "This ain't right." As Kelly and Turnbull dragged him along the landing, he saw his girlfriend. "You call my lawyer, baby, his number's on the fridge. Tell him the pigs have hauled me in but I ain't done nothing." He glared at Fogg. "Where you taking me, man?"

"Ask me nicely," said Fogg.

"Fuck you, where you taking me? I got the right to know."

Fogg ignored him and jerked his thumb at Kelly. "On the bus," he said.

Alleyne began to scream abuse at Fogg, the TSG and the Metropolitan Police in general as he was dragged down the stairs and outside. When his yells had faded into the background, Fogg went into the smaller bedroom, removing his helmet and gloves. He smiled at the woman and her two children. "Shayla, my name's Roy Fogg," he said. "I'm a sergeant, based at Paddington Green." He handed her a business card. "I'm sorry about the way we stormed in, but we had to do it to make sure that no one got hurt. We'll pay for any damage and we'll check that your house is secure until everything's made good. Are your children okay?"

"They're scared," she said. She kissed them. "You ain't got no right to scare kids like you did."

"Again, I'm sorry for that, but we were worried that Jerome might have started fighting if we hadn't come in quickly, and we didn't want him hurt. We certainly didn't intend to scare your children." He smiled at the little girl with dreadlocks. "I'm sorry we were so noisy, but we're not bad men," he said to her.

The child smiled through her tears.

"We're going to have to search your house, I'm afraid, to see if Jerome left any drugs or weapons here," Fogg continued. "It'd make things a lot easier if you could tell me about any weapons or drugs you know about."

"He don't have no gun," said the woman. "I told him, no guns in the house."

"That's good," said Fogg. "But we're still going to have to look. And any damage that's done during the search, we'll repair it." He gestured up at the ceiling. "We'll be removing all the chemicals and equipment from the attic, and that's going to take some time, I'm afraid. But I've arranged for someone to take care of you and the children while we make the house safe."

"I don't want to go. This is my house," said the woman. She hugged the two toddlers tightly. "You can't make me go."

Fogg smiled reassuringly. "They'll give you breakfast and help entertain the kids, and as soon as we've finished they'll bring you right back," he said. He nodded at Castle. "This is Carolyn, she'll take you outside. And if you have any problems in getting the damage repaired, you call me — all right? Roy Fogg. Okay?"

The woman nodded. "Okay."

"If you want to take anything with you, tell Carolyn and she'll help," he said.

Castle took the woman and the two small children out of the bedroom and down the stairs. Shepherd flipped up his visor as Fogg came out of the bedroom. "You've got a soft side, then, Sarge," he said.

"She's not the villain here," Fogg said. "And you've got to be careful because entries like this can very easily turn racial. If she goes out screaming and alleging abuse then the neighbours will get riled up and before long bottles'll be thrown and all hell breaks loose. But if she goes quietly then all's sweetness and light."

Parry came up the stairs. "Just putting him on the bus now, Sarge," he said.

"Any problems?"

"He's a bit verbal but KFC and Colgate have him under control."

Fogg jerked a thumb at the main bedroom. "You help Nipple give that room a going over, then do downstairs."

"What about me, Sarge?" asked Shepherd.

"You stay where you are," said Fogg. "Keep the hatch secure until the Noddy suits get here. We don't want Alleyne claiming we planted a meth lab on him." Fogg headed downstairs. "Lurpak, start on the kids' bedroom. No stone unturned."

Coker removed his protective gloves and took a pair of purple search gloves from the pouch on the back of his belt. He put them on as he climbed the stairs. "I just hope they're not bed-wetters," he said, as he passed Shepherd.

Shepherd took off his helmet. He watched Parry and Simmons methodically searching the main bedroom. Parry went through the drawers of a pine chest while Simmons stripped off the bedding and tilted the mattress on its side. Shepherd heard footsteps on the stairs and turned to see Kelly and Turnbull heading up. They, too, had taken off their helmets and replaced their bulky protective gloves with purple plastic ones.

"How did it go?" asked Shepherd.

"He banged his head a bit getting onto the bus," said Kelly.

"Against KFC's knee," said Turnbull.

The two officers went into the small bedroom where Coker was sorting through a large tea chest full of toys. Turnbull went down on his hands and knees and checked under the bunk bed, while Kelly opened the doors to a wardrobe and began pulling out clothes and dropping them onto the floor.

There was a crash from the main bedroom and Shepherd jumped. He went to the door. Simmons was standing in the middle of the room, looking at the shards of what had once been a glass vase. "Whoops," he said.

"Butterfingers!" shouted Turnbull.

"I'd give you a hand but Foggy says I've got to guard the hatch," said Shepherd.

"Yeah, in case it runs off," said Turnbull, pulling off a pillowcase and feeling his way along the pillow.

Shepherd turned. Across the hallway he saw Coker holding something. It looked like a towel, but when he unwrapped it Shepherd saw that it was a gun. A revolver. Coker held it up and said something to Kelly, who turned from the wardrobe. As he did so, Coker slid the gun inside his stab vest. As he adjusted the vest, he saw Shepherd. Their eyes locked. There was no telltale bulge where Coker had put the gun, and for a second Shepherd wondered if he'd imagined it. But there was no mistaking the hardness in Coker's eyes. Shepherd swallowed but his mouth had gone dry. He coughed to cover his discomfort. Coker continued to stare at him, his face impassive. It felt as if they had locked eyes for hours but Shepherd knew that it had only been a few seconds at most. He gave Coker the slightest of nods, then turned his back on him and watched Simmons carefully picking up the pieces of glass in the main bedroom.

Coker and Kelly said nothing in the van as the team headed back to Paddington Green and they went off to the canteen together as soon as they'd parked up. By the time Shepherd had changed out of his uniform there was still no sign of them. He waited until he was back in the house in Kilburn before phoning Charlotte Button and telling her what he'd seen. "So Coker's bad," she said.

"I can't see any other reason for him taking the gun," said Shepherd.

"And he hasn't spoken to you?"

"Went AWOL as soon as we got back to base. I'm guessing he was hiding the gun somewhere."

"And Kelly saw it?"

"Coker said something to him just before he slid it inside his vest."

"So that's two," said Button. "Well done. What about Fogg? Or Dawson?"

"Dawson was at the back of the house, and I didn't see him connect with Coker or Kelly. Fogg was downstairs when Coker took the gun."

"Be nice to know if either of them knows what Coker did."

"Agreed," said Shepherd. "But it's a difficult subject to bring up in general conversation. Coker knows I saw him, so I guess he's going to have to mention it at some point. If nothing else he's going to want to know what I'm going to do."

"There's no doubt about what you saw, or that he knows you saw him?"

"It was definitely a gun, a revolver, and we had eye-contact. He was looking right at me."

"Okay," said Button. "So let's let it run a while longer, see who else you can nail."

"No problem," said Shepherd.

"You don't think Coker will see you as a threat now?"

"It's possible, but I'm a big boy, I can take care of myself."

"I've no doubt on that score," said Button. "But if you need anything, let me know." She ended the call.

Shepherd switched on the kettle and opened the fridge door to see what he had to eat. He'd been so busy at work that he hadn't had time to do any shopping so all he had was a pack of corned beef and two eggs that had passed their sell-by date. His mobile rang and he closed the fridge door. The caller had withheld his ID. Shepherd pressed the green button to accept the call. "Is that Mr Shepherd?"

"Yes," said Shepherd, hesitantly. "Who's this?"

"DC Cooper at Hereford. Where are you, Mr Shepherd?"

"I'm not sure that's any business of yours," said Shepherd.

"Are you in Hereford?"

"Why do you want to know?"

"I'd be grateful if you'd answer my questions, Mr Shepherd."

"How grateful?"

"What do you mean?" said Cooper, confused.

"You said you'd be grateful. I asked how grateful." The kettle switched itself off and Shepherd held the phone between neck and shoulder as he spooned coffee into the cafetière.

"I hope you're not going to be difficult."

"Why? Are you going to arrest me for being difficult?"

"I don't understand your attitude," said the detective.

"I think there's a lot that you don't understand," said Shepherd. "Why are you bothering me?" He poured hot water onto the coffee grounds.

"I need to know where you are, Mr Shepherd."

"And I need to know why you need to know. And if you don't tell me I'm going to end this call right now."

There was a long pause, and Shepherd guessed that Cooper had put his hand over the mouthpiece and was talking to someone else, probably his sergeant. Eventually Cooper came back on the line. "Jorgji Talovic has gone missing, and I need to rule you out as a suspect," he said.

"I don't know anyone called Jorgji Talovic," said Shepherd.

494

"The man who was threatening you," said Cooper. "The man you claimed poisoned your dog."

"The man who threatened me and the man who killed my dog was called Imer Lekstakaj," said Shepherd.

"Mr Shepherd, I don't understand your hostility," said Cooper.

"This isn't hostility, this is contempt," said Shepherd. "Put Hollis on the phone."

"I'm handling this inquiry," said Cooper.

"Put Hollis on now or I'm ending this call," said Shepherd.

"Mr Shepherd . . ."

Shepherd pressed the red button to end the call. He poured himself a mug of coffee and took it through to the sitting room. He was channel-surfing when his phone rang again. This time there was a number on the phone's screen. Sergeant Hollis. Shepherd took the call.

"You've managed to upset my colleague somewhat, Mr Shepherd," said Hollis.

"You can't imagine how happy that makes me," said Shepherd.

"He's all for dragging you in here for questioning," said Hollis.

"He'd have to find me first and I get the feeling that he couldn't find his dick even if he used both hands," said Shepherd. "I don't owe the little shit any favours and you can tell him that for me."

"I understand your position entirely," said the sergeant. Shepherd figured that Cooper was standing next to Hollis and could hear his side of the conversation. "As my colleague explained to you, Imer Lekstakaj has disappeared and we believe that there is a good chance he has been killed."

"More bad news," said Shepherd. "My cup runneth over."

"In view of the problems you'd been having with Mr Lekstakaj, we'd like you to account for your movements yesterday."

"There you go calling him Mr again," said Shepherd. "He's a wanted murderer who threatened my family and poisoned my dog. He doesn't have the right to be called Mr. If something's happened to him it's nothing to do with me."

"Where are you, Mr Shepherd?"

"On my sofa."

Hollis sighed. "Which city?"

"London."

"Why London?"

"I can't tell you that. It's classified."

"And how long have you been in London, Mr Shepherd?"

"I got here Sunday evening and I'll be here until Friday."

"I'm going to need someone to corroborate that."

"My word won't do, then?"

Hollis chuckled. "Much as I enjoy your sense of humour, Mr Shepherd, this is a murder inquiry. I'm going to need you to account for your whereabouts."

"I already said — I'm in London."

"Where specifically?"

"I can't tell you."

"Because?"

"Because I'm in the middle of a very sensitive investigation, and I can't risk you or PCDC jeopardising that investigation."

"So how do you suggest I verify your whereabouts?"

"What happened to Lekstakaj?"

"We're not sure."

"That doesn't make any sense. How can you be involved in a murder investigation if you don't know what happened?"

"Mr Lekstakaj has disappeared. And there are signs of a struggle."

"What sort of signs?"

"I'm not at liberty to divulge that information, but we do suspect that a crime has been committed."

"Well, not by me," said Shepherd. "I already told you that I work for SOCA. I solve crimes, I don't commit them."

"Nevertheless I need to know your movements over the past week."

"Look, Sergeant, what do you want me to say? I'm in London, and I've been in London all week. I'm on a SOCA case and there's no way that I can give you details of that case. The best I can do is to give you the number of my boss and she can confirm that I'm working and give you a character reference if you need one."

"Who is your boss, Mr Shepherd?"

Shepherd gave him Charlotte Button's number. "Can you at least tell me why you think there's been foul play?" he asked.

"A neighbour reported hearing sounds of a struggle at the house," said Hollis. "And she heard a vehicle being driven away at high speed. There's a small amount of blood splatter on the garage floor, and damage to the wing mirror of his car. It looks as if he got home from work and we think that someone was waiting for him in his garage and they attacked him"

"One of the wing mirrors was cracked when I went around to his house."

"When was that?"

"The time he threatened me. After he threw the brick through my window. You should check your notes."

"And you can remember a cracked mirror?"

"I've a good memory," said Shepherd. "Basically, you've no real evidence that he's been the victim of a crime, have you? Not like when I told you about the brick through my window and my dead dog."

"It's not the same thing, Mr Shepherd."

"No, it's not, is it?" said Shepherd. "You have a nice evening." Shepherd ended the call. He smiled to himself as he tapped out Jack Bradford's number. He told his friend that he and his brother could drop the surveillance on his house. Again, Jack didn't ask any questions. "I owe you and Billy, big-time," said Shepherd.

"Happy to be of service. Gave us the chance to get a good look at Katra again. She's fit, Spider."

"She's family," laughed Shepherd.

"She's not my family," said Jack. "Put in a good word for me, will you?"

"I'll see what I can do," said Shepherd.

"That means no, doesn't it? Bastard."

"Take care, Jack. And thanks."

Shepherd spent most of Thursday helping to secure a crime scene in Wembley. Four black teenagers had fired more than two dozen shots at a Turkish takeaway where a rival gang had been buying kebabs. The gang members had escaped unscathed but the owner of the restaurant and his teenage daughter had been wounded. By chance an armed-response vehicle had been in the area but they had been forced to give up the chase after a hail of bullets ripped through their vehicle. The getaway car was later found burned out in Harlesden. Detectives from Operation Trident were on the case and reckoned that it was part of an ongoing drugs dispute between two north-London gangs.

Over a five-hour period Shepherd had knocked on more than eighty doors of flats overlooking the street where the shooting had taken place. Most of the residents hadn't answered, and those who had just said they hadn't seen anything.

The team were given sandwiches and cans of soft drink for lunch. Shepherd sat next to Kelly while he ate. There was the usual banter and ribbing, and no indication that Kelly was in any way uncomfortable being around him. Coker, too, was his usual self. Shepherd was used to hiding his emotions and real feelings while working under cover and knew how difficult it was. He kept looking for signs of tension in the two men and the way they acted, but there was nothing to suggest they were anything other than part of a tightly knit team.

They got back to Paddington Green just after six. Shepherd had taken the Tube to work, and on the way home he stopped off at Marks & Spencer to stock up on groceries. When he got back to his house in Kilburn he made himself two bacon sandwiches and some coffee before going through to the sitting room. He was just reaching for the TV remote when the doorbell rang. He got up, went through to the hall and opened the front door. It was Coker. He was wearing a waterproof jacket and black leather gloves. He grinned. "Hey, Three-amp," he said. "Got any beer?"

"Fridgeful," said Shepherd, holding the door open. "Just made bacon sandwiches if you want one."

He showed Coker into the sitting room and went to get him a can of Heineken. When he got back, Coker had taken off his gloves and was tucking into one of the sandwiches. Shepherd put the can in front of him and sat on the sofa.

Coker held up the sandwich. "You said I could, right?"

"Knock yourself out," said Shepherd. Coker had taken off his coat and hung it on the door handle. Shepherd was surprisingly reassured that Coker had also taken off his gloves. He reached for the remaining sandwich and took a bite. "So, how did you get the nickname Lurpak?" he asked.

Coker wiped his mouth with the back of his hand. "No one told you?"

"I didn't ask."

"But you're asking now?"

"Yeah, I'm asking now."

"It's because I'm a butter," he said.

"A butter?"

"A head-butter," said Coker. "We were doing a rapid entry — into a house not far from here, as it happens. I was third in. Carpets was first, obviously, and Pelican had nagged to be number two so that she could show us how big her balls were. So we go piling in and Carpets bundles the guy up against a wall so all's good, and then this woman gets up from behind a sofa and grabs Pelican from behind and starts scratching her. She had these long nails, like bloody talons they were, and she was going for Pelican's eyes. We were in a tiny bloody flat, not enough room to swing a cat, so I could barely move. I grab the woman and try to pull her off Pelican and she turns and starts spitting at me. Then she tries to knee me in the groin and I'm losing it but I can't use my baton so I head-butt her. Bang. She goes down like a sack of spanners." Coker laughed, then popped the tab on his can of lager and drank.

"Any comebacks?" asked Shepherd.

Coker shook his head. "Necessary force, mate," he said. He put down his lager and took another bite of his sandwich.

Shepherd wondered when he was going to explain why he'd turned up on his doorstep. "Pelican wasn't happy when I hit that slag for her," he said.

"Yeah, she likes to show that she's one of the guys," agreed Coker. "Hates it when we stand up for her. But at the end of the day she's a female and if anyone takes liberties with her then it's up to us to step in."

"Can't argue with that," said Shepherd.

Coker sipped his lager, his eyes never leaving Shepherd. He put the can down slowly. "Get yourself a beer, Three-amp. Coffee's for wimps."

Shepherd chuckled and went through to the kitchen to get himself a lager. He popped the tab, clunked his can against Coker's and toasted him. "Down the hatch," he said.

"Yeah," said Coker. They both drank. Coker's eyes narrowed as he studied Shepherd — perhaps he was trying to work out what was going through his mind. Shepherd smiled back amiably. "I wanted to talk about what happened yesterday," said Coker, quietly.

"Yeah, I figured," said Shepherd.

"You didn't say anything?"

"To who?"

"To anybody."

"None of my business, Lurpak."

"But you must have wondered, right?"

Shepherd shrugged. "If you want a souvenir, it's nothing to do with me," he said.

Coker laughed, spraying bits of bacon and bread over the coffee-table. "I like you, Three-amp," he said, when he'd finished laughing.

"Yeah, I like you too," said Shepherd. "Shall we get married?"

Coker laughed again. Then he put his head on one side, watching Shepherd. "Why do you think I wanted the gun, Three-amp?"

502

"I have no bloody idea," said Shepherd. "Why don't you tell me?"

"First I want to know why you didn't go running to the sarge. Or the commander. Or the rubber heels. Professional Standards?"

"Because I'm the newbie. If that's the way things are done, it's nothing to do with me."

Coker picked up his can and sat back. "I don't get you, Three-amp. You're not even curious?"

"Of course I'm curious, you stupid sod, but I'm on very thin ice here, aren't I? I like this job, I worked bloody hard to get it, and if I don't fit in I could be out on my arse."

Coker studied Shepherd with unblinking blue eyes. Then he nodded slowly. "Remember that story KFC told you, about the drug-dealer who threatened his family?"

"Wilkes. Yeah, I remember."

"Yeah, and remember how you said he should have given Wilkes a good kicking?"

"The bastard deserved it," said Shepherd.

"No question," said Coker. "The thing is, somebody did kick his arse. Kicked it good and proper."

"KFC said Wilkes was in prison in the States."

"Yeah, he is. But before that he was warned off."

"By who?"

Coker tapped the side of his nose. "Need to know, Three-amp. One step at a time. What I can tell you is that it got sorted for KFC, well and truly sorted."

"How?"

Coker shoved the last bit of sandwich into his mouth and chewed, then washed it down with lager. "Someone went around to Wilkes and showed him the error of his ways."

"And that sorted it?"

Coker grinned. "Oh, yeah, it straightened him out perfectly." He leaned forward. "He poured petrol over Wilkes and his wife, took out a lighter and told Wilkes that he had two choices. He could swear to never go near KFC and his family or he could go up in flames."

"Who was he?"

"The Masked Avenger," said Coker. "Wilkes didn't know who it was. The guy was wearing a mask and he told Wilkes that if anything ever happened to KFC he'd be back. Then he gave him a good kicking and went on his way. From that day on KFC didn't have any problems with Wilkes."

"That's a good story, Lurpak," said Shepherd. "Want another beer?"

"Okay," said Coker.

Shepherd went to the kitchen to get two more cans of lager. He gave one to Coker and opened one for himself. He didn't want to drink but he wanted to appear relaxed. He put his feet up on the coffee-table. "The thing is, I don't see how what happened to Wilkes has anything to do with what happened at the house. Unless you're going to tell me that you're the Masked Avenger."

Coker laughed. "Nah, I'm not the Caped Crusader," he said. "I'm more like Robin."

"A sidekick?"

Coker drank his lager and smacked his lips. "Yeah, a sidekick. Here's the thing, Three-amp. What happened to Wilkes wasn't legal, no question about that. But it worked. It worked a treat. Wilkes never went near KFC again, and when he did come across him it was 'Yes, sir, no, sir, three bags full, sir.' And when we saw that it worked, well, that got us thinking."

"And by 'we' you mean . . .?"

Coker waved the question away as he burped loudly. "That's for down the line," he said. "What I'm telling you now is by way of background." He leaned forward. "I know you're a sheep-shagger, but you've been in London long enough to see the way things are here, right?"

"I'm not Welsh, Lurpak. And I don't shag sheep."

"You're not from the city, though. And the city is a whole different ballgame. We've got gangbangers on every street corner, feral kids running wild, no-go areas, knife crime, drive-by shootings, and we've got a criminal justice system that can't cope. We've got beat cops who are so weighed down with paperwork that they're scared of making arrests. We've got fat cops, short cops, cops who've been hired because of their ethnic background rather than their abilities, we've got magistrates who think that burglars and muggers can be punished with warnings and probation, and we've got prisons so full that murderers and rapists are being put back on the streets early. But more than anything what we've got is a criminal population who don't fear the system any more. They know that the cops are powerless, that the judges are weak and that in prison they'll get TV and PlayStations and gyms and the European Court of Human Rights to appeal to if they feel hard done by, all at the taxpayer's expense."

"Bloody hell, Lurpak, that's one hell of a speech."

"I'm telling you what most cops think. It's just that in the PC world we live in, no one can say it."

"But I get the feeling you're not just talking, right?"

"Right," agreed Coker.

"So what's the gun for? Keeping it for a rainy day?"

Coker put down his lager, interlinked his fingers and leaned forward. "I'm taking a risk, talking to you like this."

"Not really," said Shepherd. "If I was going to say anything about the gun the time to say it was when we were in the room or back at the station. The fact I didn't means I'm in deep shit if it comes out now."

"You could go running to the commander."

"I could, but then I'd have to explain why I didn't say anything at the time."

"And why didn't you?"

"Like I said, I'm the newbie. I don't want to make waves while I'm still wet behind the ears." He smiled. "Besides, worst that can happen is that I just say I didn't say anything. I can't be punished for that."

"And that's what you'd say if you were asked?"

"Hear no, see no, speak no," said Shepherd.

Coker nodded thoughtfully, then drained his can and stood up. "Okay," he said.

"Okay?" said Shepherd. "What does that mean?"

"It means I'm off," said Coker.

"And then what?"

"I've got to talk to someone."

"The Masked Avenger?"

Coker grinned. "Yeah."

"And then what?"

"Then we'll see what he says."

Shepherd frowned. "Lurpak, I don't understand what's happening here. Did you just come to see if I was going to drop you in the shit? Or is there something more going on?"

Coker tapped the side of his nose. "Secret Squirrel," he said.

"Screw you." Shepherd drank from his can. "Screw you and screw the Masked Avenger."

"Look, we have to take this slowly," said Coker.

"Take what slowly?"

Coker sighed. "You're a good guy, Three-amp. I know that. And I want you on board."

"On board what?"

"I can't tell you, not until we all agree."

"Who's we?"

Coker tapped the side of his nose again.

"I know, I know, Secret bloody Squirrel," said Shepherd, feigning irritation. "If it helps you decide, I'll do whatever I have to do if it means putting the bad guys away. If it's a matter of egging the pudding, I'm up for it."

"That's good to hear."

"But it's not you that calls the shots, right?"

"There are others involved, yeah."

"Gary Dawson?"

Coker frowned. "What?"

"Just a feeling I had, that's all. He doesn't seem happy with the way things are going."

"Gary's a straight arrow."

"Foggy, then?"

"We're not playing Twenty Questions here," said Coker, putting on his gloves. "See you tomorrow."

Shepherd raised his can in salute. "Drive carefully," he said. "You can see yourself out, yeah?"

Coker flashed him a thumbs-up. Shepherd waited until he heard the front door close before hurrying upstairs. He went into the front bedroom and watched Coker drive away, then pulled out his mobile and called Charlotte Button. He brought her up to speed on what Coker had said.

"Excellent," said Button. "Did Coker say when you'd get to meet the rest of them?"

"He'll get back to me. I think his first concern was what I was going to say about the gun."

"And this Masked-Avenger, Caped-Crusader character? Any idea who he might be?"

"He was cagey about that," said Shepherd. "He was feeling me out. But it's not Gary Dawson. He definitely ruled him out."

"And you made all the right noises?"

"No, I said I was calling three nines and turning them in," said Shepherd.

"I wasn't trying to teach my grandmother to suck eggs," said Button. "So what happens next?"

"I guess he reports back to the rest of them, and if I get a vote of confidence they take me into the fold."

"Excellent," said Button. "Full steam ahead."

508

"How far do I take it?" asked Shepherd.

"All the way," said Button. "We need to catch them in the act. I doubt that we'll be able to get any of them to roll over on the others so we need them red-handed."

Shepherd felt his stomach lurch. He didn't like the idea of betraying the men in the first place, but doing it up close and personal made it that much worse. The last thing he wanted was to be there when they were arrested.

"And I'm going to need you wired up. I'll send Amar around."

"I strip off in front of these guys every morning and night," said Shepherd.

"How lovely for you," said Button. "I think Amar can be creative on that front so don't worry."

"I'm not worried," said Shepherd.

"Good to hear it. So, I had a very strange phone call from a detective sergeant in Hereford."

"Hollis," said Shepherd.

"Wanted to know your whereabouts during the week."

"Yeah, sorry about that. Some guy I had an argument with has disappeared. I think they're checking up on everyone. Were you able to put him right?"

"He wanted details of the operation you're on so I had his assistant chief constable call him to explain the error of his ways. He won't be bothering you again."

"Thanks for that, Charlie."

"That's what I'm here for," she said. "Anyway, well done with Coker. Call me as soon as you know more." She ended the call.

Shepherd went down to the sitting room and sat on the sofa. The remains of his bacon sandwich lay on its plate but he had lost his appetite.

Early on Friday morning Shepherd was dragged out of a dreamless sleep by the insistent ringing of his mobile phone. The caller had blocked their number but Shepherd took the call, rubbing the sleep from his eyes.

"Rise and shine," said a voice. Amar Singh.

"Bloody hell, what time is it?" said Shepherd, sitting up.

"Six," said Singh. "Charlie said I should catch you before you go to work."

"Where are you?"

"Outside."

"Give me a minute." Shepherd ended the call, pulled on a shirt and trousers and padded downstairs.

Singh was on his doorstep, wearing a different leather jacket from the one he'd had on last time they'd met, and a pair of pristine jet black jeans. He nodded at his car in the road. "Do you think it's safe to leave it there?" he asked. "It's not the best of areas."

"The car-jackers will be fast asleep this time of the morning," said Shepherd. "Like I should be." He stepped aside to let Singh in. "How much do you spend on clothes, Amar?" he asked, as he showed the technician into the kitchen.

"It's my only vice," said Singh.

"That jacket's Armani, right?" said Shepherd, switching on the kettle.

"This one? Nah, this is Prada. Red deer." He held out his arm. "Feel it, it's like butter."

"Thanks but I'll pass," said Shepherd. "How do you afford gear like that?"

Singh laughed. "Overtime," he said. "Lots and lots of overtime."

"Is that the real reason why you turned up on my doorstep at this unearthly hour? They give you time and a half?"

"I resent the implication of that," said Singh. He nodded at the kettle. "White with two sugars," he said.

"You know Charlie's leaving SOCA?" asked Shepherd, leaning against the kitchen counter.

"That's the word on the street."

"She didn't tell you?"

Singh shrugged. "Why would she? I'm just a foot-soldier."

"Would you go with her to Five? If she asked?"

"I don't see that she would," said Singh. "Five's got the best techs in the business — it's not as if I'd be taking anything to the table. They get stuff direct from the CIA and the Pentagon, gear that we'll never see at SOCA. Plus the pay deal I'm on would take some beating. I don't think Five get the overtime rates we get, and I can't believe what a great pension they gave me when I moved over from the Met."

"Might get a better class of work," suggested Shepherd.

"I'm technical, remember? The job's pretty much the same for me no matter who the target is. Speaking of which . . ." He reached into his jacket and took out a black Nokia N95, a double of the one Shepherd already had. "Let me have your phone and I'll swap the Sim card," he said.

Shepherd handed it over and then made two mugs of coffee. Singh opened the back of Shepherd's phone and slotted the Sim card into the one he'd brought with him. "Same make, same style, looks the same, but this one acts as a listening device as well," said Singh, as he powered up the phone. "It's got GPS too so we'll always know where it is. The neat thing is that the microphone only kicks in when you switch the phone off. The GPS is on all the time, whether the phone is off or on." He scrolled through the menu. "So, when you think you're in a situation that you want recording, switch it off." He showed Shepherd the button on the top of the phone. "Keep pressing it until it powers down. Once you do that it starts sending everything it hears through the telecom system to our computer. So there's no range problems, so long as you're in contact with a mobile-phone mast, we can hear everything you say and we know exactly where you are." He handed the Nokia to Shepherd. "The one problem is the battery," he said. "Perversely, when it's switched off the power consumption goes up because it starts transmitting. The battery will go flat in about six hours. So the way to go is to keep it switched on normally and only switch it off when you're ready to transmit. And charge it as often as you can."

"How do you know when it's transmitting?"

"It goes through to a SOCA monitoring station, and as soon as it starts transmitting Charlie will get a call. They can then tell her what's being said or provide her with a live feed. And, of course, it's all recorded." He put Shepherd's original phone into his pocket. "Charlie says we should work out a code phrase so that we can send in the cavalry if necessary."

"Good idea," said Shepherd. "How about 'I'm not happy about this'? That covers a multitude of sins."

"I'll tell her," said Singh.

"Do you want to write it down?"

Singh laughed. "My memory isn't as good as yours, but I'll manage. I'll tell you what else — we can program it in so that when you say those words a red flag flashes."

"That's good to hear," said Shepherd. "I just hope that the cavalry is ready to ride because the guys I'll be with won't mess around."

"Heavy?"

"Very," said Shepherd. He gave Singh his coffee.

"Thanks. So, what about you? Have you heard who'll be taking over from Charlie?"

"She said as soon as she knows I'll know."

"And will you go with her to Five?"

"She hasn't asked."

"Think she will?"

"I just don't know, Amar," he said. "I get the feeling that at the moment she's more concerned about her own career prospects."

★ ★ ★

Shepherd's team spent Friday morning carrying out high-visibility stop-and-searches in Wembley. They were heading to Wembley police station for lunch when Fogg got a call on his radio. Parry was driving and the sergeant called out for him to turn around and head to Harlesden. "We've got a bailiff who's bitten off more than he can chew," said Fogg.

Helping bailiffs was a regular part of the TSG's workload. With rising unemployment and a faltering economy, more and more people were falling into debt, and the banks and building societies were sending in bailiffs to get what money they could. To Shepherd it appeared, more often than not, that the financial institutions were trying to get blood out of a stone. Not surprisingly, people wanted to keep what little they had in the way of assets, and at the first sign of trouble the bailiffs would call the police. The locals cops didn't like dealing with house seizures so whenever they could they'd try to pass the buck to the TSG.

By the time they had reached the address, Gary Dawson's team was already there and out of their van, putting on riot gear and stacking up their long shields. "What's the story, Gary?" asked Fogg.

Dawson gestured at the house. It was semi-detached with a garage next to it. The garage door was open revealing a ten-year-old Renault. "Bailiffs called around about an hour ago. A white male and a black female inside. Keith and Pearl Johnson. Mr Johnson is behind on his mortgage repayments to the tune of eight grand and the building society wants him out." He nodded at a middle-aged man in a rumpled suit who was standing next to two heavily built men in bomber jackets. "The suit is a lawyer from the building society, the heavies with him are the bailiffs. All the paperwork's in order."

"So what's the problem?" asked Fogg.

"The problem is that Mr Johnson has kept his wife in the dark about his problems. Didn't tell her that he'd lost his job, didn't tell her that he was behind with the mortgage, hid all the court letters from her. First she knew there was a problem was when they rang her doorbell. Now Mr Johnson has barricaded himself inside and Mrs Johnson is with him. Every time they knock on the door he screams that he's got a gun and he's going to kill anyone who steps inside."

"Is the threat a serious one?"

"Unlikely in the extreme," Dawson said. "But not surprisingly the bailiffs don't want to go in."

"And the wife?"

"We haven't heard a peep from her. According to the suit she was screaming the odds at the husband before he slammed the door."

"So we're not sure if she's in there willingly or not?"

Dawson nodded. "We're going to give him one more chance to open the door and if that doesn't work we're going in."

"What about a negotiator?"

"I called it in but they said that, with the best will in the world, it's going to be three or four hours before they have anyone, and even then we're low priority unless we're sure there's a threat."

"How do you want to handle it, Gary?"

"Slow entry, full gear and shields, talking to him every step of the way. He's not violent — a couple of convictions for drunk and disorderly about ten years ago but nothing recent. If he sees what he's up against I'm guessing he'll come out. He hasn't hit anybody — he swore at the bailiffs and threatened them but they won't be looking to charge him."

"Where do you want my guys?"

Shepherd and the rest of the team were already out of the van. Parry had opened the rear doors and was handing out their kitbags.

"I've only got four today," said Dawson, "one off sick and two have got Taser training. Be handy if you could go in the back while we take the front. There's a kitchen door — you go from there to the hall. We'll meet you halfway, and presumably we'll have him there unless he moves upstairs."

"Anyone else in the house?"

"They've got two boys but, according to the neighbours, they're at school. They're good people, Foggy. The neighbours say the kids are always well turned out. The wife takes them to school, and the dad helps with the school soccer team at weekends. They've just got themselves into a situation, that's all. I think my wife would probably kick off if she found out I hadn't been paying the mortgage for six months."

"Mind if I have a word?" said Fogg, gesturing at the front door.

"Knock yourself out."

Fogg went over to the van and explained the situation to his team. "Full kit on and long shields," he

516

said. "We'll be going in the back." He walked towards the house as they began opening their bags and taking out their gear.

Fogg went up to the front door. There was a letterbox at chest level and he slipped a hand through it and peered down the hall. He could see a West Indian woman in the kitchen, dabbing her eyes with a tea-towel. "Mrs Johnson!" he called. "Are you okay?" She flinched, then slammed the kitchen door. "Mrs Johnson, can you come here so that we can talk to you?"

"I've got a gun!" shouted a male voice. "You come through that door and I'll shoot you."

Fogg looked as far to the left and right of the hallway as he could, but he couldn't see Johnson. He was either up the stairs or in one of the two rooms leading off to the left of the hallway. "Mr Johnson, can you at least allow your wife to leave the house?" said Fogg.

"She's not going anywhere. No one is. This is our house. Just go away and leave us alone."

"That's not going to happen, Mr Johnson. The bailiffs have the legal right to enter the premises."

"This ain't premises, this is my home!" screamed Johnson. He came running out of the sitting room. Fogg caught a glimpse of a middle-aged white man with a shaved head and a West Ham tattoo on his forearm before the letterbox slammed shut, just a fraction of a second after he had slipped out his fingers.

Foggy walked back to Dawson's van. "I see what you mean," he said. "The wife's in the kitchen, he was in the sitting room. I don't think he's hurt her but she's

517

crying. She just slammed the door so she's in there on her own."

Dawson's team had lined up by their van, each with a long shield on their left arm. "Okay, let's get this over with," he said. "You let me know when you're in position and we'll go in together."

Fogg went over to his van. "Carpets, you're on the enforcer. I don't think the back door'll give you any trouble. She's alone in the kitchen at the moment. Pelican, you go in first. Give her every chance to come quietly — she's under a lot of stress."

"Got it, Skip."

"KFC, you and Three-amp go in after Pelican. Everyone stay back unless needed. I'll follow them in. Everyone got it?" They all nodded. "Okay, helmets on and off we go."

They put on their helmets and jogged alongside the garage to the rear of the house. Parry followed, carrying the orange enforcer. Fogg held them back, out of sight of the kitchen window, while he called up Dawson on the radio. "In position," he said.

"We're going in on three," said Dawson.

Fogg pointed at Parry, then at the door, then held up three fingers, then two. Then he nodded. Parry ran to the door, swung back the enforcer and smashed it against the lock. The door splintered and crashed inwards. He stepped aside and Castle ran into the house, her shield up. They could hear crashes and shouts from the front.

Mrs Johnson stood facing them. Her cheeks glistened with tears and her eyes were red from crying.

518

Her hair was in short dreadlocks, tied back with a polka-dotted scrunchie, and she was wearing a denim dress that buttoned up the front. On any other day she would have been pretty, but her lips were drawn back into a snarl and she was shaking like a trapped animal. As the police moved towards her, she screamed and grabbed a knife from a wooden block by the sink. "Knife!" shouted Castle, and stood where she was, her shield out in front of her. Shepherd and Kelly moved into the kitchen behind her and stood either side so that the three shields formed a Perspex wall.

"Put down the knife, Mrs Johnson," said Castle, calmly. "There's no need for that."

The woman was panicking, swishing the blade from side to side and making soft whimpering noises. Her left hand was clutching a small crucifix at her throat. She was in her late twenties but she had the eyes of a frightened child. On the other side of the kitchen door they heard thumps and bangs and a scream.

Fogg stepped into the kitchen. "Mrs Johnson, please, let's not get over-excited. We can sort this out."

The woman pulled open the kitchen door and ran down the hallway, her skirt flapping around her knees. Castle, Shepherd and Kelly followed her.

Dawson's team had used their shields to force the husband against the far wall of the sitting room. One of the men had dropped his shield and was trying to handcuff Johnson but he was resisting, swearing and shouting that he was going to kill them.

As Mrs Johnson hurtled down the hallway, Dawson stepped out of the sitting room. When she saw him she swerved to the right and up the stairs. She stopped halfway and turned around, still waving the knife.

Shepherd, Castle and Kelly held back. Fogg came up behind them. Dawson was nearest so Fogg kept quiet and left it to the other sergeant to do the talking.

Dawson kept his arms out to the sides. "It's okay, Foggy. Mrs Johnson doesn't want to hurt anyone."

"You're not taking my house," said the woman. She whipped the knife from side to side. "Just go away, leave us alone."

"Pearl, relax," said Dawson. "No one's going to hurt you."

"You can't take away my house," she said.

Dawson nodded. "Okay, just relax, all right? There's no reason for you to get upset." He reached his hand slowly to his neck strap and undid it, then took off his helmet.

"I didn't know — I didn't know that Keith had lost his job."

"I know that, Pearl."

"He lied to me. He went out every day, same as always. He said money was tight but money's always tight, right?" She reached up and grasped her crucifix.

"That's right," said Dawson. He took off his gloves and held out his right hand. "Just give me the knife, Pearl. I know you don't want to hurt anyone."

"Gary, keep away from her," said Fogg, removing his Taser from the holster on his hip.

"Foggy, it's okay," said Dawson, his eyes still on the woman. "Pearl's going to give me the knife and we're all going to walk out of here. No one's in any trouble, no one's been hurt, it's just a misunderstanding, isn't it, Pearl?" Dawson nodded, trying to get the woman to agree with him, but she just stared at him with wide eyes. "Pearl, your children are going to be home soon, aren't they? You don't want them to see you like this, do you?"

"Don't you talk about my kids," she snapped. "You leave my kids out of this." She released the crucifix and pointed her finger at Dawson. "This is nothing to do with my kids!" she hissed.

"I'm just saying, we don't want to upset them, do we? Two boys you've got, right?"

The woman nodded. "You can't take my boys away from me."

"No one's going to take your boys, Pearl, you have my word." Dawson took a step towards her, his arm extended. "We can find somewhere for you and your boys to stay."

"This is our home," she said. "We're staying here."

Dawson took another step towards her. "That's not possible, Pearl. The court says you have to move out and that's the end of it. But the council have to find you somewhere to live so you won't be on the streets. And someone can wait with you until the boys come home."

"No!" screamed the woman, and lashed out with the knife. Dawson tried to get out of the way but he was too slow and the blade caught him under the chin. Blood spurted across the stair carpet as he staggered back. Fogg pulled the trigger of the Taser and two prongs shot out trailing thin wires behind them. They

521

hit Mrs Johnson in the chest and half a second later thousands of volts pulsed through her. She convulsed and dropped like a stone onto the stairs.

Shepherd threw his shield to the side and rushed to Dawson, who was slowly sliding down the side of the banisters, his hands clasped to his neck. Blood was seeping through his fingers. Shepherd could see the panic in his eyes. He grabbed the sergeant's arms and gently helped him to the floor. "You'll be okay, Gary, just relax." He looked up at Fogg. "Get the paramedics in here now, Sarge," he said. Fogg hurried down the corridor and out of the front door. Two of Dawson's men came over but Shepherd told them to keep back, that Dawson needed room.

Kelly leaned his shield against the wall and joined Shepherd on the floor. "How bad is it?" he asked. Behind him, Castle and Simmons put down their shields and went past Shepherd to get to the unconscious woman. They picked her up by the arms and carried her down the stairs and out of the front door. She was mumbling incoherently and shaking her head.

"I don't think she cut anything serious," said Shepherd. "Get me a kitchen roll or something." He pulled off his gloves and threw them onto the floor. Kelly nodded and dashed to the kitchen.

Dawson's mouth was working but there was only a gurgling sound. Blood trickled between his lips. Kelly appeared with a roll of kitchen paper and a tea-towel.

"Gary, don't try to talk," said Shepherd, gazing directly into the man's eyes. "You're cut but it's not life-threatening, okay? If an artery had been severed you'd have passed out already, so you've just got to stay calm, all right? The blood in your mouth is coming from the throat wound so lean forward a bit so that it doesn't go down your air passage. Concentrate on breathing slowly and shallowly. If your mouth fills up then swallow it but don't let it go down into your lungs. And try to relax. You're going to get through this."

Shepherd helped him lean forward. Dawson opened his lips and blood spilled out over the front of his stab vest. Shepherd took the roll of kitchen paper from Kelly and pulled off a dozen sheets, folding them into a thick wad. He looked into Dawson's eyes again. "Gary, I need you to take your hands away from your neck, so that I can apply this to the wound. On the count of three. Don't worry, it'll take less than a second. One, two, three."

On three, Dawson removed his hands and Shepherd slapped the wad of kitchen roll over the gash in his neck. "Good man," he said. He kept the paper in place with his left hand while he took the tea-towel from Kelly. He placed the towel over the wad of paper. "Okay, Gary, you can put your hands back now," he said. "Keep the pressure on as much as you can, okay?" Dawson put his hands up to the makeshift bandage and Shepherd moved his away. Blood was still oozing from Dawson's mouth but not as much as there had been at first. "Keep breathing slowly and evenly and you'll be just fine," he said.

There was a heavy footfall outside and two paramedics in green jackets with fluorescent stripes burst into the hall carrying bulky medical kits. Shepherd stood up so that they had room to work. Kelly put an arm around his shoulders. "Nice work, Terry," he said.

"Basic first aid," said Shepherd.

"You're one cool bastard," said Kelly.

"Does that mean I can have a different nickname?" asked Shepherd. "I'm not happy with Three-amp." The two paramedics knelt beside Dawson. Shepherd picked up his gloves. "Come on, I need some air," he said.

Shepherd and Fogg watched as the paramedics wheeled Dawson on a stretcher towards the waiting ambulance. Mrs Johnson and her husband were sitting in the back of a local response car, waiting to be taken to Harlesden police station. Inspector Smith arrived in a TSG van, accompanied by three patrol cars. He had a quick word with the paramedics, then walked over to Fogg and Shepherd. "He'll be okay," said the inspector. "What the hell happened in there?"

"He was talking to her and she kicked off," said Fogg.

"He knew she had a knife?"

"He wanted to talk to her," said Fogg.

"He should have stayed behind the shields. That's procedure," said Smith. "How did he let her get so close?"

"He was trying to take the knife off her," said Fogg.

Smith was more annoyed than upset. "That's why we train for these situations," he said. "We have procedures in place so this doesn't happen. He could have died."

524

"He didn't want her hurt," said Shepherd.

"Yeah, well, it didn't work out that way, did it?" said the inspector. "And she got Tasered anyway. And that doesn't make the TSG look good either, does it? Tasering a housewife and mother."

"She had just stabbed Gary in the throat, sir," said Fogg.

"Yeah, but even so," said Smith. He shook his head. "What a mess." He nodded at Shepherd. "Paramedics said you helped Gary, stopped the bleeding."

"I just put a compress on the wound, sir, that's all," said Shepherd.

"Good job," said Smith. "But get back to base ASAP and wash that blood off you. It's not good for our image."

They drove back to Paddington Green. This time there was none of the banter and horseplay that usually heralded the end of a shift. They walked in through the rear entrance of the building and Shepherd went straight to the shower room. He took off his stab vest and held it under the shower to wash off Dawson's blood, then did the same with his overalls. There were only a few spots on his boots and he wiped them with a paper towel. Then he stripped off the rest of his clothes and showered himself clean. He wrapped his towel around his waist and carried his clothing through to the locker room to change. Fogg was there, putting on a pair of jeans. "Gary's in the hospital, doing fine," he said.

"That's good to hear," said Shepherd. He rolled his overalls around his stab vest and put them in the bottom of his locker.

"Didn't realise you did first aid," said Fogg.

"Did some in the army," said Shepherd. "Battlefield injuries, but the principle's the same. Stop the bleeding, keep them calm, get a medic."

Fogg pulled on a Belstaff waterproof jacket and took his motorcycle helmet out of his locker. "I'm glad you were there, Terry. You're a real asset to this team."

"Thanks, Skip."

Fogg winked and closed his locker. "See you next week," he said, and left.

Shepherd pulled on a clean polo shirt. He jumped as a hand fell on his shoulder. "Fancy a Spanish, hero?" asked Coker. "Drop of Rioja?"

"I've got the bike," said Shepherd.

"Nah, come and have Spanish with us over at San Miguel," said Coker. "Colgate can drive you home if you get too pissed. And put your uniform on."

"What?"

"Just do as you're told, Three-amp," said Coker: "Shirt, tie, trousers, boots. Casual jacket on top. Trust me, I'm a policeman."

"Who else is going?" asked Shepherd, taking off his polo shirt.

"It's a surprise," said Coker.

Shepherd put on one of his long-sleeved white shirts, a pair of black trousers and his tie. Coker folded his arms and watched him get dressed. "Come on, Lurpak, fill me in."

"I don't want to spoil the surprise," he said.

Turnbull appeared at the door wearing an overcoat over his uniform. "Is he coming?" he asked Coker.

"Yeah, he's cool," said Coker.

Shepherd pulled on his sports jacket. He switched off his mobile phone and slid it into the inside pocket of his jacket. "I wish someone would tell me what's going on," he said.

Coker put on his waterproof jacket and flipped the collar up at the back. "Let's go," he said.

Shepherd walked out of the station flanked by Coker and Turnbull, feeling like a prisoner being escorted to his cell. The two men kept up a cheerful banter as they crossed Edgware Road and walked to San Miguel. He felt as if he was being abducted by two Mafia hitmen, but doubted that anything would happen in a Spanish restaurant across the road from the most secure police station in England.

They went downstairs. Shepherd and Coker sat at a corner table while Turnbull went to the bar.

"What's the story, Lurpak?" asked Shepherd. "Is this about that other business?"

"Thought you might want to meet the guys, that's all," said Coker.

"The guys? You mean the Caped Crusader?"

"Masked Avenger, you prat," said Coker. "And we don't call him that, we call him the sergeant."

"Foggy?"

Coker laughed and shook his head. "No, not Foggy," he said. "Foggy plays it by the book. He'd hit the roof if he knew what was going on."

527

Kelly and Parry came into the restaurant, both wearing dark padded jackets over their uniforms. They sat down at the table. A waiter brought over a basket of crusty bread. "You all right, Three-amp?" asked Kelly, reaching for a chunk.

"All good," said Shepherd.

Turnbull came over with two bottles of Rioja and six glasses. He sloshed wine into the glasses, then sat down. He took one and raised it. "To crime!" he said.

Everyone at the table raised their glasses and drank except Shepherd. Kelly pointed a finger at him. "Don't even start to say you've got your bloody bike," he said.

Shepherd grinned and raised his glass. "Yes, sir," he said, and drank.

"That's better," said Kelly. He reached across and clinked his glass against Shepherd's.

"I'm getting fed up with the bike anyway," said Shepherd. "Too many nutters on the roads here."

"Too many nutters everywhere," agreed Turnbull.

"Where's the sergeant?" asked Shepherd, nodding at the untouched glass.

"On his way," said Kelly, picking up another chunk of bread. The waiter returned with menus. Kelly ordered half a dozen tapas and another bottle of Rioja.

"So you're okay with this, Three-amp?" asked Turnbull, when the waiter had gone.

"Okay with what?" said Shepherd.

Turnbull looked at Kelly. "He's okay," said Kelly.

"I'm okay," said Shepherd.

"You'd better be, because there's no turning back," said Turnbull.

"Bit dramatic," said Kelly. He bit into his bread and chewed noisily.

"I'm serious, Three-amp," said Turnbull. "No one's going to think any less of you if you don't want to move forward."

"Not everyone can do it," agreed Parry.

"You guys don't have a problem with it, right?" asked Shepherd. All the men around the table shook their heads. "Then I'm with you. But I've a question."

"Fire away," said Kelly.

"There's the four of you," said Shepherd. "Did you ask anyone else in the Serial?"

Coker and Kelly exchanged a look and they both sniggered. "KFC wanted to ask Pelican but we said no girlies," said Coker.

"I thought she'd be up for it," said Kelly. "I still do."

"Pelican's a great TSG officer, but what we do requires something extra," said Coker.

"Balls?" suggested Shepherd.

All the men laughed. Coker banged the table with the flat of his hand. "Got it in one," he said. He looked at the door. "Here's the sergeant now."

Shepherd turned to see Ross Mayhew walking towards them. He'd changed out of his CSO uniform and was wearing a black overcoat over a dark blue suit.

"Sergeant?" said Shepherd.

"He was a sergeant in the army," said Kelly.

Mayhew sat down at the table. "I was promoted not long before I left," he said. "These guys started calling me that when they found out." He grinned at Kelly. "KFC here started it, I think."

"Beer?" asked Kelly.

"Bottle of Corona," said Mayhew. "And tell them to forget the lime — there's no bloody flies down here."

Kelly went over to the bar. Mayhew leaned over the table. "So, what were you guys talking about?" he said.

"I was asking who else was on board," said Shepherd. "They were telling me that Pelican didn't have the balls for it."

Mayhew chuckled. "That's funny. She's got balls but she doesn't have what it takes to do what we do."

"But I do?"

Mayhew nodded. "I'm a pretty good judge of character," he said. "And we only take someone on when we're one hundred per cent sure of them."

"What about Nipple?" asked Shepherd.

"Graduate entry, fast-tracked to stardom," said Mayhew. "He'll be a chief constable one day, maybe even running the Met. He's not going to risk that, even if it means doing what's right."

Kelly returned with a bottle of Corona. He gave it to Mayhew and sat down again.

"Plus we weren't too sure about him when he joined nine months ago," said Coker.

"Why was that?" asked Shepherd.

"Seemed a strange posting for a graduate entrant," said Turnbull. "And he'd done a year with the rubber heels. We thought he might have been put in to check up on us."

"Yeah," agreed Kelly. "For a while back there we were calling him Triffid."

"Triffid?" repeated Shepherd.

"Yeah, because we thought he was a dangerous plant."

Shepherd laughed. "And Foggy's too straight as well?" he asked Mayhew.

"Foggy's the salt of the earth and a bloody good copper," said Mayhew. "But he's not right for what we do. So mum's the word when he's around. We don't talk about this with outsiders, ever."

"Like *Fight Club*?" said Shepherd.

"What?" said Mayhew.

Kelly laughed. "He's right," he said. "The first rule of Fight Club is you never talk about Fight Club. The Brad Pitt movie. Yeah, it's the same. Because if anyone talks, we're screwed."

"No one's going to talk," said Mayhew. "Because we're all in this together, and we all believe in what we're doing."

"Like the five musketeers," said Turnbull.

"Six," said Shepherd. "I'm in, remember?"

"Have you done something like this before?" asked Turnbull.

"Like what, Colgate?"

"Like taking the law into your own hands?"

Shepherd shrugged. "I got heavy with a drug-dealer in my last job. In Hereford."

"Any repercussions?" asked Parry.

"I'm here now, aren't I?" said Shepherd. He leaned forward. "How far do you guys go?"

"As far as we want," said Kelly. "As far as we bloody well want."

"No limits?"

Kelly reached for more bread. "We do what we have to do," he said. "And it's working. Just look at the crime stats for our area. Housebreaking down, street muggings down, drive-by shootings down. All major crime down."

"Can't argue with that," said Shepherd.

"We get results," said Mayhew. "We do what we have to do and it works. And before long there'll be others following our example."

"You're not planning on going public, are you?" asked Shepherd.

"Of course not," said Mayhew. "It has to be done on the QT. But we can recruit slowly, spread the philosophy throughout the Met, then on to other forces. We can show that it works, that a few good men can take back the streets."

Shepherd nodded appreciatively. "Sounds like a plan."

"It is," said Mayhew. "And it's a plan that'll work. And tonight you show us what you can do."

"Tonight?" said Shepherd.

"Strike while the iron's hot."

Shepherd nodded slowly. "Okay," he said. "What's the story?"

"Two guys in Queen's Park," said Mayhew. "Paul Hanratty and Mike Trelawny. Pavement artists. Done at least a dozen banks and building societies over the past couple of years. They shot a pensioner in the legs, blinded a cashier with ammonia, kicked a manager in the nuts. Nasty bastards."

"And never charged?"

"Never been caught in the act," said Mayhew. "Loads of CCTV and eye-witness reports but they wear masks and they're careful with the old forensics. They steal a motor the day before and torch it afterwards."

"So how do we know they're the ones?"

"Because they like to throw their money around when they're flush," said Mayhew. "Casinos, top restaurants, high-class hookers."

"I've never understood how a hooker can be high class," said Kelly. "Hookers sell their pussies, which means high class doesn't come into it."

Mayhew glowered at him. "Let's stay focused," he said.

Kelly shoved more bread into his mouth. The waiter reappeared with two plates of ham. He put them on the table and Kelly grabbed a couple of slices.

Mayhew waited until the waiter had left before continuing. "Anyway, these guys have boasted about doing jobs in the past, so there's no doubt it's them. The Flying Squad have turned them over a couple of times and in January they staked them out for a week, waiting for them to do a Nationwide branch in Acton. Never happened." Mayhew sat back in his chair. "You ask me, they're getting intel from someone at the Yard. Maybe even the Sweeney itself. The Yard leaks like a sieve, these days."

The waiter came back with bowls of garlic mushrooms, chicken in red wine, *patatas bravas* and a large tortilla. Kelly was the first to help himself.

Mayhew sipped his wine. "So, if the Sweeney can't bring these guys down, it's up to us."

"What have you got in mind?" asked Shepherd.

"We stop them," said Mayhew. "We explain the error of their ways and we show them that we're serious."

"How exactly?" asked Shepherd.

"By beating the crap out of them," said Kelly.

"We hurt them," said Mayhew, quietly. "We hurt them so bad that they stop shooting pensioners."

Shepherd nodded slowly. "Okay," he said.

"You're up for it?" said Mayhew.

"Yeah, I'm up for it," said Shepherd.

Mayhew smiled and raised his bottle of Corona. "Good man," he said. "Let's eat, and then we go."

A Chinese nurse took Jimmy Sharpe from Reception and opened the door to Gary Dawson's private room for him. "Visitor for you, Sergeant Dawson," she said brightly.

Dawson smiled when he saw Sharpe. "Brian, what are you doing here?"

"Just wanted to drop by and say hail to the hero."

The nurse checked the dressing around Dawson's neck. "Try not to talk too much," she said, then left them alone in the room.

Dawson waved at the armchair next to the bed. "Take the weight off your feet."

Sharpe looked around the room as he sat down. There was a decent-sized LCD television on one wall, complete with a DVD player, a side table with a range of soft drinks and a view over a garden. It was better than a lot of hotel rooms Sharpe had stayed in. "They're looking after you all right," he said.

"How did you know I was here?" asked Dawson.

"Friends in low places," said Sharpe. "I was going to bring you fruit but then I figured you wouldn't be eating for a while, having been stabbed in the throat and all."

"Yeah, it'll be a week or so before I can chew," said Dawson. "No solids until then."

"Sounds like you were lucky," said Sharpe. "The nurse outside said the knife missed your larynx and most of the major blood vessels."

"Could have been worse," agreed Dawson.

Sharpe nodded thoughtfully, but didn't say anything.

"Something on your mind, Brian?" said Dawson, eventually.

Sharpe sighed and folded his arms. "Yeah, I'm afraid so," he said.

"Better out than in, as they say," said Dawson. "What's wrong?"

"My name's not Brian Parker," said Sharpe, quietly.

"Okay," said Dawson, hesitantly.

"I shouldn't be here, Gary. And I sure as hell shouldn't be having this conversation with you."

"We're not having a conversation yet," said Dawson. "Spit it out, whatever it is."

"You're a mate, Gary. I mean that."

"You're a mate too." Dawson smiled. "I hope you're not going to tell me you're gay," he said, "because I've got a wife and two kids."

Sharpe laughed, then shook his head. "It's worse than that," he said.

Dawson frowned, and then he swore under his breath. "You're with Professional Standards," he said.

"No, I'm with SOCA, that much is true. But, yeah, I'm doing Professional Standards' dirty work."

Dawson closed his eyes. "Shit," he said.

"They've been on to you for months, Gary," said Sharpe. "They got hold of a phone number on a membership list."

Dawson opened his eyes again. "You were spying on me."

"I like to think of it as gathering intelligence but, yeah, pretty much."

"And that's why you're here, to arrest me?"

"I'm SOCA," said Sharpe, "we don't arrest people."

"So why did you come?"

"Like I said, to say hail to the hero."

"Thanks. Now fuck off and die."

"Gary . . ."

"Don't bloody 'Gary' me. You lied to me, you set me up and now you're going to screw me over." His eyes narrowed. "Lenny — is he in this too? Lenny Brennan? Is he working for you?"

"Brennan's just a guy I met at the England First meeting," said Sharpe. "He doesn't know me from Adam."

"Small mercies," said Dawson.

"Look, the reason I'm here . . ." Sharpe sighed mournfully. "You have to know they have everything they need to sack you, Gary. You'll lose your job, your pension, the works."

"I'd figured that out already," said Dawson, his voice loaded with sarcasm.

"My reports are already with SOCA and they'll be sent to the Met. There's nothing I can do about that. And you know that membership of an organisation like England First is grounds for instant dismissal."

"I'm not a racist," said Dawson, quickly.

"I know you're not," said Sharpe. "But whether you are or not has nothing to do with what's going to happen. Membership alone means you're out. There's nothing you can do to change that. But there is something you can do. You can get your resignation in first. Medical reasons. That wound in your throat is enough reason for you to be invalided out, and even if it isn't, you can get a doctor to sign you off on stress or PTSD or whatever they want to call it. If you quit on medical grounds, they can't then sack you. Your pension is safe and you leave covered in glory."

"I was going to quit anyway," said Dawson. "The job's not what it was."

"Can't say I blame you," said Sharpe. "But you're going to have to do it quickly, Gary. Strike while the iron's hot. At the moment you're a hero, so if you quit now they won't dare do anything to queer your pitch."

Dawson nodded. "I get it," he said.

Sharpe stood up. "I'm sorry," he said.

"You were just doing your job," said Dawson. "You can tell me one thing, though."

"Sure."

"Who are you really?"

Sharpe smiled. "Jimmy," he said.

Dawson held out his hand. "Thanks for letting me know where I stand, Jimmy," he said.

Sharpe shook it. "No problem," he said.

"Now fuck off and leave me in peace."

Shepherd was in the prisoner seat and Richard Parry was in his regular spot, sitting by the door, leaning forward with his elbows resting on his knees. Turnbull was driving and Coker was in the front passenger seat.

Mayhew was sitting directly in front of Shepherd, and Kelly was on his left. It was dark outside and starting to rain. Turnbull switched on the wipers and they whispered as they flicked across the windscreen.

"So where are we going?" Shepherd asked Mayhew. He had no way of knowing if Button or Singh were listening in, but he had to assume that they were and give them as much information as he could. They would know where he was from the tracking device on the van and the GPS in his phone but they wouldn't know where he was going. If Mayhew was going to tackle two professional armed robbers he and his men would probably have guns themselves, which meant that Button would need to send in an armed-response unit.

"Queen's Park," said Mayhew. "We'll pick Hanratty up first and then grab Trelawny."

"They're going to be armed, right?" asked Shepherd.

"Maybe, maybe not," said Mayhew. "They're pros so they're not likely to have guns in their homes."

538

"But we've got it covered if they are," said Coker. He bent down and pulled a carrier bag from under the seat in front of him. He opened it and showed Shepherd the barrel of a sawn-off shotgun.

"Tell me that's not a sawn-off," said Shepherd, for the benefit of anyone listening.

"Picked it up on a raid a few months back," said Coker. "Totally clean, totally untraceable."

"But not loaded, right?"

"Oh, it's loaded," said Coker, putting the gun back under the seat.

"And what's the plan?" asked Shepherd. "Where do we take them?"

"I've got a warehouse fixed up," said Mayhew. "Been empty for ages. There's a few other businesses nearby but they'll be closed this time of night. Bare minimum of security so we won't be disturbed."

"How do you get that sorted?" asked Shepherd.

"No one pays any attention to a CSO doing his rounds," said Mayhew. "I get to check premises, look at locks and alarms, and no one gives a toss."

Shepherd folded his arms. He really wanted an address but he didn't see how he could ask for that without drawing attention to himself. He forced himself to relax, stretching out his legs and sighing. "I tell you, you could have chosen a quieter day."

"I heard you guys had a run-in with a mad woman."

"She wasn't mad, she was just under pressure," said Shepherd. "I don't think she knew what she was doing."

"She damn near killed Gary — the bitch deserves to rot in hell for that," said Mayhew.

"Gary's not on your crew, is he?" asked Shepherd.

Mayhew shook his head. "Straight as an arrow," he said. "Funny thing is, he's as disillusioned as we all are, but he won't cross the line. Keeps saying that we need a political solution but he's so wrong. The politicians we've got aren't going to solve anything — they're too busy feathering their own nests."

"Did you try to convert him?"

"It doesn't work like that, Terry," said Mayhew. "It's not about converting people to our cause. It's about finding like-minded individuals who've already seen the light."

"That's how we knew you'd be on side," said Coker. "You saw me take the gun and you didn't say anything. You crossed the line yourself. No one made you do it."

"That's true." Shepherd looked out of the window. They were driving through Kilburn, not far from his rented house. He nodded at Mayhew. "So when did you cross the line, Ross? Here or in Afghanistan?"

Mayhew frowned. "What do you mean?"

"I'm guessing you spent some time planning this," said Shepherd. "Or did it just come to you when you started working as a CSO?"

"The situation in Afghanistan isn't that different from what we've got in London," said Mayhew. "The vast majority of the Afghans just want to get on with their lives. They want to work, get married, raise their kids, have a bit of fun now and again. That's all anyone wants, right? But a hardcore percentage don't want

540

that. They want to cause mayhem and destruction, they want to kill and maim — and for why? For money. And for power. They want to have power over others. They say it's about religion but it's not. It's about power."

"But London's not a war zone," said Shepherd.

"Isn't it?" said Mayhew. "You've got more guns out there than ever before, a murder rate well above New York's, you've got areas where the police just won't go unless they're mob-handed, you've got people living in fear of gangs, you've got children being stabbed to death in the streets. That's pretty close to the definition of a war zone in my book, Terry."

"I can't argue with that, Ross," said Shepherd. Actually he could, but Shepherd wasn't looking for an argument: he was looking for Mayhew to hang himself. Every word being said in the van was being transmitted by the bug in Shepherd's mobile phone and recorded by Amar Singh or one of his people. "At least in Afghanistan you get the chance to shoot back," said Shepherd.

"You know that's not the way it works," said Mayhew. "The troops out there are hampered by the same sort of stupid rules and regulations as the cops here. The Taliban plant IEDs, they use children and women as suicide bombers, they ambush our guys, then they throw away their guns and hold up their hands and say that, no, they're just civilians, they're innocent. And then when we want to question them to get the truth, we're told that we can't be too rough with them, we can't do this, we can't do that, they've got human rights et cetera, et cetera. It's a bloody nonsense. They want

541

soldiers out there fighting for whatever it is we're fighting for, but they want them doing it with one hand tied behind their backs. The Taliban think we're weak. They laugh at the way they can run rings around us, and they laugh at the way we treat our prisoners. You know what the Taliban do with their prisoners? They hack off their heads with a blunt knife, that's what they do. And yet we treat their people according to the Geneva Convention."

"Madness," said Shepherd.

"Yeah, madness," agreed Mayhew.

"Is that why you left? You'd had enough?"

Mayhew's eyes narrowed. "You're asking a lot of questions, Terry."

Shepherd put up his hands. "Sorry, just curious," he said. "I was out there, I hear what you're saying. There were times when I wished I could just let rip with my weapon. You'd be looking at guys in the street and you'd know, you'd just know, that the night before they were shelling us with mortars, but you couldn't do anything."

"They fight like cowards, not like men," said Mayhew. "I told my captain — I said that regular soldiering won't work against scum like the Taliban. They don't fight like soldiers so they don't deserve to be treated like soldiers."

"There's a lot of squaddies that'd agree with you there," said Shepherd. "It's only the politicians and the armchair generals who think there's honour in war, these days. You do what you have to do, right?"

542

"Yeah, but my captain didn't see it that way. Put me on report, said I was a loose cannon." He shrugged. "I'd rather be a loose cannon than shipped back on a stretcher with my legs blown off." He tapped on Turnbull's shoulder. "Park up here, Colgate," he said.

Turnbull brought the van to a stop. "KFC, you and Carpets bring Hanratty to us. Nice and easy, you know the drill. We just need him down at the station for an ID parade."

Parry opened the door and he and Kelly headed down the street.

"I think it's a damn shame they didn't let you join the Met," said Shepherd.

"Yeah, you and me both," said Mayhew.

"The Met's got quotas to fill," said Turnbull, twisting round in the driver's seat. "Women, ethnic minorities, Muslims."

"And my face doesn't fit," said Mayhew.

"There's got to be more to it than that," said Shepherd. "They need guys like you with military training. You'd be perfect for the TSG." He scratched his chin. "The army probably screwed you over."

"What do you mean?" asked Mayhew.

"Maybe the psych report stuffed you," said Shepherd. "Maybe they gave you a shit reference. The loose-cannon thing." He grinned. "You didn't get heavy with civilians, did you?"

"Only if they asked for it," said Mayhew. "That's the thing with the ragheads. They sling mortars and set booby-traps, then wander around in their man dresses pretending to be civilians. They don't fight fair.

Anyway, me and a few of the guys got fed up with the way things were going so we took care of half a dozen ragheads that we knew were Ansar al-Islam."

"Ansar al-Islam?" said Shepherd.

"An offshoot of al-Qaeda," said Mayhew. "Vehemently anti-women. They were burning down beauty salons, throwing acid in the faces of women who didn't wear full burkhas, murdering women who talked to men they didn't know. We knew who they were but our officers said we were to leave them alone. Said it was politics and nothing to do with our mission. Morons."

"But you took care of them anyway?"

"Damn right," said Mayhew. "Rounded them up at night, drove them out into the desert and did what needed to be done."

"And there were no repercussions?"

"The captain had his suspicions, but nothing he could prove. That's how it works. If no one sees you and there's no forensics and no one talks, then no one can get to you."

Kelly and Parry came around the corner. Between them was a short, stocky man, his hands bound in front of him with a plastic tie. He was balding with a Mexican-style moustache and he was talking animatedly to the two policemen.

Coker pulled open the door. "Who's in charge here?" said Hanratty. He was wearing a brown leather bomber jacket, khaki cargo pants and Timberland boots.

"Just sit down and shut up," said Parry, pushing him into the van.

Mayhew grabbed Hanratty by the shoulders and shoved him onto a seat. "You the boss?" asked Hanratty.

"Like my colleague said, shut the fuck up," said Mayhew.

Parry and Kelly climbed into the van. Parry slid onto the jump seat and Kelly sat next to Shepherd. Turnbull drove off. Now that Hanratty was on board there was no chatter: everyone sat in silence — except Hanratty, but the team ignored him.

Hanratty's partner, Mike Trelawny, lived a couple of miles away in a council tower block. Kelly and Parry went to get him. They returned after five minutes with a lanky black man in his twenties wearing a black Nike tracksuit. "He was just going for a run," said Kelly, pushing Trelawny into the van. His wrists were also bound with a plastic tie.

"What the fuck's going on?" said Hanratty. "What's he doing here? You said it was a line-up."

"Shut up," snarled Mayhew.

"Nah, you shut up," said Hanratty. "I know my rights. Fuck this — if you want me to come with you then you need to arrest me and I need my lawyer."

"Yeah, we want lawyers," said Trelawny.

Mayhew punched Hanratty in the face. Cartilage splintered and blood spurted across the floor of the van. Hanratty fell back, his hands over his face, and his head banged on the window. Trelawny began to struggle but Kelly and Parry wrestled him to the floor. Coker had a roll of duct tape. He pulled off a strip, ripped it with his teeth and gave it to Parry, who slapped it across Trelawny's mouth. Coker ripped off another piece of tape and used that to gag Hanratty. Then he pulled the man off the prisoner seat and made him lie on the floor next to Trelawny.

Mayhew pressed his foot against Hanratty's back. "Right, Colgate," he said. "Hit the gas."

The van stopped at a metal-sided building with a large for-rent sign above its main door. They were on a small industrial estate to the south of the North Circular Road, close to Muswell Hill golf course. Parry pulled open the door and jumped out of the van. Kelly nodded at Shepherd and the two men grabbed Trelawny. They pulled him off the floor and across the Tarmac towards the building. Coker gave Mayhew the bag containing the shotgun, then bundled Hanratty out of the van. Turnbull climbed out of the driver's side and helped Coker drag Hanratty after Trelawny.

Mayhew jogged to the side of the building where there was a door. He took a key from his pocket and opened it, then stepped aside to give Kelly and Shepherd room to push Trelawny inside. Mayhew followed them, switching on the lights and pointing at a doorway. "Take him through there," he said.

Trelawny was struggling but his wrists were bound and Kelly and Shepherd were gripping his arms tightly. He was trying to speak but the duct tape muffled his words.

The doorway led to a large open area with metal girders overhead and metal tables lining the walls.

546

Mayhew flicked a light switch and overhead fluorescent lights flickered into life.

Kelly put his knee against the back of Trelawny's left leg and forced him to the floor, then planted his foot in the small of the man's back, pinning him down. As Mayhew took the sawn-off shotgun out of the bag, Turnbull and Coker dragged Hanratty in and threw him down next to Trelawny.

Hanratty tried to roll onto his back but Coker kicked him in the side and told him to lie still.

Mayhew broke the shotgun open, checked the two shells, then clicked it closed. He grinned at Shepherd. "See, Three-amp? Easy-peasy," he said.

"Now what happens?" said Shepherd.

"Now we give them a taste of their own medicine."

Parry walked in and stood watching, his massive fists on his hips.

"You're going to shoot them?"

"In the legs," said Mayhew.

The two men began to struggle but Kelly still had foot in the middle of Trelawny's back and Coker did the same with Hanratty.

"And then what? You leave them to bleed to death?"

"We'll call it in and an ambulance will pick them up before that happens." Mayhew bent down and tapped the barrel of the shotgun against Hanratty's head. "You hear that? You hear what's going to happen to you? You're not going to die, not today, but if you ever tell anyone what happened here, we'll come back and finish you. Do you understand?"

Hanratty nodded.

"What about you, Mike? You hear what I'm saying? You turn stool pigeon and you're dead meat. Understand?"

Trelawny grunted.

"I'm not happy about this," said Shepherd, raising his voice so that it was sure to be picked up by the transmitter in his phone.

"What?" said Mayhew.

"I said I'm not happy about this."

"About what exactly?"

"About shooting unarmed men," said Shepherd.

"That's just a matter of timing," said Mayhew. "When these guys are working, they're tooled up. They've shot at little old ladies, housewives, anyone who gets in their way."

"So why not take them in and charge them?"

Mayhew scowled at Coker. "You said he was squared away, Lurpak."

"He is," said Coker. He put a hand on Shepherd's shoulder. "What's your problem, Terry? You know why we're here — it's a bit bloody late for getting cold feet."

"I'm just saying shotguns aren't an exact science. A pellet can go through an artery and before we know it he's bled out and we're all up on murder charges. It's one thing to add a bit of extra evidence here and there, but I didn't sign up for murder."

"Hell, if you're that worried, shoot them yourself," said Mayhew, holding the shotgun out. "Shoot their knees."

As Shepherd reached for the weapon he heard rapid footsteps behind him and shouts of "Armed police!"

Mayhew jumped back and held the shotgun against his chest.

Three armed policemen in Kevlar helmets, goggles and armoured vests over black fatigues burst through the door with Heckler & Koch MP5s at their shoulders. An inspector followed, and behind him three more men, all wearing helmets and vests and sweeping their MP5s around. There were laser sights on all the weapons and red dots flickered across the men standing in the middle of the building.

"Armed police — down on the floor now!" yelled the inspector.

Parry dropped to the floor, his hands behind his head.

"Drop your weapon!" the inspector screamed at Mayhew. "Drop the weapon or we will fire!"

There were now seven armed officers fanning around the door, moving cautiously, their weapons constantly on the move.

"Don't shoot!" shouted Kelly. He held up his hands and slowly knelt down. Turnbull did the same.

"On the floor, face down!" shouted the inspector. Kelly and Turnbull lowered themselves and lay with their arms outstretched.

"Drop your weapon!" the inspector screamed again.

"You're not taking me in!" shouted Mayhew.

"Drop your weapon or we'll fire!" yelled the inspector. Red dots danced on Mayhew's chest.

"Don't fire!" shouted Shepherd, holding his arms up. "He's not a danger to anyone — he's not going to shoot."

"Get out of the way, Three-amp," said Mayhew.

Shepherd stepped between Mayhew and the armed police. The red dots disappeared from Mayhew's chest and Shepherd knew that the laser sights were now trained on his back.

"Get out of the way! We will fire!" screamed the inspector.

"I'm not armed," shouted Shepherd. "You're not stupid enough to shoot an unarmed man in the back. Now, keep quiet, I'm talking here!" He gestured at the shotgun in Mayhew's hands. "It's over, Ross."

"It's over when I say it's over," said Mayhew.

"If you pull the trigger, they'll shoot you, and probably catch me in the crossfire, too."

"Are you scared of dying, Three-amp? Because I'm not. After what I've seen, what I've been through. Death's nothing to fear. Least of all a warrior's death."

"Is that what you want? Cop suicide?"

"What I want is to get out of here." He pointed the gun at Hanratty. "And I can think of worse ways to go. At least I'll take these scumbags with me."

"You want to die with guys like them? Where's the honour in that?"

"This isn't about honour. I'm screwed, I know that, but at least this way I go out fighting."

"If you shoot them the cops shoot you. That's not fighting. That's suicide. The coward's way out."

"I'm no coward," Mayhew snarled.

"So prove it," said Shepherd. He heard scuffing sounds behind him and he knew that the armed police were moving, trying to get a clear shot. Shepherd took a step closer to Mayhew. "I'm moving so that they can't shoot you," he explained.

"Why are you doing this?"

"Because I don't want anyone to die here," said Shepherd.

"Tell them to put their guns down, then."

Shepherd smiled. "They're not going to listen to me, Ross. They want you to put the shotgun down."

"And then what?" said Mayhew. "I rot in a cell for the rest of my life?"

"Maybe not," said Shepherd.

Mayhew frowned. "What do you mean?"

"What you did, most people would agree with. Have your day in court, tell the jury why you did what you did. You might be surprised."

"You think they'd let me walk?"

"That's for the jury to decide. But either way, the whole world will be listening."

"Drop the weapon!" screamed the inspector behind Shepherd. "Drop the weapon or we will fire!"

"Ignore them," said Shepherd, keeping his eyes fixed on Mayhew. "When you started this, what did you want to achieve?"

"I wanted to do the right thing," said Mayhew. "I wanted to reclaim the streets, get rid of the shits that make life a misery for regular people."

"So tell the world that," said Shepherd. "Have your day in court, explain why you did what you did, and I bet you'll have people queuing up to continue what you started." Mayhew bit down on his lower lip. A red dot moved across his forehead and came to rest between his eyebrows. Shepherd moved to the left and the dot vanished. "We don't have much time, Ross," he said.

"If I die here, the result will be the same," said Mayhew.

"If you die they'll control the way the story's told," said Shepherd. "They'll make out that you're some maverick nutter, dig up psych reports from the army, get officers saying that you were a loose cannon, ramp up the Walter Mitty angle — they'll leak all the shit they can to the tabloids."

Mayhew gestured at the cops lying on the ground. "They'll tell it like it is," he said.

"They'll be too busy cutting deals to save their own skins," said Shepherd. "If you die, any good you did will be lost for ever. But if you stand up in court and tell your story, the whole world listens."

Mayhew began to lower the shotgun. Shepherd held up his hands. "Put the gun down on the floor, Ross. Do it nice and slowly, don't give them any excuse to —"

Three dots flickered across Mayhew's chest and Shepherd flinched as he heard three simultaneous bangs behind him. Mayhew staggered back, blood trickling from three wounds under his left shoulder. The shotgun slipped from his fingers as his mouth worked soundlessly. Red froth spilled from between his lips and he fell to his knees, then pitched forward.

Shepherd whirled around. The inspector and two other heavy-set men with MP5s advanced towards him, their weapons aimed at his chest. "He was giving up, you bastards! He was bloody well giving up."

"Down on your knees, your hands behind your neck!" shouted the inspector. "If you do not comply, we will shoot."

"I'm not armed."

"Down on the floor, now!"

Shepherd glared at the inspector. "I'm going to remember you," he said quietly. "And one day . . ."

"Down on the floor!" The inspector's finger tightened on the trigger.

Shepherd slowly put his hands behind his neck and went down on his knees, his eyes never leaving the inspector's face. "One day . . ." he said.

"Are you okay with wine?" asked Charlotte Button. She pulled the bottle out of the cooler. "It's a Pinot Grigio and very drinkable."

"That's fine," said Shepherd. He didn't care what sort of wine it was: he was there to talk, not to drink. It was forty-eight hours after the armed police had stormed into the industrial unit and shot Ross Mayhew. And just one hour after Shepherd had been released from police custody. They were in a wine bar in Covent Garden, sitting at a quiet table overlooking a square where a young man in a top hat was standing on stilts and juggling fire extinguishers.

Button poured wine into a glass and gave it to him, then raised her glass in salute. "Congratulations," she said. "Job well done."

Shepherd nodded and sipped his wine. He put down the glass but kept his fingers on the stem. "I've had enough, Charlie."

"Of what exactly?" asked Button.

"The cops. SOCA. Law enforcement. It's a waste of time."

"That's a bit of a sweeping statement, Spider. You're just annoyed because CO 19 were a tad trigger happy."

"There was no need to shoot Mayhew. And no need to threaten to shoot me."

"It was all seat-of-the-pants," said Button. "There was no time for a full briefing. So far as they were concerned you were one of the bad guys."

"Yeah, well, I'm not." He swirled his wine around the glass. "The prick that shot Mayhew, I want him out of the job."

"He's been suspended. There'll be a full investigation."

"After which he'll be cleared and back working." He shook his head. "I want him out. I want him sacked and I want him to lose his pension. Mayhew was surrendering. He was no threat to anyone."

"There were three different slugs in him, Spider," said Button.

"It was the inspector who pushed them — he had something to prove. And if I'd given him any excuse he'd have shot me too." He glared at Button. "I'm serious about this, Charlie. I want him out. And before you give me any of that crap about you not having enough weight, if he isn't out I'll go public. I'll go to the press and, if necessary, I'll stand up in court and give evidence against him."

"Then your career would be over," she said quietly.

"I'm past caring," Shepherd said. "That's twice this year that an armed cop has almost killed me, and it's twice too many times. That bastard killed Mayhew when he was surrendering and he threatened to kill me. I want him out."

"Okay," said Button. "I'll see what can be done."

"I'm serious about this, Charlie," said Shepherd.

"I can see that. Is that why you said you'd had enough? Because you were almost shot?"

"It's more than that," said Shepherd. "CO19 isn't the issue. My job is. SOCA is a waste of time. It's the truth and you know it. We're the Serious Organised Crime Agency, but how many big-time criminals have we put away? How many of the really big villains are behind bars because of SOCA?"

"There's a lot of ongoing investigations that have yet to bear fruit," she said.

Shepherd snorted. "With respect, that's bollocks," he said. "Over the last two years I've put forward half a dozen villains that I think we should be looking at, and each time they've been knocked back because of budgetary considerations. I ask you, Charlie, what the hell are we doing worrying about budgetary considerations? We're supposed to be putting criminals in prison, not worrying about profit and loss accounts."

"There's always a cost element in investigations," said Button.

"Yeah, but with SOCA it feels like money's the driving force. If it's too expensive to go after a big-time villain then he gets a free pass. That's not right."

"It's not as simple as that, Spider."

"I'm sorry but it is," said Shepherd. "You and I both know who are responsible for bringing most of the cocaine into this country. But because they live in Amsterdam we don't do a thing about them. There are gangs in north London that run protection rackets earning millions a year and we don't go after them. We know the names of three gangland assassins who between them have killed — what? — sixteen people over the last decade. Do we try and take them down? No. Our country is full of foreign murderers and rapists and we let them live here because nobody can be bothered to send them home. And what am I told to do? I'm told to investigate coppers. Why? Because it's the easy option. Send good old Spider in to infiltrate a group of cops, make friends with them and then betray them. Looks good for the figures and doesn't break the bank."

"They were vigilantes, Spider. They were breaking the law."

"Were they, Charlie?" said Shepherd. "Were they breaking the law or were they upholding it? What were they doing? They were driving drug-dealers out of the country, they were getting rid of paedophiles, they were castrating pimps and rapists. Isn't that what the police are supposed to be doing? Isn't that SOCA's job?"

"Castration and murder? No, that's most definitely not SOCA's remit."

"I'm talking about justice," said Shepherd. "Rough justice, maybe. But real justice. That's the problem, Charlie. There's no justice in the world, these days. We put pensioners in prison for not paying their council tax and we let murderers and rapists roam the streets."

"The system breaks down sometimes, but systems are never infallible."

Shepherd shook his head. "It's not that the system occasionally breaks down," he said. "It's just plain broken. The cops have no power, the courts are biased towards the villains rather than the victims, the prisons are so crowded that we're putting the bad guys back on the street before they've finished their sentences, and the probation service is so overworked that they can't keep track of the criminals who are released." He sighed. "I've just had enough. I don't want to be part of the system any more."

Button tilted her head to one side and narrowed her eyes. "Is the failure of the criminal justice system the issue, Spider? Is that really the issue?"

Shepherd frowned. "What do you mean?"

"Is it the vigilante cops that have got you all riled up, or is it something more personal?"

"Like what?" he said.

"Oh, I don't know," she said, her voice barely a whisper. "Perhaps the reason you're not happy about bringing the vigilantes to justice has more to do with you crossing a line of your own than about SOCA not having the right priorities."

"What exactly are you accusing me of, Charlie?"

She locked eyes with him. "I don't know, Spider. What exactly have you done?" she said.

As he stared into her eyes, he realised what a skilled interrogator she was. She was smiling but her eyes were hard, and he could see that she was studying him intently, looking for the body language and reflexes that would give a clue to his innermost thoughts. He was also very well aware of the first rule of interrogation — never ask a question that you don't know the answer to. He swallowed but his mouth had gone dry and he almost gagged. He saw a small gleam of triumph in Button's eyes. "Why don't you tell me?" he said, wishing he felt half as confident as he sounded.

"Did you really think I wouldn't find out?" she said. "Did you think for one minute that the disappearance of the Fox brothers wouldn't appear on my radar? Especially coming so quickly after the assassination of Allan Gannon's nephew. Did you think that you and he could zip across the Irish Sea without me knowing?" She smiled thinly. "And that just because you leave your mobile phones behind I wouldn't be able to track you? I'm not sure what annoys me most, Spider. The fact that you went behind my back, or the fact that you misunderestimated me, as George W liked to say."

Shepherd put his hands on the table and linked his fingers, trying to stay calm. He felt like a poker player whose opponent had just turned over two aces. If she knew that he'd helped Gannon kill the Fox brothers, then she knew everything.

"I worked for MI5, Spider," she continued. "I'll be back working for MI5 next month. I have access to intelligence material at a level so high that you'd need a hot-air balloon to keep up with me."

"You've been spying on me," he said quietly.

"I've been watching your back," she said. "Like I said I would."

"Does anyone else know?"

558

"Give me some credit, Spider."

He nodded. "Sorry."

"Sorry for what?"

He felt like a pupil being given a dressing down by a headmistress and that at any minute she was going to tell him he'd let her down, let the school down, but that more than anything he'd let himself down. "You know, I'm not sure. If I could turn the clock back, I wouldn't. I did what I did and I have no problems with it."

"Funnily enough, neither do I," said Button.

Shepherd raised his eyebrows. "That's not what I expected to hear," he said.

"Why am I not surprised?" she said. "I'm starting to wonder if you really know me, Spider." She sipped her wine, her eyes never leaving his. "Is there anything else you want to share with me?" she added. "Something else you've been keeping from me?"

"Charlie, it sounds like you know pretty much everything," he said.

"You don't know the half of it," she said. "Didn't you think that my curiosity would be aroused when the cops from Hereford starting asking me where you were when Imer Lekstakaj was murdered? And why did you even think that you could start asking the SOCA lab at Tamworth to start doing private DNA analysis without me finding out? Or waving your Terry Halligan warrant card around New Scotland Yard and accessing Europol databases without raising a red flag?" She sighed. "I set the right man on the trail of vigilantes, didn't I? Set a thief to catch a thief."

"Do you know what Lekstakaj did?"

"I know he was a shit of the first order back in Albania. And I know that he killed your dog and threatened your family."

Shepherd sat back in his chair. Button was right: he had underestimated her. He'd assumed that he could run rings around her but within a few minutes she had proved comprehensively how wrong he'd been. He wanted to apologise, but not for what he'd done. He wasn't sorry that he'd helped the Major kill the Fox brothers and he certainly had no regrets about the way he'd dealt with Lekstakaj, but he sincerely regretted going behind her back. She was right: he'd treated her like a fool and Charlotte Button was nobody's fool.

"Lekstakaj had a wife and child, didn't he?" asked Button.

"They're fine," said Shepherd. "The wife did a runner with the boy after the police went around. I made it clear that they weren't to be hurt."

"That's very big of you, Spider," she said, her voice loaded with sarcasm.

"I'm not justifying what I did. I did what I had to do to protect my family. And you, more than anyone, should understand that." Button's eyes narrowed and she looked as if she was about to say something, but then she relaxed and poured more wine into her glass. She went to top up his too, but he shook his head. "I'm driving," he said. She shrugged and put the bottle back in the cooler. "So, what happens now?" he asked.

"In what respect?"

Shepherd was pretty sure that she knew what he meant. She knew more than enough to finish his career and put him in the dock charged with conspiracy to murder, and more.

"I'm leaving SOCA, you know that," said Button. "What lines you did or didn't cross are no concern of mine."

Shepherd nodded. "Thank you."

She shook her head fiercely. "You don't have to thank me, Spider. I always take care of my people. I always have and I always will, even when they don't appreciate it."

"I do appreciate it, Charlie. Really. I just . . ." He struggled to find the right words. "I guess I didn't want anyone else to get dragged into what I was doing."

"You don't have to explain anything." She leaned towards him and lowered her voice. "I understand why you did what you did, and maybe in your place I would have done the same. And strictly between you and me, and I'd deny that I ever said this, but so far as SOCA goes I think you're right. SOCA isn't fit for purpose, as our beloved politicians love to say. It isn't bringing in the major villains and is doing precious little to bring down the crime rate. But ours not to reason why, Spider. We don't make policy, we implement it."

"We were doing a better job when we were a police unit," said Shepherd. "At least then we were called in when local forces had a problem they wanted solving. We went after real villains."

"Is that what you want to do? Go back to being a cop?"

"Maybe," he said. "Or go back to the Regiment. I could be an instructor."

Button smiled. "I never had you down as a teacher. What is it they say? If you can't do, teach. You're a doer, Spider, not a teacher."

"It's just a thought. There aren't too many career options for an SAS trooper turned undercover cop."

Button studied him closely. "You could come to Five with me," she said quietly.

"Are you serious?" he said. "Do you see me as a spook?"

"I see you as a talented undercover operative who could be used in a multitude of situations," she said. "And you've got other talents that I'm sure Five could make use of."

"Such as?"

She smiled slyly. "You know, those hidden talents that, if you use them off your own bat, could get you into all sorts of trouble, but if you used them for Queen and country could win you a medal or two."

"Do spooks get medals?"

"Absolutely they do. And knighthoods." She leaned forward again. "Think about it. It's an option." She smiled. "And, you never know, it might be fun."

Major Gannon tapped out the alarm code and left his house as the console beeped. He double-locked the front door and whistled softly to himself as he walked towards his silver Jaguar. He hadn't got back until late the previous night and hadn't wanted to disturb the neighbours in his mews by opening the garage door and reversing in so he had left the car parked outside his kitchen window. As always, he did a quick walk-around to convince himself that his car hadn't been tampered with, then opened the boot and put away the small metal suitcase that contained his satellite phone.

He had a busy day ahead of him. He was due at New Scotland Yard to give a briefing to senior officers in the Met on the new weapons he'd been testing at Hereford. Then he had to attend a Foreign Office discussion group who had to prepare a policy paper for the Foreign Secretary on the seizure of a British ship off the coast of Somalia by pirates who were demanding a ransom of half a million pounds. So far as the Major was concerned, the best way of dealing with the growing problem of ships being seized was to send in the Increment with guns blazing, but official policy over the past few years had been to negotiate and pay. The government had long ago backtracked on its promise never to negotiate with terrorists, and the Somalian pirates knew that, providing they didn't hurt their hostages and kept their demands to a reasonable level, there was every chance they would continue to be paid. The Major hoped to sway the group towards his point of view, that enough was enough and that if they took out one of the pirate gangs they would probably leave British ships alone in future. It wouldn't stop them, but it would keep them off British vessels.

After the Foreign Office meeting he had to drive to Hereford to prepare for a tour of visiting dignitaries from the Gulf, a trio of Arab princes who were keen to see what the SAS could do and had specifically asked for a look at the hi-tech Killing House where the troopers sharpened their hostage-rescue skills with live ammunition.

He slammed the boot shut, walked around to the driver's side and climbed in. The car was only two months old and still had its new-car smell. The Major had always been a fan of Jaguars, and the silver X-Type was his sixth. He put in the ignition key. As he started to turn it he noticed a greasy smear close to the insignia on the bonnet, a smear he'd never noticed before.

The explosion shattered all the windows in the street. The alarm in the Major's house was one of a dozen that went off, but his was the only one linked to the local police station. By the time a patrol car arrived the Fire Brigade were already on the scene, dousing the burning car with their hoses as a thick plume of black smoke curled into the sky, and two paramedics were tending a pensioner who had been injured by flying shards of steel.

Just thirty minutes after the explosion, a phone call was made to the news desk of the *Belfast Telegraph*. A recognised codeword was given and the caller identified himself as a member of the Real IRA. He said that the organisation was claiming responsibility for the justified execution of an enemy of the Irish people who had been responsible for dozens of deaths in the province, including those of the freedom fighters Padraig and Sean Fox. More assassinations were to follow until the deaths of the Fox brothers had been avenged. "*Tiocfaidh ár lá*," said the caller, before hanging up. "Our day will come."

Also available in ISIS Large Print:

Nightfall

Stephen Leather

"You're going to hell, Jack Nightingale": They are words that ended his career as a police negotiator. Now Jack's a struggling private detective — and the chilling words come back to haunt him.

Nightingale's life is turned upside down the day that he inherits a mansion with a priceless library; it comes from a man who claims to be his father, and it comes with a warning. That Nightingale's soul was sold at birth and a devil will come to claim it on his 33rd birthday — just three weeks away.

Jack doesn't believe in Hell, probably doesn't believe in Heaven either. But when people close to him start to die horribly, he is led to the inescapable conclusion that real evil may be at work. And that if he doesn't find a way out he'll be damned in hell for eternity.

ISBN 978-0-7531-8624-4 (hb)
ISBN 978-0-7531-8625-1 (pb)

Live Fire

Stephen Leather

Mickey and Mark Moore are Ordinary Decent Criminals — hard men who live by their own code and leaders of a gang that has made millions at gunpoint. But when Dan "Spider" Shepherd is sent to infiltrate the tightly-knit team of bank robbers, he discovers that he has more in common with them then he first thought. And that perhaps being a career criminal isn't the worst thing in the world. As Shepherd and his Serious Organised Crime Agency colleagues plot the downfall of the Moore brothers, a more sinister threat stalks the streets of London. A group of home-grown Islamic fundamentalist fanatics embark on a campaign of terror the like of which Britain has never seen. Car bombs and beheadings are only the prelude of what they have planned. And Shepherd is the only man who can stop them.

ISBN 978-0-7531-8418-9 (hb)
ISBN 978-0-7531-8419-6 (pb)

The Vets

Stephen Leather

Hong Kong. The British administration is preparing to hand the capitalist colony back to communist China with the minimum of fuss. But Colonel Joel Tyler has other plans for the British Colony, plans which involve four Vietnam War veterans and a spectacular mission, making use of their unique skills. Vietnam was the one thing the four men had in common before Tyler moulded them into a team capable of pulling off a sensational robbery.

But while the vets are preparing to take Hong Kong by storm, their paymaster, Anthony Chung, puts the final touches to an audacious betrayal. At stake is the future of Hong Kong . . .

ISBN 978-0-7531-8296-3 (hb)
ISBN 978-0-7531-8297-0 (pb)

The Fireman

Stephen Leather

Young, talented, in love with life — why should Sally have thrown herself 15 floors to her death? But as suicide is the verdict of the uncompromising Hong Kong authorities, Sally's brother, a London-based crime reporter, begins his own investigations.

As he delves into the details of Sally's unaccountably opulent lifestyle and her mysterious work as a journalist, he is forced to recognise a very different girl from the fun-loving kid sister he remembers. He uncovers a trail that leads him through the decadent haunts of Hong Kong ex-pat society, the ruthless wheeler-dealing of international big-business and the violent Chinese mafia underworld — to an ultimate, shocking act of revenge.

ISBN 978-0-7531-7964-2 (hb)
ISBN 978-0-7531-7965-9 (pb)

Hot Blood

Stephen Leather

Dan "Spider" Shepherd is used to putting his life on the line. It goes with the turf when you're an undercover cop.

Now working for the Serious Organised Crime Agency, Shepherd is pitting his wits against the toughest criminals in the country. But when the man who once saved his life is kidnapped in the badlands of Iraq, thrown into a basement and threatened with execution, Shepherd has to decide whether his loyalties lie with his country, his career or his friend.

Shepherd and his former SAS colleagues realise that the hostage has been abandoned by the Government and that officially nothing is being done to rescue him. And with the execution deadline only days away, Shepherd knows that the only way to stop his friend being murdered is to put himself in the firing line in the most dangerous city in the world — Baghdad.

ISBN 978-0-7531-7840-9 (hb)
ISBN 978-0-7531-7841-6 (pb)

Staffordshire Library and Information Services

Please return or renew by the last date shown

If not required by other readers, this item may may be renewed in person, by post or telephone, online or by email.
To renew, either the book or ticket are required

24 Hour Renewal Line
0845 33 00 740

Staffordshire
County Council